A FAINT
COLD FEAR

A FAINT COLD FEAR

Karin Slaughter

THORNDIKE
WINDSOR
PARAGON

This Large Print edition is published by Thorndike Press®, Waterville, Maine USA and by BBC Audiobooks, Ltd, Bath, England.

Published in 2004 in the U.S. by arrangement with William Morrow, an imprint of HarperCollins Publishers, Inc.

Published in 2004 in the U.K. by arrangement with The Random House Group Limited.

U.S. Hardcover 0-7862-6118-8 (Americana)
U.K. Hardcover 0-7540-9560-0 (Windsor Large Print)
U.K. Softcover 0-7540-9578-9 (Paragon Large Print)

The text of this Large Print edition is unabridged.
Other aspects of the book may vary from the original edition.

Set in 16 pt. Plantin by Elena Picard.

Printed in the United States on permanent paper.

British Library Cataloguing-in-Publication Data available

Library of Congress Cataloging-in-Publication Data

Slaughter, Karin, 1971–
    A faint cold fear : a novel / Karin Slaughter.
        p. cm.
    ISBN 0-7862-6118-8 (lg. print : hc : alk. paper)
    1. Police — Georgia — Fiction. 2. Women physicians — Fiction. 3. Police chiefs — Fiction. 4. Georgia — Fiction. 5. Large type books. I. Title.
    PS3569.L275F35 2004

                                                    2003066324

For VS —
in consideration of love and affection

Sunday

1

Sara Linton stared at the entrance to the Dairy Queen, watching her very pregnant sister walk out with a cup of chocolate-covered ice cream in each hand. As Tessa crossed the parking lot, the wind picked up, and her purple dress rose above her knees. She struggled to keep the jumper down without spilling the ice cream, and Sara could hear her cursing as she got closer to the car.

Sara tried not to laugh as she leaned over to open the door, asking, "Need help?"

"No," Tessa said, wedging her body into the car. She settled in, handing Sara her ice cream. "And you can shut up laughing at me."

Sara winced as her sister kicked off her sandals and propped her bare feet on the dashboard. The BMW 330i was less than two weeks old, and Tessa had already left a

9

bag of Goobers to melt in the backseat and spilled an orange Fanta on the carpet in the front. Had Tessa not been nearly eight months pregnant, Sara would have strangled her.

Sara asked, "What took you so long?"

"I had to pee."

"Again?"

"No, I just like being in the bathroom at the damn Dairy Queen," Tessa snapped. She fanned her hand in front of her face. "Jesus, it's hot."

Sara kept her mouth shut as she turned up the air-conditioning. As a doctor, she knew that Tessa was merely a victim of her own hormones, but there were times when Sara thought that the best thing for all concerned would be to lock Tessa in a box and not open it until they heard a baby crying.

"That place was packed," Tessa managed around a mouthful of chocolate syrup. "Goddamn, shouldn't all those people be at church or something?"

"Hm," Sara said.

"The whole place was filthy. Look at this parking lot," Tessa said, swooping her spoon in the air. "People just dump their trash here and don't even care about who has to pick it up. Like they think the trash

10

fairy's gonna do it or something."

Sara murmured some words of agreement, eating her ice cream as Tessa continued a litany of complaints about everyone in the Dairy Queen, from the man who was talking on his cell phone to the woman who waited in line for ten minutes and then couldn't decide what she wanted when she got to the counter. After a while Sara zoned out, staring at the parking lot, thinking about the busy week she had ahead of her.

Several years ago Sara had taken on the part-time job of county coroner to help buy out her retiring partner at the Heartsdale Children's Clinic, and lately Sara's work at the morgue was playing havoc with her schedule at the clinic. Normally the county job did not require much of Sara's time, but a court appearance had taken her out of the clinic for two days last week, and she was going to have to make up for it this week by putting in overtime.

Increasingly, Sara's work at the morgue was infringing on clinic time, and she knew that in a couple of years she would have to make a choice between the two. When the time came, the decision would be a hard one. The medical examiner's job was a challenge, one Sara had sorely needed thirteen years ago when she had left Atlanta and moved back to Grant County. Part of her thought her brain would atrophy without the constant obstacles presented by forensic medicine. Still, there was something restorative about treating children, and Sara, who could not have children of her own, knew that she would miss the contact. She vacillated daily on which job was better. Generally, a bad day at one made the other look ideal.

"Getting on up there!" Tessa screeched, loud enough to get Sara's attention. "I'm thirty-four, not fifty. What the hell kind of thing is that for a nurse to say to a pregnant woman?"

Sara stared at her sister. "What?"

"Have you heard a word I've said?"

She tried to sound convincing. "Yes. Of course I have."

Tessa frowned. "You're thinking about Jeffrey, aren't you?"

Sara was surprised by the question. For once her ex-husband had been the last thing on her mind. "No."

"Sara, don't lie to me," Tessa countered. "Everybody in town saw that sign girl up at the station Friday."

"She was lettering the new police car,"

Sara answered, feeling a warm flush come to her cheeks.

Tessa gave a disbelieving look. "Wasn't that his excuse the last time?"

Sara did not answer. She could still remember the day she'd come home early from work to find Jeffrey in bed with the owner of the local sign shop. The whole Linton family was both amazed and irritated that Sara was dating Jeffrey again, and while Sara for the most part shared their sentiments, she felt incapable of making a clean break. Logic eluded her where Jeffrey was concerned.

Tessa warned, "You just need to be careful with him. Don't let him get too comfortable."

"I'm not an idiot."

"Sometimes you are."

"Well, you are, too," Sara shot back, feeling foolish even before the words came out of her mouth.

But for the whir of the air-conditioning, the car was quiet. Finally Tessa offered, "You should've said, 'I know you are, but what am I?'"

Sara wanted to laugh it off, but she was too irritated. "Tessie, it's none of your business."

Tessa barked a loud laugh that rattled in

Sara's ears. "Well, hell, honey, that's never stopped anybody before. I'm sure damn Marla Simms was on the phone before the little bitch even got out of her truck."

"Don't call her that."

Tessa waved her spoon in the air again. "What do you want me to call her? Slut?"

"Nothing," Sara told her, and meant it. "Don't call her anything."

"Oh, I think she deserves a few choice words."

"Jeffrey's the one who cheated. She just took advantage of a good opportunity."

"You know," Tessa began. "I took advantage of plenty of good opportunities in my time, but I never chased after a married one."

Sara closed her eyes, willing her sister to stop. She did not want to have this conversation.

Tessa added, "Marla told Penny Brock she's put on weight."

"What were you doing talking to Penny Brock?"

"Stopped-up drain in their kitchen," Tessa said, smacking her mouth around her spoon. Tessa had quit working full-time with their father in the family plumbing business when her swollen belly made it impossible to navigate crawl spaces, but she was still capable of taking a plunger to a drain.

Tessa said, "According to Penny, she's big as a house."

Despite her better intentions, Sara could not help but feel a moment of triumph, followed by a wave of guilt that she could take pleasure in another woman's widening hips. And ass. The sign girl was already a little too full in the flank for her own good.

Tessa said, "I see you smiling."

Sara was; her cheeks hurt from the strain of keeping her mouth closed. "This is horrible."

"Since when?"

"Since . . ." Sara let her voice trail off. "Since it makes me feel like an absolute idiot."

"Well, you am what you am, as Popeye would say." Tessa made a great show of scraping her plastic spoon around the cardboard cup as she wiped it clean. She sighed heavily, as if her day had just taken a turn for the worse. "Can I have the rest of yours?"

"No."

"I'm pregnant!" Tessa squeaked.

"That's not my fault."

Tessa went back to scraping her cup. To add to the annoyance, she started scratching the bottom of her foot on the dashboard's burled wood inlay.

A full minute passed before Sara felt an older sister's guilt hit her like a sledgehammer. She tried to fight it by eating more ice cream, but it stuck in her throat.

"Here, you big baby." Sara handed over her cup.

"Thank you," Tessa answered sweetly. "Maybe we can get some more for later?" she suggested. "Only, can you go back in and get it? I don't want them to think I'm a pig, and" — she smiled sweetly, batting her eyelids — "I might have ticked off the kid behind the counter."

"I can't imagine how."

Tessa blinked innocently. "Some people are just sensitive."

Sara opened the door, glad for a reason to get out of the car. She was three feet away when Tessa rolled down the window.

"I know," Sara said. "Extra chocolate."

"Yeah, but hold up." Tessa paused to lick ice cream off the side of her cell phone before she handed it out the window. "It's Jeffrey."

Sara pulled up onto a gravel embankment between a police cruiser and Jeffrey's car, frowning as she heard stones kicking up against the side of her car. The only reason Sara had traded in her two-seater convertible for the larger model was to accommodate a child's car seat. Between Tessa and the elements, the BMW was going to be trashed before the baby came.

"This it?" Tessa asked.

"Yep." Sara yanked up the parking brake and looked out at the dry river basin in front of them. Georgia had been suffering from a drought since the mid-1990s, and the huge river that had once slithered through the forest like a fat, lazy snake had shriveled to little more than a trickling stream. A cracked, dry carcass was all that remained, and the concrete bridge thirty feet overhead seemed out of place, though Sara could remember when people had fished from it.

"Is that the body?" Tessa asked, pointing to a group of men standing in a semicircle.

"Probably," Sara answered, wondering if they were on college property. Grant County comprised three cities: Heartsdale, Madison, and Avondale. Heartsdale, which housed the Grant Institute of Technology, was the jewel of the county, and any crime that happened inside its city limits was considered that much more horrible. A crime on college property would be a nightmare.

"What happened?" Tessa asked eagerly, though she had never been interested in this side of Sara's job before.

"That's what I'm supposed to find out," Sara reminded her, reaching over to the glove box for her stethoscope. The clearance was tight, and Sara's hand rested on the back of Tessa's stomach. She let it stay there for a moment.

"Oh, Sissy," Tessa breathed, grabbing Sara's hand. "I love you so much."

Sara laughed at the sudden tears in Tessa's eyes, but for some reason she could feel herself tearing up as well. "I love you, too, Tessie." She squeezed her sister's hand, saying, "Stay in the car. This won't take long."

Jeffrey was walking to meet Sara as she shut the car door. His dark hair was combed back neatly, still a little wet at the nape. He was dressed in a charcoal gray suit, perfectly pressed and tailored, with a gold police badge tucked into the breast pocket.

Sara was in sweatpants that had seen better days and a T-shirt that had given up on being white sometime during the Reagan administration. She wore sneakers with no socks, the laces loosely tied so she could slip in and out of them with as little effort as possible.

"You didn't have to dress up," Jeffrey joked, but she could hear the tension in his voice.

"What is it?"

"I'm not sure, but I think there's something hinky —" He stopped, looking back at the car. "You brought Tess?"

"It was on the way, and she wanted to come. . . ." Sara let her voice trail off, because there really was no explanation, other than that Sara's goal in life at the moment was to keep Tessa happy — or, at the very least, to keep her from whining.

Jeffrey recognized the situation. "I guess arguing with her wasn't worth it?"

"She promised to stay in the car," Sara said, just as she heard the car door slam closed behind her. She tucked her hands into her hips as she turned around, but Tessa was already waving her off.

"I've gotta go," Tessa said, pointing toward a line of trees in the distance.

Jeffrey asked, "She's gonna walk home?"

"She's going to the bathroom," Sara explained, watching Tessa head up the hill toward the forest.

They both watched Tessa navigate the steep slope, her hands hooked under her belly as if she were carrying a basket. Jeffrey asked, "Are you gonna be mad at me if I laugh when she rolls back down that hill?"

Sara laughed with him instead of answering his question.

He asked, "You think she'll be okay up there?"

"She'll be fine," Sara told him. "It won't kill her to get some exercise."

"Are you sure?" Jeffrey pressed, concerned.

"She's fine," Sara reassured, knowing that Jeffrey had never been around a pregnant woman for any length of time in his life. He was probably scared Tessa would go into labor before she got to the trees at the top of the hill. They should all be so lucky.

Sara started to walk toward the scene but stopped when he did not follow. She turned around, waiting for what she knew was coming.

He said, "You left pretty early this morning."

"I figured you needed the sleep." She walked back and took a pair of latex gloves out of his coat pocket, asking, "What's hinky?"

"I wasn't that tired," he said, in the same suggestive tone he would have used this morning if she'd stuck around.

She fidgeted with the gloves, trying to think of something to say. "I had to let the dogs out."

"You could start bringing them."

Sara gave the police cruiser a pointed look. "Is that new?" she asked, feigning curiosity. Grant County was a small place. Sara had heard about the new patrol car before it was even parked in front of the station.

He said, "Got it a couple of days ago."

"Lettering looks good," she said, keeping her tone casual.

"How about that," he said, an annoying phrase he had lately picked up when he did not know what else to say.

Sara did not let him get away with it. "She did a really nice job."

Jeffrey kept his gaze steady, as if he had nothing to hide. Sara would have been impressed had he not used the exact same expression the last time he'd assured her he was not cheating.

She gave a tight smile, repeating, "What's hinky?"

He let out a short, irritated breath. "You'll see," he told her, heading toward the river.

Sara walked at her normal pace, but Jeffrey slowed enough for her to catch up

21

with him. She could see that he was angry, but Sara had never let Jeffrey's moods intimidate her.

She asked, "Is it a student?"

"Probably," he said, his tone still clipped. "We checked his pockets. There wasn't any ID on him, but this side of the river is college land."

"Great," Sara mumbled, wondering how long it would be before Chuck Gaines, the new head of security at the college, showed up and started questioning everything they did. Chuck was easy to dismiss as a nuisance, but Jeffrey's prime directive as chief of police for Grant County was to keep the college happy. Chuck knew this better than anyone, and he exploited his advantage whenever he could.

Sara noticed a very attractive blonde sitting on a cluster of rocks. Beside her was Brad Stephens, a young patrolman who had been a patient of Sara's a long time ago.

"Ellen Schaffer," Jeffrey provided. "She was jogging toward the woods. Crossed the bridge and saw the body."

"When did she find it?"

"About an hour ago. She called it in on her cell phone."

"She jogs with her phone?" Sara asked,

wondering why she was surprised. People could not go to the bathroom anymore without taking their phones in case they got bored.

Jeffrey said, "I want to try to talk to her again after you examine the body. She was too upset before. Maybe Brad will help calm her down."

"Did she know the victim?"

"Doesn't look like it," he said. "She was probably just in the wrong place at the wrong time."

Most witnesses suffered from this same sort of bad luck, seeing something in a few moments that stayed with them for the rest of their lives. Fortunately, from what Sara could see of the body in the center of the riverbed, the girl had gotten off lightly.

"Here," Jeffrey said, taking Sara's arm as they approached the bank. The land was hilly, with a downward slope toward the river. A path had been worn into the ground by rain falloff, but the silt was porous and loose.

Sara judged that the bed was at least forty feet wide at this spot, but Jeffrey would have someone measure that later. The ground was parched beneath their feet, and she could feel grit and clay working their way into her tennis shoes as they kicked up dust walking toward the body. Twelve years ago they would have been up to their necks in water by now.

Sara stopped halfway to the scene, looking up at the bridge. The design was a simple concrete beam with a low railing. A ledge jutted out a couple of inches from the bottom, and between this and the railing, someone had spray-painted in black letters DIE NIGGER and a large swastika.

Sara got a sour taste in her mouth. She said derisively, "Well, that's nice."

"Ain't it, though," Jeffrey replied, just as disgusted as she was. "It's all over campus."

"When did it start?" Sara asked. The graffiti looked faded, probably a couple of weeks old.

"Who knows?" Jeffrey said. "The college hasn't even acknowledged it."

"If they acknowledged it, they'd have to do something about it," Sara pointed out, looking over her shoulder for Tessa. "Do you know who's doing it?"

"Students," he said, giving the word a nasty spin as he resumed walking. "Probably a bunch of idiot Yankees who think it's funny coming down south to play hicks and crackers."

"I hate amateur racists," Sara mumbled, putting on a smile as they approached Matt Hogan and Frank Wallace.

"Afternoon, Sara," Matt said. He held an instant camera in one hand and several Polaroids in the other.

Frank, Jeffrey's second in command, told her, "We just finished the pictures."

"Thanks," Sara told them, snapping on the latex gloves.

The victim was lying directly under the bridge, facedown on the ground. His arms were splayed out to the side and his pants and underwear were bunched up around his ankles. Judging from his size and the lack of hair on his smooth back and buttocks, he was a young man, probably in his twenties. His blond hair was long to the collar and parted on the back of his head. He could have been sleeping but for the splattering of blood and tissue coming out of his anus.

"Ah," she said, understanding Jeffrey's concern.

As a formality Sara knelt down and pressed her stethoscope to the dead boy's back. She could feel and hear his ribs move under her hand. There was no heartbeat.

Sara looped the stethoscope around her neck and examined the body, calling out her findings. "There's no sign of the kind of trauma you'd expect with forcible sodomy. No bruises, no lacerations." She glanced up at his hands and wrists. His left arm was turned awkwardly, and she could see a nasty pink scar running up the forearm. From the look of it, the injury had happened within the last four to six months. "He wasn't tied up."

The young man was wearing a dark green T-shirt, which Sara lifted to check for further signs of damage. A long scrape was at the base of his spine, the skin broken, but not enough to bleed.

"What is it?" Jeffrey asked.

Sara did not answer, though something about the scrape seemed odd to her.

She picked up the boy's right leg to move it aside but stopped when the foot did not come with it. Sara slid her hand under the pant leg, feeling for the bones of the ankle, then the tibia and fibula; it was like squeezing a balloon filled with oatmeal. She checked the other leg, finding the same consistency. The bones were not just broken, they were pulverized.

A set of car doors slammed, and Sara heard Jeffrey whisper, "Shit," under his breath.

Seconds later Chuck Gaines walked

down the bank, the shirt of his tan security uniform stretched tight across his chest as he tried to navigate the slope. Sara had known Chuck since elementary school, where he had teased her mercilessly about everything from her height to her good grades to her red hair, and she was just as happy seeing him now as she had been on the playground those many years ago.

Lena Adams stood beside Chuck wearing an identical uniform that was at least two sizes too big for her small frame. A belt kept the pants up, and, with her aviator sunglasses and hair tucked under a wide-brimmed baseball cap, she looked like a little boy playing dress-up in his father's clothes, especially when she lost her footing on the bank and slid the rest of the way down on her bottom.

Frank moved to help her, but Jeffrey stopped him with a look of warning. Lena had been a detective — one of them — up until seven months ago. Jeffrey had not forgiven Lena for leaving, and he was bound and determined to make sure no one else under his command did either.

"Damn," Chuck said, taking the last few steps at a jog. There was a light sheen of sweat over his lip despite the cool day, and his face was red from the effort of walking down the bank. Chuck was extremely muscular, but there was something unhealthy about him. He was always perspiring, and a thin layer of fat made his skin look tight and bloated. His face was round and moonish, his eyes a bit too wide. Sara did not know if this was from steroids or poor weight training, but he looked like a heart attack waiting to happen.

Chuck gave Sara a flirty wink, saying, "Hey, Red," before jutting out his meaty hand toward Jeffrey. "How they hanging, Chief?"

"Chuck," Jeffrey said, reluctantly shaking his hand. He gave Lena a cursory glance, then turned back to the scene. "This was called in about an hour ago. Sara just got here."

Sara said, "Hey, Lena."

Lena gave a slight nod, but Sara could not read her expression behind the dark sunglasses. Jeffrey's disapproval of this exchange was obvious, and if they had been alone, Sara would have told him what he could do with it.

Chuck clapped his hands together, as if to assert his authority. "Whatcha got here, Doc?"

"Probably a suicide," Sara answered, trying to remember how many times she had asked Chuck not to call her "Doc." Probably not nearly as many times as she had asked him not to call her "Red."

"That so?" Chuck asked, craning his neck. "Don't it look to you like he's been fiddled with?" Chuck indicated the lower half of the body. "Looks like it to me."

Sara sat back on her heels, not answering. She glanced at Lena again, wondering how she was holding up. Lena had lost her sister a year ago this month, then gone through hell during the investigation. Even though Sara could think of a lot of things she did not like about Lena Adams, she would not wish Chuck Gaines on anyone.

Chuck seemed to realize no one was paying attention to him. He clapped his hands together again, ordering, "Adams, check the periphery. See if you can sniff up anything."

Surprisingly, Lena acquiesced, walking downstream.

Sara looked up at the bridge, shielding her eyes from the sun. "Frank, can you go up there and look for a note or something?"

"A note?" Chuck echoed.

Sara addressed Jeffrey. "I imagine he jumped from the bridge," she said. "He

29

landed on his feet. You can see his shoe treads punched into the dirt. The impact pulled down his pants and broke most if not all of the bones in his feet and legs." She looked at the tag on the back of the jeans, checking the size. "They were baggy, and the force from that height would be pretty substantial. I imagine the blood is from his intestines detaching. You can see where part of the rectum was turned inside out and forced from the anus."

Chuck gave a low whistle, and before she could think to stop herself, Sara looked up at him. She saw his lips move as he read the racial epithet on the bridge. He flashed a bright, obvious smile at Sara before asking, "How's your sister?"

Sara saw Jeffrey's jaw lock as he gritted his teeth. Devon Lockwood, the father of Tessa's child, was black.

"She's fine, Chuck," Sara answered, forcing herself not to rise to the bait. "Why do you ask?"

He flashed another smile, making sure she saw him looking at the bridge. "No reason."

She kept staring at Chuck, appalled at how little had changed about him since high school.

"This scar on his arm," Jeffrey inter-

30

rupted. "It looks recent."

Sara forced herself to look at the victim's arm, but her anger caught in her throat when she answered, "Yes."

"Yes?" Jeffrey repeated, a definite question behind the word.

"Yes," Sara said, letting him know she could fight her own battles. She took a deep, calming breath before saying, "My best guess is it was deliberate, straight up the radial artery. He would've been taken to the hospital for that."

Chuck was suddenly interested in Lena's progress. "Adams!" he yelled. "Check up thataway." He pointed away from the bridge, the opposite direction she had been heading.

Sara put her hands on the dead boy's hips, asking Jeffrey, "Can you help me turn him?"

As she waited for Jeffrey to put on a pair of gloves, Sara searched the tree line for Tessa. There was no sign of her. For once Sara was grateful Tessa was in her car.

"Ready," Jeffrey said, his hands on the dead boy's shoulders.

Sara counted off, and they turned the body as carefully as they could.

"Oh, fuck," Chuck squeaked, his voice going up three octaves. He stepped back

31

quickly, as if the body had suddenly burst into flames. Jeffrey stood up fast, a look of total horror on his face. Matt gave what sounded like a dry heave as he turned his back to them.

"Well," Sara said, for lack of anything better to say.

The bottom side of the victim's penis had been almost completely skinned off. A four-inch flap of skin hung loosely from the glans, a series of dumbbell-style earrings piercing the flesh at staggered intervals.

Sara knelt by the pelvic area, examining the damage. She heard someone suck wind through his teeth as she stretched the skin back to its normal position, studying the jagged edges where the flesh had been ripped from the organ.

Jeffrey was the first to speak. "What the hell is that?"

"Body piercing," she said. "It's called a frenum ladder." Sara indicated the metal studs. "They're pretty heavy. The impact must have pulled the skin off like a sock."

"Fuck," Chuck muttered again, staring openly at the damage.

Jeffrey was incredulous. "He did this to himself?"

Sara shrugged. Genital piercings were

hardly commonplace in Grant County, but Sara had dealt with enough piercing-related infections at the clinic to know that this sort of thing was out there.

"Je-sus," Matt muttered, kicking at some dirt, still turned away from them.

Sara indicated a thin gold hoop piercing the boy's nostril. "The skin is thicker here, so it didn't pull out. His eyebrow . . ." She looked around on the ground, spotting another gold hoop pressed into the clay where the body had fallen. "Maybe the clasp popped open on impact."

Jeffrey pointed to the chest. "What about here?"

A thin trickle of blood stopped about two inches below the boy's right nipple, which was torn in two. Sara took a guess and rolled back the waistband of the jeans. Caught between the zip and a pair of Joe Boxers was a third hoop earring. "Pierced nipple," she said, picking up the hoop. "Do you have a bag for this?"

Jeffrey took out a small paper evidence bag, holding it open for her, asking with great distaste, "Is that it?"

"Probably not," she answered.

Cupping the young man's jaw between her thumb and forefinger, Sara pressed open the mouth. She reached in carefully with her fingers, trying not to cut herself.

"His tongue was probably pierced, too," she told Jeffrey, feeling the muscle. "It's bisected at the tip. I'll know when I get him on the table, but I imagine the tongue stud is in his throat."

She sat back on her heels, removing her gloves and studying the victim as a whole rather than by his pierced parts. He was an average-looking kid except for the line of blood dribbling from his nose and pooling around his lips. A reddish blond goatee hugged his soft chin, and his sideburns were thin and long, curving around his jawline like a piece of multicolored yarn.

Chuck took a step forward for a better look, his mouth dropping open. "Aw, shit. That's — Shit . . ." He groaned, thumping himself in the head. "I can't remember his name. His mama works at the college."

Sara saw Jeffrey's shoulders slump at the news. The case had just gotten ten times more complicated.

From the bridge Frank yelled, "Found a note."

Sara was surprised at the news, even though she had been the one to send Frank to search in the first place. Sara had seen a number of suicides in her time, and something about this one did not feel right.

Jeffrey was watching her closely, as if he could read her mind. He asked Sara, "You still think he jumped?"

Sara left it open, saying, "It looks that way, doesn't it?"

Jeffrey waited a beat before deciding. "We'll canvass the area."

Chuck started to volunteer help, but Jeffrey smoothly cut him off, asking, "Chuck, can you stay here with Matt and get a picture of his face? I want to show it to the woman who found the body."

"Uh . . ." Chuck seemed to be trying to think of an excuse, not because he did not want to stick around but because he did not want to take an order from Jeffrey.

Jeffrey motioned to Matt, who had finally turned back around. "Get some pictures."

Matt gave a stiff nod, and Sara wondered how he would take pictures without looking at the victim. Chuck, on the other hand, could not look away. He had probably never seen a dead body before. Knowing what kind of person he was, Sara was not surprised by Chuck's reaction. He could have been watching a movie for all the emotion he showed in his face.

"Here," Jeffrey said, helping Sara stand.

"I've already called Carlos," Sara told

him, meaning her assistant at the morgue. "He should be here soon. We'll know more from the autopsy."

"Good," Jeffrey said. He told Matt, "Try to get a good one of his face. When Frank gets down here, tell him to meet me by the cars."

Matt gave him a salute, still not saying much.

Sara tucked her stethoscope into her pocket as they walked along the riverbed. She glanced up at the car, looking for Tessa. The sun struck the windshield at an angle, turning the glass into a bright mirror.

Jeffrey waited until they were out of Chuck's earshot before asking, "What aren't you saying?"

Sara paused, not knowing how to articulate her feelings. "Something about this doesn't feel right."

"That could be because of Chuck."

"No," she told him. "Chuck's a jerk. I've known that for thirty years."

Jeffrey allowed a smile. "Then what is it?"

Sara turned around to look at the boy on the ground, then back up at the bridge. "The scrape on his back. Why would he have that?"

Jeffrey suggested, "From the railing on the bridge?"

"How? The railing isn't that high. He probably sat on it and swung his feet over."

"There's a ledge under the railing," Jeffrey pointed out. "He could have scraped it on the way down."

Sara kept staring at the bridge, trying to imagine the right scenario. "I know it sounds stupid, but if it was me, I wouldn't want to hit myself on the way down. I would stand on the railing and jump out, away from the ledge. Away from everything."

"Maybe he climbed down to the ledge and scraped his back on part of the bridge."

"Check it for skin," Sara suggested, though for some reason she doubted they would find anything.

"What about landing on his feet?"

"It's not as unusual as you think."

"You think he did that on purpose?"

"Jumped?"

"The thing." Jeffrey indicated his lower half.

"The piercing?" Sara asked. "He's probably had it for a while. It's well healed."

Jeffrey winced. "Why would somebody do that to himself?"

"Supposedly it heightens sexual sensation."

Jeffrey was skeptical. "For the man?"

"And the woman," Sara told him, though the thought of it made her shudder.

She looked toward the car again, hoping to see Tessa. Sara had a clear view of the parking pad. Except for Brad Stephens and the witness, no one else was in sight.

Jeffrey asked, "Where's Tessa?"

"Who knows?" Sara answered, irritated. She should have taken Tessa home instead of letting her tag along.

"Brad," Jeffrey called to the patrolman as they walked up to the cars. "Did Tessa come back down the hill?"

"No, sir," he answered.

Sara looked in the backseat of her car, expecting to see Tessa curled up for a nap. The car was empty.

Jeffrey asked, "Sara?"

"It's okay," Sara told him, thinking Tessa had probably started down the hill then had to go back up again. The baby had been tap-dancing on her bladder the last few weeks.

Jeffrey offered, "You want me to go look for her?"

"She's probably just sitting down somewhere, taking a break."

"You sure?" Jeffrey asked.

She waved him off, following the same path Tessa had walked up the hill. Students from the college jogged the trails in the woods, which led from one side of the town to the other. If Sara went east a mile or so, she would eventually run into the children's clinic. West would take her to the highway, and north would dump her out on the opposite side of town, close to the Linton house. If Tessa had decided to walk home without letting anyone know, Sara was going to kill her.

The grade was steeper than Sara had imagined, and she stopped at the top of the hill to catch her breath. Trash littered the area, beer cans scattered like dead leaves. She looked back down at the parking pad, where Jeffrey was interviewing the woman who had found the body. Brad Stephens waved, and Sara waved back, thinking that if she was winded from the climb, Tessa must have been panting by now. Maybe Tessa had stopped to catch her breath before going back down. Maybe she had come across a wild animal. Maybe she had gone into labor. On this last thought, Sara turned back to the trees, following a worn trail into the woods. A few feet inside, she scanned the immediate area, looking for any sign of her sister.

"Tess?" Sara called, trying not to let herself get angry. Tessa had probably wondered off and lost track of the time. She had stopped wearing her watch a few months ago when her wrists had gotten too swollen for the metal band.

Sara walked deeper into the woods, raising her voice as she repeated, "Tessa?"

Despite the sunny day, the forest was dark, the limbs from the tall trees linking together like fingers in a child's game, blocking out most of the light. Still Sara shielded her eyes, as if that would help her see better.

"Tess?" she tried again, then waited to the count of twenty.

There was no answer.

A breeze stirred the leaves overhead, and Sara felt a disconcerting prickling on the back of her neck. Rubbing her bare arms, she took a few more steps down the trail. After about fifteen feet, the path forked. Sara tried to decide which way to go. Both trails looked well traveled, and she could see overlays of tennis-shoe prints in the dirt. Sara was kneeling, trying to make out the flat tread of Tessa's sandals among the ribbed and zigzagged treads, when a sound came from behind her.

She jumped, saying, "Tess?" but it was only a raccoon who was just as startled to see Sara as she was to see him. They stared at each other for a few beats before the raccoon scampered off into the forest.

Sara stood, clapping the dirt off her hands. She started down the trail to the right, then backtracked to the fork, drawing a simple arrow in the dirt with the heel of her shoe to indicate which direction she had taken. As soon as she made the mark, Sara felt silly, but she could laugh about the precaution later, when she was driving Tessa home.

"Tess?" Sara said, breaking off a twig from a low-hanging branch as she walked down the trail. "Tess?" she called again, then stopped, waiting, but there was still no answer.

Ahead Sara could see that the path took a slight turn, then forked again. She debated whether or not to get Jeffrey to help but decided against it. Part of her felt foolish for considering it, but another, deeper part of her could not quell her fear.

Sara moved forward, calling Tessa's name as she walked. At the next fork, she shielded her eyes with her hand again, looking both ways. The trails gradually curved away from each other, the one on the right making a sharp turn about eighty feet ahead. The forest was darker here, and Sara had to strain her eyes to see. She started to draw a mark toward the left trail, but something flashed in her mind, as if her eyes had taken their time relaying an image to her brain. Sara scanned the trail on the right, seeing an oddly shaped rock just before the sharp bend. She took a few steps forward, then ran, realizing that the rock was actually one of Tessa's sandals.

"Tessa!" Sara yelled, snatching the shoe from the ground, holding it to her chest as she spun around, frantically searching for her sister. Sara dropped the sandal, feeling a wave of dizziness. Her throat constricted as the dread she had been suppressing all along flowered into full-blown terror. In a clearing ahead, Tessa lay on her back, one hand to her stomach, the other out to the side. Her head was turned awkwardly, her lips slightly parted, her eyes closed.

"No —" Sara exhaled, running toward her sister. The distance between them could not have been more than twenty feet, but it felt like miles. A million possibilities went through Sara's mind as she raced toward Tessa, but none of them prepared her for what she found.

"Oh, God," Sara gasped, her knees buckling as she sank to the ground. "Oh, no . . ."

Tessa had been stabbed at least twice in the stomach and once in the chest. Blood was everywhere, turning the dark purple of her dress into a deep, wet black. Sara looked at her sister's face. Her scalp had been ripped open, part of it hanging into her left eye, the bright red on the underside of the flesh a stark contrast to her pale white skin.

Sara cried, "No . . . Tess . . . no . . . !" putting her hand to Tessa's cheek, trying to make her open her eyes. "Tessie?" she said. "Oh, God, what happened?"

Tessa did not respond. She was slack and unresisting as Sara pressed her torn scalp into place and forced open Tessa's eyelids, trying to see the pupils. Sara tried to check for a carotid pulse, but her hand was shaking so much all she managed to do was smear blood in a macabre finger painting on Tessa's neck. She pressed her ear to Tessa's chest, the wet dress sticking to her cheek as she tried to find signs of life.

Listening, Sara looked down at the stomach, at the baby. Blood and amniotic fluid oozed from the lower incisions like a dribbling faucet. A piece of intestine pushed out through a wide tear in the purple jumper, and Sara closed her eyes to the sight, holding her breath until she heard the faint beat of Tessa's heart and felt the almost imperceptible rise and fall of Tessa's chest as she took breath into her lungs.

"Tess?" Sara asked, sitting up, wiping blood from her face with the back of her arm. "Tessie, please wake up."

Someone stepped on a twig behind Sara, and she turned at the loud snap, her heart in her throat. Brad Stephens stood there, his mouth open in shock. They stared at each other, both speechless for several seconds.

"Dr. Linton?" he finally asked, his voice small in the large clearing. He had the same startled expression as the raccoon back up the trail.

Sara could do nothing more than stare at him. In her mind she was yelling at him to go get Jeffrey, to do something, but in reality the words would not come out.

"I'll get help," he said, his shoes clomping on the ground as he turned and ran back up the trail.

Sara watched Brad until he disappeared around the bend before she let herself look

44

back at Tessa. This was not happening. They were both trapped in some horrible nightmare, and soon Sara would wake up and it would be over. This was not Tessa — not her baby sister who had insisted on tagging along like she used to when they were little. Tessa had just gone for a walk, gone to find a place to relieve her bladder. She wasn't lying here on the ground bleeding out while Sara could think of nothing to do but hold her hand and cry.

"It's going to be okay," she told her sister, reaching over to take Tessa's other hand. She felt something sticking between their skin, and when she looked in Tessa's right hand, there was a piece of white plastic stuck to her palm.

"What's this?" she asked. Tessa's fist clenched, and she groaned.

"Tessa?" Sara said, forgetting the plastic. "Tessa, look at me."

Her eyelids fluttered but did not open.

"Tess?" Sara said. "Tess, stay with me. Look at me."

Slowly Tessa opened her eyes and breathed, "Sara . . ." before her eyelids started to flutter closed.

"Tessa, don't close your eyes!" Sara ordered, squeezing Tessa's hand, asking, "Can you feel that? Talk to me. Can you feel me squeezing your hand?"

Tessa nodded, her eyes opening wide as if she had just been startled out of a deep sleep.

"Can you breathe okay?" Sara asked, aware of the shrill panic in her voice. She tried to take the edge off, knowing she was only making things worse. "Are you having trouble breathing?"

Tessa mouthed a no, her lips trembling from the effort.

"Tess?" Sara said. "Where's the pain? Where does it hurt most?"

Tessa did not answer. Hesitantly her hand moved up to her head, fingers hovering over the torn scalp. Her voice was barely more than a whisper when she asked, "What happened?"

"I don't know," Sara told her, not sure of anything but the need to keep Tessa awake.

Tessa's fingers found her scalp, the skin moving underneath until Sara took her hand away. Tessa said, "What . . . ?" her voice trailing off with the word.

There was a large rock near her head, blood and hair scraped onto the surface of the stone. "Did you hit your head when you fell?" Sara asked, thinking she must have. "Is that what you did?"

"I don't . . ."

"Did someone stab you, Tess?" Sara asked. "Do you remember what happened?"

Tessa's face contorted with fear as her hand reached down to her stomach.

"No," Sara said, taking Tessa's hand, stopping her from feeling the damage.

More branches snapped as Jeffrey ran toward them. He dropped down to his knees opposite Sara, demanding, "What happened?"

At the sight of him, Sara burst into tears.

"Sara?" he asked, but she was crying too hard to answer. "Sara," Jeffrey repeated. He grabbed her by the shoulders, ordering, "Sara, focus. Did you see who did this?"

She looked around, just now realizing that the person who stabbed Tessa might still be here.

"Sara?"

She shook her head. "I don't . . . I didn't . . ."

Jeffrey patted her front pockets, finding her stethoscope and putting it into her limp hand. When he said "Frank is calling an ambulance," his voice sounded so far away that Sara felt as if she were reading his lips instead of hearing his words.

"Sara?"

She was paralyzed by her emotions and could not think what to do. Her vision tunneled, and all she could see was Tessa, bloodied, terrified, her eyes wide with shock. Something passed between them: abject horror, pain, blinding fear. Sara was utterly helpless.

Jeffrey repeated, "Sara?," putting his hand on her arm. Her hearing came back in a sudden rush, like water sluicing through a dam.

He squeezed her arm hard enough to cause pain. "Tell me what to do."

Somehow his words brought her back to the moment. Still, her voice caught when she said, "Take off your shirt. We need to control the bleeding."

Sara watched as Jeffrey pulled off his jacket and tie, then ripped through the buttons of his shirt. Gradually she felt her mind start to work. She could do this. She knew what to do.

He asked, "How bad is it?"

Sara did not answer, because she knew that voicing the harm done would give it more power. Instead she pressed his shirt to Tessa's belly, then put Jeffrey's hand over it, saying, "Like this," so he would know how much pressure to exert.

"Tess?" Sara asked, trying to be strong for her sister. "I want you to look at me, okay, sweetie? Just look at me and let me know if anything changes, all right?"

Tessa nodded, her eyes darting to the side as Frank made his way toward them.

Frank dropped down beside Jeffrey. "They've got Life Flight less than ten minutes away." He started to unbutton his shirt just as Lena Adams came into the clearing. Matt Hogan was behind her, his hands clenched at his sides.

"He must have gone that way," Jeffrey told them, indicating the path that led deeper into the forest. The two ran off without another word.

"Tess," Sara said, pressing open the chest wound to see how deep it went. The trajectory of the knife would have put the blade dangerously close to the heart. "I know this hurts, but just hang on. Okay? Can you hang on for me?"

Tessa gave a tight nod, her eyes still darting around.

Sara used the stethoscope to listen to Tessa's chest, her heartbeat like a fast drum, her breathing a sharp staccato. Sara's hand began to shake again as she pressed the bell of the stethoscope against Tessa's abdomen, checking for a fetal heart rate. A stab to the belly was a stab to the fetus, and Sara was not surprised when she could not find a second heartbeat.

Amniotic fluid had gushed from the wound, destroying the baby's protective environment. If the knife blade had not damaged the fetus, the loss of blood and fluid certainly would.

Sara could feel Tessa's eyes boring into her, asking a question Sara could not bring herself to answer. If Tessa went into shock, or her adrenaline surged, her heart would pump blood more quickly out of the body.

"It's faint," Sara said, feeling her stomach lurch at the depth of the lie. She made herself look Tessa in the eye, taking her hand, saying, "The heartbeat is faint, but I can hear it."

Tessa's right hand lifted to feel her stomach, but Jeffrey stopped her. He looked down at her palm.

"What's this?" Jeffrey asked. "Tessa? What's this in your hand?"

He held up Tessa's hand so she could see what he meant. A look of confusion came to her face as the plastic fluttered in the breeze.

"Did you get it from him?" Jeffrey asked. "The person who attacked you?"

"Jeffrey," Sara said, her voice low. His shirt had soaked through with blood, covering his hand to the wrist. He saw what she meant and started to take off his undershirt but she told him no, grabbing his coat because it was quicker.

Tessa groaned at the momentary change in pressure, air hissing out between her teeth.

"Tess?" Sara asked loudly, taking her sister's hand again. "Are you holding up okay?"

Tessa gave a tight nod, her lips pressed together, nostrils flaring as she labored to breathe. She squeezed Sara's hand so hard that Sara felt the bones move.

Sara asked, "You're not having trouble breathing, right?" Tessa did not respond, but her eyes were alert, darting from Jeffrey to Sara.

Sara tried to keep the fear out of her voice, repeating, "Are you breathing all right?" If Tessa became incapable of breathing on her own, Sara could do only so much to help her.

Jeffrey's voice was tight and controlled. "Sara?" His hand was tensed over Tessa's belly. "It felt like a contraction."

Sara shook her head in a quick no, putting her hand next to Jeffrey's. She could feel uterine contractions.

Sara raised her voice, asking, "Tessa? Are you feeling more pain down here? Pelvic pain?"

Tessa did not answer, but her teeth chattered as if she were cold.

"I'm going to check for dilation, okay?" Sara warned, lifting Tessa's dress. Blood and fluid covered Tessa's thighs in a sticky black matt. Sara pressed her fingers into the canal. The body's reaction to any trauma was to tense up, and Tessa's was doing just that. Sara felt as if she were putting her hand into a vise.

"Try to relax," Sara told Tessa, feeling for the cervix. Sara's obstetrics rotation had been years ago, and even the reading she'd done lately in preparation for the birth was sorely lacking.

Still, Sara told her, "You're fine. You're doing fine."

Jeffrey said, "I felt it again."

Sara cut him with a look, willing him to be quiet. She had felt the contraction, too, but there was nothing they could do about it. Even if there was a chance that the baby was alive, a cesarean section in this setting would kill Tessa. If the knife had cut through her uterus, she would bleed out before they reached the hospital.

"That's good," Sara said, pulling out Tessa's hand. "You're not dilated. Everything is okay. All right, Tess? Everything's okay."

Tessa's lips still moved, but the only sound she made was the sharp pant of her breathing. She was hyperventilating, throwing herself into hypocapnia.

"Slow down, sweetie," Sara said, putting her face close to Tessa's. "Try to slow down your breathing, okay?"

Sara showed her, breathing in deeply, letting it go slowly, thinking all the time that they had done this same thing in Lamaze class weeks ago.

"That's right," Sara said as Tessa's breathing started to slow. "Nice and slow."

Sara had a moment's relief but then every muscle in Tessa's face tensed up at once. Tessa's head started to tremble, and Sara's hand then her arm absorbed the vibration like a tuning fork. A gurgling noise came from Tessa's lips, and then a thin stream of clear liquid dribbled out. Her eyes were still glassy, her stare blank and cold.

Sara kept her voice low, asking Frank, "What's the ETA on the ambulance?"

"Shouldn't be much longer," Frank said.

"Tessa," Sara said, making her voice stern, threatening. She had not talked to her sister this way since Tessa was twelve and wanted to do a somersault off the roof of the house. "Tessa, hold on. Hold on just a little bit longer. Listen to me. Hold on. I'm telling you to —"

Tessa's body gave a sudden, violent jerk, her jaw clamping tight, eyes rolling back in her head, guttural sounds coming from her throat. The seizure erupted with frightening intensity, working through Tessa's body like a current of electricity.

Sara tried to use her body as a barrier so Tessa would not hurt herself more. Tessa shook uncontrollably, grunting, her eyes rolling. Her bladder released, the smell of her urine strongly acidic. Her jaw was clenched so tight that the muscles in her neck stood out like steel cords.

Sara heard the whir of an engine in the distance, then the distinctive chopping of a helicopter's blades. When the air ambulance hovered overhead before circling toward the riverbed, Sara felt tears stinging her eyes.

"Hurry," she whispered. "Please hurry."

2

Jeffrey could see Sara through the window of the helicopter as it lifted into the air. She was holding Tessa's hand to her chest, head bent down as if in prayer. Neither he nor Sara had ever been particularly religious, but Jeffrey found himself thinking a prayer to anyone who would listen, begging for Tessa to be okay. He kept watching Sara, kept silently praying, until the helicopter made a wide right turn, angling over the tree line. The farther away it got, the less easily the words came to mind, so that by the time the machine turned west toward Atlanta, all he felt was anger and helplessness.

Jeffrey looked down at the thin white strip of plastic he'd found clutched in Tessa's hand. He had peeled it off her palm before they loaded her into the helicopter, hoping that perhaps it would lead them to the person who had attacked her. Staring at it now, he felt a crushing sense of hopelessness bearing down on him. Both he and Sara had touched the plastic. There were no obvious fingerprints in the blood. There was no telling if it even had anything to do with the attack.

"Chief?" Frank handed Jeffrey his suit jacket and shirt, both of which were dripping with blood.

"Jesus," Jeffrey said, extracting his police badge and wallet. They were as soaked as his clothes. He found an evidence bag and sealed the plastic strip inside, asking, "What the hell happened?"

Frank held out his hands, speechless.

The gesture irritated Jeffrey, and he bit back the cutting comment that came to mind, knowing that what had happened to Tessa Linton was not Frank's fault. If anything, it was Jeffrey's. He had been standing with his thumb up his ass less than a hundred yards away when Tessa had been attacked; he'd known something was wrong when Tessa was not at the car, and he should have insisted on going with Sara to look for her.

He tucked the bag into his pants pocket, asking, "Where are Lena and Matt?"

Frank flipped open his cell phone.

"No," Jeffrey told him. The worst thing that could happen to Matt in the middle of the forest was to have his phone ring. "Give them ten minutes." He glanced at his watch, not sure how much time had already passed. "If they're not out by then, we'll go look for them."

"Right."

Jeffrey dropped his clothes on the ground, resting his wallet and badge on top. He continued, "Call the station. Get six units out here."

Frank started to dial in the number, asking, "You want to cut the witness loose?"

"No," Jeffrey told him. Without another word he started down the hill toward the parked cars.

He tried to get his thoughts together as he walked. Sara had felt there was something suspicious about the suicide. Tessa's being stabbed in the immediate vicinity made that possibility even more likely. If the kid in the riverbed had been murdered, it was possible Tessa Linton had surprised his assailant in the woods.

"Chief," Brad said, his voice lowered so as not to be rude. Behind him Ellen Schaffer was on her cell phone.

Jeffrey cut his eyes at Brad. Within ten minutes everyone on campus would know exactly what had happened.

Brad winced, understanding the mistake he had made. "Sorry."

Ellen Schaffer followed the exchange, giving a quick "Gotta go" into her cell phone before ending the call.

She was an attractive young blonde with hazel eyes and one of the most off-putting Yankee accents Jeffrey had heard in a long time. She wore a pair of tight running shorts and an even tighter cropped Lycra shirt. A belt with a CD player sat low on her hips, and an intricately designed sunburst was tattooed in a circle around her belly button.

Jeffrey began, "Ms. Schaffer —"

Schaffer's voice was more grating than he remembered when she asked, "Is she going to be all right?"

"I think so," Jeffrey said, though his gut twisted into a knot over the question. Tessa had been unconscious when they loaded her onto the stretcher. There was no telling if she would ever wake up again. He wanted to be with her now — with Sara — but there was nothing Jeffrey could do at the hospital except wait. At least this way he might be able to find some answers for Sara's family.

Jeffrey asked, "Can you tell me again what happened?"

Schaffer's lower lip trembled at the question.

He prompted, "You saw the body from the bridge?"

"I was jogging. I always jog in the morning."

He looked at his watch again. "This exact time?"

"Yes."

"Always alone?"

"Usually. Sometimes."

Jeffrey made a conscious effort to be polite when what he really wanted to do was shake the girl and make her tell him what he wanted to know. "You usually jog alone?"

"Yes," she answered. "I'm sorry."

"Do you normally take this trail?"

"Normally," she echoed. "I go down the bridge and then up into the woods. There are paths . . ." Her voice trailed off as she realized he must know this.

"So," he said, getting her back on track, "you jog this same path every day?"

Ellen nodded, a quick up-and-down. "I don't usually stop at the bridge, but something didn't feel right. I don't know why I stopped." She pressed her lips into a thin line as she considered it. "There are usually birds, nature sounds. It felt too still.

Do you know what I mean?"

Jeffrey knew. He had sensed that same eerie feeling when he was running through the woods looking for Sara and Tessa. The only sounds had been those of his own feet pounding into the ground and his heart pounding even more loudly in his head.

Ellen continued, "So I stopped to stretch, and then I looked over the railing — and there he was."

"You didn't go down to check on him?"

She looked embarrassed. "I didn't. . . . Should I have?"

"No," he said and then, to be kind, added, "it's better that you didn't contaminate the scene."

She seemed relieved. "I could tell . . ." She looked down at her hands, silently crying.

Jeffrey glanced back at the woods, nervous that Matt and Lena were not back by now, especially with the noise the helicopter had made. Sending them out into the forest was probably not one of his better ideas.

Schaffer interrupted his thoughts, asking, "Did he suffer?"

"No," he assured her, though he had no idea. He said, "We think he jumped from the bridge."

She seemed surprised. "I just assumed . . ."

He did not give her time to dwell on her feelings. "So you saw him. You called the police. Then what did you do?"

"I stayed on the bridge until the officer got here." She indicated Brad, who gave a sheepish smile. "Then the others came, and I stayed with him."

"Did you see anyone else? Someone in the woods?"

"Just the girl going up the hill," she said.

"Anyone else?"

"No. No one," she answered, looking over Jeffrey's shoulder. He turned, seeing Matt and Lena walking out of the woods. Lena was limping, her hands out to the side in case she fell. Matt offered his hand to help her down the hill, but she waved him off.

Jeffrey told Ellen Schaffer, "I'll follow up with you tomorrow. Thank you for making yourself available." Then, to Brad, "Make sure she gets back to the dorm."

"Yes, sir," Brad said, but Jeffrey was already running up the hill.

The soles of Jeffrey's loafers slipped on the ground as he ran toward Lena and Matt, but all he could think was that he had jeopardized another woman by sending Lena into the woods. By the time he reached them, remorse was a tight band around his chest. He put his hand under Lena's arm to help her sit.

"What happened?" Jeffrey asked, feeling like a parrot, thinking he'd asked that question a million times today and still had not gotten a satisfactory answer. "Are you okay?"

"Yes," Lena said, shrugging him off so quickly that she fell the rest of the way down. Frank started to help her, taking her arm, but Lena jerked away, saying, "Jesus, I'm all right," though she winced as her foot touched the ground.

The three men stood transfixed as Lena untied the laces of her shoe, and Jeffrey knew they were feeling the same emotions he was. When he glanced up, both Matt and Frank leveled him with an accusatory glare. Lena could have been seriously hurt in the woods. Whatever had happened to her — and whatever could have hap-pened — was Jeffrey's fault.

Lena broke the spell, saying, "He was still out there."

"Where?" Jeffrey asked, feeling his pulse quicken.

"The bastard was hiding behind a tree, looking to see what was going on."

Frank muttered an angry "Jesus," but Jeffrey did not know if his anger was for the attacker or for Jeffrey.

"I chased him," Lena continued, oblivious to the tension, or perhaps just choosing to ignore it. "I tripped on something. A log. I don't know. I can show you where he was hiding."

Jeffrey tried to get his head around this. Was the attacker staying around to make sure Tessa got help, or was he watching what happened like a home movie, sucking up the drama?

Frank had an edge to his voice when he asked Matt, "Where were you when all this was happening?"

Matt used the same sharp tone. "We spread out to cover more area. Say, a coupla minutes later, I saw the kid running."

Frank grumbled, "You shouldn'ta left her in the first place."

Matt grumbled back, "I was just following procedure."

"Both of you," Jeffrey said, trying to stop them. "We don't have time for this." He turned his attention to Lena again. "How close was he to the scene?"

"Close," she said. "Off the trail, about fifty yards away. I backtracked, thinking if he was still hanging around, it'd be close, so he could see the action."

Jeffrey asked, "Did you get a good look at him?"

"No," she told him. "He saw me before I saw him. He was crouching behind a tree. Maybe he was getting off on watching Sara freak out."

"I didn't ask for speculation," Jeffrey snapped, not liking the condescending way she had said Sara's name. Lena had never gotten along with Sara, but now was hardly the time to bring up the grudge, especially considering the state Tessa was in.

He said, "You saw the guy. Then what?"

"I didn't see him," she shot back, her anger ignited. Jeffrey realized too late that he had pushed the wrong buttons. He looked to Frank and Matt for help, but their faces were just as hard as Lena's.

"Go on," Jeffrey said.

Lena was terse. "I saw a blur. Movement. He stood up and took off. I ran after him."

"Which way did he go?"

Lena took her time, looking up to find the sun. "West, probably toward the highway."

"Black? White?"

"White," she said, then added a flippant, "maybe."

"Maybe?" Jeffrey demanded, aware that he was fueling the fire but incapable of stopping himself.

"I told you," she said, defensive. "He turned and ran. What was I going to do, ask him to slow down so I could ascertain his ethnicity?"

Jeffrey paused a moment, trying to hold back his temper. "What was he wearing?"

"Something dark."

"A coat? Jeans?"

"Jeans, maybe a coat. I don't know. It was dark."

"Long coat, short coat?"

"A jacket . . . I think."

"Did he have a weapon?"

"I couldn't see."

"What color was his hair?"

"I don't know."

"You don't know?"

"I think he was wearing a hat."

"You *think* he was?" Suddenly, all the helplessness that had been building up since he had seen Tessa lying near death exploded out of him. "Jesus Christ, Lena, how long were you a cop?"

Lena stared at him with the kind of burning hatred he was used to seeing in suspects he interrogated.

He demanded, "You chase a fucking suspect, and you can't even tell me if he was wearing a hat or not? What the fuck were you doing out there, picking daisies?"

Lena kept staring up at him, her jaw working as she held back what she wanted to say.

"It's a damn good thing he didn't go after you," Jeffrey said. "We'd be looking at two girls on that chopper instead of one."

She snapped, "I can take care of myself."

"You think that little knife on your ankle's gonna protect you?" He was disgusted by the surprised look on her face, mostly because he had taught Lena better than that. Jeffrey had seen her ankle sheath when she'd slid on her ass down the riverbank.

He said, "I should run you in for carrying concealed."

She continued to stare, her hatred palpable.

"You better check that look," he warned her.

Lena's teeth were so tightly clenched that her words were hard to make out. "I don't work for you anymore, *asshole*."

Something inside Jeffrey was very close to snapping. His vision sharpened, everything coming into startling focus.

"Chief," Frank said, putting his hand on Jeffrey's shoulder. Jeffrey backed down, knowing he was acting insane. He saw his bloody clothes on the ground, Tessa's blood. Everything rushed in on him in that moment: The tears on Sara's face making tracks on her bloodstained cheek. Tessa's arm, limp, dangling off the stretcher as they lifted her.

Jeffrey turned away so they could not see his expression, picking up his badge, polishing it with the tail of his undershirt, trying to buy himself time to calm down.

Brad Stephens chose that moment to walk up, twirling his hat in his hand. He asked, "What's going on, Chief?"

Anger made Jeffrey's throat tight. "I told you to walk Schaffer to her dorm."

"She ran into a couple of friends," Brad said, turning pale. "She wanted to go with them." His clear blue eyes were wide with fright, and he stuttered, "I-I-I figured she'd be better off with them. They're with her house. Keyes House. I didn't think —"

"All right," Jeffrey interrupted, knowing that taking out his anger on Brad would only make him feel worse. He told Frank, "Get some of our people on the highway. Tell them we're looking for someone walking. Anyone walking. Maybe in a jacket, maybe not." He did not look at Lena on this last part, though she must have known a description would make all the difference.

Frank said, "The units should be here soon."

Jeffrey nodded. "I want a grid search from this area up to the last point where Lena saw the attacker. We're looking for a knife. Anything that doesn't belong."

"He had something in his hand," Lena said, like she was offering up a prize. "A white bag."

Brad Stephens gasped, then blushed when everyone looked at him.

Jeffrey asked, "What is it?"

Brad spoke with a mixture of apprehension and apology. "I saw Tessa picking up some stuff on the way up the hill," he said.

"What kind of stuff?"

"Trash and things, I guess. She had a plastic bag, like the kind they give out at the Pig." He meant the Piggly Wiggly, the town's grocery store. Thousands of people shopped there every week.

Jeffrey forced himself not to speak for a few seconds. He thought about the piece of plastic he had found in Tessa's hand. The scrap very well could have been the torn handle of a plastic grocery bag.

Jeffrey asked Brad, "Tessa found the bag on the hill?" noticing for the first time how much trash littered the area. The college grounds crew spent most of their energy maintaining the land closest to the college. They had probably not cleaned up out here all year.

"Yes, sir," Brad said. "She just kind of picked it up and started putting some stuff in it while she walked up the hill."

"What stuff?" Jeffrey asked.

Brad stuttered again, something that happened only when he was nervous. "T-trash, I reckon. Wrappers and cans and stuff."

Jeffrey tried to moderate his tone with Brad, mostly because for some reason the stutter made his own anger boil back up. "You didn't think to go up there and ask her what she was doing?"

"You told me to stay with the witness," Brad reminded him. Another blush crept up his pasty cheeks. "And I . . . uh . . . didn't want to interfere with what she was doing up there. You know, p-p-personal stuff."

Jeffrey told Matt, "Put that out on the radio. Dark clothes, maybe carrying a white bag."

"You think he stole the trash?" Lena asked, skeptical.

Matt cupped his cell phone to his ear

and walked a few feet away to carry out Jeffrey's orders. Frank was looking down at Lena, but there was no telling what he was thinking.

Jeffrey saw Chuck taking his time walking up the hill. When the other man stopped and bent to the ground, Jeffrey tensed, but Chuck was only tying his shoe.

When Chuck reached them, he said, "I was staying with the body. Securing the scene."

Lena ignored him, asking Jeffrey, "You think this is connected?"

Jeffrey could tell from Frank's expression that, with all that had happened, he was only now considering the question. The old cop would have gotten to it eventually, but Lena was leaps and bounds ahead of the more senior officers on the squad. Her quick mind was the thing Jeffrey missed most now that she was gone.

Lena repeated, "There's got to be some kind of connection."

Jeffrey shut her out, and not just because Chuck was taking all of this in. Lena had chosen to stop being a cop seven months ago. She was not part of Jeffrey's team anymore.

He told Frank, "Let me see the suicide note."

"It was under a rock at the end of the bridge," Frank said. He reached into his back pocket and pulled out a folded sheet of notebook paper. Jeffrey did not have it in him to reprimand Frank for not putting the note in an evidence bag. Both of their hands were bloody enough to stain the page.

Jeffrey glanced at it, his eyes not really focusing.

Chuck put his hand to his chin in a thinking pose. "You still think he took a swan dive on his own?"

"Yeah," Jeffrey said, staring at the college security guard. Chuck was a walking sieve where secrets were concerned. Jeffrey had heard him gossip about enough people to know that the man could not be trusted.

Frank backed up Jeffrey, explaining, "A killer would have stabbed him, not pushed him off the bridge. They don't change their MOs like that."

"Makes sense," Chuck agreed, though anyone with an ounce of intelligence would have asked more questions.

Jeffrey handed the note back to Frank, saying, "When a team gets here, you take the other side of the river. I want a fingertip search if we have to. You understand?"

"Yeah," Frank told him. "We'll start at the river and go to the highway."

"Good."

Matt had finished his calls and Jeffrey gave him another assignment. "Call over to Macon and see if we can get some dogs out here."

Chuck crossed his arms over his chest. "I'll get a couple of my people —"

Jeffrey jabbed a finger at the other man. "Keep your people the fuck out of my crime scene," he ordered.

Chuck stood his ground. "This is college property."

Jeffrey pointed toward the dead boy on the riverbed. "The only college business you've got is finding out who that kid is and telling his mama."

"It's Rosen," Chuck said, defensive. "Andy Rosen."

"Rosen?" Lena echoed.

Jeffrey asked, "Did you know him?"

Lena shook her head no, but Jeffrey could tell she was hiding something.

"Lena?" he said, giving her the opportunity to come clean.

"I said no," she snapped, and Jeffrey was no longer sure if she was lying or just dicking around with him. Either way he didn't have time for her games.

"You're in charge of the search," Jeffrey told Frank. "I've got something to do."

Frank nodded, probably guessing where Jeffrey had to go.

Jeffrey told Chuck, "Have the mother in the library for me to talk to in an hour." He indicated Lena with his thumb. "If I were you, I'd take Lena to do the notification. She's had a lot more experience at this kind of thing than you have."

Jeffrey let himself look at Lena again, thinking she would be appreciative. From the way she looked back, he could tell she didn't think he'd done her any favors.

Jeffrey always kept a spare shirt in his car, but no amount of rubbing would get all the blood off his hands. He had used a bottle of water to clean his chest and upper body, but his fingernails were still rimmed with red. His Auburn class ring was caked in it, dried blood around the numbers from his football jersey and the year he would have graduated if he'd stuck around. Jeffrey thought about the famous line from Macbeth, knowing guilt was magnifying the blood, making it seem worse than it really was. Tessa should never have been on that hill. Three seasoned cops with guns less than a hundred feet away, and she'd been stabbed nearly to death. Jeffrey should have protected her. He should have done something.

Jeffrey pulled into the Linton driveway, parking behind Eddie's van. Dread filled him like a virus as he forced himself to get out of the car. Since Sara and Jeffrey's divorce, Eddie Linton had made it clear that he thought Jeffrey was no better than a piece of shit smeared onto his eldest daughter's shoe. Despite this, Jeffrey felt a real affinity for the old man. Eddie was a good father, the kind of father Jeffrey had wanted when he was a kid. Jeffrey had known the Lintons for over ten years, and, during his marriage to Sara, he'd felt for the first time in his life like he belonged to a family. In a lot of ways, Tessa was like a little sister to him.

Jeffrey took a deep breath as he walked up the driveway. A cool breeze brought a chill, and he realized he was sweating. Music was coming from the back of the house, and Jeffrey decided to walk around rather than knock on the front door. He stopped suddenly, recognizing the song on the radio.

Sara did not like a lot of fuss and formality, so their wedding had been held at the Linton house. They'd exchanged vows in the living room, then had a small reception for family and friends in the backyard. Their first dance as husband and wife had been to this song. He could remember what it had felt like to hold her, feeling her hand on the back of his neck, lightly stroking the nape, her body close to his in a way that was at once chaste and the most sensual thing he'd ever felt. Sara was a terrible dancer, but either the wine or the moment had conferred upon her some kind of miraculous coordination, and they had danced until Sara's mother reminded them they had a plane to catch. Eddie had tried to stop her; even then he did not want to let Sara go.

Jeffrey pushed himself to move again. He had taken one daughter away from the Lintons that long-ago day, and he was about to tell them they might have lost another.

As Jeffrey rounded the corner, Cathy Linton was laughing at something Eddie had said. They were sitting on the back deck, oblivious as they listened to Shelby Lynne and enjoyed a lazy Sunday afternoon the way most everybody else in Grant County was doing today. Cathy sat in a sling-back chair, her feet propped up on a stool as Eddie painted her toenails.

Sara's mother was a beautiful woman

with just a little gray in her long blond hair. She must have been close to sixty, but she still had a lot going for her. There was something sexy and down-to-earth about Cathy that Jeffrey had always found appealing. Though Sara insisted she was nothing like her mother — tall where Cathy was petite, curvy where Cathy was almost boyishly thin — there were a lot of things the two women shared. Sara had her mother's perfect skin and that smile that made you feel like you were the most important thing on the planet when it was directed at you. She also had her mother's biting wit, and she knew how to put you in your place while making it sound like a compliment.

Cathy smiled at Jeffrey when she saw him, saying, "We missed you at lunch."

Eddie sat up in his chair, screwing the top back onto the fingernail polish, grumbling something Jeffrey was glad he could not hear.

Cathy turned up the music, obviously remembering it from the wedding. She sang along in a low, throaty voice, "I'm confessin' that I love you . . ." with such a joyful teasing in her eyes, her eyes that looked so much like Sara's, that he had to look away.

She turned the music down, sensing that something was wrong, probably thinking he was having an argument with Sara. She said, "The girls should be back soon. I don't know what's taking them so long."

Jeffrey made himself walk closer. His legs felt unsteady, and he knew that what he was about to say would change everything. Cathy and Eddie would always remember this afternoon, this time when their lives had been completely turned upside down. As a cop, Jeffrey had done hundreds of notifications, told hundreds of parents and spouses and friends that their loved one had been hurt or, worse, would not be coming home. None had struck him as closely as this one did. Telling the Lintons would be almost as bad as being in that clearing again, watching Sara break down as Tessa bled out, knowing that there was nothing he could do to help either of them.

Jeffrey realized they were staring at him because he had been quiet for too long. He asked, "Where's Devon?" not wanting to do this twice.

Cathy gave him a questioning look. "He's at his mama's," she said, using the same tone Sara had used less than an hour ago with Tessa: tight, controlled, scared.

She opened her mouth to ask the question, but nothing came out.

Jeffrey climbed the steps slowly, wondering how he could do this. He stood on the top step, tucking his hands into his pockets. Cathy's eyes followed his hands, his bloody, guilt-stained hands.

He saw her throat move as she swallowed. She put her hand to her mouth, sudden tears glistening in her eyes.

Eddie finally spoke for his wife, giving voice to the only question the parent of two children can ask, "Which one?"

3

Lena used her twisted ankle as an excuse to lag behind Chuck, knowing that her temper would flare if he tried to make conversation. She needed a couple of minutes to herself to think about what had happened with Jeffrey. Her mind would not let go of the way he had looked at her. Jeffrey had been angry with Lena before, but never like today. Today he'd actually hated her.

In the last year, Lena's life had been one long series of fuck-ups, from losing her job to sliding on her ass down the riverbed. No wonder Jeffrey had pushed her off the force. He was right; she was unreliable. He could not trust her because time and time again Lena had proved she did not deserve it. This time she might have cost him the man who'd stabbed Tessa Linton.

"Keep up, Adams," Chuck tossed over his shoulder. He was a couple of feet in front of her, and she stared at his wide back, willing all her hatred into him.

"Come on, Adams," Chuck said. "Walk it off."

"It's fine."

"Yeah," Chuck said, slowing down. He gave her a wet smile. "So . . . guess the chief don't want you back anytime soon."

"You either," she reminded him.

Chuck snorted, as if she'd made a joke instead of pointed out the truth. Lena had never met anyone who was so good at ignoring the obvious.

Chuck said, "He just don't like me because I dated his girlfriend back in high school."

"You dated Sara Linton?" Lena asked, thinking that was about as likely as Chuck's dating the queen of England.

Chuck shrugged casually. "Long time ago. You friends with her or something?"

"Yeah," Lena lied. Sara was far from a close friend. "She never mentioned it."

"Sore spot for her," Chuck covered. "I left her for another girl."

"Right," Lena said, thinking this was typical Chuck. He thought that everything that came out of his mouth was believed, and he labored under the false impression that he was well respected on campus, even though it was common knowledge that the only reason Chuck had gotten his job was his daddy had made a phone call to Kevin Blake, the dean of Grant Tech. Albert Gaines, president of the Grant Trust and Loan, had a lot of pull in town, especially with the college. When Chuck had moved back home after eight years in the army, he walked right into the job as director of campus security with no questions asked.

Answering to a man like Chuck was a bitter pill Lena had to swallow every day. She had not been presented with a lot of choices after resigning her badge. At thirty-four, Lena didn't know anything other than being a cop. She'd entered the academy right out of high school and never looked back. The only things she was qualified for were flipping burgers or cleaning houses, neither of which appealed.

In the days after Lena left the force, she'd considered going somewhere far away, maybe visiting Mexico and finding her grandmother's people or volunteering somewhere overseas, but then reality caught up with her, and she realized that the bank did not care if Lena needed a change of scenery — they still expected her mortgage and car payments every month. Even with the paltry disability payments she received from the police department and what little money she'd managed to make from selling her house, things were tight.

The college job offered free campus housing and health benefits in lieu of a living wage. Granted, the housing sucked and the health insurance had a deductible so high Lena panicked if she so much as sneezed, but it was a steady job and meant she did not have to move in with her uncle Hank. Moving back to Reece, where Hank had raised Lena and Sibyl, her twin sister, would have been too easy. It would've been too easy to take up space at the bar Hank owned and drink away her nightmares. It would have been too easy to hide from the rest of the world, until thirty years had passed and she was still holding down a barstool, the scars on her hands the only reminder of why she'd started drinking in the first place.

Lena had been raped a little over a year ago; not just raped but kidnapped, held in her abductor's home for days. Her memories from that time were scattered because she was drugged during most of the attack, her mind sent to a safer place while her body was brutalized. Scars on her hands and feet served as a permanent reminder that she'd been nailed spread-eagle to the floor to keep her open to her attacker at all times. Her hands still ached on cold days, but the pain could not match the fear she'd experienced watching the long nails being hammered into her flesh.

Before setting his sights on Lena, this same animal had killed Sibyl, Lena's sister, and the fact that he was gone now offered no comfort. He still showed up in Lena's dreams, giving her such vivid nightmares that she sometimes woke in a cold sweat, clutching the covers, feeling his presence in the room. Worse still were the dreams that were not nightmares, when he touched her so softly that her skin tingled, and she woke disoriented and aroused, her body shaking in response to the erotic images her sleeping mind had conjured. She knew the drugs she had been given during the attack had tricked her body into responding, but Lena still could not forgive herself. Sometimes the memory of his touch on her body would cover her like the fine silk of a spiderweb, and she would find herself shaking so hard that only a scalding-hot shower could make her skin feel like her own again.

Lena didn't know if it was desperation or stupidity that had made her call the college's counseling center a month ago.

Whatever had compelled her, the three and a half sessions she'd managed to attend were a huge mistake. Talking to a stranger about what had happened — not that Lena had actually gotten around to that part of it — was too much. There were some things that were too private to discuss. Ten minutes into a particularly painful fourth session, Lena had gotten up and left the clinic, never to return. At least not until now, when she would have to tell that same doctor that her son was dead.

"Adams," Chuck said, glancing over his shoulder, "you know this chick?"

Women were always chicks or bitches to Chuck, depending on whether or not he thought they would fuck him. Lena hoped to God he knew she was a bitch, but sometimes she got the feeling that Chuck thought it was just a matter of time before she threw herself at his feet.

She told him, "I've never met her." Then, just in case, she added, "I've seen her around campus."

He looked back at her again, but Chuck was as good at reading people as he was at making friends.

"Rosen," Chuck said. "That sound Jewish to you?"

Lena shrugged; she'd never given it

much thought. Grant Tech was fairly well integrated, and except for one or two assholes who had recently decided to take up spray-painting racial slurs on anything that wasn't moving, there was an easy balance on campus.

"Hope she's not —" Chuck made a whistling noise, whirling his finger near his temple. Of course Chuck would assume that anyone working in a mental-health clinic was nuts.

Lena did not give him the satisfaction of a response. She was trying to think whether anyone at the clinic would recognize her. The clinic closed at two on Sundays, but Rosen had agreed to see Lena after hours, probably because of the notoriety attached to Lena's case. Anyone who could read a newspaper knew the lurid details of Lena's kidnapping and rape. Rosen had probably been overjoyed to hear Lena's voice on the line.

"Here go," Chuck said, opening the door to the counseling center.

Lena caught the door before it closed in her face and followed Chuck into the crowded waiting room.

Like most colleges, Grant Tech was seriously underfunded in the mental-health department. Especially in Georgia, where the lottery-backed Hope Scholarship pretty much ensured that anybody who could pencil in a circle got into a state university, more and more kids were coming to college who could not handle the emotional stress of being away from home or having to work. As a technical college, Grant tended toward math nerds and overachievers anyway. These type-A personalities did not take failure well, and the counseling center was practically bulging at the seams from the influx of new students. If their insurance plans were anything like Lena's, the students had no choice but to turn to the college.

Chuck hitched up his pants as he walked to the counter. Lena could almost read his mind as he looked around the room, taking in the fact that most of the patients were young women wearing cropped T-shirts and bell-bottom jeans. Lena had her own thoughts about the girls, whose worst difficulties probably centered on boys and missing Fido back home. They probably had no idea what it was like to have real problems, problems that kept you up at night, sweating it out until morning came and you could breathe again.

"Hello?" Chuck said, popping his palm against the bell on the counter. Some of the women jumped at the sound, giving Lena a nasty glance, as if they expected her to be able to control him.

"Hello?" He leaned over the counter, trying to see down the hallway.

His voice was so loud in the small room that Lena wanted to put her hands over her ears. Instead she stared at the floor, trying not to look as embarrassed as she felt.

The receptionist, a tall strawberry blonde with an irritated look on her face, finally appeared. She glanced at Lena with no sign of recognition.

"There you are," Chuck said, smiling like they were old friends.

"Yes?"

"Carla?" Chuck asked, reading her name tag. His eyes lingered at her chest.

She crossed her arms. "What is it?"

Lena stepped in, keeping her voice low. "We need to see Dr. Rosen."

"She's in session. She can't be disturbed."

Lena was about to take the woman aside and privately explain the situation when Chuck blurted out, "Her son killed himself about an hour ago."

There was a collective gasp around the room. Magazines were dropped, and two girls walked out the door within seconds of each other.

Carla took a moment to recover from her shock before offering, "I'll go get her."

Lena stopped her, saying, "I'll tell her. Just take me to her office."

The younger woman exhaled with relief. "Thank you."

Chuck was at Lena's heels as they followed the girl down the long, narrow hallway. Claustrophobia struck Lena like a sudden flame, and she found herself sweating by the time they reached Jill Rosen's office. With his usual flair for knowing how to make things worse, Chuck stood close to Lena, almost hovering over her. She could smell his aftershave mixed with the sickly sweet smell of his gum, which he smacked loudly in her ear. She held her breath, turning her head away from him, trying not to be sick.

The receptionist rapped lightly on the door. "Jill?"

Lena pulled at her collar, trying to get more air.

Rosen sounded exasperated as she opened the door, asking, "Yes?" Then she saw Lena, recognition bringing a curious smile. Her mouth opened to say something, but Lena cut her off.

"Are you Dr. Rosen?" Lena asked, aware her voice sounded tinny.

Rosen looked from Lena to Chuck, hesitating for a moment before she turned back to the patient in her office, saying, "Lily, I'll be right back."

She pulled the door closed, saying, "This way."

Lena glared at Chuck before following her, but he still kept close to her heels.

Rosen stopped at an open doorway, gesturing into the room. "We can talk in here."

Lena had only ever been in the waiting room or Rosen's office, so she was surprised to find herself in a large conference room. The space was warm and open, with lots of plants, just like Jill Rosen's office. The walls were painted a soothing light gray. There were chairs covered in mauve fabric tucked under a long mahogany conference table. Large four-drawer filing cabinets filled one side of the room, and Lena was glad to see they were padlocked to keep people from prying.

The doctor turned around, pushing her hair out of her eyes. Jill Rosen had a narrow face and shoulder-length dark brown hair. She was attractive for her age, which was probably early forties, and dressed in an earthy style, with long, flowing blouses and skirts that suited her figure. There was a no-nonsense manner about her that had been very off-putting to Lena, especially when the doctor took it upon herself to diagnose Lena as an alcoholic after only three sessions. Lena wondered that the woman had any patients at all with that kind of attitude. Come to think of it, there was not much to be said for a shrink who couldn't keep her own son from taking a deep dive into a shallow river.

Predictably, Rosen got straight to the point. "What's the problem?"

Lena took a deep breath, wondering how strained this was going to be, considering her past with Rosen. She decided to be direct. "We've come about your son."

"Andy?" Rosen asked, sinking into one of the chairs like a slowly deflating balloon. She sat there, back straight, hands clasped in her lap, perfectly composed but for the look of sheer panic in her eyes. Lena had never read anyone's expression so clearly in her life. The woman was terrified.

"Is he —" Rosen stopped to clear her throat, and tears sprang into her eyes. "Has he gotten into trouble?"

Lena remembered Chuck. He was

standing in the doorway, hands tucked into his pockets as if he were watching a talk show. Before Chuck could protest, she shut the door in his face.

"I'm sorry," Lena said, pressing her palms against the table as she sat down. The apology was for Chuck, but Rosen took it a different way.

"What?" the doctor pleaded, a sudden desperation filling her voice.

"I meant —"

Without warning, Rosen reached across the table and grabbed Lena's hands. Lena flinched, but Rosen did not seem to notice. Since the rape, the thought of touching someone — or worse, being touched — made Lena break into a cold sweat. The intimacy of the moment brought bile to the back of her throat.

Rosen asked, "Where is he?"

Lena's leg started to shake, the heel of her foot bobbing up and down uncontrollably. When she spoke, her voice caught, but not from sympathy. "I need you to look at a picture."

"No," Rosen refused, holding on to Lena's hands as if she were hanging over a cliff and Lena was the only thing keeping her from falling. "No."

With difficulty Lena freed one of her

hands and took the Polaroid out of her pocket. She held up the picture, but Rosen looked away, closing her eyes like a child.

"Dr. Rosen," Lena began. Then, moderating her tone, "Jill, is this your son?"

She looked at Lena, not the photograph, hatred glowing like white-hot coals.

"Tell me if it's him," Lena persisted, willing her to get this over with.

Rosen finally looked at the Polaroid. Her nostrils flared and her lips pressed into a thin line as she fought back tears. Lena could tell from the woman's expression that the dead boy was her son, but Rosen was taking her time, staring at the picture, trying to let her mind accept what her eyes were seeing. Probably without thinking, Rosen stroked the scar on the back of Lena's hand with her thumb as though it were a talisman. The sensation was like sandpaper on a blackboard, and Lena gritted her teeth together so she would not scream.

Rosen finally asked, "Where?"

"We found him on the west side of campus," Lena told her, so taken by the urge to jerk back her hand that her arm began to shake.

Rosen, oblivious, asked, "What happened?"

Lena licked her lips, though her mouth was as dry as a desert. "He jumped," she said, trying to breathe. "From a bridge." She stopped. Then, "We think he —"

"What?" Rosen asked, her hand still clamped onto Lena's.

Lena could take no more, and she found herself begging, "Please, I'm sorry . . ." A look of confusion crossed Rosen's face, which made Lena feel even more trapped. The level of her voice rose with each word, until she was screaming, "Let go of my hand!"

Rosen recoiled quickly, and Lena stood, knocking over her chair, moving away from the other woman until she felt her back against the door.

A look of horror was on Rosen's face. "I'm sorry."

"No." Lena leaned against the door, rubbing her hands on her thighs like she was wiping off dirt. "It's okay," she said, her heart shaking in her chest. "I shouldn't have yelled at you."

"I should have known . . ."

"Please," Lena said, feeling heat on her thighs from the friction. She stopped the motion, clasping her hands, rubbing them together as if she were cold.

"Lena," Rosen said, sitting up in her

chair but not standing. She said, "It's okay. You're safe here."

"I know that," Lena said, but her voice was weak, and the taste of fear was still sour in her mouth. "I'm fine," she insisted, but she was still wringing her hands. Lena looked down, pressing her thumb into the scar on her palm, rubbing into it as if she could rub it away. "I'm okay," she said. "I'm okay."

"Lena . . . ," Rosen began, but she did not finish the thought.

Lena concentrated on her breathing, calming herself. Her hands were red and sticky from sweat, the scars standing out in angry relief. She forced herself to stop, tucking her hands under her arms. She was acting like a head case. This was the kind of thing mentally ill people did. Rosen was probably ready to commit her.

Rosen tried again. "Lena?"

Lena tried to laugh it off. "I just got nervous," she said, pushing her hair behind her ear. Sweat made it stick to her scalp.

Inexplicably, Lena wanted to say something mean, something that would cut Rosen in two and put them both back on a level playing field.

Maybe Rosen sensed what was coming, because she asked, "Who should I talk to at the police station?"

Lena stared, because for a split second she could not remember why she was here.

"Lena?" Rosen asked. She had retreated back into herself, her hands clasped in her lap, her posture ramrod straight.

"I —" Lena stopped. "Chief Tolliver will be at the library in about half an hour."

Rosen stared, as if she could not decide what to do. For a mother, thirty minutes of waiting to hear the details of what had happened to her son was probably a life-time.

Lena said, "Jeffrey doesn't know about . . ." She indicated the space between them.

"Therapy?" Rosen provided, as if Lena were stupid for not being able to say the word.

"I'm sorry," Lena said, and this time she genuinely felt the emotion. She was supposed to be here comforting Jill Rosen, not yelling at her. Jeffrey had told Chuck that Lena would be an asset, and she had fucked everything up in the space of five minutes.

Lena tried again. "I'm really sorry."

Rosen raised her chin, acknowledging the apology but not accepting it.

Lena uprighted the chair. The desire to

bolt from the room was so strong that her legs ached.

Rosen said, "Tell me what happened. I need to know what happened."

Lena folded her hands over the back of the chair, holding on to it tightly. "It looks like he jumped from the bridge by the woods," she said. "A student found him and called 911. The coroner got there a little while later and pronounced him."

Rosen inhaled, holding the air in her chest for a few beats. "He walks to school that way."

"The bridge?" Lena asked, realizing that Rosen must have a house near Main Street, where a lot of professors lived.

"His bike kept getting stolen," she said, and Lena nodded. Bicycles were constantly being stolen on campus, and the security team had no idea who was doing it.

Rosen sighed again, as if she were letting out her grief in little spurts. She asked, "Was it fast?"

"I don't know," Lena said. "I think so. That kind of thing . . . it would have to happen fast."

"Andy's manic-depressive," Rosen told her. "He's always been sensitive, but his father and I are . . ." She let her voice trail off, as if she did not want to trust Lena with too much information. Considering her recent outburst, Lena could not blame her.

Rosen asked, "Did he leave a note?"

Lena took the note out of her back pocket and put it down on the table. Rosen hesitated before picking it up.

"That's not from Andy," Lena said, indicating the bloody fingerprints Frank and Jeffrey had left on the paper. Even considering everything that had happened with Tessa, Lena was surprised Frank had let her take the note to Andy's mother.

"It's blood?"

Lena nodded but did not explain. She would leave it to Jeffrey to decide how much information to give the mother.

Rosen put on her glasses, which were hanging by a chain around her neck. Though Lena had not asked her to, she read aloud, " 'I can't take it anymore. I love you, Mama. Andy.' "

The older woman took another deep breath, as if she could hold it in along with her emotions. Carefully she took off her glasses, putting the suicide note on the table. She stared at it as if she could still read it, saying, "It's almost identical to the one he wrote before."

"When was this?" Lena asked, her mind

clicking onto the investigation.

"January second. He slit his arm up the center. I found him before he lost too much blood, but . . ." She leaned her head on her hand, looking down at the note. She put her fingers on it, like she was touching a part of her son — the only part that he had left her.

"I'll need that back," Lena told her, even though Jeffrey and Frank had destroyed its value as evidence.

"Oh." Rosen moved her hand away. "Will I be able to get it back?"

"Yes, when everything's finished."

"Oh," Rosen repeated. She started to fidget with the chain holding her glasses. "Can I see him?"

"They'll need to perform an autopsy."

Rosen latched on to the news. "Why? Did you find something suspicious?"

"No," Lena said, though she was still unsure. "It's just routine because the death was unattended. No one was there."

"Was his body badly . . . damaged?"

"Not really," she said, knowing that the answer was subjective. Lena could still remember seeing her sister in the morgue last year. Though Sara had cleaned her up, the small bruises and cuts on Sibyl's face had seemed like a thousand wounds.

"Where is he now?"

"At the morgue. They'll release him to the funeral home in a day or so," Lena told her, then realized from Rosen's shocked expression that the mother had not let her mind think through the steps to the point where she would actually have to bury her son. Lena thought about apologizing, but she knew what a pointless gesture the words would be.

"He wanted to be cremated," Rosen said. "I don't think I can do that. I don't think I can let them . . ." She shook her head, not finishing. Her hand went to her mouth, and Lena noticed a wedding ring.

"Do you want me to tell your husband?"

"Brian's out of town," she said. "He's been working on a grant."

"He's at the college, too?"

"Yes." Her brow furrowed as she fought back emotions. "Andy was working with him, trying to help. We thought he was doing better —" She tried to suppress a sob but finally broke down.

Lena clutched the back of the chair, watching the other woman. Rosen was a silent crier, her lips parted but no sound coming out. She put her hand to her chest, squeezing her eyes closed as tears poured down her face. Her thin shoulders folded inward, and her chin trembled as it dropped to her chest.

Lena was overwhelmed with the urge to leave. Even before the rape, she had never been good at comforting people. There was something about neediness that threatened her, like Lena would have to give up part of herself in order to console someone. She wanted to go home now to fortify herself, to wash the taste of fear out of her mouth. Lena had to find a way to regain her strength before she went out into the world again. Especially before she saw Jeffrey.

Rosen must have sensed Lena's feelings. She wiped away a tear, her tone turning brisk. "I need to call my husband," she said. "Can you give me a moment?"

"Of course," Lena told her, relieved. "I'll meet you in the library." She put her hand on the doorknob but stopped, not looking at the doctor. "I know I don't have a right to ask this," she began, aware that Jeffrey would write her off completely if Rosen told him what had happened.

Rosen seemed to sense exactly what Lena was worried about. She snapped, "No, you *don't* have a right to ask."

Lena turned the knob, but she could feel Rosen's stare burrowing into her. Lena felt trapped, but she managed to ask, "What?"

Rosen offered what seemed like a compromise. She said, "If you're sober, I won't tell him."

Lena swallowed, and her mouth could almost taste the shot of whiskey her mind had been conjuring for the last two minutes. Without answering, she shut the door behind her.

Lena sat at an empty table by the circulation desk at the library, watching Chuck making a fool of himself with Nan Thomas, the school librarian. Setting aside the fact that Nan, with her mousy brown hair and thick glasses, was hardly worth the effort, Lena happened to know that the woman was gay. Nan had been Sibyl's lover for four years. The two women had been living together when Sibyl was murdered.

To take her mind off Chuck, Lena glanced around the library, looking at the students working at the long tables lining the middle of the room. Midterms were on the horizon, and the place was pretty packed for a Sunday. Other than the cafeteria and the counseling center, the library was the only building open today.

As libraries went, Grant Tech's was pretty impressive. Lena supposed that the school's not having a football team meant more money could be spent on the facilities, but she still thought they would have been better off with some sort of athletic department. Five years ago two Grant professors had developed some kind of shot or magic pill that made pigs grow fatter in a shorter amount of time. Farmers had gone nuts over the discovery, and there was a framed cover of *Porcine & Poultry* by the library entrance with a picture of the two professors looking rich and satisfied on the cover. The headline read "High on the Hog," and judging by the smiles on the professors' faces, they certainly were not hurting for money. As with most research institutes, the school got a chunk of the proceeds from anything its professors worked on, and Kevin Blake, the dean, had used some of the money to completely refurbish the library.

Large stained-glass windows facing the eastern side of the campus had been reglazed so that heat and air-conditioning didn't seep outside. The dark wood paneling on the walls and the two stories of floor-to-ceiling bookshelves had been lightened so that they were still imposing but not oppressive. The overall atmosphere was soothing, and Lena liked coming here at night as part of her after-work routine. She would sit in one of the cubicles in the front and thumb through whatever book was handy until around ten, when she would return to her room, have a drink or two to take the edge off, and try to go to sleep. All in all, the routine worked for her. There was something comforting about having a schedule.

"Fuck," Lena groaned as Richard Carter walked toward her.

Without waiting for an invitation, Richard slumped down in the chair opposite Lena.

"Hey, girl," he said, flashing a smile.

"Hey," she said, injecting as much dislike into her tone as possible.

"Whatcha know good?"

Lena stared at him, wishing he would go away. Sibyl's ex–teaching assistant was a short, husky man who had only recently traded in his thick glasses for contact lenses. Richard was three years younger than Lena, but he already had a large bald spot on the crown of his head, which he tried to cover by brushing the rest of his hair straight back. Between the new contacts, which had him constantly blinking, and the widow's peak on his forehead, he had the appearance of a confused owl.

Since Sibyl's death Richard had been promoted to an associate professorship in the biology department where, considering his repellent personality, his career would probably stall. Richard was a lot like Chuck in that he tried to cover his suffocating stupidity with an air of completely unfounded superiority. He could not even order breakfast at a restaurant without implying to everyone around that he knew more about the eggs than the cook did.

"Did you hear about that kid?" Richard made a low whistle like a plane going down, waving his hand in the air and slapping it on the table for emphasis. "Jumped right off the bridge."

"Yeah," she told him, not offering more.

"Assassination plots abound," Richard said, almost giddy. He loved gossip more than a woman; appropriate, considering he was queer as a three-dollar bill. "Both his parents work at the school. His mother is in the counseling department. Can you imagine the scandal?"

Lena felt a flush of shame as she thought about Jill Rosen. She told Richard, "I imagine they're both pretty broken up. Their son is dead."

Richard twisted his lips to the side, openly appraising Lena. He was very perceptive for a self-involved asshole, and she hoped she wasn't giving anything away.

He asked, "Do you know them?"

"Who?"

"Brian and Jill," he said, glancing over Lena's shoulder. He gave a silly little-girl wave to someone before turning his focus back to Lena.

She stared, not answering his question.

"Have you lost weight?"

"No," she said, though she had. Her pants were looser than they had been last week. Lena had not felt much like eating lately. "Was he one of your kids?"

"Andy?" Richard asked. "Sibyl had him for a quarter right before —"

"What kind of kid was he?"

"Nasty, if you ask me. His parents couldn't do enough for him."

"He was spoiled?"

"Rotten," Richard confirmed. "He nearly failed Sibyl's class. Organic biology. How hard is that? He's supposed to be the next Einstein, and he can't pass OB?" Richard gave a snort of disgust. "Brian tried to lean on her, call in some favors to get the grade bumped up."

"Sibyl didn't do favors like that."

"Of course she didn't," Richard said, as if he had never called it into question. "Sib was very polite, as usual, but Brian was ticked." He lowered his voice. "Let's be honest. Brian was always jealous of Sibyl. He lobbied night and day for her position as department head."

Lena wondered if Richard was really being honest or just stirring up shit. He had a habit of putting himself in the middle of things. At one point during the investigation of Sibyl's murder, Richard's big mouth had nearly talked him onto the list of suspects, even though he was as capable of murder as Lena was of sprouting wings.

She tried to put him on the spot. "It sounds like you know Brian pretty well."

He shrugged, waving at someone else behind Lena as he said, "It's a small department. We all work together. That was Sibyl's doing. You know her motto was 'Teamwork.' "

He waved again.

She was half curious to turn around and see if anyone was really there but decided she would be better served pumping Richard for information.

"Anyway," Richard began, "Andy ended up dropping out, and of course Daddy found a job for him at the lab." He puffed an irritated breath. "Not that I'd call sitting on your ass listening to rap music for six hours a day a job. And God forbid you complain to Brian about it."

"I guess he'll take the news pretty hard."

"Who wouldn't?" Richard asked. "I imagine both of them will be devastated."

"What does Brian do?"

"Biomedical research. He's working on a grant right now, and between you and me . . ." He didn't finish, but Lena knew that it was between Richard and the entire school. "Well, let's just say that if he doesn't get this grant, he's out of here."

"He doesn't have tenure?"

"Oh," Richard said knowingly, "he has tenure."

Lena waited for more, but Richard was uncharacteristically silent. She had worked on campus for only a few months, but Lena could guess how the school would get rid of a professor who was under-performing. Richard, who taught remedial biology to drooling freshmen all day, was a perfect example of how the administration could punish professors without exactly firing them. The only difference was, someone like Richard would never leave.

She asked, "Was he smart?"

"Andy?" Richard shrugged. "He was here, wasn't he?"

Lena knew that that could be taken a

couple of different ways. Grant Tech was a good school, but any geek worth his salt wanted to go to Georgia Tech in Atlanta. Like Emory University in Decatur, Georgia Tech was considered one of the South's Ivy League schools. Sibyl had gone to Georgia Tech on a full scholarship, and it had given her instant cachet on staff. She could have taught anywhere she wanted to, but something had drawn her to Grant.

Richard sounded reflective. "I wanted to go to Georgia Tech, you know. For as long as I could remember. That was going to be my way out of Perry." He smiled, and for just a second he seemed like a regular human being. "When I was a kid, I had posters all over my walls. I was a Ramblin' Wreck," he said, citing one of Georgia Tech's many school mottos. "I was going to show them all."

"Why didn't you go?" Lena asked, thinking she would embarrass him.

"Oh, I got accepted," Richard said, waiting for her to be impressed. "But my mother had just died and . . ." He let his voice trail off. "Oh, well. Nothing I can do about that now." He pointed his finger at Lena. "I learned a lot from your sister. She was a very good teacher. She was a role model for me."

Lena let his compliment hang in the air between them. She did not want to talk about Sibyl with Richard.

"Oh, God." Richard sat up quickly. "There's Jill."

Rosen stood at the door, looking around for Lena. The woman seemed lost, and Lena was debating whether to say something to her when Richard tossed one of his girlie waves.

Jill Rosen smiled weakly, walking toward them.

Richard stood, saying, "Oh, honey," as he took both of Rosen's hands.

"Brian's coming in from Washington," she told him. "They're going to try to get him on the next flight out."

Richard frowned, offering, "If there's anything I can do for you or Brian . . ."

"Thank you," Rosen said, but she was looking at Lena.

Lena told Richard, "I'll see you later."

Richard raised his eyebrows but bowed out gracefully, offering a final, "Anything you need," to Jill Rosen.

Rosen gave a tight smile of thanks as he left. She asked Lena, "Is Chief Tolliver here yet?"

"Not yet."

Rosen stared at her, probably trying to

ascertain if Lena had held up her side of the bargain. Lena had, actually. She was sober. The two drinks she had grabbed at her apartment after telling Rosen about her son were hardly enough to make her drunk.

Lena said, "He had some things to deal with first."

"Do you mean the girl?" Rosen asked, and Lena guessed she'd heard the news about Tessa Linton at least twenty times walking from the counseling center to the library.

Lena explained, "I didn't want to tell you."

The woman's tone was clipped. "Of course you didn't."

"No, not because of that," Lena said. "We're not even sure if it has anything to do with Andy. I didn't want you to think —"

"It was her blood on the note?"

"That came after," Lena said. "They just had it and . . ."

Tears welled into Rosen's eyes. She rested her hands on the table as though she needed help standing up.

Lena said, "I could leave you alone if you wanted," hoping like hell the woman would take her up on the offer.

"No," Rosen said, blowing her nose

again. She did not offer an explanation as to why she wanted to keep Lena around.

They both stood there, staring aimlessly at the people in the library. Lena realized she was rubbing the scars on her hands and forced herself to stop. She said, "I'm really sorry about your son. I know what it's like to lose someone."

Rosen nodded, still looking away. "After the first time" — she indicated her arm, and Lena took it that she meant Andy's earlier suicide attempt — "he was getting better. We'd gotten his medication balanced. He seemed like he was doing better." She smiled. "We'd just bought him a car."

Lena asked, "He was enrolled in school here?"

"Richard told you, I suppose," she said, but there was no bitterness to her tone. "We took him out this last quarter so he could concentrate on getting better. He was helping his father at the lab, doing some things around the clinic for me." She smiled, remembering. "Thursdays he had art lessons. He was very good."

Lena wished she had her notebook so she could write down this information, but there was really no reason for her to do so. As Jeffrey had pointed out, Lena was not a cop. She was just Chuck's security gofer, and barely that.

Rosen asked, "What will Chief Tolliver want from me?"

"Probably a list of your son's friends, where he hung out." Lena took a wild guess, unable to stop herself from thinking like a cop. "Was Andy using drugs?"

Rosen seemed surprised. "What makes you ask that question?"

"Depressed people tend to self-medicate."

Rosen tilted her head to the side, giving Lena a knowing look. When Lena did not respond, Rosen said, "Yes, he did drugs. Pot at first, but he was moving into the heavier stuff this time last year. We sent him to a treatment facility. He came out a month later." She paused. "He told me he was clean, but you can never be certain."

Lena admired the fact that the woman admitted she did not know everything about her son. In Lena's experience parents tended to insist they knew their kid better than anyone else did, even the kid.

"When he came out of the program, none of his friends would talk to him. No one who's using wants to be around someone who's not." She added almost as an afterthought, "He was always lonely, though. He never really fit in. He was very smart, and other kids found that off-putting. I suppose you could say he felt a bit alienated."

"Were any of his friends mad at him? Mad enough to wish him harm?"

Lena could see a spark of hope glimmer in Rosen's eyes when the mother asked, "You think he could've been pushed?"

"No," Lena answered, knowing that Jeffrey would kill her for putting the thought into Rosen's head. At the thought of Jeffrey, Lena felt her heart drop.

"Listen," she told Rosen, "are you going to tell Jeffrey about today or not?"

Rosen took her time answering, moving closer to Lena, as if she wanted to smell her breath. All she would sniff was minty-fresh gel, but Lena still felt a moment of panic.

"No," Rosen decided. "I won't tell him about today."

"What about before?"

Rosen seemed confused. "Therapy?" She shook her head. "That's confidential, Lena. I told you that in the beginning. I'm not in the habit of revealing who my patients are."

Lena could only nod, overcome with relief. Jeffrey had given Lena an ultimatum seven months ago: Go to a shrink or go find another job. The choice had seemed simple at the time, and she had tossed both her badge and her gun onto his desk without reservation. Now Lena would put a bullet in her head before she admitted to Jeffrey that she had weakened last month and gone to the clinic. Her pride could not take it.

As if on cue, the large oak doors at the front of the room opened and Jeffrey came in, looking around the room. Chuck walked over to meet him, but Jeffrey must have said something to cut him off, because the next thing Lena knew, Chuck was leaving the room with his tail tucked between his legs.

Lena had never seen Jeffrey look as bad as he did now. He had changed clothes from before, but his suit was rumpled and he was not wearing a tie. The closer he got, the worse he looked.

"Dr. Rosen," Jeffrey said. "I'm sorry about your loss." He did not shake her hand or wait for her to acknowledge his words, which struck Lena as very unlike Jeffrey.

He held out a chair for Rosen. "I need to ask you some questions."

Rosen sat, asking, "Is the girl okay?"

114

His expression changed just enough to make Lena feel sorry for him. "We don't know anything yet," he said. "The family is driving into Atlanta right now."

Rosen folded the tissue in her hand. "Do you think the person who attacked her could have killed my son?"

"Right now," Jeffrey said, "we're treating Andy's death as a suicide." He paused, probably to let his words sink in. "I talked to your husband earlier."

"Brian?" She was surprised.

"He called at the station after he spoke with you," Jeffrey told her, and Lena could tell from the way he squared his shoulders that the father had been far from polite.

Rosen must have picked up on this. "Brian can be abrupt," she said by way of apology.

Jeffrey said, "Dr. Rosen, all I can tell you is what I told him. We're following every possible lead we can, but with your son's history, suicide seems the most likely scenario."

Rosen told him, "I've been talking to Detective Adams —"

"I'm sorry, ma'am," Jeffrey interrupted her. "Ms. Adams isn't on the police force. She works for campus security."

Rosen's tone said she wasn't going to get

caught in the middle of this. "I'm not sure what the hierarchy has to do with the fact that my son is dead, Mr. Tolliver."

Jeffrey looked only a little contrite. "I'm sorry," he repeated, taking something out of his coat pocket. "We found this in the forest," he said, holding up a silver chain with a Star of David hanging from it. "There weren't any fingerprints on it, so —"

Rosen gasped, grabbing the chain. Tears sprang into her eyes again, and her face seemed to crumple into her neck as she held the charm to her lips, saying, "Andy, oh, Andy . . ."

Jeffrey glanced at Lena, and when she made no move to comfort Jill Rosen, he put his hand on the woman's shoulder, trying to do the job himself. He patted her like a dog, and Lena wondered why it was perfectly acceptable for a man to be bad at this, but the same deficiency in a woman made her somehow less of a person.

Rosen wiped her eyes with the back of her hand. "I'm sorry."

"It's perfectly understandable," Jeffrey told her, patting her shoulder a few more times.

Rosen fingered the necklace, still keeping it close to her mouth. "He hadn't worn it for a while. I thought he might have given it away or sold it."

"Sold it?" Jeffrey asked.

Lena provided, "She thinks he might have been using drugs."

Jeffrey said, "The father says he was clean."

Lena shrugged.

Jeffrey asked Rosen, "Did your son have a girlfriend?"

"He's never really dated." She gave a humorless laugh. "Girls or boys, not that we would have minded. We just wanted him to be happy."

Jeffrey asked, "Was there any particular person he hung around with?"

"No," she said. "I think he was probably very alone."

Lena watched Rosen, waiting for more, but the doctor's composure had started to slip again. She closed her eyes, squeezing them tight. Her lips moved silently, but Lena could not tell what she was saying.

Jeffrey gave the mother some time before saying, "Dr. Rosen?"

"Could I see him?" she asked.

"Of course." Jeffrey stood, offering the woman his hand. "I'll drive you to the morgue," he said, then told Lena, "Chuck went to see Kevin Blake."

Lena said, "All right."

Rosen seemed lost in her own thoughts, but she told Lena, "Thank you."

"It's okay." Lena forced herself to touch Jill Rosen's arm in what she hoped was a comforting gesture.

Jeffrey took in the exchange with a glance. He told Lena, "I'll talk to you later," in a tone that sounded more like a threat than anything else.

Lena rubbed her thumb into the back of her hand as she watched them leave. There were noises on the second-floor balcony, where a couple of guys were horsing around, but Lena ignored them. She sat down, going over the last ten minutes in her mind, trying to figure out what she should have done differently. She was a couple of minutes into the process before she realized that what she really needed to do to make things right was relive the whole damn year.

"God," Nan Thomas groaned, plopping into the chair across from Lena. "How do you work with that jerk?"

"Chuck?" Lena shrugged, but she was glad for the distraction. "It's a job."

"I'd rather shelve books in hell," Nan said as she pulled her stringy brown hair into a red rubber band. There was a huge thumbprint on the right lens of her glasses, but Nan did not seem to notice. She wore a Pepto-Bismol pink T-shirt tucked into an elastic-waisted denim skirt. Red Converse All-Stars completed the ensemble, worn with matching pink socks.

Nan asked, "What are you doing this weekend?"

Lena shrugged again. "I don't know. Why?"

"I thought I'd have Hank come up for Easter. Maybe cook a ham."

Lena tried to think of an excuse, but she'd been blindsided by the invitation. She looked at a calendar only to see when she was going to get paid, not to figure out which holiday was coming up. Easter came as a surprise.

Lena said, "I'll think about it," and, to her relief, Nan took it well.

There was a shout from above, and they both turned to look at the boys playing on the balcony. One of them must have sensed Nan's displeasure, because he gave her an apologetic smile before opening the book in his hand and pretending to read it.

"Idiots," Lena said.

"Nah, they're good kids," Nan told her, but she kept her eye on them for a few beats to make sure they stayed settled down.

Nan was the last person on earth Lena would have thought herself capable of being friends with, but over the past few months, something had shifted. They weren't friends in the normal sense — Lena wasn't interested in going to the movies with her or hearing about the gay side of Nan's life — but they talked about Sibyl, and, for Lena, talking about Sibyl with someone who really knew her was like having her back.

"I tried to call you last night," Nan said. "I don't know why you don't get an answering machine."

"I'll get around to it," Lena said, though she already had one sitting in the bottom of her closet. Lena had unplugged the damn thing her first week living on campus. The only people who called were Nan and Hank, both of them leaving the same concerned messages, wondering how she was doing. Now Lena had Caller ID hooked up, and that was all she needed to screen her calls, such as they were.

"Richard was here," Lena said.

"Oh, Lena." Nan frowned. "I hope you weren't rude to him."

"He was trying to dig up dirt."

As usual, Nan tried to defend Richard. "Brian works in his department. I'm sure

Richard just wanted to know what happened."

"Did you know him? The kid, I mean?"

Nan shook her head. "We saw Jill and Brian at the faculty Christmas party every year, but we never really socialized. Maybe you should talk to Richard," she suggested. "They work together in the same lab."

"Richard is an asshole."

"He was very good to Sibyl."

"Sibyl could take care of herself," Lena insisted, though they both knew that was not necessarily true. Sibyl had been blind. Richard had been her eyes on campus, making her life a hell of a lot easier.

Nan changed the subject, saying, "I wish you would talk to me about taking some of the insurance —"

"No," Lena cut her off. Sibyl had taken out a life-insurance policy through the college that paid out double for accidental death. Nan had been the beneficiary, and she had been offering half to Lena since the check cleared.

"Sibyl left that to *you*," Lena told her for what felt like the millionth time. "She wanted you to have it."

"She didn't even have a will," Nan countered. "She didn't like to think about death, let alone plan for it. You know how she was."

Lena felt tears well into her eyes.

Nan said, "The only reason she had the policy was the college offered it for free with her health insurance. She just put me because —"

"Because she wanted you to have it," Lena finished for her, using the back of her hand to wipe her eyes. She had cried so much in the last year that it no longer embarrassed her to do it in public. "Listen, Nan, I appreciate it, but it's your money. Sibyl wanted you to have it."

"She wouldn't have wanted you working for Chuck. She would've hated that."

"I'm not too crazy about it myself," Lena admitted, though the only person she had ever said this to was Jill Rosen. "It's just something to get by until I decide what I want to do with my life."

"You could go back to school."

Lena laughed. "I'm a little old to be going back to school."

"Sibby always said you'd rather sweat your butt off running a marathon in the middle of August than spend ten minutes inside an air-conditioned classroom."

Lena smiled, feeling the release as her mind conjured Sibyl's voice saying this exact thing. Sometimes it was like a click in Lena's brain, where the bad things were shut off and the good things came on.

Nan said, "It's hard to believe it's been a year."

Lena stared out the window, thinking how odd it was that she was talking to Nan like this. Except for Sibyl, Lena would have stayed as far away as possible from someone like Nan Thomas.

"I was thinking about her this morning," Lena said. Something about the fear on Sara Linton's face as they loaded her sister into the helicopter had cut Lena deeper than anything had in a long while. "Sibyl used to love this time of year."

"She loved walking in the woods," Nan said. "I always tried to leave early on Fridays so we could go for a walk before it got too dark."

Lena swallowed, afraid that if she opened her mouth, a sob would escape.

"Anyway," Nan said, putting her palms flat on the table as she stood, "I'd better start cataloging some books before Chuck comes back and asks me to dinner."

Lena stood, too. "Why don't you just tell him you're gay?"

"So he can get off on it?" Nan asked. "No thank you."

Lena conceded the point. She herself had worried about Chuck's reading the paper and the lurid details of Lena's attack.

"Besides," Nan said, "a guy like that will just say the only reason I don't want him around is because I'm a lesbian and lesbians hate men." Nan leaned forward conspiratorially. "When the truth is, we don't hate all men. We just hate him."

Lena shook her head, thinking if that was the criteria, every woman on campus was a lesbian.

4

Grady Hospital was one of the most respected level-one trauma centers in the country, but its reputation among Atlantans was notoriously bad. Operated by the Fulton-DeKalb Hospital Authority, Grady was one of the few remaining public hospitals in the area, and despite the fact that it housed one of the nation's largest burn units, had the most comprehensive HIV/AIDS program in the nation, and served as a regional treatment center for high-risk mothers and infants. If you came in with an upset stomach or a bad earache, you were more than likely looking at a two-hour wait to see a doctor — if you were lucky.

Grady was a teaching hospital, and Emory University, Sara's alma mater, as well as Morehouse College supplied a steady stream of interns. The emergency-room slot was highly sought by students, as Grady was said to be the best place in the country to learn emergency medicine. Fifteen years ago Sara had fought tooth and nail to win a position on the pediatric team, and she'd learned more in one year than most doctors learned in a lifetime. When she left Atlanta to move back to Grant County, Sara had never thought she would see Grady again, especially under these circumstances.

"Somebody's coming," the man beside Sara said, and everyone in the waiting room — thirty people at least — looked up at the nurse expectantly.

"Ms. Linton?"

Sara's heart lifted, and for a split second she thought her mother had finally arrived. Sara stood, putting down a magazine to save her chair, though she had been taking turns saving places with the old man beside her for the last two hours.

"Is she out of surgery?" Sara asked, unable to keep the tremble from her voice. The surgeon had estimated four hours at least, a conservative guess to Sara's thinking.

"No," the nurse told her, leading Sara to the nurses' station. "You have a phone call."

"Is it my parents?" Sara asked, raising her voice to be heard. The hallway was crowded with people; doctors and nurses whizzing by with purpose in their step as they tried to keep a handle on their ever-increasing patient load.

"He said he's a police officer." The nurse handed the phone to Sara, saying, "Keep it brief. We're really not supposed to allow private calls on this line."

"Thanks." Sara took the phone, leaning her back against the nurses' station, trying to stay out of the way.

"Jeffrey?" she asked.

"Hey," he said, sounding as stressed as she felt. "Is she out of surgery?"

"No," she told him, glancing up the hallway toward the surgical suites. Several times she had thought about walking through the doors, trying to find out what was happening, but there was a guard posted who seemed very intent on doing his job.

"Sara?"

"I'm here."

Jeffrey asked, "What about the baby?"

Sara felt her throat tighten at the question. She could not talk about Tessa with him. Not like this. She asked, "Did you find out anything?"

"I talked to Jill Rosen, the suicide's mom. She couldn't tell me much. We found a chain, some kind of necklace with a Star of David, that belonged to the kid in the woods."

When Sara did not respond, Jeffrey told her, "Andy, the suicide, was either in the woods or someone who took the chain from him went into the woods."

Sara made herself respond. "Which do you think is likely?"

"I don't know," he answered. "Brad saw Tessa pick up a white plastic bag on the way up the hill."

"She had something in her hand," Sara remembered.

"Is there any reason she would be picking up trash?"

Sara tried to think. "Why?"

"Brad said that looked like what she was doing on the hill. She found a bag and started putting trash in it."

"She might," Sara said, confused. "She was complaining about people littering earlier. I don't know."

"Maybe she found something on the hill and put it in the bag? We found the Star of David that belonged to the victim, but that was deeper in the forest."

"If Tessa did pick up something, that would mean someone was watching us while we were with the body. What's his name again — Andy?"

"Andy Rosen," he confirmed. "Do you still think something's suspicious?"

Sara did not know how to answer. Examining Rosen seemed like a lifetime away. She could barely recall what the boy had looked like.

"Sara?"

She told him the truth. "I don't know anymore."

"You were right that he tried it before," he said. "His mom confirmed it. Slit his arm open."

"A previous attempt and a note," Sara said, thinking that, barring something that might jump out in the autopsy, those two factors would generally be conclusive enough to rule the death a suicide. She said, "We could run a tox screen. He wouldn't have gone over that bridge without a struggle."

"His back was scraped."

"Not in a violent way."

"I can get Brock to check that out," he offered. Dan Brock, a local mortician, had been the county coroner before Sara had taken the job. "I haven't let it out that there's anything suspicious. Brock can keep a secret."

She said, "He can pull blood samples,

but I want to do the autopsy."

"Do you think you'll be able to?"

"If this is connected," she began. "If whoever did this to Tess . . ." Sara couldn't finish, but she had never in her life felt such a need for vengeance. Finally she said, "Yes. I'll be able to do it."

Jeffrey seemed doubtful, but he told her, "We're checking Andy's apartment. They found a pipe in his room. The mom says he had a drug problem a while back, but the dad says he kicked it."

"Right," Sara said, feeling her anger flare at the thought of her sister's being caught in the crossfire of something as stupid and pointless as a drug transaction gone wrong. Tessa's stabbing was the sort of violence that people who said drugs were harmless fun tended to ignore.

"We're dusting his room, trying to get prints to run through the computer. I'm going to talk to his parents tomorrow. The mother gave me a couple of names, but they've already transferred out of school or graduated." Jeffrey paused, and she could tell he was feeling frustrated.

The surgical doors burst open, but the patient was not Tessa. Sara pressed her heels into the baseboard of the nurses' station so the team could pass by. An older woman with dark blond hair was on the gurney, her eyelids still taped closed from surgery.

"How did his parents take the news?" Sara asked, thinking of her own parents.

"Okay, considering." Jeffrey paused. "She really broke down in the car. There was something going on with her and Lena. I can't put my finger on it."

"Like what?" Sara asked, though Lena Adams was the last person in the world she cared about right now.

"I don't know," he said, unsurprisingly. She could hear him drumming his fingers on something. "Rosen lost it in the car. Just lost it." The drumming stopped. "Her husband called me when he found out. They routed him through from the station." He paused for a moment. "They're both pretty torn up. This kind of thing can be hard on people. They tend to —"

"Jeffrey," Sara interrupted, "I need you . . ." She felt her throat closing again, as if the words were choking her. "I need you here."

"I know," he told her, resignation in his voice. "I don't think I can."

Sara wiped her eyes with the back of her hand. One of the passing doctors looked up at her, then quickly back down at the chart he held in his hands. Feeling foolish and exposed, Sara tried to steel herself against the emotions that wanted to come. She said, "Sure, okay. I understand."

"No, Sara —"

"I'd better get off this phone. It's the one at the nurses' station. Some guy's been on the phone in the waiting room for an hour." She laughed, just to get some release. "He's speaking in Russian, but I think he's been making drug deals."

"Sara," Jeffrey stopped her, "it's your dad. He asked me — he *told* me not to come."

"What?" Sara said the word so loudly that several people looked up from their work.

"He was upset. I don't know. He told me not to come to the hospital, that it was a family matter."

Sara lowered her voice. "He doesn't get to decide —"

"Sara, listen to me," Jeffrey said, his voice calmer than she felt. "It's your dad. I've got to respect that." He paused. "And it's not just your dad. Cathy said the same thing."

She felt foolish repeating herself, but all she could say was, "What?"

"They're right," he said. "Tessa

shouldn't have been there. I shouldn't have let her —"

"I'm the one who brought her to the scene," Sara reminded him, the guilt she'd been feeling for the last few hours suddenly raging back up inside her.

"They're just upset right now. Understandably upset." He stopped, like he was trying to think how to phrase his words. "They need some time."

"Time to see what happens?" she asked. "So if Tessa makes it, then you're welcome back to Sunday dinner, but if she doesn't . . ." Sara could not complete the sentence.

"They're angry. That's how people get when something like this happens. They feel helpless, and they get angry at whoever's around."

"I was around, too," she reminded him. "Yeah, well . . ."

For a moment Sara felt too shocked to speak. Finally she asked, "Are they mad at me?" but she knew that her parents had every reason to be. Sara was in charge of Tessa. She always had been.

Jeffrey said, "They just want time, Sara. I have to give them that. I won't upset them any more."

She nodded, though he couldn't see her.

"I want to see you. I want to be there for you and for Tessa." She could hear the grief in his voice and knew how hard this was for him. Still, she could not help feeling betrayed by his absence. Jeffrey had a history of not being around when she needed him most. He was doing the right thing, the respectful thing, now, but Sara was in no mood for noble gestures.

"Sara?"

"All right," she said. "You're right."

"I'll go by and feed the dogs, okay? Take care of the house." He paused again. "Cathy said they'd go by your house on the way to bring you some clothes."

"I don't need clothes," Sara told him, feeling her emotions rise up again. She could only whisper, "I need you."

His voice was soft. "I know, baby."

Sara felt tears threatening to come again. She had not let herself cry yet. There had not been time when Tessa was in the helicopter, and then the emergency room and the waiting room — even the bathroom, where Sara had changed into a pair of scrubs one of the nurses had found for her — had been too crowded for her to take a private moment to let herself give in to the grief she felt.

The nurse chose this moment to interrupt. "Ms. Linton?" she said. "We really need the phone."

"I'm sorry," Sara told her. Then, to Jeffrey, "I have to get off this line."

"Can you call me from somewhere else?"

"I can't leave this area," Sara said, watching an older couple walking up the hallway. The man was slightly stooped, the woman holding him up by the arm as they shuffled along, reading the signs on the doors.

Jeffrey said, "There's a McDonald's across the street, right? Near the university parking decks?"

"I don't know," Sara answered, because she had not been into this part of Atlanta in years. "Is there?"

"I think there is," he told her. "I'll meet you there at six tomorrow morning, okay?"

"No," she said, watching the older couple come closer. "Take care of the dogs."

"Are you sure?"

Sara continued watching the man and his wife. With a start, Sara realized that she had not recognized her own parents.

Jeffrey said, "Sara?"

"I'll call you later," she said. "They're here. I've got to go."

Sara leaned over the counter to hang up

the phone, feeling disoriented and afraid. She walked down the hall, hugging her arms to her stomach, waiting for her parents to start looking like her parents again. With a startling clarity, she realized how old they were. Like most grown children, Sara had always pictured her mother and father as somehow not going past a certain age, yet here they were, elderly and so frail-looking she wondered how they managed to walk.

"Mama?" Sara said.

Cathy did not reach for her, as Sara had thought she would, had wanted her to do. One arm stayed around Eddie's waist, as if she needed to hold him up. The other she held at her side. "Where is she?"

"She's still in surgery," Sara told her, wanting to go to her, knowing from Cathy's hard expression that she should not. "Mama —"

"What happened?"

Sara felt a lump in her throat, thinking that Cathy did not even sound like her mother. There was an impenetrable edge to her voice, and her mouth was set in a straight, cold line. Sara took them to the side of the busy hallway so they could talk. Everything felt so formal, as if they had just met.

Sara began, "She wanted to come along with me —"

"And you let her," Eddie said, and the accusation behind his words cut deep. "Why in God's name did you let her?"

Sara bit her lip to keep from trying. "I didn't think —"

He cut her off. "No, you didn't."

"Eddie," Cathy said, not to reprimand him but to tell him that now was not the time.

Sara was quiet for a moment, willing herself not to get more upset than she already felt. "They've got her in surgery now. She should be in for another couple of hours." They all looked up as the doors opened again, but it was just a nurse, probably taking a break from surgery.

Sara continued, "She was stabbed in the belly and the chest. There was a grazing head wound." Sara put her hand to her own head, showing them where Tessa's head had hit the rock. She paused there, thinking about the wound, feeling the same panic well up. She wondered not for the first time if it had all been a terrible dream. As if to snap her out of it, the surgical doors popped open again, and an orderly pushing an empty wheelchair passed through.

Cathy said, "And?"

"I tried to control the bleeding," Sara continued, seeing the scene playing out in her mind. In the waiting room, she had been going over and over what had happened, trying to figure out what she could have done differently, only to realize how hopeless the situation had been.

"And?" Cathy tersely repeated.

Sara cleared her throat, trying to distance herself from her feelings. She spoke to them as if they were just the parents of a patient. "She had a grand mal seizure about a minute before the helicopter came. I did what I could to help her." Sara stopped, remembering how Tessa's spasms had felt under her hands. She stared at her father, realizing he had not looked at her once since they'd arrived.

Sara said, "She had two more seizures during the flight. Her left lung collapsed. They put a tube in her chest to help her breathe."

Cathy asked, "What are they doing now?"

"Controlling the bleeding. A neurologic consult was called, but I don't know what they found. Their primary focus is to stop the bleeding. They'll do a C-section to remove —" Sara stopped, holding her breath.

"The baby," Cathy finished, and Eddie slumped against her.

Sara slowly let the breath go.

"What else?" Cathy asked. "What are you not telling us?"

Sara looked away but told them, "They might have to perform a hysterectomy if they can't get the bleeding under control."

Her parents were both quiet at the news, though Sara knew what they were thinking as clearly as if they were screaming it at her. Tessa had been their only hope for grandchildren.

"Who did this?" Cathy finally asked. "Who would do such a thing?"

"I don't know," Sara whispered, the question echoing in her mind. What kind of monster would stab a pregnant woman and leave her for dead?

"Does Jeffrey know anything?" Eddie asked, and Sara could tell the effort it took for her father to say Jeffrey's name.

"He's doing everything he can," Sara told him. "I'll go back to Grant as soon as . . ." She could not finish.

Cathy asked, "What can we expect when she wakes up?"

Sara stared at her father, wanting to say something that would make him look up at her. If Eddie and Cathy had been anyone else, Sara would have told them the truth: that she had no idea what they should expect. Jeffrey often said that he didn't like to talk to the relatives or friends of victims until he had something concrete to tell them. Sara had always thought this was a little cowardly on his part, but now she saw it was necessary, that people needed some kind of hope, some assurance that at least one thing would turn out all right.

"Sara?" Cathy prompted.

"They'll want to monitor cranial activity. Probably do an EEG to make sure her brain isn't damaged." Sara grappled for something positive to say. Finally she told them the only thing she knew for certain. "There are a lot of things that could have gone wrong."

Cathy had no more questions. She turned toward Eddie, closing her eyes, pressing her lips to his head.

Eddie finally spoke, but he still would not look at Sara. "You're sure about the baby?"

Sara found she had trouble speaking. Her throat felt as dry as the riverbed when she managed to whisper, "Yes, Daddy."

Sara stood at the vending machine outside the hospital cafeteria, punching the button on the snack machine until she felt a sharp pain in her knuckles. Nothing happened, and she bent down, checking the hopper, thinking she might have missed something. The bin was empty.

"Dammit," she said, kicking the machine. With little fanfare, a KitKat dropped down.

Sara unwrapped the package, walking down the hallway to get away from the noise of the cafeteria. The food service had changed since she'd worked at the hospital. They served everything from Thai cuisine to Italian to juicy, thick hamburgers now. She imagined that it was a money pit for the hospital, but it did not make sense that a place dedicated to healing sold such unhealthy food.

Even at close to midnight, the hospital was throbbing with people, and the constant noise made it like walking around a beehive. Sara could not remember the noise from her internship, but she was certain it had been the same. Fear and sleeplessness had probably kept her from noticing. Back before interns had gotten organized and started to demand more humane hours, shifts at Grady ran twenty-four to thirty-six hours long. To this day Sara felt she had yet to catch up on her sleep.

She leaned her back against a door marked LINEN, knowing that she would never get up if she sat down again. Tessa had been out of surgery for three hours, and they had moved her to the ICU, where the family was taking turns staying with her. She was heavily sedated and had not yet woken up from surgery. Her condition was listed as guarded, but the surgeon thought the bleeding was under control. Tessa could still have children if she ever recovered enough from the ordeal in the forest to want one again.

Being in the tiny ICU room with Tessa, feeling Eddie and Cathy's blame though they had not said one word to Sara about it, had been too much. Even Devon had avoided talking to Sara, skulking in the corner, his eyes wide with shock over what had happened to his lover and his child. Sara felt very near her breaking point, but there was no one around who could help her put the pieces together again.

She leaned her head back and closed her eyes, trying to remember the last thing her sister had said to her. In the helicopter Tessa had been post-ictal from the seizure and beyond communication. The last coherent thing she had said was in the car, when she told Sara that she loved her.

Sara bit into the KitKat even though she was not hungry.

"Evenin', ma'am," an older man said, tipping his hat to Sara as he walked by.

She made herself smile, watching him go up the stairs. The man was around Eddie's age, but what she could see of his hair was completely white. His skin was almost translucent in the artificial light of the hospital, and though his dark blue pants and light blue shirt were clean-looking, she could smell something like grease or machine oil in his wake. He could have been a mechanic or a maintenance man at the hospital, or maybe he had someone upstairs holding on to life, just like Tessa.

A group of doctors stopped in front of the cafeteria doors, their scrubs wrinkled, their white jackets stained with various substances. They were young, probably students or interns. Their eyes were bloodshot, and there was something world-weary about them that Sara recognized from her own time here at Grady.

They were obviously waiting for someone as they talked among themselves, their voices a low hum. Sara looked down at the chocolate in her hand, her eyes not really focusing on the label, as she heard them passing around hospital gossip, tossing out procedures they would like to get in on.

A man's voice said, "Sara?"

Sara kept her eyes on the label, assuming that the man was talking to another Sara.

"Sara Linton?" the voice repeated, and she glanced up at the group of interns, wondering if one of her patients from the Heartsdale Children's Clinic was working at Emory now. She felt ancient looking at their young faces until she caught sight of a tall, older man standing behind them.

"Mason?" she asked, recognition finally dawning. "Mason James?"

"That's me," he said, pushing through the group of interns. He put his hand on her shoulder. "I ran into your folks upstairs."

"Oh," Sara said, not knowing what else to say.

"I work here now. Pediatric trauma."

"Right." Sara nodded as if she remembered. She had dated Mason when she worked at Grady, but they'd lost touch after she moved back to Grant.

"Cathy told me you were down here getting something to eat."

She held up the KitKat.

He laughed. "I see your culinary tastes haven't changed."

"They were out of filet mignon," she told

him, and Mason laughed again.

"You look great," he said, an obvious lie that good breeding and manners helped him pull off smoothly. Mason's father had been a cardiologist, just like his grandfather. Sara had always thought that part of Mason's attraction to her lay in the fact that Eddie was a plumber. Growing up in a world of boarding schools and country clubs, Mason had not had much contact with the working class, beyond writing checks for their services.

"How . . . uh . . ." Sara struggled for something to say. "How have you been?"

"Great," he said. "I heard about Tessa downstairs. It's all over the ER."

Sara knew that even in a hospital as large as Grady, a case like Tessa's stuck out. Any violence involving a child was considered that much more horrific.

"I checked in on her. Hope you don't mind."

"No," Sara told him. "Not at all."

"Beth Tindall's her doc," he said. "She's a good surgeon."

"Yes," Sara agreed.

He gave her a warm smile. "Your mother is still as pretty as ever."

Sara tried to smile back. "I'm sure she was glad to see you."

145

"Well, under the circumstances . . ." he allowed. "Do they know who did it?"

She shook her head, feeling her composure slip. "No idea."

"Sara," he said, brushing the back of her hand with his fingers, "I'm so sorry."

She looked away, willing herself not to cry. No one had tried to console her since Tessa had been stabbed. Her skin prickled at his touch, and she felt foolish for taking comfort in such a small gesture.

Mason noticed the change. He cupped his hand to her face, making her look up at him. "Are you okay?"

"I should go back up," she said.

He took her elbow, saying, "Come on," as he led her down the hallway.

Sara listened to him talk as they walked toward the ICU, not really paying attention to his words but liking the soft, soothing monotone of his voice as he told her about the hospital and his life since Sara had left Atlanta. Mason James was the type of man who seemed to take everything in stride. When she'd been fresh from Grant County, Mason had seemed so cosmopolitan and grown-up to Sara, whose only dating experience at that point had been Steve Mann, a guy who thought that a good date ended with him fondling

Sara in the backseat of his father's Buick.

They turned the corner, and Sara could see her father and mother in the hallway, having what looked like a heated discussion. Eddie was the first to spot Sara and Mason, and he stopped whatever he was saying.

Eddie's eyelids were drooped, and he looked more tired than Sara had ever seen him. Her mother seemed to have aged more in the last hour than she had in the last twenty years. They looked so vulnerable that Sara felt a lump come into her throat.

"I'm going to go check on Tess," she said, excusing herself. She pushed the button to the right of the doors and walked into the ICU.

Like most hospitals, the intensive-care unit at Grady was small and secluded. The lights were darkened in the rooms and corridors, and the atmosphere was cool and soothing, as much for the few visitors who were allowed in every two hours as for the patients. All the rooms had sliding glass doors and afforded little privacy, but most of the patients were too sick to complain. Sara could hear the beeps of heart monitors and the slow breathing of ventilators as she walked to the back. Tessa's room was directly across from the nurses' station, which said something about how critical her case was.

Devon was in the room with her, standing a few feet from the bed with his hands tucked into his pockets. He leaned against the wall, though there was a comfortable chair right beside him.

"Hey," Sara said.

He barely acknowledged her. His eyes were red-rimmed, and his dark skin looked pale in the artificial light of the room.

"Has she said anything?"

He took his time answering. "She opened her eyes a couple of times, but I don't know."

"She's trying to wake up," Sara told him. "That's good."

His Adam's apple bobbed as he swallowed.

"If you need a break . . . ," she began, but Devon did not wait for her to finish. He walked from the room without a backward glance.

Sara pulled the chair over to Tessa's bed and sat down. She had been sitting most of the day waiting for news, but she felt exhausted.

Bandages covered Tessa's head where they had stitched her scalp back into place.

Two drains were attached to her belly to draw off fluid. A catheter hung from the bed rail, only partially full. The room was dark, the only light coming from the various monitors. Tessa had been taken off the ventilator an hour before, but the heart monitor was still attached, its metallic beep announcing every beat of her heart.

Sara stroked her sister's fingers, thinking that she'd never noticed what small hands Tessa had. She could still remember Tessa's first day of school, when Sara had taken her hand to walk her to the bus stop. Before they left, Cathy had lectured Sara to take care of her little sister. The theme was a familiar one throughout their childhood. Even Eddie had told Sara to take care of her sister, though Sara later figured the real reason her father had always encouraged Tessa to tag along on Sara's dates with Steve Mann: Eddie knew about the Buick's large backseat.

Tessa's head moved, as if she sensed someone was there.

"Tess?" Sara said, holding her hand, gently squeezing. "Tess?"

Tessa made a noise that sounded more like a groan. Her hand moved to her stomach, as it had a million times over the last eight months.

Slowly Tessa's eyes opened. She looked around the room, her eyes finding Sara.

"Hey," Sara said, feeling a relieved smile come to her face. "Hey, sweetie."

Tessa's lips moved. She put her hand to her throat.

"Are you thirsty?"

Tessa nodded, and Sara looked for the cup of ice chips the nurse had left by the bed. The ice had mostly melted, but Sara managed to find a few slivers for her sister.

"They put a tube down your throat," Sara explained, sliding the ice into Tessa's mouth. "You'll feel sore from that for a while, and it'll be hard to talk."

Tessa closed her eyes as she swallowed.

"Do you have much pain?" Sara asked. "Do you want me to get the nurse?"

Sara started to stand, but Tessa did not let go of her hand. She didn't have to vocalize the first question on her mind. Sara could read it in her eyes.

"No, Tessie," she said, feeling tears stream down her face. "We lost it. We lost her." Sara pressed Tessa's hand to her lips. "I'm so sorry. I'm so —"

Tessa stopped her without saying a word. The beep of the heart monitor was the only sound in the room, a metallic testament to Tessa's life.

"Do you remember?" Sara asked. "Do you know what happened?"

Tessa's head moved once to the side for no.

"You went into the woods," Sara said. "Brad saw you pick up a bag and put trash in it. Do you remember that?"

Again she indicated no.

"We think someone was there." Sara stopped herself. "We know someone was in the woods. Maybe he wanted the bag. Maybe he . . ." She did not finish her train of thought. Too much information would only confuse her sister, and Sara was not sure of the facts herself.

Sara said, "Someone stabbed you."

Tessa waited for more.

"I found you in the woods. You were lying in the clearing and I . . . I tried to do what I could. I tried to help. I couldn't." Sara felt her composure slip again. "Oh, God, Tessie, I tried to help."

Sara put her head down on the bed, ashamed that she was crying. She needed to be strong for her sister, needed to show her that they would get through this together, but the only thing she could think about was her own blame in all of this. After a lifetime of looking out for Tessa, Sara had failed her at the one time she was needed most.

"Oh, Tess," Sara sobbed, needing her sister's forgiveness more than anything else in her life. "I'm so sorry."

She felt Tessa's hand on the back of her head. The touch was awkward at first, but Tessa was trying to pull Sara toward her.

Sara looked up, her face inches from Tessa's.

Tessa moved her lips, not yet used to using her mouth. She breathed the word "Who?" She wanted to know who had done this to her, who had killed her child.

"I don't know," Sara said. "We're trying, sweetie. Jeffrey's out there right now doing everything he can." Sara's voice caught. "He'll make sure whoever did this to you never hurts anybody again."

Tessa touched her fingers to Sara's cheek, just under her eye. With a trembling hand, she wiped away Sara's tears.

"I'm so sorry, Tessie. I'm so sorry." Sara begged, "Tell me what I can do. Tell me."

When Tessa spoke, her voice was scratchy, little above a whisper. Sara watched her lips move, but she could hear Tessa speak as plainly as if she had shouted.

"Find him."

Monday

5

Jeffrey leaned down to pick up the newspaper off Sara's front porch before going into the house. He had told her he would be there by six this morning so she could call him with an update on Tessa. She had sounded awful on the phone last night. More than anything, Jeffrey hated to hear Sara cry. It made him feel useless and weak, two characteristics he despised in anyone, especially himself.

Jeffrey switched on the lights in the hallway. On the other side of the house, he heard the dogs stirring, their collars jingling, their loud yawns, but they did not come out to see who had arrived. After spending two years racing around the dog track in Ebro, Sara's two greyhounds were loath to expend any energy unless they had to.

Jeffrey whistled, tossing the paper onto the kitchen counter, glancing at the front page while he waited for the dogs. The photograph above the fold showed Chuck Gaines standing between his father and Kevin Blake. Apparently the three men had won some sort of golf tournament in Augusta on Saturday. Underneath was a story encouraging voters to support a new bond referendum that would help replace the trailers outside the school with permanent classrooms. The *Grant Observer* had its priorities right in giving Albert Gaines top billing. The man owned half the buildings in town and his bank carried the mortgages on the others.

Jeffrey whistled for the dogs again, wondering what was taking them so long. They finally sauntered into the kitchen, their nails tip-tapping against the black and white tiles on the floor. He let them outside into the fenced-in yard, leaving the door open for when they had finished their business.

Before he forgot, Jeffrey took two tomatoes out of his coat pocket and put them in Sara's refrigerator beside a funny-looking green ball that might have been food at some point in its sad, short life. Marla Simms, his secretary at the office, was an amateur gardener, and she was always giving Jeffrey more food than he could possibly eat on his own. Knowing Marla and her penchant for sticking her nose into places where it did not belong, she probably did this on purpose, hoping Jeffrey would share some with Sara.

Jeffrey scooped some kibble for Bubba, Sara's cat, even though Bubba would not come out until after Jeffrey had left. The cat would only drink from a bowl left by the utility closet, and when Jeffrey had lived here, he was constantly kicking it over by accident. The cat took this and many other things personally. Jeffrey and Sara had a love-hate relationship with the animal. Sara loved the thing, and Jeffrey hated it.

The dogs came trotting back into the kitchen just as Jeffrey was opening up a can of food. Bob leaned against Jeffrey's leg for petting while Billy lay down on the floor, heaving a sigh as if he had just climbed Mount Everest. Jeffrey had never understood how such large animals could be house dogs, but the two greyhounds seemed perfectly content to stay indoors all day. If they were left in the yard for too long, they would get lonely and jump the fence to go looking for Sara.

Bob nuzzled him again, pushing him toward the counter.

"Hold on a minute," Jeffrey told him, picking up their bowls. He tossed in a couple of scoops of dry food, then mixed in the canned using a soup spoon. Jeffrey knew for a fact that the dogs would eat whatever was put in the bowls — Billy saw the cat box as his own personal snack tray — but Sara liked to mix their food for them, so that's what he did.

"Here you go," Jeffrey said, putting down the food.

They walked to the bowls, showing him their slim behinds as they ate. Jeffrey watched them for a moment before deciding to make himself useful and clean the kitchen. Sara was not the neatest person even on a good day, and the stack of dishes from their dinner Friday night was still piled in the sink. He draped his jacket over the back of a kitchen chair and rolled up his sleeves.

A large window over the sink offered a tranquil view of the lake, and Jeffrey stared absently at the water as he scrubbed the dishes. Jeffrey liked being here in Sara's house, liked the homey feeling of her kitchen and the deep, comfortable chairs she had in the den. He liked making love to her with the windows open, hearing the birds on the lake, smelling the shampoo in her hair, watching her eyes close as she held on to him. He liked all of this so much that Sara must have sensed it; they spent the majority of their time together at his house.

The phone rang as he was washing the last plate, and Jeffrey was so absorbed in his own thoughts that he almost dropped it.

He picked up the phone on the third ring.

"Hey," Sara said, her voice soft and tired.

He grabbed a towel to dry his hands. "How is she?"

"Better."

"Has she remembered anything?"

"No." She was silent, and he couldn't tell if she was crying or too tired to talk.

Jeffrey's vision blurred, and in his mind he was in the forest again, his hand pressed into Tessa's belly, his shirt soaked through with her blood. Billy looked over his shoulder at Jeffrey as if he sensed something wrong, then turned back to his breakfast, the metal tag on his collar clinking against the bowl.

Jeffrey asked, "Are you holding up okay?"

She made a noncommittal noise. "I

talked to Brock and told him what needs to be done. We should be able to get the lab results back tomorrow. Carlos knows to put a rush on it."

Jeffrey did not let her sidetrack him. "Did you get any sleep last night?"

"Not really."

Neither had Jeffrey. Around three that morning, he had gotten out of bed and gone for a six-mile run, thinking it would tire him out enough to sleep. He'd been wrong.

Sara told him, "Mama and Daddy are in with her now."

"How are they doing?"

"They're so mad."

"At me?"

She did not answer.

"At you?"

He could hear her blowing her nose. Then, "I shouldn't have taken her with me."

"Sara, you had no way of knowing." He was angry that he couldn't think of anything more comforting than that. "We've been to a hundred scenes before and nothing bad has ever happened. Ever."

"It was still a crime scene."

"Right, a place where a crime already happened. There's no way we could've anticipated —"

"I'll drive Mama's car back later to-night," she said. "They're going to move Tessa sometime after lunch. I want to make sure she's settled in." She paused. "I'll do the autopsy as soon as I get in."

"Let me come get you."

"No," she told him. "That's too long a drive, and —"

"I don't care," he interrupted. He'd made the mistake before of not being there when Sara needed him, and he was not going to do it again. "I'll meet you in the lobby at four."

"That's too close to rush hour. It'll take you forever."

"I'll be going the opposite way," Jeffrey said, though that hardly mattered in At-lanta, where everyone over the age of fif-teen owned a car. "I don't want you driving back by yourself. You're too tired."

She was silent.

"I'm not asking you, Sara. I'm telling you," he said, keeping his voice firm. "I'll be there around four, all right?"

She finally gave in. "All right."

"Four o'clock in the front lobby."

"Okay."

Jeffrey told her good-bye and hung up before she could change her mind. He started to roll down his sleeves but reconsidered when he saw his watch. He was supposed to pick up Dan Brock and drive him to the morgue in an hour so Brock could take blood samples from Andy Rosen. After that, Jeffrey was scheduled to talk to the Rosens about their son and see if they had thought of anything useful during the night.

There was nothing Jeffrey could do at the office until the crime techs finished processing Andy's one-room apartment over his parents' garage. Any fingerprints would be checked through the computer, but that was always hit-and-miss, because the computer could make comparisons only against known prints on file. Frank would call Jeffrey on his cell phone when the reports were in, but for now there wasn't really anything Jeffrey could do. Unless they came up with some earth-shattering revelation, Jeffrey would drop by Ellen Schaffer's dorm room and see if she recognized the picture of Andy Rosen's face. The young woman had seen the body only from the back, but, considering how gossip traveled around the campus, Schaffer probably already knew more about Andy Rosen than anyone on the police force did.

Again Jeffrey decided to make himself

useful. He headed for the bedroom, picking up Sara's socks and shoes, then a skirt and underwear, as he walked down the hallway. Obviously she had discarded her clothes as she walked through the house. Jeffrey smiled, thinking about how this used to irritate him when they were living together.

Billy and Bob were settled back on the bed when he tossed Sara's clothes over the chair by the window. Jeffrey sat beside them, petting them both in equal turns. There were a couple of framed pictures by Sara's bed, and he paused to look at them. Tessa and Sara were in the first photo, both of them standing in front of the lake with fishing poles in their hands. Tessa wore a ratty fishing hat that Jeffrey recognized as Eddie's. The second picture was from Tessa's graduation. Eddie, Cathy, Tessa, and Sara stood with their arms around one another, big smiles on their faces.

Sara, with her dark red hair and pale skin, standing a few inches taller than her father, always looked like a neighbor child who had wandered into the family photos, but there was no mistaking that the smile on her face was the same as her father's. Tessa had her mother's blond hair, blue

163

eyes, and petite build, but all three women shared the same almond shape to their eyes. There was something more womanly about Sara, though, and Jeffrey had always been attracted to the fact that she curved just enough in all the right places.

He put down the photo and noticed a streak of dust on the table where another frame had been. Jeffrey looked on the floor, then opened the drawer and pushed around a couple of magazines before he found the silver-edged frame buried at the bottom. He knew this picture well; a passing stranger on the beach had taken it for them on Sara and Jeffrey's honeymoon.

He used the corner of the bedsheet to dust off the frame before putting it back in the drawer.

Brock's Funeral Home operated out of a large Victorian house that was the kind of place Jeffrey had dreamed about living in when he was a kid. Back in Sylacauga, Alabama, Jeffrey and his mother — and less often his father — lived in a two-bedroom, one-bath house that even on a good day could not be called a home. His mother had never been a happy person, and for as long as Jeffrey could remember, there were no pictures on the walls or carpets on the floors or anything that might add a personal touch to the house. It was as if May Tolliver did everything she could to avoid setting down roots. Not that she had a lot to work with even if she wanted to.

Poorly insulated windows rattled when you closed the front door, and the kitchen floor sloped so severely toward the back that dropped food collected under the baseboards. On particularly cold winter nights, Jeffrey had slept in his sleeping bag on the floor of the hall closet, the warmest room in the house.

Jeffrey had been a cop for too long to think that a crappy childhood was a good excuse for anything, but he understood why some people used it as a justification. Jimmy Tolliver was a nasty drunk, and he had knocked Jeffrey around plenty of times when Jeffrey had made the mistake of getting in his father's way. Most of the time, Jeffrey got hit when he inserted himself between his mother and Jimmy's fists. That was in the past, though, and Jeffrey had moved on long ago. Everybody had something horrible happen to them at one time or another in their life; it was part of the human condition. How they struggled through adversity proved what kind of people they were. Maybe that was why

Jeffrey was having such a hard time with Lena. He wanted her to be a different person than who she really was.

Dan Brock came tumbling out of the front door, then stopped as his mother called to him. She handed him two Styrofoam cups, and Jeffrey hoped to God one of them was meant for him. Penny Brock made a mean cup of coffee.

Jeffrey tried not to smile as he watched mother and son say good-bye. Brock leaned down for his mama to kiss his cheek, and she took the opportunity to brush something off the shoulder of his black suit. There was a reason Dan Brock was nearly forty and had never married.

Brock gave a toothy smile as he walked toward the car. He was a lanky man who had the great misfortune of looking like what he was: a third-generation mortician. He had long, bony fingers and a blank face that lent itself to comforting the bereaved. Brock didn't get to talk much to people who weren't crying their hearts out, so he tended to be incredibly chatty around anyone who was not in mourning. He had a very dry wit and a sometimes alarming sense of humor. When he laughed, he put his whole face into it, his mouth cracking open like a Muppet's.

Jeffrey leaned over to open the door, but Brock had already managed, switching the two cups to one large hand.

"Hey, Chief," he said, climbing into the car. He handed Jeffrey a cup. "From my mama."

"Tell her I said thanks," Jeffrey said, taking the cup. He peeled off the top and inhaled the steam, thinking it would wake him up. Straightening up Sara's house was not exactly a debilitating task, but he was in a funk after seeing she had put that picture of them in the drawer, like she did not want to be reminded of the fact that they had been married. He couldn't help but laugh at himself; he was acting like a love-sick girl.

"What's that?" Brock asked, having a mortician's sense for someone who was letting his emotions get the better of him.

Jeffrey put the car in gear. "Nothing."

Brock settled in happily, his long legs stretched out in front of him like two bent toothpicks. "Thanks for picking me up. I don't know when the hearse is gonna be ready, and Mama has her Jazzercise on Mondays."

"That's not a problem," Jeffrey told him, trying not to snort at the thought of Penny Brock in leotards. The image of a lumpy

167

sack of potatoes came to mind.

Brock asked, "Any word on Tessa?"

"I talked to Sara this morning," Jeffrey told him. "She's doing a little better, it sounds like."

"Well, praise the Lord," Brock said, putting his hand up in the air. "I've been praying for her." He dropped his hand, slapping it against his thigh. "And that sweet little baby. Jesus has a special place for children."

Jeffrey did not respond, but he hoped Jesus had an even better place for whoever stabbed them to death.

Brock asked, "How's the family holding up?"

"They seem okay," Jeffrey told him before changing the subject. "You haven't worked for the county in a while, have you?"

"Oh, no," Brock balked, even though he had been the county coroner for years. "I have to say I was really glad when Sara took over. Not that the money wasn't nice, but Grant was just getting a little too big for me back then. Lots of people coming in from the city, bringing their city ways. I didn't want to miss something. It's an awesome responsibility. My hat's off to her."

Jeffrey knew that by "city" Brock meant

Atlanta. Like most small towns in the early nineties, Grant had seen an influx of urbanites seeking a slower way of life. They moved out of the larger cities, thinking they would find a peaceful Mayberry at the end of the interstate. For the most part, they would have — if they'd left their children at home. Part of the reason Jeffrey had been hired as chief of police was his experience with working on a gang task force in Birmingham, Alabama. By the time Jeffrey had signed his contract, the powers-that-be in Grant would have taken up goat sacrifices if they thought it would solve their youth-gang problem.

Brock said, "This one's pretty straightforward, Sara said. You just need blood and urine, right?"

"Yeah," Jeffrey told him.

"I hear Hare's helping out with her practice," Brock said.

"Yeah." Jeffrey said around a sip of coffee. Sara's cousin Hareton Earnshaw was also a doctor, though not a pediatrician. He was filling in at the clinic while Sara was in Atlanta.

"My daddy, rest his soul, used to play cards with Eddie and them," Brock said. "I remember sometimes he'd take me over to play with Sara and Tessie." He guffawed loud enough for it to echo in the car. "They were the only two girls in school who would talk to me!" He had real regret in his voice when he explained, "The rest of them thought I had cootie hands."

Jeffrey looked at him.

Brock held out a hand to illustrate. "From touching dead people. Not that I did that when I was young. That didn't come until later."

"Uh-huh," Jeffrey said, wondering how they'd gotten onto this subject.

"Now, my brother Roger, he was the one who touched them. Roger was a real scamp."

Jeffrey braced himself, hoping this was leading to a sick joke.

"He'd charge a quarter a person to take some of the kids down to the embalming room at night after Daddy'd gone to bed. He'd get 'em all in there with the lights off and nothing but a flashlight to show the way, then he'd press right here on the departed's chest, like this." Despite his better judgment, Jeffrey looked to see where. "And the body'd let out this low moan."

Brock opened his mouth and gave out a low, soulless moan. The sound was horrific — terrifying — something Jeffrey hoped to God he would forget when he tried to go to bed that night.

"Jesus, that's creepy," Jeffrey said, feeling a shudder well up, like someone had walked over his grave. "Don't do that again, Brock. Jesus."

Brock seemed contrite, but he handled it well, drinking his coffee and remaining silent the rest of the way to the morgue.

When Jeffrey pulled up to the Rosen house, the first thing he noticed was a shiny red Ford Mustang parked in the driveway. Instead of going to the front door, Jeffrey went over to the car, admiring its sleek lines. When he was Andy Rosen's age, Jeffrey had dreamed about driving a red Mustang, and seeing one here gave him an unreasonable pang of jealousy. He ran his fingers along the hood, tracing the black racing stripes, thinking that Andy had a hell of a lot more to live for than he had at that age.

Someone else loved this car, too. Despite the early hour, there was no dew on the paint. A bucket was upended near the back fender, a sponge on top. The garden hose was still reeled out to the car. Jeffrey looked at his watch, thinking it was an odd time to be out washing a car, especially considering that the owner had died the day before.

As he approached the front porch, Jeffrey could hear the Rosens having what sounded like a nasty argument. He had been a cop long enough to know that people were more likely to tell the truth when they were angry. He waited by the door, eavesdropping but trying not to look obvious in case any early-morning joggers wondered what he was up to.

"Why the hell do you care about this now, Brian?" Jill Rosen demanded. "You never cared about him before."

"That's fucking bullshit, and you know it."

"Don't use that language with me."

"Fuck you! I'll talk to you however I fucking please."

A moment passed. Jill Rosen's voice was softer, and Jeffrey could not make out what the woman was saying. When the man responded, his voice was equally low.

Jeffrey gave them a full minute to rile up again before knocking on the door. He could hear them moving around inside and guessed that one or both of them were crying.

Jill Rosen answered the door, and he could tell from the well-used Kleenex grasped in her hand that she'd spent the morning in tears. Jeffrey had a flash of

Cathy Linton on the deck at her house yesterday, and he felt a sympathy that he'd never imagined himself capable of.

"Chief Tolliver," Rosen said. "This is Dr. Brian Keller, my husband."

"We talked on the phone," Jeffrey reminded him.

Keller had an air of devastation about him. Judging by his thinning gray hair and soft jaw, he was probably in his late fifties, but grief made him look twenty years older. His trousers were pin-striped, and though they obviously belonged with a suit, Keller was wearing a yellowing undershirt with a deep V-neck that revealed a smattering of gray hair on his chest. He had a Star of David chain like his son, or maybe it was the one they had found in the woods. Incongruously, his feet were bare, and Jeffrey guessed that Keller had been the one to wash the car.

"I'm sorry about that," Keller said. "Yesterday on the phone. I was upset."

Jeffrey said, "I'm sorry for your loss, Dr. Keller," taking the man's hand, wondering how to ask tactfully if Andy was his natural son or adopted. A lot of women kept their maiden names when they married, but usually the children took their father's name.

Jeffrey asked Keller, "You're Andy's biological father?"

Rosen said, "We let Andy choose which name he wanted to take when he was old enough to make an informed decision."

Jeffrey nodded his understanding, though he was of the opinion that kids' being given too many choices was one of the reasons he saw so many of them at the station, shocked that their bad decisions had actually landed them in trouble.

"Come in," Rosen offered, indicating Jeffrey should follow the short hallway to the living room.

Like most professors, they lived on Willow Drive, which was just off Main Street and a short distance from the university. The school had worked out something with the bank to guarantee low-interest home loans for new professors, and they all ended up taking the nicest houses in town. Jeffrey wondered if all of the professors let their houses fall into disrepair as Keller had. There were stains on the ceiling from a recent rainfall, and the walls were in serious need of a fresh coat of paint.

"I'm sorry about the mess," Jill Rosen said in a practiced tone.

"It's fine," Jeffrey said, though he wondered how anyone could live in such clutter. "Dr. Rosen —"

"Jill."

"Jill," he said. "Can you tell me, do you know Lena Adams?"

"The woman from yesterday?" she asked, her voice going up at the end.

"I was wondering if you knew her from before."

"She came to my office earlier. She's the one who told me about Andy."

He held her gaze for a moment, not knowing the woman well enough to tell if there was something more to her words, which could be taken any number of ways. Jeffrey's gut told him that something was going on between Lena and Jill Rosen, but he was not sure how it pertained to the case.

"We can sit in here," Rosen said, indicating a cramped living room.

"Thanks," Jeffrey said, glancing around the room.

Rosen had obviously taken great care decorating the house when she moved in, but that had been many years ago. The furniture was nice, but looked a little too lived in. The wallpaper was dated, and the carpet showed high-traffic areas as clearly as a path in the forest. Even without these cosmetic problems, the place was crowding in on itself. Stacks of books and magazines spilled over in piles. There were newspapers Jeffrey recognized from last week spread around one of the armchairs by the window. Unlike the Linton house, which arguably had the same amount of clutter and certainly more books, there was something stifling about the place, as if no one had been happy here for a very long time.

"We talked to the funeral home about the service," Keller told him. "Jill and I were just trying to decide what we should do. My son had very definite feelings about cremation." His bottom lip quivered. "Will they be able to do that after the autopsy?"

"Yes," Jeffrey told them. "Of course."

Rosen said, "We want to support his wishes, but . . ."

Keller told her, "It's what he wanted, Jill."

Jeffrey could sense the tension between them and did not offer his opinion.

Rosen indicated a large chair. "Please, have a seat."

"Thank you," Jeffrey said, tucking in his tie, sitting on the edge of the cushion so he would not sink back into the lumpy chair.

She asked, "Would you like something to drink?"

Before Jeffrey could refuse, Keller said, "Water would be nice."

Keller stared at the floor until his wife left the room. He seemed to be waiting for something, but Jeffrey was not sure what. When the faucet in the kitchen was turned on, he opened his mouth, but no words came out.

Jeffrey said, "Nice car outside."

"Yes," he agreed, clasping his hands in his lap. His shoulders were stooped and Jeffrey realized Keller was a larger man than he had initially thought.

"You washed it this morning?"

"Andy took good care of that car," he said, but Jeffrey noticed he did not answer the question.

"You're in the biology department?"

"Research," Keller clarified.

Jeffrey began, "If there's something you want to tell me . . . ?"

Keller opened his mouth again, but just then Rosen came into the room, handing both Jeffrey and her husband a glass of water.

"Thank you," Jeffrey said, taking a sip, even though the glass had a funny smell. He set it down on the coffee table, glancing at Keller to see if the man had anything to say, before getting down to business.

He said, "I know y'all have other things to worry about. I just need to ask you some routine questions, and then I'll get out of your way."

"Take all the time you need," Keller offered.

Rosen said, "Your people were up in Andy's apartment until late last night."

"Yes," Jeffrey answered. Contrary to what cops did on television, Jeffrey liked to stay as far away from a fresh crime scene as he could until the technicians were finished processing it. The riverbed where Andy had killed himself was too expansive and public to be of much use. Andy's apartment was a different matter.

Keller waited for his wife to sit down, then sat beside her on the couch. He tried to take her hand, but she pulled away. Obviously the fight they'd been having was still going on.

Rosen asked, "Do you think he could have been pushed?"

Jeffrey wondered if anything had been said to Rosen or if she had come up with the scenario on her own. He asked, "Did anyone ever threaten to hurt your son?"

They looked at each other as if they had talked about this earlier. "Not that we know of."

Jeffrey asked, "And Andy attempted to kill himself before?"

They nodded in unison.

"You saw the note?"

Rosen whispered, "Yes."

"It's not likely," he told the parents. No matter what Jeffrey suspected at this point, it was just that: speculation. He did not want to give Andy's parents something to hold on to, only to have to disappoint them later. "We'll investigate every possibility, but I don't want to get your hopes up." He paused, regretting his choice of words. What parents would *hope* that their child was murdered?

Keller told his wife, "They'll find anything irregular in the autopsy. They can find out all kinds of things. It's amazing what science can do these days." He said this with the conviction of a man who worked in the field and relied on scientific method to prove any point.

Rosen held the tissue to her nose, not acknowledging what her husband had said. Jeffrey wondered if the tension between them was from the recent argument or if there had been problems in the marriage for a while. He would need to ask some discreet questions around campus to find out.

Keller interrupted Jeffrey's thoughts. "We've been trying to think of something to tell you," he said. "Andy had some friends from before —"

"We never really knew them," Rosen interrupted. "His drug friends."

"No," Keller agreed. "As far as we know, there was no one lately."

Rosen conceded, "At least no one Andy introduced us to."

"I should have been here more," Keller said, regret making his voice thick.

Rosen did not dispute this, and Keller's face turned red with the effort to keep from crying.

"You were in Washington?" Jeffrey asked the man, but it was his wife who answered.

She explained, "Brian's working on a very complicated grant application right now."

Keller shook his head, like it was nothing. "What does it mean now?" he asked no one in particular. "All that wasted time and for what?"

"Your work could help people one day," she said, but Jeffrey sensed some animosity in her tone. This wouldn't be the first time a wife resented her husband working long hours.

"That's his car in the driveway?" Jeffrey

asked the mother. He noticed Keller look away.

Rosen said, "We'd just bought it for him. Something to . . . I don't know. Brian wanted to reward him for doing so well."

The unsaid implication was that Rosen had not agreed with her husband's decision. The car was an extravagant purchase, and professors were hardly millionaires. Jeffrey guessed he was probably paid more money than Keller, which was not a hell of a lot.

Jeffrey asked, "Did he usually drive it to school?"

"It was easier walking," Rosen said. "Sometimes we all walked over together."

"Did he tell you where he was going yesterday morning?"

"I was already at the clinic," Rosen answered. "I assumed he would be home all day. When Lena came . . ."

Her tone of voice put a familiarity on Lena's name that Jeffrey would have liked to pursue, but he could think of no way to introduce it into the conversation.

Jeffrey took out his notebook instead, confirming, "Andy worked for you, Dr. Keller?"

"Yes," Keller answered. "There wasn't much for him to do, but I didn't want him spending a lot of time by himself at home."

Rosen added, "He helped at the clinic as well. Our receptionist isn't that reliable. Sometimes he would man the desk or do some filing."

Jeffrey wondered, "Did he ever have access to patient information?"

"Oh, never," Rosen said, as if the thought alarmed her. "That's kept under lock and key. Andy handled expense reports, scheduling, phone calls. That sort of thing." Her voice trembled. "It was just busywork to keep him occupied during the day."

"The same at the lab," Keller provided. "He wasn't really qualified to help with research. That work belongs to the graduate students." Keller sat up, hands on his knees. "I just wanted him close so I could keep an eye on him."

"You were worried he would do something like this?" Jeffrey asked.

"No," Rosen said. "Or, I don't know. Perhaps subconsciously I thought he might be considering it. He was acting very strange lately, like he was concealing something."

"Did you have any idea what he was hiding?"

"No telling," she said with true regret.

"Boys that age are difficult. Girls, too, for that matter. They're trying to make the transition between being a teenager and being an adult. Parents go back and forth between being a liability and a crutch, depending on the day of the week."

"Or whether or not he needs cash," Keller added. The parents smiled at this, like it was a shared joke between them.

Keller asked, "Do you have a son, Chief Tolliver?"

"No." Jeffrey sat back, not liking the question. When he was younger, Jeffrey never thought he would want a kid of his own. Knowing Sara's circumstances, he had put it out of his mind. Something about the last case he had worked on with Lena had made Jeffrey wonder what it would be like to be a father.

Keller said, "They'll tear your heart out," in a hoarse whisper, dropping his head into his hands. Rosen seemed to go through some silent debate with herself before reaching over and rubbing his back. Keller looked up, surprised, as if she had just given him some kind of gift.

Jeffrey waited a few moments before asking, "Did Andy tell you that he was having problems coping?" They both shook their heads. "Was there someone or

183

something that might have been upsetting him?"

Keller shrugged. "He was trying very hard to forge his own identity." He waved his hand toward the back of the house. "That was why we let him live over the garage."

"He was taking an interest in art," Rosen said. She pointed to the wall behind Jeffrey.

"Nice." Jeffrey glanced at the canvas, trying not to do a double take. The drawing was a rather one-dimensional rendering of a nude woman reclining on a rock. Her legs were wide open, her genitals the only color in the picture, so that it looked as if she had a plate of lasagna between her thighs.

"He had a real gift," Rosen said.

Jeffrey nodded, thinking that only a deluded mother or the editor of *Screw* magazine would think whoever drew the picture had a gift. He turned around, his eyes finding Keller. The man looked squeamishly uncomfortable, mirroring Jeffrey's own reaction.

"Did Andy date much?" Jeffrey asked, because as detailed as the drawing was, the boy seemed to have missed some important parts.

"Not that we know of," Rosen answered. "We never saw anyone going to his room, but the garage is in the back of the house."

Keller glanced at his wife before saying, "Jill thinks he could have been doing drugs again."

Jeffrey told them, "We found some paraphernalia in his room." He did not wait for the question Rosen was obviously about to ask. "Squares of tinfoil and a pipe. There's no telling when they were last used."

Rosen slumped, and her husband wrapped his arm around her, holding her close to his chest. Still, she seemed apart from him, and Jeffrey wondered again about the condition of their marriage.

Jeffrey continued, "There was nothing else in his room that pointed to a drug problem."

"He had mood swings," Keller said. "Sometimes he would be very melancholy. Sullen. It was hard to tell if it was from drugs or just his natural disposition."

Jeffrey thought now was as good a time as any to bring up Andy's piercings. "I noticed he had a pierced eyebrow."

Keller rolled his eyes. "It nearly killed his mother."

"His nose, too," Rosen added with a disapproving frown. "I think he had something done to his tongue recently. He wouldn't show me, but he kept chewing it."

Jeffrey pressed, "Anything else unusual?"

Keller and Rosen both looked at him in wide-eyed innocence. Keller spoke for both of them. "I don't think there was anything else left to pierce!" he said, not exactly laughing.

Jeffrey moved along. "What about the suicide attempt in January?"

"In retrospect, I'm not sure he meant anything by it," Keller said. "He knew that Jill would find the note when she woke that morning. He timed it so she would find him before anything got desperate." The father paused. "We thought he was just trying to get our attention."

Jeffrey waited for Rosen to say something, but her eyes were closed, her body folded into her husband's.

Keller said, "He acted out sometimes. He didn't think of the ramifications."

Rosen did not protest.

Keller shook his head. "I don't know, maybe I shouldn't say something like that."

"No," Rosen whispered. "It's true."

"We should have noticed," Keller insisted. "There must have been something."

Death was bad enough, but suicides

were always particularly horrible for the people who were left behind. Either the survivors blamed themselves for not seeing the signs or they felt betrayed by their selfish loved ones who'd left them to clean up the mess. Jeffrey imagined that Andy Rosen's parents would spend the rest of their lives swinging back and forth between the two emotions.

Rosen sat up, wiping her nose. She took another tissue out of the box and dried her eyes. "It's a wonder you found anything in that apartment at all," she said. "He was so messy." She had been trying to collect herself, but something about her words brought it all back to her.

Rosen broke down slowly, her mouth twitching as she tried to hold back her sobs, until she finally covered her face with her hands.

Keller put his arm around his wife again, pulling her close. "I'm so sorry," he said, burying his face in her hair. "I should have been here," he said. "I should have been here."

They stayed like this for several minutes, as if Jeffrey were no longer there.

He cleared his throat. "I thought I'd go out back and look at the apartment, if you don't mind."

Keller was the only one to look up. He nodded his head, then went back to comforting his wife. Rosen slumped into him. She could have been a rag doll in his hands.

Jeffrey turned to leave, coming face-to-face with Andy's reclining nude. There was something oddly familiar about the woman that he could not place.

Aware that he might be gawking, Jeffrey let himself out of the house. He wanted to follow up with Keller and find out exactly what it was the man could not speak about in front of his wife. He also needed to talk to Ellen Schaffer again. Maybe getting some distance from the crime scene had helped jog her memory.

Jeffrey stopped in front of the Mustang, admiring its lines again. Washing the car this early in the morning so soon after Andy Rosen's death was odd, but certainly not a crime. Maybe Keller had done it to honor his son. Maybe he'd been trying to hide evidence, though Jeffrey was hard-pressed to think of anything that could connect the car to this crime. Other than the attack on Tessa Linton, Jeffrey was not even sure a crime had been committed.

He leaned down, running his hand over the tire treads. The road leading to the parking pad by the bridge was paved, and the pad itself was gravel. Even if they were able to match treads, Andy might have driven the car to the site himself a hundred times before. Jeffrey knew from patrol reports that the area was a prime make-out spot.

Jeffrey flipped open his phone to call Frank but stopped when he noticed Richard Carter coming up the walk carrying a large casserole dish in his hands.

Richard's face broke into a wide grin when he saw Jeffrey, but then he seemed to catch himself and put on a more serious expression.

"Dr. Carter," Jeffrey said, trying to sound pleasant. Jeffrey had more important things to do than field prying questions so Richard could look like a big man on campus.

Richard said, "I made a casserole for Brian and Jill. Are they in?"

Jeffrey glanced back at the house, thinking of the oppressive atmosphere, the raw grief the parents were experiencing now. "Maybe now wouldn't be the right time."

Richard's face fell. "I just wanted to help."

"They're pretty upset," Jeffrey told him,

wondering how he could ask Richard some questions about Brian Keller without looking obvious about it. Knowing how Richard operated, he decided to approach the subject from a different angle. "Were you friends with Andy?" he asked, thinking that Richard could not have been more than eight or nine years older than the boy.

"God, no." Richard guffawed. "He was a student. Barring that, he was an obnoxious brat."

Jeffrey had gathered as much about Andy Rosen on his own, but he was surprised by the vehemence behind Richard's words. He asked, "But you're pretty close to Brian and Jill?"

"Oh, they're great," Richard said. "Everybody likes everybody on campus. The whole faculty is like a little family."

"Yeah," Jeffrey agreed. "Brian seems like a solid family man."

"Oh, he is," Richard agreed. "The best father in the world to Andy. I wish I'd had a father like that." There was an edge of curiosity to his voice, and Jeffrey could tell that Richard had realized he was being questioned. With this realization came a sense of power, and Richard had a smirk on his face as he waited for Jeffrey to ask him for dirt.

Jeffrey jumped in with both feet. "They seem to have a good marriage."

Richard twisted his lips to the side. "You think?"

Jeffrey did not answer, and Richard seemed to take this as a good thing.

"Well," Richard began, "I don't like to spread rumors . . ."

Jeffrey suppressed the *bullshit* that wanted to come.

"And it was just that — a rumor. I never saw anything to give it credence, but I can tell you that Jill was acting mighty strange around Brian at the last department Christmas party."

"Y'all are in the same department?"

"Like I said," Richard reminded him. "small campus."

Jeffrey stared silently, which was all the encouragement Richard needed.

"There was rumor of a problem a while back."

He seemed to need Jeffrey to say something, so Jeffrey provided, "Yes?"

"Mind you, just a rumor." He paused like a true showman. "About a student." Again he paused. "A female student."

"An affair?" Jeffrey guessed, though it was hardly a difficult leap. This would certainly be something that Keller would not want to talk about in front of his wife, especially if Rosen already knew about it. Jeffrey knew from his own experience that Sara's even alluding to the circumstances that had ended their marriage made him feel like he was dangling his feet over the Grand Canyon.

"Do you know the girl's name?"

"No idea, but if you believe the gossip, she transferred after Jill found out."

Jeffrey was dubious, and he was sick of people holding things back. "Do you remember what she looked like? What her major was?"

"I'm not sure if I believe she even existed. As I said, it was just a rumor." Richard frowned. "And now I feel bad for talking out of school." He laughed at the double meaning.

"Richard, if there's something you're not telling me . . ."

"I've told you everything I know. Or at least heard. Like I said —"

"It was just a rumor," Jeffrey completed.

"Was there anything else?" Richard asked, a pronounced pout to his lips.

Jeffrey decided to parry. "That's nice of you to bring them food."

The corners of Richard's mouth turned down. "I know when my mother passed away a few years ago, having people bring things was like a ray of sunshine in what was arguably the darkest period of my life."

Jeffrey played back Richard's words in his head, alarms going off like crazy.

"Chief?" Richard asked.

"Sunshine," Jeffrey said. Now he knew what was so familiar about Andy Rosen's lewd drawing. The girl in the picture had a sunburst tattooed around her belly button.

A patrol car and Frank Wallace's unmarked Taurus were parked outside Ellen Schaffer's sorority house when Jeffrey pulled up, though Jeffrey had asked for neither.

"Shit," Jeffrey said, pulling into the space by Frank's car. He knew that something was horribly wrong even before he saw two girls coming out of the dorm with their arms around each other, sobbing.

Jeffrey jogged to the house, taking the front steps two at a time. Keyes House had burned down years ago, but the college had replaced it with a close duplicate of the old antebellum mansion, with formal front parlors and a grand dining room that seated thirty. Frank was standing in one of the front parlors waiting for him.

"Chief," Frank said, motioning Jeffrey into the room, "we've been trying to call you."

Jeffrey slipped his phone out of his pocket. The battery level was fine, but there were areas around town where signals would not reach.

Jeffrey asked, "What happened?"

Frank closed the pocket doors to give them some privacy before answering. "Blew her head off."

"Fuck," Jeffrey cursed. He knew the answer, but had to ask, "Schaffer?"

Frank nodded.

"Deliberately?"

Frank lowered his voice. "After yesterday who knows?"

Jeffrey sat on the edge of the couch, feeling dread creep up again. Two suicides in as many days were not unheard of, but Tessa Linton's stabbing was casting a shadow over everything that happened on campus.

Jeffrey said, "I just talked to Brian Keller, Andy Rosen's father."

"That his stepson?"

"No, he took his mother's name." When Jeffrey saw Frank's confusion, he said, "Don't ask. Keller's his biological father."

"All right," Frank agreed, a baffled expression still on his face. For a split second, Jeffrey wished he had Lena here instead of Frank. Not that Frank was a bad cop, but Lena was more intuitive, and she and Jeffrey knew how to work off of each other. Frank was what Jeffrey thought of as a gumshoe, meaning he was better at wearing down the soles of his shoes tracking down leads than he was at making the mental leaps that solved cases.

Jeffrey walked to the swinging door that led to the kitchen, making sure they weren't being overheard. "Richard Carter said —"

Frank snorted out a breath. Jeffrey was not sure if this was because of Richard's sexual orientation or his abhorrent personality. Only the latter was acceptable to Jeffrey, but he had learned a long time ago that Frank was set in his ways.

Jeffrey said, "Carter knows campus gossip."

"What'd he say?" Frank relented.

"That Keller was having an affair with a student."

"Okay," Frank said, his tone contrary to the word.

"I want you to do some digging around about Keller. Find out his background. Let's see if this rumor is true."

"You think his son found out about an affair and the dad shut him up to keep it from the wife?"

"No," Jeffrey said. "Richard said the wife knew."

Frank said, "As far as you can trust that fruit."

"Cut it out, Frank," Jeffrey ordered. "If Keller was having an affair, it could play out real nice for a suicide. Maybe the son couldn't forgive his father, so he jumped off the bridge to punish him. The parents were fighting this morning. Rosen told Keller he never cared about him when he was alive."

"Could be just her being mean. You know women can get that way sometimes."

Jeffrey was not going to debate the point. "Rosen seemed pretty clearheaded to me."

"You think she did it?"

"What would she have to gain?"

Frank's answer was the same one Jeffrey had: "I don't know."

Jeffrey stared at the fireplace, wishing again he had Lena or even Sara to talk this through with. He told Frank, "I'm gonna be looking at a lawsuit if I stir up shit around his parents and the kid really killed himself."

"That's true."

"Go ahead and check if Keller was really in D.C. when this happened," Jeffrey said. "Ask some discreet questions around campus and see if we can substantiate this rumor."

"The flights are easy enough to check," Frank said, taking out his notebook. "I can ask around about the affair, but the kid would probably be better for that than me."

"Lena's not a cop, Frank."

"She could help. She's already on campus. She probably knows some students."

"She's not a cop."

"Yeah, but —"

"But nothing," Jeffrey said, shutting him up. Lena had proved in the library yesterday that she was not interested in helping out. Jeffrey had given her plenty of opportunities to talk to Jill Rosen, but she had kept her mouth shut, not even offering to comfort the other woman.

Frank said, "What about Schaffer? How's she fit into this?"

"There was a painting," Jeffrey told him, giving Frank the details of the drawing in the Keller-Rosen living room.

"The mom had that hanging up?"

"She was proud of him," Jeffrey guessed,

though his own mother would have slapped the crap out of him and ignited the painting with one of her cigarettes. "Both of them said the son wasn't seeing anybody."

"Maybe he didn't tell them," Frank said.

"He might not have," Jeffrey agreed. "But if Schaffer was having sex with Andy, why didn't she recognize him yesterday?"

"He was ass up," Frank said. "If it was Carter not recognizing him, then I'd be suspicious."

Jeffrey gave Frank a look of warning.

"All right." Frank held up his hands. "Lookit, though, she was upset. He was about fifty feet below her. What's she supposed to recognize?"

"True," Jeffrey conceded. "Do you think this could have been some kind of suicide pact?"

"They'd do it together, not a day apart," Jeffrey pointed out. "Did we lift anything off the suicide note?"

"Everybody and his mother touched it," Frank said, and Jeffrey wondered if he was making a joke.

"If it was a pact, they'd say so in the note."

"Maybe Andy broke up with her," Frank suggested. "So she gets him back by throwing him over the bridge."

"You think she's strong enough to do that?" Jeffrey asked, and Frank shrugged. "I don't buy it," Jeffrey said. "Girls don't act out like that."

"It's not like she could divorce him."

"Watch it," Jeffrey warned, taking the remark personally. He continued before Frank could embarrass them both trying to apologize. "*Young* girls don't do that," he amended. "They shame the guy, or they lie about him to his friends, or they get pregnant, or they take a load of pills —"

"Or they blow their brains out?" Frank interrupted.

"All of this is assuming that Andy Rosen was murdered. He still could have killed himself."

"You got anything on that?"

"Brock took some blood this morning. We'll have the lab report back tomorrow. There's no evidence of foul play right now. Tessa's the only reason we're looking at this funny, and who the hell knows if there's a connection?"

Frank said, "Hell of a coincidence if it's not."

"I'm going to give Keller a day to stew, then go at him hard to see what he knows. There was something he wanted to tell me this morning that he didn't want to discuss in front of his wife. Maybe after Sara does the autopsy tonight, I'll have more to go on."

"She's coming back tonight?"

"Yeah," Jeffrey said. "I'm picking her up this afternoon."

"She doin' okay?"

"It's a hard time," Jeffrey said, then cut off the conversation. "Where's Schaffer?"

"This way," Frank told him, opening up the pocket doors. "You wanna talk to the roommate first?"

Jeffrey was going to tell him no but changed his mind when he saw the crying woman sitting in the window seat at the end of the hall. Two girls flanked her, offering their support. They could have all been carbon copies of each other, with their blond hair and blue eyes. Any one of them could have passed for Ellen Schaffer's sister.

"Ma'am," Jeffrey said, trying to sound consoling, "I'm Chief Tolli—"

The woman cut him off by bursting into tears. "It's so horrible!" the girl cried. "She was fine just this morning!"

Jeffrey glanced at Frank. "That's the last time you saw her?"

She nodded, her head bobbing like a fishing line.

"What time was that?" Jeffrey asked.

"Eight," she said, and Jeffrey knew that he had been with the Rosen-Kellers during that time.

She said, "I had to go to class. . . . Ellen said she was going to sleep in. She was so upset about Andy. . . ."

Jeffrey asked, "She knew Andy Rosen?"

At this the girl burst into tears again, putting her whole body into it. "No!" she wailed. "That's what was so tragic. He was in her art class, and she didn't even know him!"

Jeffrey exchanged a look with Frank. Oftentimes in police work, they ran across people who felt a lot closer to victims of crime than they ever had when the victim was living. In Andy's case, an alleged suicide, the melodrama would be heightened.

"So," Jeffrey began, "you saw Ellen at eight? Did anyone else see her?"

One of the girls beside the roommate spoke up. "We all have early classes."

"Did Ellen?"

The three nodded in unison. One of them said, "Everyone in the house does."

"What's her major?" Jeffrey asked, wondering if the girl was linked to Keller in some way.

"Cell biology," the third girl provided.

"She was supposed to hand in her labs to-morrow."

Jeffrey asked, "Did she have Dr. Keller for any classes?"

They all shook their heads. One of them said, "Is that Andy's father?" but Jeffrey didn't answer her.

He told Frank, "Let's get copies of her schedule and see what classes she's had since she's been here." To the girls he said, "Was Ellen dating anyone in particular?"

"Um," the first girl began, looking nervously at her friends. Before Jeffrey could coax her along, she said, "Ellen was seeing *lots* of different guys." The emphasis implied thousands.

"No one had a grudge against her?" Jeffrey asked.

"Of course not," the first girl defended. "Everyone loved her."

"Did y'all see anyone suspicious hanging around the house this morning?"

The three shook their heads.

Jeffrey turned to Frank. "Did you do a canvass?"

"Most of them were gone," Frank said. "We're rounding them up. No one heard the gunshot."

Jeffrey raised his eyebrows in surprise but didn't comment in front of the girls.

He told them, "Thank you for your time," and gave them each one of his cards in case they thought of anything else that might be useful.

It was not until Frank was taking him up the hallways to Schaffer's ground-floor room that Jeffrey asked, "What'd she use?"

"Remington 870."

"The Wingmaster?" Jeffrey asked, wondering what a girl like Ellen Schaffer was doing with such a weapon. The pump-action rifle was one of the most popular weapons used by law enforcement.

"She shoots skeet," Frank said. "She's on the team."

Jeffrey vaguely recalled that Grant Tech had a shooting team, but he still could not reconcile the perky blonde he had met the day before with a skeet shooter.

Frank indicated a closed door. "She's in there."

Jeffrey did not know what he was expecting when he walked into Ellen Schaffer's room, but his jaw dropped at what he saw. The young woman was on the couch, her legs wrapped around the barrel of the pump-action rifle. The muzzle was pointed at her head — or what was left of her head.

His eyes watered as a strong odor hit

him. "What's that smell?"

Frank pointed to the bare lightbulb over the desk. A piece of scalp clung to the frosted white glass, smoke wafting up to the ceiling as it cooked from the heat.

Jeffrey covered his mouth and nose with his hand, trying to block out the odor. He walked over to the window, which was opened about twelve inches. Glancing out behind the house, he could see a lawn with a gazebo and a sitting area. Beyond this was the national forest. A trail that half the kids on campus probably used led into the woods.

"Where's Matt?"

"Canvassing," Frank told him.

"Get him outside this window to look for footprints."

Frank flipped open his phone and made the call as Jeffrey studied every inch of the window. After a full minute of staring, he found nothing. It was not until he started to turn away that the light caught a streak of grease near the latch. "Did you see this?" he asked.

Frank walked over, bending his knees for a better look. "Oil?" he asked, then indicated the desk beside the couch. A wire breech brush, a patch, and a small bottle of Elton gun-cleaning oil were laid out on the top. On the floor a cloth that had obviously been used to clean the barrel of the rifle was crumpled into a ball.

"She cleaned the gun before she shot herself?" Jeffrey asked, thinking that was the last thing he would do.

Frank shrugged. "Maybe she wanted to make sure it was working right."

"You think?" Jeffrey asked, standing in front of the couch. Schaffer was wearing a pair of tight jeans and a cropped T-shirt. Her feet were bare, her toe caught in the trigger mechanism. The sun tattoo around her belly button was visible beneath a backspray of blood. Her hands were resting on the muzzle of the rifle, probably to keep it pointed toward her head.

Using a pen from his pocket, Jeffrey pushed the right hand away. The palm was clean of blood where it had rested against the rifle, which meant that Schaffer had had her hand on the gun at the time she'd shot herself. Or been shot. An examination of the other hand revealed the same.

Stuck between the cushions on the couch was a spent shot shell that had been ejected from the chamber when the trigger was pulled. Jeffrey pushed it with his pen, wondering why it didn't look right. He checked the fine print on the muzzle to make sure, then said to Frank, "She's got a twelve-gauge rifle and she used a twenty-gauge shell."

Frank stared at him for a moment. "Why'd she use a twenty?"

Jeffrey stood up, shaking his head. The circumference of the rifle's muzzle was larger than the circumference of the bullet. Probably one of the most dangerous things you can do with a rifle is load the wrong ammunition. Manufacturers had standardized the jacket colors of shells to prevent just this from happening.

"How long was she on the skeet team?" Jeffrey asked.

Frank took out his notebook and turned to the right page. "Just this year. Her roommate said she wanted to get into decathlons."

"She color-blind?" Jeffrey asked. The bright yellow shell was hard to mistake for the green twenty-gauge.

"I can check," Frank said, making a note.

Jeffrey examined the tip of the muzzle, holding his breath as he tried to get a closer look. "She had a skeet choke on it," he noticed. The choke would constrict the barrel, making it much more likely that the smaller shell would lodge.

Jeffrey stood. "This isn't adding up."

Frank said, "Look at the wall."

Jeffrey did as he was told, walking around a pool of blood by the head of the couch to examine the wall behind the body. The shot blast had displaced most of the skull, fragmenting pieces of the head against the wall at a high velocity.

Jeffrey strained his eyes, trying to make sense of the blood and tissue that riddled the white wall. The lead shot pellets had left several large holes, some of them going through to the next room.

"Something next door?" Jeffrey asked, saying a small prayer of thanks that no one had been in the other room when the trigger was pulled.

"That's not what I meant," Frank said. "Do you see what's in the wall?"

"Hold on," Jeffrey told him. He stared as hard as he could until he realized that something was staring back.

Ellen Schaffer's eyeball was embedded in the Sheetrock.

"Christ," Jeffrey said, turning away. He went back to the window, wanting to open it up and let out the smell. Being in this room was like being trapped in a shithouse on the last day of the state fair.

Jeffrey looked back at the girl, trying to

get some distance. He should have talked to her earlier. Maybe if he'd been here first thing, Ellen Schaffer would still be alive. He wondered what else he had missed. The caliber discrepancy on the rifle was suspicious, but anybody could make a mistake, especially if the person thought he — or she — wasn't going to have to hang around to clean up the mess. Then again, the whole thing could have been staged. Did someone else have a bull's-eye painted on their head?

Jeffrey asked, "When did they find her?"

"About thirty minutes ago," Frank told him, taking out his handkerchief and patting his forehead. "They didn't touch anything. Just closed the door and called us."

"Christ," Jeffrey repeated, taking out his own handkerchief. He glanced back at the desk.

"There's Matt," Frank said, and Jeffrey saw Matt walk into the backyard, hands in his pockets as he stared at the ground, looking for anything that seemed out of place. He stopped at one particular spot and knelt down for a better look.

"What?" Jeffrey called, just as Frank's cell phone started to ring.

Matt raised his voice to be heard. "It looks like an arrow."

"A what?" Jeffrey yelled, thinking he did not have time for this.

"An arrow," Matt said. "Like somebody drew it into the ground."

"Chief," Frank said, holding the phone to his chest.

Jeffrey called to Matt, "Are you sure?"

"Come see for yourself," Matt answered. "It sure looks like it."

Frank repeated, "Chief."

"What, Frank?" Jeffrey snapped.

"One of the fingerprints from Rosen's apartment came back with a positive match on the computer."

"Yeah?" Jeffrey demanded.

Frank shook his head. He looked down at the floor, then seemed to think better of it. "You don't want to know."

6

Lena lay on her back, staring up at the ceiling, trying to breathe and relax the way Eileen, the yoga instructor, had told them to. Lena could hold every yoga pose longer than anyone else in class, but when it came to the cool-down period, she was a complete failure. The concept of "letting go" was against Lena's personal religion of being in control of herself at every point in her life, especially where her body was concerned.

Their first therapy session, Jill Rosen had recommended Lena take up yoga to help her relax and sleep better. Rosen had given Lena a lot of coping advice in their short time together, but this was the only bit that took. Part of Lena's problem after the attack was that she'd felt like her body was not her own. Because she was athletic from a young age, her muscles were not used to this idle life of moping around and feeling sorry for herself. Something about

210

stretching and pushing her body, watching her biceps and calves return to their normal hardness, had given Lena hope, like maybe she could get back to her old self. Then the cool-down period came, and Lena felt the same way she had felt the first time she took Algebra in school. And the second time she had taken it in summer school.

She closed her eyes, concentrating on the small of her back, trying to release the tension, but the effort made her shoulders draw up to her ears. Her body was as tight as a rubber band, and Lena did not understand why Eileen insisted this was the most important part of the class. All the enjoyment Lena got from stretching evaporated as soon as the music turned low and they were told to get on their backs and breathe. Instead of picturing a winding stream or the rolling waves of an ocean, all Lena pictured was a clock ticking away, and the millions of things she had to do as soon as she left the gym, even though today was her day off.

"Breathe," Eileen reminded them in her irritatingly content monotone. She was a young woman of about twenty-five with the kind of sunny disposition that made Lena want to punch her.

"Soften your back," Eileen suggested, her voice a low whisper designed to soothe. Lena's eyes popped open as Eileen pressed her palm to Lena's stomach. The contact only made Lena tense more, but the instructor did not seem to notice. She told Lena, "That's better," a smile spreading across her narrow face.

Lena waited for the woman to walk away before closing her eyes again. She opened her mouth, letting out the air in a steady stream, and was just starting to feel like it might be working when Eileen clapped her hands together.

"That's good," Eileen said, and Lena stood up so quickly she got a head rush. The rest of the students were smiling at one another or hugging the perky instructor, but Lena grabbed her towel and headed for the locker room.

Lena spun the combination on her lock, glad she had the room to herself. She glanced at herself in the mirror, then did a double take. Since the attack Lena had stopped looking in the mirror, but for some reason today she felt drawn to her reflection. Her eyes were rimmed with dark circles, and her cheekbones were more pronounced than usual. She was getting too thin, because most days the mere thought of food was enough to make her feel sick.

She took the clip out of her hair, letting the long brown strands fall around her face and neck. Lately she felt more comfortable with her hair down, like a curtain. Knowing that no one would be able to get a good look at her made Lena feel safe.

Someone came in, and Lena walked back to her locker, feeling stupid for being caught in front of the mirror. A skinny guy stood beside her, taking his backpack out of the locker next to hers. He was standing so close that she felt the hair on the back of her neck stand up. Lena turned around and snatched up her shoes, thinking she could put them on outside.

"Hi," he said.

Lena waited. He was blocking the door.

"That hugging stuff," he said, shaking his head like this was something they joked about all the time.

Lena looked him over, knowing she'd never talked to this kid before in her life. He was short for a guy, just a little taller than she was. His body was wiry and small-framed, but she could see his well-defined arms and shoulders beneath the black long-sleeved T-shirt he wore. His hair was cropped close to his head in a military style, and he was wearing lime green socks that were so bright they were almost painful to look at.

He held out his hand. "Ethan Green. I joined the class a couple of weeks ago."

Lena sat down on the bench to put on her shoes.

Ethan sat at the other end. "You're Lena, right?"

"Read it in the papers?" she asked, working at a knot in her tennis shoe, thinking that fucking article they ran on Sibyl had made her life even more difficult than it had to be.

"Noo-o," he said, drawing out the word. "I mean, yeah, I know about you, but I heard Eileen call you Lena, so I put two and two together." He flashed a nervous smile. "And I recognized the picture."

"Smart kid," she said, giving up on the knot. She stood, forcing her foot into the shoe.

He stood, too, holding his backpack close. There were only three or four guys who took yoga, and they invariably ended up in the locker room after class, spewing some line about how they did yoga to get in touch with their feelings and explore their inner selves. It was a great ploy, and Lena guessed that the male yoga students got laid more often than any other guys on campus.

She said, "I've got to go."

"Wait a minute," he said, a half smile at his lips. He was an attractive kid, probably used to having girls fall all over him.

"What?" She looked at him, waiting. A small bead of sweat rolled down the side of his face, past a two-pronged scar just below his ear. He must have gotten the wound dirty before it closed, because there was a dark tint to the scar that made it stand out against his jawline.

He smiled nervously, asking, "Would you like to go get some coffee?"

"No," she told him, hoping that would end it.

The door opened, and a stream of girls flowed in, banging lockers open and shut.

He said, "You don't like coffee?"

"I don't like kids," she said, grabbing her bag and leaving before he could say anything more.

Lena felt rattled as she left the gym, and pissed off that she'd let that kid catch her off guard. Even after climbing the uphill battle called relaxation, Lena always felt calmer when she left a yoga class than she did when it started. Now that was gone. She felt tense again, jumpy. Maybe she would drop off her bag at her room, change, and go for a long run until her body was so tired that she could sleep away the rest of the day.

"Lena?"

Lena turned, expecting to see the kid again. It was Jeffrey.

"What?" she asked, instantly feeling her defenses go up. Something about the way he stood close to her, his stance wide apart, his shoulders squared, told her this was not a social visit.

"I need you to come down to the station with me."

She laughed, but even as she did, Lena knew he wasn't joking.

"It'll just be a minute." Jeffrey tucked his hands into his pockets. "I've got some questions to ask you about yesterday."

"Tessa Linton?" Lena said. "Did she die?"

"No." He looked over his shoulder, and Lena could see Ethan about fifty yards behind him. Jeffrey stepped closer, lowering his voice, saying, "We found your fingerprints in Andy Rosen's apartment."

She could not hide her surprise. "In his apartment?"

"Why didn't you tell me you knew him?"

"Because I didn't," Lena snapped. She

started to walk away, but Jeffrey put his hand on her arm. His grip wasn't tight, but she knew it could be.

He said, "You know we can run your underwear for DNA."

Lena could not remember the last time she had felt so shocked. "What underwear?" she asked, too surprised by what he was saying to react to the physical contact.

"The underwear you left in Andy's room."

"What are you talking about?"

He loosened his grip on her arm, but it had the opposite effect for Lena. He told her, "Let's go."

Lena said what anybody with half a brain would say to a cop who was looking at her the way Jeffrey was now. "I don't think so."

"Just a few minutes." His voice was friendly, but Lena had worked with Jeffrey long enough to know what his real intentions were.

She asked, "Am I under arrest?"

He seemed insulted. "Of course not."

She tried to keep her voice calm. "Then let me go."

"I just want to talk to you."

"Make an appointment with my social secretary." Lena tried to pull her arm out of his grasp just as Jeffrey's hand tightened again. Panic welled up inside her. "Stop it," she hissed, trying to jerk her arm away from him.

"Lena —" he said, as if she were overreacting.

"Let me go!" she screamed, yanking away so hard that she fell back onto the sidewalk. Her tailbone connected with the cement like a sledgehammer, pain shooting up her spine.

Suddenly Jeffrey lurched forward. Lena thought he might fall on her, but he caught himself at the last minute, taking two big steps around her.

"What the . . . ?" Her mouth opened in surprise. Ethan had pushed Jeffrey from behind.

Jeffrey recovered quickly, and he was in Ethan's face before Lena could tell what was going on. "What the fuck do you think you're doing?"

Ethan's voice was a low growl. The goofy boy Lena had talked to back in the locker room had been replaced by a nasty pit bull of a man. "Fuck off."

Jeffrey held up his badge a few inches from Ethan's nose. "What did you say, boy?"

Ethan stared at Jeffrey, not the shield.

The muscles in his neck stood in stark relief, and a vein near his eye pulsed strongly enough to give him a visible tic. "I said fuck off, you goddamn pig."

Jeffrey pulled out his handcuffs. "What's your name?"

"Witness," Ethan said, his tone hard and even. He obviously knew enough about the law to realize he had leverage. "Eyewitness."

Jeffrey laughed. "To what?"

"To you knocking this woman down." Ethan pulled Lena up by the arm, his back to Jeffrey. He slapped dirt off her pants, ignoring Jeffrey, telling her, "Let's go."

Lena was so shocked by the authority in his tone that she started to follow.

"Lena," Jeffrey said, as if he were the only one being reasonable. "Don't make this harder than it has to be."

Ethan turned, his fists clenched, ready for a fight. Lena thought he was not only stupid but insane. Jeffrey had at least fifty pounds on the younger man, and he knew how to use them. Not to mention that Jeffrey had a gun.

Lena said, "Come on," jerking Ethan away by the arm like she was tugging his leash. When she dared look back over her shoulder, Jeffrey stood where they had left him, the look on his face telling her this was far from over.

Ethan put two ceramic mugs down on the table, coffee for Lena, tea for him.

"Sugar?" he asked, taking a couple of packets out of his pants pocket. He was back to being a goofy nice kid again. The transformation was so complete that Lena was not sure whom she had seen earlier. Today was so fucked up, she did not know if she could trust her memory on anything.

"No," she said, wishing he were offering her whiskey instead. No matter what Jill Rosen said, Lena had rules, and one of them was that she never drank before eight at night.

Ethan sat down across from Lena before she could think to tell him to go away. She would go home in a minute, after she got over the shock of what had happened with Jeffrey. Lena's heart was still pounding in her chest, and her hands shook around the mug. She'd never met Andy Rosen in her life. Why would her fingerprints be in his apartment? Never mind the fingerprints — why would Jeffrey think he had Lena's underwear?

"Cops," Ethan said, the same way someone might say "pedophiles." He sipped his tea, shaking his head.

"You shouldn't have interfered," she told him. "And you shouldn't have pissed off Jeffrey like that. He'll remember you the next time he sees you."

Ethan shrugged. "I'm not worried."

"You should be," she said, thinking he sounded just like every other disaffected suburban punk whose parents had been too busy arranging golf dates to teach their kids to respect authority. If they had been in an interview room at the police station, she would have slapped that smug look right off his face.

She told him, "You should've listened to Jeffrey."

Anger flashed in his eyes, but he kept it under control. "Like you did?"

"You know what I mean," Lena told him, taking another sip of coffee. The liquid was hot enough to scorch her tongue, but she drank it anyway.

"I wasn't gonna stand around and watch him push you like that."

"What're you, my big brother?"

"It's just cops," Ethan said, playing with the string on his tea bag. "They think they can push you around because they've got a badge."

Lena took umbrage at his remark and

spoke before she could think about what had just happened. "It's not easy being a cop, mostly because people like you have that same shitty attitude."

"Hey, now." He held up his hands, giving her a puzzled look. "I know you used to be one of them, but you gotta admit that guy was pushing you around."

"He was not," Lena said, hoping he gathered from her tone that *no one* pushed her around. "Not until you came along." She let that sink in. "And speaking of which, where the fuck do you get off putting your hands on a cop?"

"Same stop he got off on," Ethan shot back, anger flashing in his eyes again. He glanced down at his mug, recovering some of his calm. When he looked up again, he smiled, as if that smoothed everything over.

Ethan said, "You always want a witness when a cop starts to go off on you like that."

"Got a lot of experience with it?" she asked. "What are you, twelve?"

"I'm twenty-three," he said, but he did not seem to take her question the way she had intended. "And I know about cops because I know about cops."

"Yeah, right." When he just shrugged, she said, "Let me guess, you went to juvie for knocking over mailboxes? No, wait, your English teacher found some pot in your book bag?"

He smiled again, not quite laughing. She could see that one of his front teeth was slightly chipped. He said, "I got mixed up in some stuff, but I'm not that way anymore. Okay?"

"You've got a temper," she said, though it was more an observation than a criticism. People were constantly telling Lena she had a quick temper, but she was Mother Teresa compared to Ethan Green.

He said, "I'm not that kind of person anymore."

She shrugged, because she could not care less what kind of person he was. What Lena cared about right now was why the hell Jeffrey thought she was connected to Andy Rosen. Had Jill Rosen told him something? How could Lena find out?

"So," he said, like he was glad they had gotten that out of the way, "did you know Andy well?"

Lena felt her guard coming back up. "Why?"

"I heard what the cop said to you about your panties."

"He didn't say 'panties,' for one."

"And for two?"

"For two, it's none of your goddamn business."

He smiled again. Either he thought it made him charming or he had some kind of weird Tourette's.

Lena stared at him, not saying anything. Ethan was a little guy, but he'd managed to make up for it by developing every muscle in his small frame. His arms did not bulge like Chuck's, but his delts stood out as he played with the tea bag hanging inside his cup. His neck looked strong but not thick. Even his face was toned, with a solid jaw and cheekbones that jutted out like pieces of granite. There was something about the way he lost and regained his control that was fascinating, and on any other day Lena would have felt tempted to see if she could force him over the edge.

He said, "You're like a porcupine. Anybody ever tell you that?"

Lena did not answer. As a matter of fact, Sibyl had said the exact thing to her all the time. As usual, the thought of Sibyl brought tears to her eyes, and she looked down, swirling the coffee in her mug, watching it cling to the sides.

She looked up when she thought she had sufficiently masked her feelings. Ethan had picked one of the trendy new coffee places on the outskirts of campus. The small space was packed even at this time of day. She looked over her shoulder, thinking Jeffrey would be there, watching her. She could still feel his anger, but beyond that, what stung was the way he had looked at her, like Lena had crossed the line. Not being a cop was one thing, but being a hindrance to a case — maybe even being involved in a case but lying about it — would put her squarely on his shit list. Over the years Lena had pissed off Jeffrey more than her share of times, but today she knew without a doubt that she had lost the one thing she had worked her ass off to get: his respect.

At the thought of this, a cold sweat broke out all over her body. Did Jeffrey really think of her as a suspect? Lena had seen Jeffrey work before, but had never been on the other end of one of his interrogations. She could see how easily someone could talk their way into a jail cell, even if it was for a couple of nights while Jeffrey worked something out. Lena could not spend even a second in a locked cell. To be a cop, even an ex-cop, in jail was a dangerous thing. What was Jeffrey thinking? What evidence did he have? There was no way her fingerprints could be in Rosen's apartment. She did not even know where the kid lived.

Ethan interrupted her thoughts. "This is about that girl who was stabbed, huh?"

She looked at him, demanding, "What are we doing here?"

He seemed surprised by her question. "I just wanted to talk to you."

"Why?" she asked. "Because you read that article in the paper? Am I fascinating to you because I was raped?"

He glanced around nervously, probably because her voice had gotten louder. She thought about taking it down a notch, but everyone in the room knew that Lena had been attacked. She could not pay for a Coke at the movie theater without the asshole kid behind the counter glancing down at the scars on her hands. No one wanted to talk to *her* about it, but they were more than happy to talk with one another behind her back.

"What do you want to know?" she asked him, trying to keep a conversational tone. "Are you doing some kind of project on it for school?"

He tried to make light of it. "That's more like sociology. I'm in materials science. Polymers. Metals. Composites. Tribomaterials."

"I was nailed to the floor." She showed

him her hands, turning them so he could see where the nails had gone all the way through. If she still had her shoes off, she would have shown him her feet, too. "He drugged me and raped me for two days. What else do you want to know?"

He shook his head, like this was some big misunderstanding. "I just wanted to take you out for coffee."

"Well, you can mark that off your list now," she told him, finishing her cup in one swallow. The hot liquid burned in her chest as she put the mug down on the table with a bang and started to stand. "See you around."

"No." Lightning fast, he reached out and wrapped his fingers tightly around her left wrist. The pain was almost unbearable, sharp jolts traveling up the nerves in her arm. Lena remained standing, keeping her expression neutral even though the pain made her stomach roll.

"Please," he said, his hand still clamped on her wrist. "Just stay for another minute."

"Why?" she asked, trying to keep her voice even. If he squeezed her wrist any tighter, the bones would probably break.

"I don't want you to think I'm that kind of guy."

"What kind of guy are you?" she asked, letting herself look down at his hand.

He waited a beat before letting go of her wrist. Lena could not stop the small gasp of relief that hissed out between her lips. She let her hand dangle beside her, not testing the bones and tendons for damage. Her wrist throbbed as the blood rushed through, but she would not give him that satisfaction of looking down.

She repeated herself. "What kind of guy are you?"

His smile was far from reassuring. "The kind of guy who likes to talk to pretty girls."

She gave a sharp laugh, looking around the coffeehouse, which had started to empty out over the last few minutes. The man behind the counter had been watching them, but when Lena caught his eye, he turned around to the espresso machine like he had been cleaning it all along.

"Come on," Ethan said. "Sit down."

Lena stared at him.

"I'm sorry I hurt you."

"What makes you think you hurt me?" she asked, though her wrist was still throbbing. She bent her hand, trying to test it, but the pain stopped her. She was going to pay him back for this. There was no way this kid would get away with hurting her.

He said, "I don't want you to be mad at me."

"I hardly know you," she told him. "And in case you didn't notice, I've got some problems of my own right now, so thanks for the coffee, but —"

"I knew Andy."

Her mind clicked back to Jeffrey and what he had said about Lena being in Andy's apartment. She tried to read Ethan's expression to see if he was lying, but she could not. The threat from Jeffrey came rushing back to Lena. She asked him, "What do you know about Andy?"

"Sit down," he said, more an order than a request.

"I can hear you fine from here."

"I'm not gonna talk to you standing up," he said, sitting back in his chair, waiting.

Lena stood beside the chair, debating her options. Ethan was a student. He was probably privy to a lot more gossip than Lena was. If she could get some information about Andy for Jeffrey, maybe Jeffrey would reconsider his crazy accusations. Lena felt herself smile at the thought of throwing Jeffrey clues that would break the case. He had made it clear that she was not a cop anymore. She would make him regret cutting her loose.

"Why are you smiling?" Ethan asked.

"It's not for you," Lena said, turning the chair around. She sat, hanging her hands over the back even though the pressure made her wrist feel like it was burning from the inside out. There was something seductive about controlling the intensity of her own pain. It made her feel strong for a change.

She dangled her hand, ignoring the ache. "Tell me what you know about Andy."

He seemed to be searching for something to tell her but finally admitted, "Not much."

"You're wasting my time." She started to stand, but he held out his hand to stop her. Ethan did not touch her this time, but the memory of his grip was enough to keep Lena in her chair.

She asked, "What?"

"I know someone who was close to him. A close friend."

"Who?"

"Do you party?"

Lena recognized the drug-culture euphemism. "Do you?" she asked. "You into E or what?"

"No," he said, sounding disappointed. "Are you?"

"What do you think?" she snapped. "Was Andy?"

Ethan stared at her for a moment, as if he was trying to figure something out about her. "Yeah."

"How do you know if you're not into it?"

"His mom's at the clinic. It's kind of like good gossip that she can't help her own kid."

Lena felt the need to take up for Jill Rosen, even though Lena had thought the same thing about the doctor. "There's only so much you can do for people. Maybe Andy didn't want to stop. Maybe he wasn't strong enough to quit."

He seemed curious. "You think so?"

"I don't know," she answered, but part of her now understood the lure of drugs like she never had before the rape. "Sometimes people just want to escape. To stop thinking about things."

"It's only temporary."

"You sound like you know about it." She glanced down at his arms, which were still covered by the sleeves of his shirt even though it was warm inside the building. She suddenly remembered him from class the week before. He had been wearing a long-sleeved T-shirt then, too. Maybe he had track marks on his arms. Lena's uncle

Hank had nasty scars from shooting up dope, but he seemed almost proud of them, as if quitting speed made him some kind of hero and the needle marks were battle scars from a noble war.

Ethan saw her looking at his covered arms. He tugged the sleeves down farther on his wrists, "Let's just say I got into some trouble and leave it at that."

"Right." She studied Ethan, wondering if he could give her anything useful. Lena wished to God she could pull his sheet — and there was no doubt in her mind that Ethan Green had one — and use it as leverage to find out what she needed to know.

She asked, "How long have you been at Grant Tech?"

"About a year," he said. "I transferred from UGA."

"Why?"

"Didn't like the atmosphere." He shrugged, and she read more in the shrug than anything else. There was something defensive about his posture, even though what he said made perfect sense. Maybe the school had kicked him out.

He continued, "I wanted to be at a smaller college. UGA is a jungle right now. Crime, violence . . . rape. It's not the kind of place I need to be."

"And Grant is?"

"I like things slower," he said, playing with the tea bag again. "I didn't like the person that being on that campus made me. It was just too much being there."

Lena understood, but she did not tell him so. Part of the reason she'd left the force — other than Jeffrey's giving her an ultimatum — was that she needed less stress in her life. She had never anticipated that working with Chuck could be even more stressful in a lot of ways. She could have found a way to bullshit Jeffrey and still keep her job. He had never asked for proof that she was seeing a shrink. Lena could have lied and made everything okay instead of ruining her life. Hell, she'd ended up ruining it anyway. Less than an hour ago, Jeffrey had looked ready to take her away in handcuffs.

Lena's tried to think of anything that would connect her to Andy Rosen. There must have been some kind of mistake. Maybe she had touched something in Jill Rosen's office that had ended up in Andy's room. That was the only explanation. As for the underwear, that would prove itself out soon enough. Though, what made Jeffrey think it was hers? Lena should have talked to him instead of pissing him off. She should have told Ethan to mind his own fucking business. He had been the one to escalate things with Jeffrey, not Lena. She hoped to God Jeffrey knew that. Lena had seen how Jeffrey could behave when he turned against somebody. He could make real trouble for her, not just in town but at the college. She could lose her job, not have a place to live or money to buy food. She could end up homeless.

"Lena?" Ethan asked, as if she had drifted off.

She said, "Who's this close friend of Andy's?"

He mistook the desperation in her voice for authority. "You sound like a cop."

"I *am* a cop," she answered automatically.

He smiled without humor, as if she had just admitted something that made him sad.

"Ethan?" she prompted, trying not to show how panicked she was.

"I like the way you say my name," he told her, like it was a joke. "All pissed off."

She gave him a scathing look. "Who was Andy hanging out with?"

He thought about it, and she could see that he liked keeping the information from her, liked holding it over her head. Ethan had the same look on his face he'd had when Lena's wrist was about to crack in his hand.

"Look, don't fuck around," she told him. "I've got too much shit in my life right now without some dumb kid holding out on me." She caught herself, knowing that Ethan was her best bet for gathering any information on Andy Rosen. "Do you have something to tell me or not?"

His mouth set in a tight line, but he did not answer her.

"Right," she said, preparing to leave again, hoping he would not see through her bluff.

"There's a party later on tonight," he relented. "Some friends of Andy's will be there. This guy I'm thinking of, too. He was pretty good friends with Andy."

"Where is it?"

He had that same superior look in his eyes. "You think you can just walk right in and start asking questions?"

"What is it you think you can get from me?" Lena asked, because it was always something. "What do you want?"

Ethan shrugged, but she could read the answer in his eyes. He was obviously attracted to her, but he liked to control things. Lena could play that game; she was a lot better at it than some twenty-three-year-old kid.

She leaned over the back of the chair, saying, "Tell me where the party is."

"We got off on the wrong foot," he said. "I'm sorry about your wrist."

Lena glanced down at her wrist, which had a dark purple bruise forming where his fingers had pressed into her bones.

She said, "It's nothing."

"You look scared of me."

Lena was incredulous. "Why would I be scared of you?"

"Because I hurt you," he said, indicating her wrist again. "Come on, I didn't mean it. I'm sorry."

"You think after what happened to me last year I'm scared of some little boy trying to hold my hand?" She gave a derisive laugh. "I'm not scared of you, you stupid twat."

His expression pulled another Jekyll and Hyde, his jaw working like a bulldozer's shovel.

"What?" Lena said, wondering how far she could push him. If he tried to grab her wrist again, she would kick the shit out of him and leave him bleeding on the floor.

Lena goaded, "Did I hurt your little feelings? Is little Ethie gonna cry?"

His voice was even and controlled. "You live in the faculty dorm."

"Is that supposed to threaten me?" Lena laughed. "Big deal, you know where I live."

"I'll be there at eight tonight."

"Is that right?" she asked, trying to see his angle.

"I'll pick you up at eight," Ethan said, standing. "We'll check out a movie, then go to the party."

"Uh," she began, waiting for the joke, "I don't think so."

"My guess is you need to talk to Andy's friend and try to get that cop off your back."

"Yeah?" she said, though she knew it was true. "Why is that?"

"Cops are like dogs; you gotta be careful around them. You never know which one is rabid."

"Great metaphor," Lena said. "But I can take care of myself."

"It's a simile, actually." He hefted his gym bag over his shoulder. "Wear your hair back."

Lena balked. "I don't think so."

"Wear it back," he repeated. "I'll see you at eight."

7

Sara sat in the main lobby of Grady Hospital, watching a steady stream of people coming and going through the large front entrance. The hospital had been built over a hundred years ago, and Atlanta had been adding on to it ever since. What started out as a small facility designed to service the city's indigent population, with only a handful of rooms, now had nearly a thousand beds and trained over 25 percent of the doctors in Georgia.

Since Sara had worked here, several new sections had been built onto the main building, but not much had been done to blend the old with the new. The new lobby was huge, almost like the entrance of a suburban shopping mall. Marble and glass were everywhere, but most of the old hallways leading off it were lined with avocado green tiles and cracked yellow floors from the forties and fifties, so that stepping from one to the other was like stepping through time. Sara guessed that the hospital authority had probably run out of money before the refurbishment was complete.

There were no benches in the lobby, probably to discourage homeless people from hanging around, but Sara had been fortunate enough to grab a plastic chair someone had left near the doorway. From where she was sitting, she could watch people coming and going through the large glass doors, starting or ending their day. Even though the view was straight onto one of the parking decks for Georgia State University, the skyline was visible, dark clouds creeping along the rooftops like cats along a fence. People sat on the front steps smoking or talking to friends, killing time before their shift started or their bus came to take them home.

Sara glanced at her watch, wondering where Jeffrey was. He had told her to meet him here at four, and it was five past. She assumed he'd been caught in traffic — rush hour on the downtown connector tended to start around two-thirty and lasted until eight — but Sara was still anxious that he might not show. Jeffrey had a history of underestimating how long things would take. Sara was gripping her mother's cell phone in her hands, thinking about calling Jeffrey, when the phone rang.

Sara answered, saying, "How late are you?"

"Late?" Hare gasped. "You told me you were on the Pill."

Sara closed her eyes, thinking that the last thing she needed right now was her silly cousin. She loved him to death, but Hare had a pathological inability to take anything seriously.

She asked, "Did you talk to Mama?"

"Ayup," he answered, but did not elaborate.

"How are things going at the clinic?"

"All that crying," he groaned. "I don't know how you stand it."

"It takes a while to get used to," Sara told him, feeling sympathetic. She still cringed when she thought of the time a six-year-old ran screaming from her in the parking lot of the Piggly Wiggly because he recognized her as the woman who gave shots.

"The whining," Hare continued. "The complaining." He pitched his voice into a pointed falsetto. " 'Put the charts back where they belong! Stop drawing doodles on the prescription pads! Tuck in your shirt! Does your mother know about that tattoo?' Good God a'mighty, that Nelly Morgan is a hard woman."

Sara found herself smiling as he made fun of the clinic's office manager. Nelly had been in charge of the clinic for years, even as far back as when Sara and Hare were patients there.

"Anyhoooooo," Hare drew out the word. "I hear you're coming back tonight?"

"Yeah," Sara told him, dreading where this might lead. She decided to make things easy for him. "I know you're supposed to be on vacation. I can work tomorrow if you want to take off."

"Oh, Carrot, don't be ridiculous," he scoffed. "I would much rather you owe me for this."

"I do," she told him, stopping just short of thanking him; not because she wasn't grateful but because Hare would find some way to turn her words into a joke.

He said, "I guess you're working on Greg Louganis tonight?"

Sara had to think about his question for a second before she understood what he was asking. Greg Louganis was a gold-medal-winning Olympic diver.

"Yes," she said, and then, because Hare worked at the emergency room in Grant, she asked, "Did you know Andy Rosen?"

"Thought you might put three and three together," he said. "He came in around New Year's with a banana split on his arm."

Working in the ER, Hare had slang for every condition known to man. "And?"

"And not much. The radial artery snapped up like a rubber band."

Sara had wondered about this. Slicing your arm straight up was not the smartest way to kill yourself. If the radial artery was cut, it tended to close itself off quickly. There were easier ways to bleed to death.

She asked, "Do you think it was a serious attempt?"

"A serious attempt to get attention," Hare said. "Mommy and Daddy were freaked out. Our golden boy basked in the rays of their love, playing the brave trouper."

"Did you call a psych consult?"

"His mother's a shrinky-dink," Hare told her. "She said she would take care of it her own damn self."

"She was rude about it?"

"Of course not!" he countered. "She was very polite. I just thought I'd editorialize to make it seem more dramatic."

"*Was* it dramatic?"

"Oh, it was for the parents. But if you

ask me, their little love was calm as a cucumber."

"You think he did it to get attention?"

"I think he did it to get a car." He made a popping sound with his mouth. "And what do you know, a week later I was walking the dog downtown and there goes Andy, driving a shiny new Mustang."

Sara put her hand to her eyes, trying to make her brain synapse. She asked, "Were you surprised when you heard he killed himself?"

"Very," Hare told her. "That boy was too self-centered to kill himself." He cleared his throat. "This is all *entre nous,* you understand. That's French for —"

"I know what it means," Sara interrupted, not wanting to hear Hare's made-up definition. "Let me know if you think of anything else."

"All right," he said, sounding disappointed.

"Is there anything else?"

He blew air through his lips, making a sputtering sound. "About your malpractice insurance . . ."

He gave Sara enough time to feel like she was having a small heart attack. She knew he was winding her up, but like every other doctor in America, Sara's malpractice premiums were higher than the national debt.

She finally prompted, "Yes?"

"Does it cover me, too?" Hare asked. "Because if I make one more claim on mine, they're gonna ask for the free steak knives back."

Sara glanced at the front doors. To her surprise, Mason James was walking toward her holding the hand of a two- or three-year-old boy.

She told Hare, "I've got to go."

"You always do."

"Hare," Sara said as Mason grew closer. She noticed for the first time that he walked with a pronounced limp.

"Yee-es?" Hare asked.

"Listen," Sara began, knowing she would regret her words. "Thank you for covering for me."

"I always have," he said, chuckling as he hung up the phone.

Mason greeted her, a warm smile lighting up his face. "I hope I'm not interrupting."

"It was just Hare," she said, ending the call. "My cousin." She started to stand, but he indicated she should stay seated.

"I know you're tired," he told her, swinging the little boy's hand. "This is Ned."

Sara smiled at the child, thinking he looked very much like his father. "How old are you, Ned?"

Ned held up two of his fingers, and Mason leaned down to peel up another one.

"Three," Sara said. "You're a big boy for three."

"He's a sleepy boy," Mason said, ruffling his hair. "How's your sister doing?"

"Better," she told him, feeling for a split second like she might cry. Other than the few words she had said to Sara, Tessa was not talking to anyone. She had spent most of her time awake staring blankly at the wall.

Sara told Mason, "She's still in a lot of pain, but her recovery looks good."

"That's great."

Ned walked to Sara, holding out his arms. Children were often drawn to Sara, which came in handy considering that more times than not she was poking and prodding them. She tucked the cell phone into her back pocket and picked him up.

Mason commented, "He knows a beautiful woman when he sees one."

She smiled, ignoring the compliment as she shifted Ned on her lap. "When did you get the limp?"

"Kid bite," he told her, laughing at her reaction. "Doctors Without Borders."

"Wow," Sara said, impressed.

"We were vaccinating kids in Angola, if you can believe it. This little girl took a chunk out of my leg." He knelt in front of her to tie Ned's shoe. "Two days later they were talking about whether or not they were going to have to chop off my leg to stop the infection." He got a wistful look in his eyes. "I always thought you'd end up doing something like that."

"Chopping off your leg?" she asked, though she knew what he meant. "Rural areas are underserved," she reminded him. "My patients depend on me."

"They're lucky to have you."

"Thank you," she said. This was the sort of compliment Sara could take.

"I can't believe you're an ME."

"Daddy finally stopped calling me Quincy after the third year."

He shook his head, laughing. "I can imagine."

Ned started to fidget in Sara's lap, and she jiggled him on her knee. "I like the science. I like the challenge."

Mason glanced around the lobby. "You could be challenged here." He paused for a moment. "You're a brilliant physician,

Sara. You should be a surgeon."

She laughed uncomfortably. "You make it sound like I'm wasting away."

"I don't mean that at all," he said. "I just think it's a shame you moved back there." As an afterthought, he added, "No matter the reasons why." He took her hand on this last note, squeezing it gently.

Sara returned the squeeze, asking, "How's your wife?"

He laughed, but did not let go of her hand. "Enjoying having the house to herself now that I'm living at the Holiday Inn."

"You're separated?"

"Six months now," he told her. "Makes being in practice with her a bit tricky."

Sara was conscious of Ned in her lap. Children understood a lot more than adults gave them credit for. "Does it look final?"

Mason smiled again, but she could tell it was forced. "Afraid so."

"How about you?" he asked, a wistful tone in his voice. Mason had tried to see Sara after she left Grady, but it had not worked out. She had wanted to cut her ties with Atlanta to make it easier to live in Grant. Seeing Mason would have made that impossible.

She tried to think of a way to answer

Mason's question, but her relationship with Jeffrey was so ill defined it was hard for her to describe. She looked toward the doors, sensing Jeffrey before she could see him. Sara stood, using both hands to shift Ned onto her shoulder.

Jeffrey was not smiling when he reached them. He looked as exhausted as she felt, and Sara thought there was a little more gray in the dark hair around his temples.

"Hi," Mason said, holding out his hand to Jeffrey.

Jeffrey took it, giving Sara a sideways glance.

"Jeffrey," she said, shifting Ned, "this is Mason James, a colleague of mine from when I worked here." Without thinking, she said to Mason, "This is Jeffrey Tolliver, my husband."

Mason seemed as shocked as Jeffrey, but neither of them could hold a candle to Sara.

"Nice to meet you," Jeffrey said, not bothering to correct the gaffe. He had such a shit-eating grin on his face that Sara felt tempted to do it herself.

Jeffrey indicated the child. "Who's this?"

"Ned," Sara told him, surprised when Jeffrey reached out and chucked Ned under the chin.

"Hello, Ned," Jeffrey said, bending down to look at him.

Sara was taken aback by Jeffrey's openness with the boy. They had talked early on in their relationship about the fact that Sara could not have children, and she often wondered if Jeffrey restrained himself around kids on purpose, trying not to hurt her feelings. He certainly was not holding back now, as he made a funny face, causing Ned to laugh.

"Well," Mason said, reaching out for Ned, "I'd better get this one home before he turns into a pumpkin."

Sara said, "It was nice seeing you." There was a long, awkward silence, and Sara looked from one man to the other. Her tastes had changed considerably since she had dated Mason, who had light blond hair and a solid build from working out in the gym. Jeffrey had a lean runner's body, and dark good looks that made him sexy in a dangerous sort of way.

"I wanted to say," Mason began, digging around in his pocket, "I had a key made for my office. It's 1242 on the south wing." He took out the key, offering it to Sara. "I thought you and your family might want to rest there. I know it's hard to find a private place in the hospital."

"Oh," Sara said, not taking the key. Jeffrey had noticeably stiffened. "I couldn't impose."

"It's no imposition. Really." He pressed the key into her hand, letting his fingers linger against her palm longer than necessary. "My main office is at Emory. I just keep a desk and a couch here to shuffle paperwork."

"Thank you," Sara said, because there was nothing else she could do. She dropped the key into her pocket as Mason held out his hand again to Jeffrey.

Mason said, "Nice meeting you, Jeffrey."

Jeffrey shook Mason's hand, his reserve somewhat diminished. He waited patiently while Sara and Mason said good-bye, his eyes following their every movement. When Mason had finally left, he said, "Nice guy," the same way he might say, "Asshole."

"Yeah," Sara agreed, walking toward the front doors. She could sense something coming and did not want it to play out in the lobby of the hospital.

"Mason." He said the name like it brought a bad taste to his mouth. "That the guy you dated when you worked here?"

"Hm," she answered, opening the door for an older couple who were going into the hospital. She told Jeffrey, "A long time ago."

"Yeah," he said, tucking his hands into his pockets. "He seems like a nice guy."

"He is," Sara allowed. "Are you in the parking deck?"

He nodded. "Nice-looking."

She walked out the door, saying, "Uh-hm."

"You sleep with him?"

Sara was too shocked to answer. She started to cross the street toward the parking deck, willing him to drop it.

He jogged to catch up with her. "Because I don't remember you naming names when we swapped lists."

She laughed, incredulous. "Because you couldn't remember half of yours, *Slick*."

He gave her a nasty look. "That isn't funny."

"Oh, for God's sakes," she groaned, incapable of believing he was being serious. "You sowed enough wild oats before we were married to qualify for farm subsidies."

A group of people milled around the entrance of the parking-deck stairwell, and Jeffrey pushed through them without a word. He opened the door, not bothering to see if Sara caught it before it closed.

"He's married," she told him, her voice

echoing in the concrete stairwell.

"So was I," he pointed out, something she did not think said much in his favor.

Jeffrey stopped on the first landing, waiting for her to catch up. "I dunno, Sara, I came a long way to get up here and see you holding some other guy's hand with his kid in your lap."

"You're jealous?" Sara could barely manage the question around a shocked laugh. She had never known Jeffrey to be jealous of anyone, mostly because he was too egotistical to consider the idea that any woman *he* wanted could possibly want someone else.

He demanded, "You wanna explain this to me?"

"No, frankly," she told him, thinking that any moment now he would say he was teasing her.

Jeffrey continued up the stairs. "If that's the way you want to play it."

Sara climbed after him. "I don't owe you an explanation for anything."

"You know what?" he said, continuing up the stairs. "Blow me."

Anger rooted Sara to the concrete. "You've got your head so far up your ass you can just reach around and do it yourself."

He stood above her, looking as if she'd deceived him and he was feeling foolish. Sara could see that he was deeply hurt, which took away some of her irritation.

Sara resumed the climb toward him. "Jeff . . ."

He said nothing.

"We're both tired," she said, stopping on the tread just below him.

He turned, walking up the next flight, saying, "I'm back home cleaning your kitchen, and you're up here —"

"I never asked you to clean my kitchen."

He stopped on the landing, leaning his hands on the railing in front of one of the large glass windows that overlooked the street. Sara knew she could either stand on her principles and spend the four-hour drive back to Grant in terse silence or make the effort to soothe his hurt ego so the trip would be bearable.

She was about to give in when Jeffrey inhaled deeply, his shoulders rising. He let the breath go slowly, and she could see him calming down.

He asked, "How's Tessie?"

"Better," she told him, leaning against the stair railing. "She's getting better."

"What about your folks?"

"I don't know," she answered, and the

truth was, she did not want to consider the question. Cathy seemed better, but her father was so angry that every time Sara looked at him, she felt like she was choking on guilt.

Footsteps announced the presence of at least two people above them. They both waited as two nurses came down the stairs, neither of them doing a good job of hiding their snickers.

When they had passed, Sara said, "We're all tired. And scared."

Jeffrey stared at the front entrance of Grady, which loomed over the parking deck like the BatCave. He said, "This has to be hard for them, being up here."

She shrugged this off, climbing the last stairs to reach the landing. "How did it go with Brock?"

"Okay, I guess." His shoulders relaxed more. "Brock is so freaking weird."

Sara started up the next flight of stairs. "You should meet his brother."

"Yeah, he told me about him." He caught up with her on the next landing. "Is Roger still in town?"

"He moved to New York. I think he's some kind of agent now."

Jeffrey gave an exaggerated shudder, and she could tell he was making an effort to get past the argument.

"Brock's not that bad," Sara told him, feeling the need to take up for the mortician. Dan had been mercilessly teased when they were growing up, something Sara could not abide even as a child. At the clinic she saw two or three kids a month who were not sick so much as tired of the relentless teasing they got at school.

"I'll be interested to see how the tox screen comes back," Jeffrey said. "Rosen's father seems to think he was clean. His mother's not so sure."

She raised an eyebrow. Parents tended to be the last to know when their kids were using drugs.

"Yeah," he said, acknowledging her skepticism. "I'm not sure about Brian Keller."

"Keller?" Sara asked, crossing yet another landing and heading up another flight of stairs.

"He's the father. The son took the mother's last name."

Sara stopped climbing, more to catch her breath than anything else. "Where the hell did you park?"

"Top floor," he said. "One more flight."

Sara grabbed the railing, pulling herself up the stairs. "What's wrong with the father?"

"There's something going on with him," he said. "This morning, he acted like he wanted to talk to me, but his wife came back into the room and he shut up."

"Are you going to interview him again?"

"Tomorrow," he said. "Frank's going to do some digging around."

"Frank?" Sara asked, surprised. "Why don't you get Lena? She's in a better position to —"

He cut her off. "She's not a cop."

Sara kept her mouth shut the last few steps, nearly collapsing with relief when he opened the door at the top of the stairs. Even this late in the day, the upper deck was packed with cars of all makes and models. Overhead, a storm was brewing, the sky turning an ominous black. Security lights flickered on as they walked toward Jeffrey's unmarked police car.

A group of young men was hanging around a large black Mercedes, their heavily muscled arms crossed over their chests. As Jeffrey walked by, the men exchanged looks, pegging him for a cop. Sara felt her heartbeat accelerate as she waited for Jeffrey to unlock the door, inexplicably scared that something horrible would happen.

Once inside the car, she felt safe

cocooned in the plush blue interior. She watched Jeffrey walk around the front to get in, his eyes locked on the group of thugs by the Mercedes. All this posturing had a point, Sara knew. If the boys thought Jeffrey was scared, they would do something to harass him. If Jeffrey thought they were vulnerable, he would probably feel compelled to force something.

"Seat belt," Jeffrey reminded Sara, closing his door. She did as she was told, clicking the belt across her lap.

Sara was quiet as they drove out of the parking deck. On the street she leaned her head on her hand, watching downtown go by, thinking how different everything was since she had last been here. The buildings were taller, and the cars in the next lane seemed to be driving too close. Sara was no longer a city person. She wanted to be back in her small town where everyone knew one another — or at least thought they did.

Jeffrey said, "I'm sorry I was late."

"It's okay," she said.

"Ellen Schaffer," he began. "The witness from yesterday."

"Did she say something?"

"No," Jeffrey said, then paused before finishing, "She killed herself this morning."

"What?" Sara demanded. Then, before he could answer, "Why didn't you tell me?"

"I'm telling you now."

"You should have called me."

"What could you have done?"

"Come back to Grant."

"You're doing that now."

Sara tried to quell her irritation. She did not like being protected like this. "Who pronounced the death?"

"Hare."

"Hare?" Sara said, some of her irritation rubbing off on her cousin for not telling her this on the phone. "Did he find anything? What did he say?"

Jeffrey put his finger to his chin and affected Hare's voice, which was a few octaves higher than Jeffrey's. " 'Don't tell me, something's missing.' "

"What was missing?"

"Her head."

Sara let out a long groan. She hated head wounds. "Are you sure it's a suicide?"

"That's what we need to find out. There was a discrepancy with the ammo."

Sara listened as he filled her in on what had happened this morning, from his interview with Andy Rosen's parents to finding Ellen Schaffer. She stopped him at the arrow Matt had found traced into the dirt outside Schaffer's window. "That's what I did," she told him. "To mark the trail when I was looking for Tessa."

"I know," he said, but offered nothing more.

"Is that why you didn't want to tell me?" Sara asked. "I don't like you withholding information from me. It's not your decision —"

With sudden vehemence he said, "I want you to be careful, Sara. I don't want you going on that school campus alone. I don't want you around any of the crime scenes. Do you understand me?"

She did not answer, mostly out of shock.

"And you're not staying at your house alone."

Sara could not stop herself. "Hold on —"

"I'll sleep on your couch if that's what it takes," he interrupted. "This is not about getting you to spend the night with me. This is about me not needing another person to worry about right now."

"Do you think you need to be worried about me?"

"Did you think you needed to be worried about Tessa?"

"That's not the same."

"That arrow could mean something. It

259

could be pointing back toward you."

"People draw marks in the dirt with their shoe all the time."

"You think it's just a coincidence? Ellen Schaffer's head is blown off —"

"Unless she did it herself."

"Don't interrupt me," he warned, and she would have laughed if his words were not tempered with his obvious concern for her safety. "I'm telling you, I'm not going to leave you alone."

"We're not even sure if this is murder, Jeffrey. Except for a few things that are out of place — and those could be explained away easily enough — this could prove to be a suicide."

"So you think Andy killed himself and Tess was stabbed and this girl today killed herself and they're all unrelated?"

Sara knew it was not likely but still said, "It's possible."

"Yeah, well," he said, "a lot of things are possible, but you're not staying alone in town tonight. Is that understood?"

Sara could only offer her silence as acquiescence.

He said, "I don't know what else to do, Sara. I can't worry about you like that. I can't feel like you're in jeopardy. I won't be able to function."

"It's okay," she finally said, trying to sound as though she understood. Sara realized that what she'd been looking forward to most was being in her own house, sleeping in her own bed, alone.

Jeffrey told her, "If it's all unconnected, you can call me an asshole later."

"You're not being an asshole," Sara said, because she knew that his concern was real. "Tell me why you were late. Did you find out anything?"

Jeffrey said, "I stopped at the tattoo parlor on the way out of town and talked to the owner."

"Hal?"

Jeffrey gave her a sideways glance as he merged onto the interstate. "How do you know Hal?"

"He was a patient of mine a long time ago," Sara said, stifling a yawn. Then, just to prove that Jeffrey did not know everything about her, she added, "Tessa and I were going to get tattoos a few years back."

"A tattoo?" Jeffrey was skeptical. "You were going to get a tattoo?"

She gave what she hoped was a sly smile. "Why didn't you?"

Sara turned in her seat so she could look at him. "You can't get them wet for a while. We were going to the beach the next day."

261

"What were you going to get?"

"Oh, I don't remember," she told him, though she did.

"Where were you going to get it?"

She shrugged.

"Right," he said, still disbelieving.

"What did he say?" Sara asked. "Hal?"

Jeffrey held her gaze a few beats before answering. "That he doesn't do tattoos on kids under twenty-two unless he talks to their parents first."

"That's smart," Sara said, thinking Hal must have done this to stop the flood of angry phone calls from parents who sent their kids to school for an education, not a permanent tattoo.

Sara suppressed another yawn. The motion of the car could easily lull her to sleep.

"There could still be a connection," Jeffrey said, but he did not sound hopeful. "Andy has the piercing. Schaffer has a tattoo. They could've gotten it done together. There are three thousand tattoo parlors between here and Savannah."

"What did his parents say?"

"It was kind of hard to ask directly. They didn't seem to know anything about it."

"That's not the thing a kid would normally ask permission for."

"I guess not," he agreed. "If Andy Rosen

262

were still alive, he would be my number-one suspect for Schaffer. The kid was obviously obsessed with her." His face took on a sour expression. "I hope to God you never have to see that drawing."

"Are you sure they didn't know each other?"

"Her friends are positive," Jeffrey said. "According to everyone at the dorm, Schaffer was used to guys having unrequited crushes on her. Happened all the time, and she never even noticed them. I talked to the art teacher. Even he noticed it. Andy mooned over Ellen, and she had no idea who he was."

"She was an attractive girl." Sara could not remember much prior to Tessa's stabbing, but Ellen Schaffer was beautiful enough to leave an impression.

"Could be a jealous rival," Jeffrey said, though he did not have much conviction in his tone. "Maybe some kid had a crush on Schaffer and took out Andy?" He paused, working through the theory. "Then, when Schaffer didn't come running to the would-be suitor, he killed her, too?"

"It's possible," Sara said, wondering how Tessa's attack would fit in.

"Schaffer could have seen something," Jeffrey continued. "Maybe she saw something in the woods, someone there."

"Or maybe whoever was waiting in the woods *thought* she saw something."

"Do you think Tessa will ever remember what happened?"

"Amnesia is common with that sort of head wound. I doubt she'll ever really remember, and even if she does, it wouldn't hold up under cross-examination." Sara did not add that she hoped her sister would never remember. The memory of Tessa's losing her child was hard enough for Sara. She could not imagine what it would be like for Tessa to live with those events constantly in her mind.

Sara changed the subject back to Ellen Schaffer. "Did anyone see anything?"

"The whole house was out."

"No one stayed home sick?" Sara asked, thinking that fifty college girls all going to class like they were supposed to was rare enough to make the papers.

"We canvassed the whole house," Jeffrey told her. "Everybody was accounted for."

"Which house?"

"Keyes."

"The smart kids," Sara said, knowing this would explain why they were all in class. "No one on campus heard the shot?"

"Some people came forward and said

they heard what sounded like a car back-firing." He drummed his fingers on the steering wheel. "She used a twelve-gauge pump-action."

"Good God," Sara said, knowing what the result of that would look like.

Jeffrey reached around to the backseat and pulled a file out of his briefcase.

"Close range," he said, taking a color photo out of the file. "The rifle was probably in her mouth. Her head could've muffled the sound like a silencer."

Sara turned on the map light to look at the photograph. It was worse than she had imagined.

"Jesus," she mumbled. The autopsy was going to be difficult. She glanced at the clock on the radio. They would not reach Grant until eight, depending on traffic. The two autopsies would take at least three to four hours each. Sara said a silent thank-you to Hare for offering to fill in for her tomorrow. The way things looked, she would need the entire day to sleep.

"Sara?" Jeffrey asked.

"Sorry," she said, taking the file from him. She opened it but her eyes blurred on the words. She concentrated on the pictures instead, flipping past the photo of the arrow drawn into the dirt to find the ones of the crime scene.

"Someone could've sneaked in through the window," Jeffrey continued. "Maybe he was there already, hiding in the closet or something. She goes to the bathroom down the hall and comes back to her room and — boom. There he is, waiting."

"Did you find prints?"

"He could have worn gloves," Jeffrey said, not exactly answering her question.

"Women don't usually shoot themselves in the face," Sara conceded, looking at a close-up of Ellen Schaffer's desk. "That's more something a man would do." Sara had always thought the statistic sounded sexist, but the numbers proved it out.

"There's something wrong with this." Jeffrey indicated the photograph. "Not just because of the arrow. Let's take that out of it, take out Tessa. The shooting still doesn't look right."

"Why?"

"I wish I could tell you. It's just like with Rosen. There's nothing I can put my finger on."

Sara thought of Tessa lying in bed back at the hospital. She could still hear her sister's words, ordering Sara to find the person who had done this to all of them. The photograph of Schaffer's room brought back a memory for Sara. She had driven to Vassar with Tessa to help her get settled in. Tessa's dorm room had been decorated the same way as Ellen Schaffer's. Posters for the World Wildlife Federation and Greenpeace were tacked to the walls along with pictures of men torn from various magazines. A calendar hanging over one of the desks had important dates circled in red. The only thing that did not jibe was the array of gun-cleaning tools on the desk.

Sara flipped back to the report. She knew that reading without her glasses would give her a headache, but she wanted to feel like she was accomplishing something. By the time she had finished reviewing all the information Jeffrey had compiled on Ellen Schaffer's death, Sara's head was pounding and her stomach was upset from reading in a moving car.

Jeffrey asked, "What do you think?"

"I think . . . ," Sara began, looking down at the closed file. "I think I don't know. Both deaths could be staged. I suppose Schaffer could have been taken by surprise. Maybe she was hit on the back of the head. Not that we know where the back of her head is."

Sara pulled out several of the photographs, putting them in some kind of order, saying, "She's lying on the couch. She could have been placed there. She could've lain down on her own. Her arm isn't long enough to reach the trigger, so she used her toe. That's not uncommon. Sometimes people use clothes hangers." She glanced back over the report, re-reading Jeffrey's notes on the ammo discrepancy. "Would she have known how dangerous it is to use the wrong ammunition?"

"I talked to her instructor. According to him, she was very careful with the gun." Jeffrey paused. "What's Grant Tech doing with a women's rifle team in the first place?"

"Title Nine," Sara told him, referring to the legislation that forced universities to give women the same access to sports that men had. If the policy had been around when Sara was in high school, the women's tennis team would at least have gotten time on the school court. As it was, they had been forced to hit balls against the wall in the gymnasium — but only when the boys' basketball team wasn't practicing.

Sara said, "I think it's great they have a chance to learn a new sport."

Surprisingly, Jeffrey conceded, "The

team's pretty good. They've won all kinds of competitions."

"So people at school who knew she was on the team would know she had a rifle."

"Maybe."

"She kept the gun in her room?"

"Both of them did," Jeffrey told her. "Her roommate was on the team, too."

Sara thought of the gun. "Did you take her prints yet?"

"Carlos took them," he told her, then anticipated her next question. "Schaffer's fingerprints are on the barrel, the pump, and what's left of the shell."

"One shell?" Sara asked. As far as she knew, a pump-action rifle carried a three-shell magazine. Pumping the fore end would put another shell in the chamber for rapid fire.

"Yeah," Jeffrey told her. "One shell, the wrong caliber for the gun, the skeet choke screwed on so the barrel would be tighter."

"Does her toe match the print on the trigger?"

Jeffrey admitted, "I didn't even think to check."

"We'll do it before the autopsy," Sara told him. "Do you think someone forced her to load the rifle, maybe someone who didn't know much about guns?"

"The first shell has a good chance of jamming in the barrel. If she didn't have another shell in the magazine, then she could buy herself some time. Maybe even turn the gun around and use it to hit the guy."

"Wouldn't the shell explode in the barrel?"

"Not necessarily. If she had a full magazine, the second shell would hit the first and they would both explode near the chamber."

Sara said, "Maybe that's why she only loaded one."

"She was either really smart or really stupid."

Sara kept staring at the pictures. A lot of her cases were suicides, and this looked just like any other. If Andy Rosen had not died the day before, and Tessa had not been hurt, Sara and Jeffrey would not be asking these questions. Even the scrape on Andy's back would not have been enough to warrant opening a full investigation.

Sara asked, "What connects them all?"

"I don't know," Jeffrey said. "Tessa's the wild card. Schaffer and Rosen have the art class, but that's —"

"Is that Jewish?" Sara interrupted. "Schaffer, I mean."

"Rosen is," Jeffrey said. "I'm not sure about Schaffer."

Sara felt anxiety take hold as she worked out a possible connection. "Andy Rosen is Jewish. Ellen Schaffer might be. Tessa is dating a black man. Not just dating him, but having his child."

"What are you saying?" Jeffrey said, though she knew he was following her.

"Either Andy was pushed or he jumped from a bridge that had racist graffiti spray-painted on it."

Jeffrey stared straight ahead at the road, not speaking for at least a full minute. "Do you think that's the connection?"

"I don't know," Sara answered. "There was a swastika on the bridge."

"Beside, 'Die Nigger,'" Jeffrey pointed out. "Not Jews." He drummed his fingers on the steering wheel. "If it was meant to be something against Andy because he was Jewish, then it would have been more specific. It would have said 'Die Jews.'"

"What about the Star of David you found in the woods?"

"Maybe Andy walked through the woods and dropped it before he killed himself. We don't have anything that links it to Tessa's attacker." He paused. "Still, Rosen and

271

Schaffer are Jewish names. That could be a connection."

"There are a lot of Jewish kids on campus."

"That's true."

"Do you think this graffiti means there's some kind of white-supremacist group working here?"

"Who else would spray-paint that kind of shit around school?"

Sara tried to see the holes in her theory. "The bridge wasn't painted recently."

"I can ask around, but, no, it looks a couple of weeks old at least."

"So what we're saying is that two weeks ago somebody painted the swastika and the slur on the bridge, knowing that yesterday he would push Andy Rosen over the side and then I would come along and bring Tessa, who would need to urinate and get stabbed in the forest?"

"It was your theory," Jeffrey reminded her.

"I didn't say it was a good one," Sara admitted. She rubbed her eyes, saying, "I can barely see straight I'm so tired."

"Do you want to try to sleep?"

She did, but Sara could only think of Tessa, and how the only thing she had asked her to do was find the man who had done this to her. She said, "Let's drop the racist angle. Let's say these were staged to look like a suicide. Do you think it's best to hide the fact that two kids have been murdered?"

"Honestly?" Jeffrey asked. "I don't know. I don't want to give the parents false hope, and I don't want to cause some sort of panic on the campus. And if these are murders, which we're not even sure they are, then maybe the guy will get cocky and make some mistakes."

Sara knew what he meant. Despite popular belief, killers seldom wanted to get caught. Murder was the ultimate exercise in risk taking, and the more they got away with, the more they wanted to push the risks.

She asked, "If someone is killing college students, what's the motivation?"

"The only thing I can come up with is drugs."

Sara was about to ask if drugs were a problem on campus, then realized what a stupid question that was. Instead she said, "Did Ellen Schaffer use?"

"As far as I can tell, she was some kind of health nut, so I doubt it." He looked in the side mirror before overtaking an eighteen-wheeler in the next lane. "Rosen might have been, but there's a good case for him being clean, too."

"What about the affair rumor?"

Jeffrey scowled. "I don't even know if I trust Richard Carter. He's like a spoon — always stirring things up. And it's obvious he couldn't stand Andy. I wouldn't put it past him to start a rumor just so he can sit back and enjoy the show."

"Well, let's say he's right," Sara said. "Could Andy's father have been having an affair with Schaffer?"

"She wasn't in any of his classes. She would have no reason to know him. She had plenty of guys her own age throwing themselves at her feet."

"That might be a reason she would be attracted to an older man. He would seem more sophisticated."

"Not Brian Keller," he said. "This guy isn't exactly Robert Redford."

"You asked around?" she persisted. "There's no connection?"

"Not that I could see," he answered. "I'm going to talk to him tomorrow, though. Maybe he'll offer something up."

"Maybe he'll confess."

Jeffrey shook his head. "He was in Washington. Frank verified it this afternoon." After a few seconds, Jeffrey allowed, "He could have hired someone."

"What was his motivation?"

"Maybe . . ." Jeffrey let his voice trail off. "Jesus, I don't know. We keep coming back to motivation. Why would anyone do this? What do they have to gain?"

"People only kill for a handful of reasons," Sara said. "Money, drugs, or some emotional reason like jealousy or rage. Random murders would suggest a serial killer."

"Christ," Jeffrey said. "Don't say that."

"I'll admit it's not likely, but nothing makes sense." Sara paused. "Then again, Andy could have jumped. Ellen Schaffer could have already been depressed, and finding the body was some kind of trigger —" Sara caught herself. "No pun intended."

Jeffrey gave her a look.

"Maybe she just killed herself. Maybe both of them did."

"What about Tess?"

"What about her?" she asked. "It could be that her attack doesn't have anything to do with the two others. If they're suicides, I mean." Sara tried to think it through, but her mind could not put together the right clues. "She could have come across someone doing something illegal in the woods."

"We went back and forth over every inch and didn't find anything except the necklace," Jeffrey said. "Even then, why would the guy stick around and watch you and Tessa?"

"Maybe it was someone else watching . . . just a jogger in the woods."

"Why would he run when he saw Lena?"

Sara exhaled slowly, thinking she was too sleep-deprived to understand any of this. "I keep going back to that scrape on Andy's back. Maybe I'll find something in the autopsy." She leaned her head in her hand, giving up on trying to be logical. "What else is bothering you?"

His jaw worked, and she knew his answer before he even said it. "Lena."

Sara suppressed a sigh as she looked out the window. Jeffrey had been worrying about Lena for as long as Sara could remember.

She asked, "What did she do?" — leaving the *this time* unsaid.

"She didn't do anything," he said. "Or maybe she did. I don't know." He paused, probably thinking it over. "I think she knew this kid, this Rosen kid. We found her fingerprints on a library book in his apartment."

"She could have checked it out."

"No," he told her. "We looked at her records."

"They let you see that?"

"We didn't actually go through the librarians," Jeffrey told her, and Sara could only imagine what kinds of strings Jeffrey had pulled to get a look at the library's records. Nan Thomas would have a screaming fit if she ever found out, and Sara would not blame the woman.

Sara suggested, "Lena could have borrowed the book without anyone knowing."

"Does Lena strike you as the type of person who would read *The Thorn Birds*?"

"I have no idea," Sara admitted, though she could not imagine Lena doing something as sedentary as reading, let alone a love story. "Did you ask her? What did she say?"

"Nothing," he said. "I tried to bring her in. She wouldn't come."

"To the station?"

He nodded.

"I wouldn't come in if you asked me to either."

He seemed genuinely curious. "Why?"

"Don't be ridiculous," she told him, not even bothering to answer. "You think Lena has something to hide?"

"I don't know." He tapped his fingers on

the steering wheel. "She seemed cagey. When we were talking on the hill — after you and Tessa left — she seemed to recognize Andy's name. When I asked her, she denied it."

"Do you remember her reaction when we turned over the body?"

"She wasn't there," Jeffrey reminded her.

"Right," Sara remembered.

He said, "We found something else, too. A pair of women's underwear in his room."

"Lena's?" Sara asked, wondering why Jeffrey had not told her this before.

He said, "I'm guessing."

"What did they look like?"

"Not like what you wear. Small."

She shot him a look. "Thanks a lot."

"You know what I mean," he said. "The kind that's thinner in the back."

Sara guessed, "A thong?"

"Probably. Silky, dark red, with lace around the legs."

"That sounds about as much like Lena as *The Thorn Birds*."

Jeffrey shrugged. "You never know."

"Could they have belonged to Andy Rosen?"

Jeffrey seemed to consider this. "We can't rule that out, considering what he did to his . . ." He didn't finish the sentence.

"He could have stolen them from Schaffer."

"The hair was dark brown," Jeffrey told her. "Schaffer's a blonde."

Sara laughed. "I wouldn't bet on it."

Jeffrey was quiet for a beat. "Lena could have been sleeping with Andy Rosen."

Sara thought this was unlikely, but with Lena there was no telling.

He said, "There was this kid there when I tried to bring Lena in. Some little prick who looked like he belonged in high school. Maybe she's seeing him. It looked like they were together."

"So she's sleeping with Andy Rosen and dating this kid?" Sara shook her head. "Considering what happened to her a year ago, I don't see Lena playing the field this soon. If ever." She crossed her arms, leaning against the door. "Are you sure it's her underwear?"

Jeffrey was quiet, like he was debating whether or not to tell her something.

"What is it?" Sara asked. Then, "Jeff?"

"There's some . . . material," he said and Sara wondered why he was being reticent. Probably his knowing Lena attached a certain taboo; he'd never been shy about this sort of thing before. He said, "Even if there's enough to run DNA, there's no way

279

in hell Lena will give us a comparison sample. If she'd just give us something to test, we could clear her and this would all be over."

"If she won't even go into the station, there's no way she'll give blood."

His voice took on an edge. "I just want to clear her out of this, Sara. If she won't help herself . . ."

Immediately Sara thought about the rape kit she had performed on Lena a year ago, but she did not volunteer this information. Something about using the DNA collected during the rape exam to possibly tie Lena to Andy Rosen did not sit right with Sara. The act struck her as a second violation. Lena would see it as a betrayal. Anyone would.

"Sara?"

She shook her head. "Just tired," she told him, trying not to remember the night she had collected the rape kit. Lena's body had been so badly damaged that she had needed seven stitches to sew her back together. Because of the drugs Lena had been given, Sara had been forced to go very light on the sedative. Until Tessa's stabbing, doing Lena's rape kit had been the most horrible event of Sara's entire medical career.

Sara asked, "What would it prove if Lena

did match? Sleeping with Andy Rosen doesn't mean she had anything to do with his death. Or Tessa's stabbing."

"Why would she lie about it?"

"Lying doesn't make her guilty."

"In my experience people only lie when they've got something to hide."

"I imagine she'd lose her job if she was having sex with a student."

"She hates Chuck. I doubt she cares whether she keeps her job or not."

Sara pointed out, "She's not your biggest fan right now. She may have lied just to spite you."

"She can't be stupid enough to impede an investigation. Not on something like this."

"Of course she can, Jeffrey. She's mad at you, and she's seeing a way to pay you back for kicking her off —"

"I didn't —"

Sara held up her hands to stop him. They had argued this point so many times already that she could already hear the rest of the sentence before he finished. What it boiled down to was that Jeffrey was angry as hell at Lena and would not admit that most of his anger stemmed from disappointment. Lena's knee-jerk response was to hate Jeffrey back just as blindly. The situation would have been comical if Sara were not caught right in the middle of it.

Sara said, "Regardless of why, Lena's not going to give you an inch on this. She pretty much proved that when she wouldn't come down to the station."

"Maybe I didn't approach her quite like I should have," he allowed, and, judging on past performance, Sara could imagine he had been quite an ass. "That kid she was with. That boy."

Sara waited, but he took his time finishing his thought.

"There's something wrong with him."

"Wrong how?"

"Dangerous," Jeffrey said. "I'd bet you ten bucks he's got a record."

Sara knew better than to take the bet. Any cop worth his salt could recognize an ex-con. That brought her to her next question. "Do you think Lena knows he's been in trouble before?"

"Who knows what the hell's going on in her head?"

Sara was just as perplexed.

Jeffrey said, "He pushed me."

"He *pushed* you?" Sara asked, certain he meant it figuratively.

"He came up from behind and pushed me."

"He pushed you?" she repeated, wondering at anyone's having the stupidity to do such a thing. "Why?"

"He probably thought I pushed Lena down."

"Did you?"

He looked at her, obviously insulted. "I put my hand on her arm. She freaked out. Jerked her arm back." Jeffrey stared at the road, silent for a moment. "She was trying so hard to get away she fell on the ground."

"That sounds like a predictable reaction."

Jeffrey skipped over her remark. "This kid, he was ready to take me on. A scrawny little shit, probably weighs less than Tess." Jeffrey shook his head, but there was something appreciative about the way he spoke. Not many people challenged him.

Sara asked, "Why haven't you run his sheet?"

"I don't have his name," Jeffrey told her. Then, "Don't worry, I followed them to a coffee shop. He left his cup on the table. I took it for prints." He smiled. "Just a matter of time until I know everything there is to know about the punk."

Sara was certain he would, and she felt more than a little sorry for Lena's white knight.

Jeffrey fell silent again, and Sara stared out the window, counting the crosses that marked traffic accidents on the highway. Some of them had wreaths laid at their bases or photographs of people Sara was glad she could not see. A pink teddy bear propped up against the foot of a small cross made her look ahead, her heart lurching in her chest. The drivers in front of them tapped their breaks, slanted red lights gleaming up ahead. The highway was getting crowded as they got closer to Macon. Jeffrey would take the bypass, but they were bound to get caught up in traffic this time of day.

Jeffrey asked, "How are your folks?"

"Angry," she said. "Angry at me. At you. I don't know. Mama will barely even talk to me."

"Has she told you why?"

"She's just worried," Sara said, but every second that passed with her parents angry at her twisted in Sara's chest. Eddie still would not talk to her, but she did not know if that was because he blamed her or because he could not deal with having both of his girls in crisis. Sara was beginning to understand just how hard it was to be strong for everyone else around you when all you really wanted to do was curl up into a ball and be comforted yourself.

"They'll be okay in a few days," Jeffrey soothed, resting his hand on her shoulder. He stroked her neck with his thumb, and she wanted to slide across the seat and put her head on his chest. Something stopped her. Without her permission, her mind kept going back to Lena in the hospital, bruised and battered, dark blood oozing from between her legs where she had been cut so deeply. Lena was a small person to begin with, but her cocky attitude normally made her seem larger than life. Lying on the hospital gurney, hands and feet bleeding through the white bandages the ambulance crew had hastily tied on, Lena had seemed more like a little child than a grown woman. Sara had never seen someone so broken.

In the car Sara felt tears in her eyes. She looked out the window, not wanting Jeffrey to see. He was still stroking her neck, but for some reason his touch no longer soothed.

She said, "I'm going to try to get some sleep," and pulled away from him as she leaned against the car door.

The Heartsdale Medical Center was not nearly as impressive as the name implied.

Two stories tall, with the morgue in the basement, the hospital was nothing more than a glorified clinic for the college, which stood on the opposite end of Main Street. As usual, the parking lot was empty but for a few cars. Jeffrey pulled up to the main parking lot in front of the emergency room, bypassing the side entrance Sara normally used. She waited patiently as he backed the car into one of the far spaces.

He put the car in park but left the engine running. "I need to check in with Frank," he said, taking out his cell phone. "Do you mind starting without me?"

"No," Sara answered, and part of her was relieved to have some time to herself.

Still, she smiled at Jeffrey before getting out of the car. He had known her for over ten years, and she could sense he understood that something was bothering her. Jeffrey did not like leaving things unresolved. Maybe he was still mad at her about what had happened in the parking deck.

Sara had not really slept during the drive back to Grant. She had been caught in that limbo between sleep and wakefulness, her mind reeling with the events from yesterday. When she did manage to nod off, Sara dreamed of Lena in the hospital last year. In the kind of horrific twist that only dreams can bring, Sara and Lena had switched places, so that it was Sara on the exam table, her feet in stirrups, her body exposed, as Lena took vaginal swabs and combed Sara's pubic hair for foreign matter. When the black light flickered on to illuminate semen and other body fluids, Sara's lower half had lit up as if it were on fire.

Sara rubbed her arms as she walked across the parking lot, though it was hardly cold. She looked up at the sky, which was dark and forbidding. She whispered, "It's coming up a storm," a phrase her Granny Earnshaw had used when they were little. Sara smiled, her tension eased by the image of her grandmother standing at the kitchen door, hands clasped worriedly to her chest, looking out at the coming storm and telling the children to make sure they all had candles before they went to bed that night.

Inside the emergency room, Sara waved at the night nurse and at Matt DeAndrea, who was filling in for Hare while he was supposed to be on vacation. Not since the summer she started puberty was Sara more glad that her cousin was not around.

"How's your mama and them?" Matt

said, giving a standard greeting. He seemed suddenly to realize what this would invite, and his face paled.

"Fine," Sara said, forcing a smile. "Everybody's doing just fine. Thanks for asking."

Neither of them had much to say after that, so Sara walked along the hallway toward the stairs down to the morgue.

Sara had never made the comparison between the morgue and Grady Hospital, but having just spent so much time in Atlanta, the similarities were glaringly obvious. The medical center had been renovated a few years back, but downstairs the morgue looked much as it had when it was first built in the 1930s. Light blue tile lined the walls, and the floors were a mixture of green and tan linoleum squares. Overhead, the ceiling was splotched with signs of water damage, the recently repaired white patches a sharp contrast against the graying old plaster. The white noise from the compressor over the freezer and the air-conditioning system made a steady hum, something Sara rarely noticed unless she'd been away for a while.

Carlos stood against the porcelain table that was bolted to the floor in the center of the room, his arms crossed over his wide chest. He was a nice kid with swarthy Hispanic looks and a thick accent that Sara had taken some time to get used to. He did not talk much, and when he did, he tended to mumble. Carlos did the shit work, literally and figuratively, and he was very well paid, but Sara felt that she did not know much about him. In the many years Carlos had worked there, he had never said anything personal about himself or complained about the work. Even when there was nothing to do, he always found a chore, sweeping the floors or cleaning the freezer. She was surprised to see him just standing at the table when she entered the morgue. He appeared to have been waiting for her.

"Carlos?" she asked.

"I am not working for Mr. Brock again," he said, in a way that let her know he was putting his foot down.

She was surprised, not just by the length of the sentence but by the passion behind it.

She asked carefully, "Is there a particular reason why?"

Carlos kept his eyes straight on hers. "He is very strange, and that is all I will say."

Sara felt a wave of relief. She realized she

had been scared he was about to quit.

"All right, Carlos," she said. "I'm sorry you're upset."

"I am not upset," he said, though obviously he was.

"Okay." Sara nodded, hoping he was finished. The truth was, she'd been taking up for Dan Brock since their first day of elementary school, when Chuck Gaines had pushed him off the monkey bars in a fit of rage that only an eight-year-old (Chuck had been kept back in kindergarten) can get away with.

Brock was not weird so much as needy, a trait not conducive to the school atmosphere, which operated on the principle of survival of the fittest. Thanks to Cathy and Eddie, Sara had never needed approval from her peers, so it had not bothered her much that she had lived in the netherworld that existed between the popular crowd and the kids who were routinely harassed and tortured. She had always been thought of as the smartest girl in her class, and between her height, her red hair, and her IQ, people had been a little intimidated by her. Brock, on the other hand, had suffered well up until high school, which is how long it took the bullies to realize that no matter how mean they were to him, Brock would always be nice back.

"Dr. Linton?" Carlos asked. Despite her repeated requests, he had never called her Sara.

"Yes?"

He said, "I am sorry about your sister."

Sara pressed her lips together, nodding her thanks. "Let's start with the girl," Sara told him, thinking it would be best to get the most difficult case out of the way first. "Did you take photos and X rays?"

He gave a curt nod but did not comment on the state of the body. He had always been professional in this manner, and she appreciated the solemn way he went about his job.

Sara walked back toward her office, which had a window looking out into the morgue. She sat down at her desk, and even though she had been sitting for the last four and a half hours, it felt good to get off her feet. She picked up the phone and dialed her father's cell-phone number.

Cathy answered before the first ring completed. "Sara?"

"We're here," she told her mother, thinking she should have called earlier. Cathy had obviously been worried.

"Did you find anything?"

"Not yet," Sara told her, watching

Carlos wheel out a black body bag on the gurney. "How's Tess?"

Cathy paused before answering. "Still quiet."

Sara watched Carlos unzip the bag and start to maneuver the body onto the porcelain table. Anyone watching would think the procedure barbaric, but the only way for one person to move a dead body onto a table was to manhandle it. Carlos started with the feet, pushing them onto the table, then jerked the rest of the body until it was in place. A plastic bag had been left around the head to help preserve evidence.

Cathy said, "I'm not mad at you."

Sara exhaled, realizing she had been holding her breath. "I'm glad."

"It wasn't your fault."

Sara did not answer, mostly because she did not agree with what her mother had said.

"When you were little," Cathy began, her voice catching, "I always counted on you to keep her out of trouble. You were always the responsible one."

Sara took a tissue from the box on her desk and patted underneath her eyes. Carlos was trying to remove the T-shirt, but he could not get it over the head. He looked up at Sara, and she made a cutting motion with her hand. The crime-scene techs had already checked for fiber evidence.

Cathy said, "It's not your fault. It's not Jeffrey's fault. It's just one of those things that happens, and we'll all get through it."

Yesterday Sara had longed to hear this, but today it did not bring comfort. For the first time in her life, she could not believe her mother.

"Baby?"

Sara wiped her eyes. "I have to go, Mama."

"All right." Cathy paused before saying, "I love you."

"I love you, too," Sara told her, hanging up the phone. She put her head in her hands, trying to clear her mind. She could not think about Tessa while she cut up Ellen Schaffer. Sara would best serve her sister by finding something that would lead to the capture of the man who had stabbed her. An autopsy was an act of violence itself, the ultimate invasion. Every body tells a story. A person's life and death can be exposed in all their glory and shame simply by looking beneath the skin.

Sara stood and walked back into the morgue just as Carlos finished cutting away the shirt along the seams so it could be put back together and studied. The material was sprayed with blood, a clean, oblong pattern indicating where the rifle had rested. Sara checked the girl's toe, noting that it, too, was sprayed with blood. The other foot had been out of range and was clean.

A girlish bra that would have been better suited for a thirteen-year-old covered the young woman's breasts. Carlos had opened the clasp and was holding a wad of toilet tissue in his hand.

"What's that?" Sara asked, though she could see what it was.

"She had it in here," Carlos said, indicating the bra. He put his hand in the other cup and pulled out another wad of tissue.

"Why would she stuff her bra if she was going to kill herself?" Sara asked, though Carlos never answered her questions.

They both turned as they heard footsteps on the stairs.

"Anything?" Jeffrey asked.

"We just started," Sara told him. "What did Frank say?"

"Nothing," Jeffrey answered, but she could tell that something was going on. Sara did not know why he was being reticent. Carlos had proved himself to be trustworthy. Most of the time, Sara forgot he had a life outside the morgue.

"Let's get these off," Sara said, and she helped Carlos remove the girl's jeans.

Jeffrey looked at the underwear, which was of the plain cotton variety, not the kind they had found in Andy Rosen's apartment.

Sara asked, "Did you check the drawers in her room?"

"They're all different kinds," he said. "Silk, cotton, thongs."

"Thongs?"

He shrugged.

Sara moved on. "We found tissue in her bra."

Jeffrey raised an eyebrow. "She stuffed her bra?"

"If she committed suicide, she would know that someone would find her, that a mortician or an ME would examine her body. Why would she do that?"

"Maybe it was just something she always did? Routine?" Jeffrey suggested, but she could tell he was skeptical.

Sara said, "The tattoo is an old one. Probably three years. That's just a best guess, but she didn't get it recently."

Carlos peeled back the underwear, and Sara and Jeffrey noticed another tattoo at the same time. A word was written in what looked like Arabic.

Jeffrey said, "That wasn't on Andy's drawing."

"It's not recent by any means," Sara noted. "You think he left it off on purpose?"

"Trust me, he would've put it in if he had seen it."

"So she wasn't involved with him," Sara said, indicating that Carlos should take a photograph of the tattoo. She placed a ruler beside the word for scale. "We'll have to scan it in and try to find someone who knows what it means."

Carlos said, *"Shalom."*

"I'm sorry?" Sara asked, surprised he had spoken.

"It's Hebrew," he said. "It means 'peace.'"

Sara could not give him the benefit of the doubt. "Are you certain?"

"I learned it in Hebrew school," he said. "My mother is Jewish."

"Oh," Sara said, wondering how so many years had passed without her ever learning this information. She glanced at Jeffrey, who was writing something in his notebook. His eyebrows were furrowed, and she wondered what connection he was making.

She turned, forgetting where she was, and hit her head on the scale above the foot of the table.

"Crap," she said, feeling her scalp for damage. She did not look at Jeffrey or Carlos to see their response. Instead she walked to the metal cabinet by the sinks and took out a sterile gown and a pair of gloves.

She asked Jeffrey, "Can you get my glasses? I think they're on my desk."

He did as she asked, and Sara slipped on the gown, then the gloves. She took another pair from the box and slipped them over the first. Carlos wheeled over the chalkboard Sara had bought from the school. Some of the information he had already gathered was filled in on the board. Blank spaces for organ weights and sizes and various other details would be recorded by Carlos through the course of the procedure. Sara liked to see everything in front of her while she performed an autopsy. Visualizing the facts was easier when they were all written down right there.

Using her foot, Sara tapped on the Dictaphone and began, "This is the unembalmed, well-developed, well-nourished body of a Caucasian nineteen-year-old female who reportedly shot herself in the head with a Wingmaster twelve-gauge rifle. She has been identified as Ellen Marjory Schaffer by responding officer. Photographs and X rays were taken under my direction. Under the provisions of the Georgia Death Investigation Act, an autopsy is performed in the morgue of the Grant County Medical Examiner's Office on . . ."

Jeffrey provided the date, and Sara continued, "Commencing at 20:33 hours, with the assistance of Carlos Quiñonez, forensic technician, and Jeffrey Tolliver, chief of police, Grant County."

She stopped, looking at the chalkboard for the right information. "She weighs approximately one hundred twenty-five pounds and measures five feet eight inches. There is extensive damage to the head consistent with a rifle blast." Sara put her hand on the abdomen. "The body has been refrigerated and is cold to the touch. Rigor mortis is full and generalized to the upper extremities."

Sara continued, calling out identifying marks as she used a pair of scissors to cut away the bag that covered Ellen Schaffer's head. Congealed blood and gray matter clung to the plastic, and bits of scalp remained in gelatinous clumps.

Carlos told her, "The rest of the scalp is in the freezer."

"I'll look at it afterward," Sara told him, peeling the bag away from what was left of Ellen Schaffer's head. Barely more than a bloody stump remained, with fragments of blond hair and teeth lodged in the brain stem. More photographs were taken before Sara picked up the scalpel to begin the internal examination. She felt punch-drunk from lack of sleep as she made the standard Y incision, and she closed her eyes for a moment to get her bearings.

Every organ was removed and weighed, cataloged and recorded, as Sara called out her findings. The stomach held what must have been Schaffer's last meal: nut-grain cereal that probably looked much the same as it had in the box.

Sara clamped off the intestines and handed them to Carlos to do what was called running the gut. He used a hose attached to one of the sinks to wash out the intestinal tract, a sieve below the drain catching what sluiced out. The odor was horrible, and Sara always felt guilty about passing along the job until she got a whiff of the contents.

She snapped off her gloves and walked to the far side of the morgue where the lightbox was set up. Carlos had snapped in the pre-autopsy X rays, and either lack of sleep or plain stupidity had made Sara forget to look at them earlier. She studied the entire series twice before noticing a familiar shape in the lungs.

"Jeff," she said, calling him over.

He stared at the film on the lightbox several seconds before asking, "Is that a tooth?"

"We'll find out soon enough." Sara double-gloved again before taking the left lung out of the viscera bag. On presentation the pleural tissue was smooth, with no evidence of consolidation. Sara had set the lungs aside to biopsy later, but she did this now using the surgically sharpened bread-loafing knife. "There's slight blood aspiration," she told Jeffrey. The tooth was found in the bottom right quadrant of the left lung.

Jeffrey asked, "Could the shot blast have knocked it down her throat?"

"She aspirated the tooth," Sara told him. "She inhaled it into her lungs."

Jeffrey rubbed his eyes with his hands. He summed up the inconsistency in plain words. "She was breathing when the tooth was knocked out."

Tuesday

8

Lena stifled a yawn as she left the movie theater with Ethan. A few hours ago she had taken a Vicodin, and while it was doing very little to help the pain in her wrist, it was making her sleepy as hell.

"What are you thinking?" Ethan asked, a line most guys used when they wanted a woman to do all the talking.

"That this party had better pan out," she told him, injecting a sense of threat into her voice.

"I hear you," he said. "Did that cop do anything else?"

"No," Lena replied, though her Caller ID had registered five calls from the station by the time she had gotten back from the coffeehouse. It was only a matter of time before Jeffrey came knocking on her door, and when he did, Lena would have to have some answers for him or suffer the consequences. She had decided during the movie that Chuck would not fire her on Jeffrey's say-so, but there were worse things the fat fuck could do to her. Chuck loved holding things over Lena's head, and — as bad as her job was now — he could make it even more miserable.

Ethan asked, "Did you like the movie?"

"Not really," she told him, trying to think about what she would do if Andy's friend did not come through. She would have to find some time during the day tomorrow to talk to Jill Rosen. Lena had called the woman's service and left three messages, but the doctor had not phoned back. Lena had to know what Rosen had told Jeffrey. She had even scrounged around in the bottom of her closet and found that damn answering machine in case the doctor called her back tonight while she was gone.

Lena looked up at the sky, taking a deep breath to try to clear her mind. She needed somebody to talk this out with, but there was no one she could trust.

"Nice night," Ethan said, probably thinking she was enjoying the stars. "Full moon."

"It's going to rain tomorrow," she told him, clenching and unclenching her hand. A nasty bluish black bruise circled her

wrist where Ethan had grabbed her, and
Lena was pretty sure something was damaged. The bone ached when she held her
hand to the side, and the swelling had
made it difficult for her to button the cuff
of her shirt. She had kept her wrist
wrapped until Ethan had knocked on the
door, but Lena would be damned if she'd
let him know she was hurting.

The problem was, Lena did not get paid
until next Monday. If she went to the
emergency room for an X ray, the fifty-
dollar co-pay her insurance required would
wipe out her checking account. She figured
that no bones were broken, because she
could still move her hand. If it was still
hurting Monday, Lena would do something about it then. She was right-handed
anyway, and besides, she had lived with
worse pain than this for longer than a
couple of days. It was almost reassuring; a
reminder that she was alive.

As if he could sense what she was
thinking, Ethan asked, "How's your
wrist?"

"Fine."

"I'm sorry I did that. I just" — he
seemed to look for the right words — "I
didn't want you to leave."

"Nice way to show it."

"I'm sorry I hurt you."

"Whatever," she mumbled. Somehow talking about it made her wrist throb more. Before she left her room, Lena had put another Vicodin and an eight-hundred-milligram Motrin in her pocket in case the pain got worse. While Ethan was looking at a group of kids in the student-union parking lot, she dry-swallowed the Motrin, coughing when it went down the wrong way.

Ethan asked, "Are you okay?"

"Fine," she managed, patting her hand to her chest.

"Are you getting a cold?"

"No," she answered, coughing again. "When does this party start?"

"It should be revving up about now." He headed toward a path between two bushes. Lena knew that it was a shortcut through the forest to the dorms on the west side of the campus, but she didn't want to walk it at night, even in full moonlight.

Ethan turned when she didn't follow, saying, "This way is faster."

For obvious reasons Lena was reluctant to follow anyone into a dark, secluded area. On the surface Ethan seemed to regret hurting her, but she had already discovered how mercurial his temper could be.

"Come on," Ethan said, trying to joke. "You're not still scared of me, are you?"

"Fuck you," she said, forcing her feet to move. She tucked her hand into her back pocket, hoping it looked like a casual move. Her fingertips brushed against a four-inch pocketknife, and she felt safer knowing it was there.

He slowed down so he could walk beside her, asking, "Have you worked here long?"

"No."

"How long?"

"A few months."

"Do you like your job?"

"It's a job."

He seemed to get the message, walking on. He dropped back again a few minutes later, though. She could see the shadow of his face but not read his expression. He sounded sincere when he said, "I'm sorry you didn't like the movie."

"It's not your fault," Lena said, though he had chosen the subtitled French film.

"I thought you'd be into that kind of thing."

She wondered if anyone in the history of the world had ever been more wrong. "If I want to read, I'll get a book."

"Do you read much?"

"Not much," she said, though lately she

307

had been sucked in by some of the sappy romances in the school library. Lena had taken to hiding the books behind the newspaper rack so no one would check them out before she finished them. She would slit her own throat before she let Nan Thomas find out what kind of trash she was reading.

"What about movies?" Ethan asked, undeterred. "What sorts of movies *do* you like?"

She tried not to sound too annoyed. "I don't know, Ethan. The kinds that make sense."

He finally got the message and shut up. Lena watched the ground, trying not to trip. She had opted for her cowboy boots tonight, and she wasn't used to walking in a shoe that had a heel — even a low one. She was wearing jeans with a dark green button-down shirt and had put on a little eyeliner as a concession to going out in the real world. She had left her hair down just to tell Ethan what she thought of his opinion.

Ethan was in baggy jeans, but he was still wearing a black long-sleeved T-shirt that covered his arms. Lena knew that it wasn't the same shirt from before, because she could smell the laundry detergent on it with just a hint of what smelled like musk cologne. Industrial-looking steel-toed work boots completed the ensemble, and Lena thought if she lost him in the woods, she would be able to track him by the deep impression the soles left in the soil.

A few minutes later, they were in the clearing behind the men's dorms. Grant Tech was pretty old-fashioned, and only one of the dorms was co-ed, but, this being a college, students had found a way around the rules, and everyone knew that Mike Burke, the professor in charge of the men's dorms, was deaf as a post and not likely to hear girls sneaking in and out at all hours. Lena thought they must have stolen his hearing aids and thrown him into a closet tonight. The music coming from the building was so loud that the ground pulsed beneath her feet.

"Dr. Burke's at his mother's for the week," Ethan explained, flashing a smile. "He left a number in case we need him."

"This is your dorm?"

He nodded, walking toward the building.

She stopped him, raising her voice over the music to tell him, "Just treat me like your date in there, okay?"

"That's what you are, right?"

She gave him a look that she hoped answered his question.

"Right." He started walking again, and Lena followed.

She cringed at the noise as they got closer to the dorm, which had every light burning, including the ones in the dormer rooms upstairs that were restricted to the housemaster. The music was somewhere between a European dance-party mix and acid jazz with a little rap thrown in, and Lena felt like her ears would start bleeding at any moment from the high decibel level.

Lena asked, "Aren't they worried about security coming?"

Ethan smiled at this, and Lena conceded the point with a frown. Most mornings when she showed up for work, whoever had been on the evening before was still in the cot in the back room, a blanket tucked under his chin and drool on the pillow from a long night's sleep. She knew from the schedule that Fletcher was on duty tonight. Of all the night men, he was the worst. In the short time Lena had been at the college, Fletcher hadn't noted one incident on his log. Of course, a lot of nighttime crimes either were unreported or went unnoticed under cover of darkness. Lena had read in an informational pamphlet that fewer than 5 percent of all women who were raped on college campuses reported their attacks to the police. She looked up at the dorm building, wondering if someone was being assaulted right now.

"Hey, Green!" A young man who was slightly taller and stockier than Ethan came up and pounded his fist into Ethan's shoulder. Ethan returned the pounding and they exchanged a complicated handshake that called for everything but a do-si-do around the dance floor.

"Lena," Ethan said, his voice straining to be heard over the music. "This is Paul."

Lena tried her best smile, wondering if this was Andy Rosen's friend.

Paul looked her up and down, as if to assess her fuckability. She did the same back, letting him know he did not meet her standards. He was pretty bland-looking in that way teenage boys can be when they're trapped between adulthood and adolescence. He wore a yellow sun visor with the bill backward, a shock of close-cropped bleached-blond hair sticking up at the crown. He had a child's pacifier and a bunch of charms that looked like they were from the Hello, Kitty collection hanging from a green metal chain around his neck. He saw her notice and put the pacifier in his mouth, smacking loudly.

"Yo," Ethan said, punching Paul's shoulder, acting a bit territorial. "Where's Scooter?"

"Inside," Paul said. "Probably trying to get them to stop playin' this nigga shit." He postured, throwing his hands around with the song.

Lena bristled at his use of the word but tried not to show it. She must not have done a good job, though, because Paul asked, "You down with the brothers?" in a heavy dialect that only a racist pig would use.

"Shut up, man," Ethan said, punching him a lot harder than he had before. Paul laughed, but he fell back into a crowd of people walking toward the woods, cat-calling racial slurs until he was far enough away for the music to drown out what he was saying.

Ethan's fists were clenched, the muscles along his shoulders rippling under his shirt. "Fucking asshole," he spit.

"Why don't you just calm down?" Lena said, but her heart was thumping in her chest when Ethan turned to her. His anger pierced her like a laser, and she put her hand into her back pocket, touching the knife like a talisman.

Ethan said, "Don't listen to him, okay? He's an idiot."

"Yeah," Lena agreed, trying to diffuse the situation, "he is."

Ethan gave her a rueful look, like it was very important for her to believe him, before heading toward the dorm.

The front door was open, a couple of students standing just inside. Lena could not tell what sex they were, but she imagined that if she hung around a couple of seconds more, she would see for herself. She walked past them, averting her eyes, trying to pin down a peculiar odor in the air. She knew the smell of pot well enough after working in a school for seven months, but this was nothing like that.

At the entrance a long central hallway with a stairway connected the three floors, with two perpendicular hallways branching off each side giving access to the rooms and the bathrooms. The dorm had the same layout as every other student dorm on campus. The unit Lena lived in was very similar, but for the fact that every room in the faculty dorm had a small suite with its own bathroom and a sitting area that doubled as a kitchenette. Here students were packed two to a room with communal bathrooms at the end of each hall.

The closer Ethan and Lena got to the end of one hallway, the better able she was to guess what at least two of the odors in the air were: piss and vomit.

"I just need to stop in here," Ethan said, pausing outside a doorway that had a HAZARDOUS WASTE sticker on the outside. "Do you mind?"

"I'll wait out here," Lena told him, leaning against the wall.

He shrugged, sticking his key into the lock and jiggling the door so it would open. Lena did not know why he bothered to lock it. Most of the kids on campus knew that if you shook the knobs hard enough the doors popped open on their own. Half the thefts Lena was called out on showed no sign of forced entry.

"Right back," he said before going in and closing the door.

She looked at the message board on the outside of his door as she waited. There was a corkboard on one half and a dry-erase board on the other. The cork had several notes thumbtacked to it that Lena was not curious enough to unfold and read. On the white board, someone had written, "Ethan gives good head" alongside a drawing that looked like a deformed monkey holding either a baseball bat or an erect penis in his three-fingered hand.

Lena sighed, wondering what the fuck

she was doing here. Maybe she should just go to the station tomorrow and talk to Jeffrey. There had to be a way to convince him that she was not involved in this case. She should just go home right now, pour herself a drink, and try to get some sleep, so that when the morning came, her head would be clear and she could plan a course of action. Or maybe she should stay and talk to Andy's friend, so that at least she had something to offer Jeffrey to show she was acting in good faith.

"Sorry," Ethan said as he returned, looking much the same as he had when he went into the room. She wondered what he had been doing in there, but not enough to ask. He had probably assumed she would go into the room with him, where he could seduce her with his boyish charms. Lena hoped she did not look as dumb as he thought she was.

"Aw, crap," he said, wiping the message board with the sleeve of his shirt. "That's just the guys playing around."

"Right," she said, bored.

"Honest," he persisted. "I stopped doing that in high school."

Lena believed him for just a beat, then allowed a smile when she realized he was joking.

He walked down the hall, asking in a loud voice, "Do you like this song?"

"Of course not," she told him, debating again whether to call this whole thing off. She could just get the kid's name and let Jeffrey handle it tomorrow.

Ethan said, "What kind of music do you like?"

"The kind that doesn't give you a headache," she said. "Are we going to talk to this friend or not?"

"This way." Ethan gestured toward the front stairs.

A piece of plaster fell from the ceiling above her as they walked into the main hall, and though Lena could hear only the music, she knew that the floor was creaking overhead.

Upstairs there would be a large central gathering room at the head of the stairs with a TV and tables for studying, not that it sounded like anyone was studying now. There would also be a community kitchen, but, judging from the other student dorms Lena had seen, probably all it contained was a hairy refrigerator, a microwave with the door stuck shut, and some vending machines. There were fewer rooms on the second floor, and even though these rooms were smaller, the second floor was more

316

coveted. Having smelled the odor from the more often used bathrooms on the lower floor, Lena could hazard a guess as to why.

"This way," Ethan yelled.

Lena followed him as they wound their way through the people sitting on the stairway. Not one of them looked older than fifteen, but they were all drinking a pink concoction that had enough alcohol in it for Lena to smell it as she walked by. She recognized the third odor in the house: hard liquor.

The upstairs hallway was more packed than the stairs, and Ethan gently took her hand so she would not get lost. Lena felt herself swallow at the sudden contact, and she glanced down at his hand in hers. He had long, delicate fingers, almost like a girl's. His wrists were bony, too, and she could see the knobs sticking out just below the sleeve of his shirt. The room was so cramped and hot she couldn't imagine how he stood the heat. No matter what Ethan hid under his sleeves, it couldn't be worth sweating to death in a room filled with at least a hundred people, all of who were jumping up and down to the beat of what could only loosely be called music.

Suddenly the music stopped. The room groaned in unison, then laughed when the lights were turned off.

Lena's heart jumped into her throat as strangers bumped into her. A man next to her whispered something, and a girl laughed loudly. Behind her another man pressed his body into Lena's, and this time there was something more purposeful to the contact.

Somebody said, "Hey, let's get the music back on!"

Another person answered, "Gimme a minute," and a flashlight was turned on over by the corner as the DJ tried to get his shit together.

Lena's eyes finally adjusted, and she could make out shapes of people all around her. She inched forward, and the man behind her followed like a shadow. He slid his hands up her waist and breathed "Hey" into her ear.

Lena froze.

"Let's go somewhere," he said, rubbing against her.

Lena tried to say "Stop," but the word caught in her throat. She lunged toward Ethan, wrapping her hands around his arm before she could restrain herself.

"What?" Ethan asked. Even in the dark, she could see him look behind her and get his answer. His muscles tensed, and he slammed his fist into the guy's chest, hissing, "Asshole."

The guy backed off, holding up his hands like it was a simple misunderstanding.

"It's okay," Ethan told Lena. He draped his arms around her, protecting her from the crowd. She should have pushed him away, but she needed a couple of seconds to calm her heart before it broke out through her ribs.

Without warning, the music started back up and black lights flicked on. The crowd cheered and started dancing again, their white T-shirts and teeth glowing purple under the light. Some started waving green and yellow glow sticks in front of one another. A few had small flashlights they used to shine in other people's eyes.

"It's a rave," Lena said. At least, she thought she did. The music was so loud she could not hear her own voice. The crowd was rolling on Ecstasy, and the lights enhanced the experience. Paul's pacifier made sense. He would use it to keep his teeth from chattering while he was rolling.

Over the music, Ethan yelled, "Come over here," making her walk backward. She reached behind her, stopping when she felt a wall.

"You okay?" he asked, his face close to hers so she could hear him.

"Of course," she said, pushing her hand to his chest to put some space between them. His body was as solid as the wall, and he did not move.

He brushed her hair back with his fingers. "I wish you had worn your hair back."

"I didn't have anything," she lied.

He smiled, watching his fingers glide through her hair. "I could get you a rubber band or something."

"No."

Ethan dropped his hand, obviously disappointed. He changed the subject, offering, "You want me to go talk to that asshole again?"

"No," she said, but part of her wanted him to — more than part of her, actually. She liked the idea of Ethan's beating the shit out of the jerk who had rubbed up against her.

"All right," Ethan said.

"I mean it," Lena told him, knowing that it would be wrong to send Ethan after the guy. She said, "This is a rave. He probably assumed —"

"All right," Ethan cut her off. "Stay here. I'll go get us something to drink."

He was gone before Lena could say anything else. She watched his back until he disappeared into the crowd, and she felt like some sort of pathetic schoolgirl. She was thirty-four, not fourteen, and she did not need some punk kid to fight her battles for her.

"Hey," somebody said, bumping into her. A perky-looking brunette offered Lena a couple of green capsules, but Lena waved her off, bumping into someone else who was standing behind her.

"Sorry," she said, stepping away and bumping into yet another person. The room started closing in on her, and Lena knew she would start screaming if she didn't get the hell out soon.

She pushed her way through the throng of people and tried to get to the stairway, but the crowd moved against her like an undertow. The room was still dark, and she felt in front of her, using her hands to push people out of her way, until she could feel another wall underneath her palms. She turned around, guessing from the light on the other side of the room that she'd gone the wrong way. The stairs were on the opposite end.

"Dammit," she cursed, feeling along the wall. Her hand found a doorknob, and she pushed the door open, blinking in the bright light. Her eyes adjusted to see a boy lying on his back in bed. He stared at Lena with a sly smile on his face while a blond girl went down on him. He motioned for her to join in, and she slammed the door, turning around and running into Ethan.

"Whoa," he said, holding a cup of orange juice to the side so it would not spill.

The pitch of the music started to wind down, Lena guessed to help the ravers trip. No matter the cause, she almost said a prayer of thanks as her eardrums stopped hurting from the noise.

"I didn't know what you wanted," Ethan said, indicating the cup. "This has vodka in it. I made it myself to be sure." He pulled a bottle of water out of the pocket of his baggy jeans. "Or you can have this."

Lena looked at the cup, wanting a drink so bad her tongue curled in her mouth. "Water," she said.

He nodded, as if she had passed a test. "I'll be right back," he said, setting the cup on a nearby table.

"You're not going to drink it?" she asked.

"I'm going to get some juice. Wait right here so I can find you."

Lena twisted off the top of the bottle of

water, watching him go again. She took a long drink, keeping her eyes open so no one could surprise her. Half the kids on the dance floor were so wasted that the other half had to hold them up.

She found herself glancing over at the table where Ethan had left the vodka. Before she could change her mind, she went over and drank the entire cup in two quick swallows. The drink was nearly neat, with just a splash of orange juice for color. Her chest contracted as the vodka went down, a slow flame filling her esophagus, like swallowing a burning match.

Lena wiped her mouth with her hand, feeling pins and needles stab into her sore wrist. She tried to remember what time she'd taken the Vicodin. The movie had lasted at least two hours. Walking to the dorm had taken half an hour. How much time were you supposed to allow between dosages?

"Fuck it," Lena said, taking the pill out of her pocket and popping it into her mouth. She looked around for something to wash it down with and saw a cup of the pink punch sitting on the table. She stared at the cup, wondering for a split second what was in it before she took a healthy gulp. The concoction tasted like vodka with just enough cherry Kool-Aid to give it its pink color. There was not much left in the cup, and Lena finished it off, banging the cup down on the table when she was done.

Lena waited three long breaths before the alcohol hit her. A few more seconds passed, and she looked around the room, feeling mellow but far from drunk. This was just a regular party with a bunch of harmless kids. She could do this. The alcohol had taken the edge off, just like she needed. The Vicodin would start working soon, and she would be feeling normal again.

The music changed to something slow and sensual, the beat lessening in her ears. Someone had apparently turned down the volume again, this time to an almost tolerable level.

Lena took another sip of water to wash the clingy feeling out of her mouth. She smacked her lips, looking around at the kids in the room. She laughed, thinking she was probably the oldest person here.

"What's funny?" Ethan was standing beside her again. He had a bottle of unopened orange juice in his hand.

Lena shook her head, feeling a sudden dizziness. She needed to move, to walk off some of the effects of the alcohol. "Let's find the friend."

He gave her a funny look, and she flushed, wondering if he noticed the empty cups on the table.

"This way," he said, trying to lead her.

"I can see," she said, slapping away his hand.

He asked, "You like this music better?"

She nodded, nearly losing her balance. If Ethan noticed, he did not say anything. Instead he ushered her to one of the side hallways leading toward the dorm rooms. She could hear different music playing in each room, and some of the doors were open, revealing kids snorting coke or fucking like rabbits, depending on how many people were around.

She asked, "Is it always like this?"

"It's because Dr. Burke's gone," he said, "but they do this sort of thing a lot."

"I bet," she said, glancing into another room, then wishing she had not.

"I'm usually at the library," he said, though she thought he might be lying. Lena had never seen him there. Of course, the library was pretty big, and Ethan looked like the kind of guy who could easily blend in. Maybe he *was* there, though. Maybe he had been watching her all along.

He paused outside a door that was remarkable only for its lack of stickers and lewd notes.

"Yo, Scooter!" he shouted, rapping his knuckles on the wood.

Lena looked down at the hardwood floor, closing her eyes, trying to make her thoughts come together.

"Scoot?" Ethan repeated, banging the door with his fist. He knocked so hard that the door bent back at the top, showing a flash of light between itself and the jamb.

Ethan said, "Come on, Scooter. Open up, you stupid fucker. I know you're in there."

Lena could not hear much going on behind the door, but she gathered that someone was moving around. Several more minutes passed before the door opened, and a wave of the worst body odor she had smelled in her life hit them like a warm bucket of shit.

"Jesus," she said, putting her hand to her nose.

"That's Scooter," Ethan said, as if it explained the smell.

Lena breathed through her mouth, trying to adjust. "Stinky" would have been a more appropriate nickname.

She said, "Hey," trying not to gag.

Scooter was remarkable in his different-ness. Where most of the boys Lena had seen so far had tightly cropped hair and wore baggy jeans and T-shirts, Scooter had long black hair and wore a pastel blue tank top and bright orange Hawaiian shorts. His left bicep had a yellow rubber tourniquet around it, the upper half of his arm bulging from the compression.

"Aw, man," Ethan said, picking at the tourniquet. "Come on." The rubber snapped off Scooter's arm and flew back into the room.

"Shit, man," Scooter groaned. He stood blocking the doorway, but completely without menace. "She's a goddamn cop. What's a cop doing here, man? Why'd you bring a cop to my pad?"

"Move," Ethan said, gently pushing him back into the room.

"Am I gonna be arrested?" he asked. "Hold on, man." He went to the floor, looking for the tourniquet. "Hold on and lemme do this hit first."

"Stand up," Ethan said, pulling Scooter up by the band of his shorts. "Come on, she's not going to arrest you."

"I can't go to jail, man."

"She's not taking you to jail," Ethan said, his voice loud in the small room.

"Yeah, all right," Scooter said, letting Ethan help him up. Scooter put his hand to his neck, and Lena noticed that he was wearing a yellow chain much like the one Paul, Ethan's friend from before, had been wearing. Scooter's was missing the pacifier and had what looked like a key collection, tiny little skeleton keys of the sort that came with a teenage girl's diary.

"Sit down, man," Ethan said, pushing him onto the bed.

"Yeah, all right," Scooter said, as if he did not realize he was already sitting.

Lena stood just inside the doorway, still breathing through her mouth. An air-conditioning unit was stuck in the window, but Scooter had not turned it on. Addicts usually liked to stay cool so the drug did not sweat out too fast, but from the smell of him, Lena imagined there was enough grease on Scooter's body to clog every last one of his pores.

The room was pretty much like all the others: longer than it was wide, with a bed, a desk, and a closet on each side. There were two large windows opposite the door, their panes fogged with grime. Stacks of books and papers lined the floor, take-out cartons and empty beer cans resting on top of them. There was a strip of blue tape down the center of the room, probably to divide the space. She wondered how Scooter's roommate felt about the smell.

A small refrigerator served as a bedside table near the bed Scooter now occupied. His roommate had gone with a more traditional small slab of plywood on two stacks of concrete blocks. He had probably stolen the blocks from the construction site over near the cafeteria. Kevin Blake had just sent out a memo two weeks ago asking Chuck to track down the missing blocks because the construction company was going to charge to replace them.

"It's okay," Ethan said, waving her into the room. "He's totally gorked."

"I can see that," Lena said, but she didn't move from the open doorway. Scooter was bigger than Ethan in every way: taller, stronger. She hooked her thumb in her back pocket, feeling the knife.

Ethan sat by Scooter on the bed, saying, "He won't talk to you if you leave the door open."

Lena debated the risks and decided she would be okay. She walked in and shut the door without turning away from them. "He doesn't look like he *can* talk — period," she said. She started to sit on the bed opposite

Scooter but stopped herself as she remembered the kinds of things that were going on in the other rooms.

"I don't blame you, man," Scooter said, laughing in short barks, like a seal.

She looked around the room, thinking there was enough drug paraphernalia in here to stock a pharmacy. Two syringes lay on a small stool by the bed. A spoon with residue sat beside them, and a small bag of what looked like large pieces of salt. They had interrupted Scooter in the process of preparing Ice, the most potent form of methamphetamine. The junk was so pure that he did not even need to filter it.

"What a fucking idiot," Lena said. Even her uncle Hank, a speed freak of the highest order, had never screwed around with Ice. It was too dangerous.

She told Ethan, "I don't see the point to this."

"He was Andy's best friend," Ethan said.

On hearing Andy's name, Scooter burst into tears. He cried like a girl, open and unashamed. Lena was torn between being disgusted and being fascinated by his reaction. Oddly enough, Ethan seemed to share her feelings.

"Come on, Scoot, straighten up," he said, pushing the other boy off him. "Jesus

Christ, what are you, a faggot?"

He glanced at Lena, probably remembering at the last minute that Lena's sister had been gay. Lena looked at her watch. She had wasted her entire night trying to talk to this stupid kid, and she was not going to give up now. She kicked the bed so hard that both boys jumped.

"Scooter," Lena said. "Listen up."

He nodded.

"You were friends with Andy?"

He nodded again.

"Was Andy depressed?"

He nodded again. Lena sighed, knowing she shouldn't have kicked the bed. He felt threatened now and would not talk.

She nodded toward the refrigerator. "Do you keep anything in there to drink?"

"Oh, yeah, man." Scooter jumped up, as if to say, *Where are my manners.* He swayed before he got his balance and opened the small refrigerator. Lena saw several bottles of beer and what looked like a plastic liter bottle of off-brand vodka. Between that and the drugs, she wondered how Scooter kept from getting kicked out of college.

Scooter began, "I got some beer and some —"

"Here," Lena said, pushing him out of the way. Maybe if she had one more drink, she'd feel more in control of herself.

"Glasses?" she asked.

Scooter reached under the bed and pulled out two plastic cups that had seen better days. Lena uprighted them on top of the fridge and took the orange juice Ethan offered. The bottle was small. There would not be much to drink for all three of them.

"None for me," Ethan said, studying her like she was one of his textbooks.

Lena did not look at him as she mixed the drink, pouring half the orange juice into one of the cups, then spilling in a little vodka. She kept the bottle of juice for herself, filling it to the top with the clear alcohol. She put her thumb over the opening and shook the bottle to mix everything, still feeling Ethan's eyes on her.

She sat on the opposite bed before she remembered she did not want to and stared at Scooter as he sipped his drink.

"This is good, man," he said. "Thanks."

Lena held the juice bottle in her lap, not taking a drink. She wanted to see how long she could last. Maybe she would not drink it after all. Maybe she would just hold it in her hand so that Scooter felt comfortable talking to her. She knew that the first thing you should do in an interview is establish a rapport. With addicts like Scooter, the easiest way to that end was to make him think she had a problem herself.

"Andy," Lena finally said, conscious of how dry her mouth felt.

"Yeah." Scooter nodded slowly. "He was a good kid."

Lena remembered what Richard Carter had said. "I heard he could be a jerk."

"Yeah, well, whoever told you that is an asshole," Scooter shot back.

He was right, but Lena kept this information to herself. "Tell me about him. Tell me about Andy."

Scooter leaned against the wall and flipped his long hair back out of his eyes. He had a startling array of pimples across his cheeks. Lena could have told him that cutting his hair, or at the very least keeping it clean, would have gone a long way toward clearing that up, but she had other things to talk about right now.

She asked, "Was he seeing anybody?"

"Who, Andy?" Scooter shook his head. "Not for a long time." He held out his cup, expecting a top-off. Lena stared at him, not wanting to share.

She said, "Talk to me first, and then we'll get you some more."

"I need a hit, man," he said, reaching toward the needles on the fridge.

"Back off a second," Ethan told him, pushing him away. "You said you'd talk to her and you're gonna, remember? You said you'd tell her what she wanted to know."

"I did?" Scooter asked, looking confused. He glanced at Lena, and she nodded her confirmation.

"Yeah, buddy," Ethan said. "You did. You promised because you want to help Andy."

"Yeah, okay," Scooter agreed, nodding his head. His hair was so filthy it didn't move.

Ethan gave Lena a sharp look. "See what this shit does to your brain?"

Lena ignored him, asking Scooter, "Was Andy seeing anyone?"

Scooter giggled. "Yeah, but she wasn't seeing him."

"Who?" Lena asked.

"Ellen, man. Ellen from his art class."

"Schaffer?" Ethan clarified, and the name didn't seem to sit well with him.

"Yeah, man, she's so fucking hot. You know what I mean?" Scooter elbowed Ethan suggestively. "So damn fine."

Lena tried to get him back on track. "She was seeing him?"

"She wouldn't see anybody like him," Scooter said. "She's a goddess. Mere mortals like Andy could only deign to sniff her panties."

"She's a walking box of come," Ethan said with obvious disgust. "She probably didn't even know he was alive."

Scooter giggled again, giving Ethan his elbow. "Maybe he's up there doing panty raids in heaven!"

Ethan scowled, pushing Scooter away.

"What?" Lena demanded, confused.

"Damn, I heard her face looked like she swallowed a fucking cherry bomb," Scooter said.

"Whose face?" Lena asked.

"Ellen!" Scooter answered, as if it were obvious. "She blew off her head, man. Where the fuck you been?"

Shock hit Lena like a brick. She had been in her dorm all day, watching the Caller ID. Nan had called a few times, but Lena had not picked up. Ellen Schaffer's death added a whole new level to the investigation. If it was staged like Andy's, then Jeffrey would be looking doubly hard at Lena.

Without thinking, Lena took a small drink from the bottle. She held the liquid in her mouth, savoring the taste before swallowing. The vodka burned as it went down, and she could feel it all the way to her stomach. She exhaled slowly, feeling calmer, sharper.

She asked, "What about the drug program his parents sent him to?"

Scooter glanced at the syringes again, licking his lips. "He did what he had to do to get out, you know? Andy liked the pipe. No getting around that. You fall in love once, you keep coming back, like a lover." Apparently Scooter enjoyed saying the word "lover," because he repeated it several times, his tongue rolling around his mouth with every repetition.

Lena tried to put him on the subject again. "So he came back and he was clean?"

Scooter nodded. "Yeah."

"How long did that last?"

"Up until Sunday, I guess," Scooter said, and laughed as if he'd made a good joke.

"When Sunday?"

"Before he died," Scooter told her. "Everybody knows the cops found a needle up there."

"Right," Lena said, thinking that Frank would have mentioned this if it were true. Rumors spread around campus as quickly as sexually transmitted diseases these days.

She said, "I thought you said he liked to smoke?"

"Yeah, yeah," he said. "That's what they found."

Lena shot Ethan a look. She asked Scooter, "Did you see Andy using prior to yesterday?"

Scooter shook his head. "No, but I know he was."

"How can you be sure?"

"Because he wanted to buy from me, man."

Beside him, Ethan noticeably stiffened.

Scooter said, "He bought a shitload Saturday night and said he was gonna take it all on Sunday. Gonna go on a magic carpet ride. Hey, you think that's what that song means?"

Lena tried again to get him back on topic. "You think he wanted to kill himself?"

Ethan stood and walked over to the window.

"Yeah, whatever," Scooter said. Again he glanced at the needles. "He, like, came to my room and he said, 'Hey, man, are you holding?' and I said, 'Fuck yeah, getting ready for Burke being gone next week,' and he was all like, 'Gimme what you got. I got money,' and I was like, 'Fuck you, no way, man, this is my shit, and you still owe me from before you went in, you fucking faggot,' and he was like —"

Lena stopped him. "He was having money trouble?"

"Yeah, like, always. His mom made him pay rent and shit. How bogus is that, man? Her own son, and she made him pay for his clothes and shit like he was on some kind of fucking welfare." He adjusted himself in his shorts. "That car was boss, though." He turned to Ethan. "Did you see that car his dad bought him?"

Lena tried to get Scooter to focus. "But he had money Saturday night? Andy had some money?"

"Hell, I dunno. I guess so. He scored."

"I thought you sold it to him."

"Hell no, man. I told you, I knew what he wanted to do. I'm not getting caught up in that shit. You sell some dope and some kid ODs, and next thing you know your ass is in jail for freaking manslaughter, and I ain't going to no jail, man. I've already got a job lined up for when I get out of here."

"Where?" Lena asked, wondering who on earth would hire such a pathetic waste.

Ethan didn't let him answer. "You knew he was gonna try to kill himself?"

"I guess." Scooter shrugged. "That's what he did last time. Bought a bag of shit and slit himself wide open with a razor blade." He drew a line up his forearm to illustrate. "Man, that was bogus. Blood *everywhere*, like you wouldn't believe. Do you think I shoulda said something, man? I didn't want to get him in trouble or nothing."

"Yeah, fuckwad," Ethan said, walking over to the bed. He slapped Scooter on the back of the head. "Yeah, you should've said something to him. You fucking killed him, is what you did."

Lena said, "Ethan —"

"Let's get out of here," Ethan said, walking toward the door. She could tell he was angry but could not understand why. He told her, "I'm sorry I wasted your time."

Scooter said, "Don't worry about it."

"Come on," Ethan said, throwing open the door so hard the knob knocked a dent in the wall behind it.

Lena followed him, but she closed the door, staying in the room.

"Lena!" The door rattled as Ethan knocked, but she locked it, hoping that would keep him out for a few minutes.

"Scooter," she said, making sure she had his attention, "who sold him the drugs?"

Scooter stared at her. "What?"

"Who sold Andy the drugs?" she repeated. "Saturday night, where did he finally get the drugs?"

"Shit," Scooter said, "I don't know." He scratched his arms, obviously uncomfortable with Ethan gone. "Leave me alone, okay?"

"No," Lena said. "Not until you tell me."

"I got rights."

"Yeah? You wanna call the cops?" She kept the bottle in one hand and scooped the loaded syringes in the other. "Let's call the cops, Scooter."

"Aw, hell, man, come on." He made a feeble attempt to reach for the needles, but Lena was faster.

"Who sold Andy the drugs?" she asked.

"Come on," Scooter whined. When he saw that this would not work, he capitulated. "You oughta know, man. You work with 'im."

Lena dropped the syringes and nearly let go of the bottle before she caught herself. "Chuck?"

Scooter fell to the ground, picking up the needles like they were found money.

"Chuck?" Lena repeated. She was too stunned to do much of anything else. She took a sip of vodka, then knocked back the whole thing. She felt so disoriented she had to sit on the bed again.

"Lena?" Ethan yelled, banging on the door.

Scooter started shooting up. Lena watched, mesmerized as he pulled back the needle to draw out some of his blood, then shot the drug into his vein. The end of the tourniquet was between his teeth, and he let it go with a snap as he pressed the plunger home.

He gasped like he'd been hit, his whole body lurching. He kept his mouth open, his body twitching as the drug took over. His eyes darted around wildly, his teeth chattering in his head. His hand shook so much that the empty syringe fell to the floor and rolled under the bed. Lena watched, unable to look away, as his body jerked from the Ice in his veins.

"Oh, man," Scooter whispered. "Oh, fuck, man. Oh, yeah."

She stared at the other syringe on the floor, thinking about it, wondering how it would feel to let go, to let a drug control your body for a while. Or to take your life.

Scooter jumped up so suddenly that Lena banged her head on the wall backing away from him.

"Oh wow it's hot in here," Scooter said, his words coming out like bullets from a machine gun as he paced the room. "You know it's so hot it's like too hot to even breathe I don't know if I can breathe can you breathe man but it feels good don't you think?" he kept chattering, tugging at his clothes like he had to get out of them.

"Lena!" Ethan yelled.

The knob shook violently, and the door popped open, slamming into the wall again.

"Asshole!" Ethan shouted, pushing Scooter so hard the other boy fell against the refrigerator. Energized by the speed in his veins, Scooter popped up again, still jabbering on and on about the temperature in the room.

Ethan saw the other syringe on the floor and stamped on it with his foot until the plastic broke into pieces, clear liquid pooling around them. Then, as if anticipating the depths to which Scooter would go for another high, Ethan slid his shoe around in the puddle until there was nothing left to draw back on.

Ethan grabbed Lena's hand, saying, "Come on."

"Shit!" she screamed. He had grabbed her hurt wrist. The pain nearly made her pass out, but Ethan did not let go until they were out in the hallway.

"Jerk!" Lena said, slamming her hand

into his shoulder. "I was getting some-where."

"Lena —"

She turned to walk away. Ethan tried to grab her arm, but she was too quick for him. He said, "Where are you going?"

"Home." She continued up the hall, her mind going over what Scooter had said. She needed to write everything down while it was still fresh. If Chuck was involved in some sort of drug ring, he could have knocked off Andy Rosen and Ellen Schaffer to shut them up. All the pieces were starting to fall together. She just had to keep them in her brain long enough to write them down.

Ethan was suddenly beside her. "Let me walk you home."

"I don't need an escort," she said, touching her wrist, wondering if he had finally broken it.

"You've had a lot to drink."

"And I'm about to have a lot more," she told him, pushing past a group of people who were blocking the doorway. After she wrote down everything, a celebratory drink would be in order. A few hours ago she was worried about losing her job. Now she might be in a position to take Chuck's place.

"Lena —"

"Go home, Ethan," she ordered, tripping over a rock in the front lawn. Lena stumbled but kept walking.

He was at her heels, jogging to keep up. "Just calm down."

"I don't need to calm down," Lena said, and it was true. The adrenaline pumping through her body was keeping her mind sharp.

"Lena, come on," Ethan said, stopping short of begging.

She turned sideways on a narrow path between two prickly shrubs, knowing she could get to the faculty dorm quicker if she cut through the quad.

Ethan followed her, but he had stopped talking.

"What are you doing?" she asked.

He did not answer.

"You're not coming into my room," she said, pushing back a low-hanging tree limb as she walked to the front entrance of her dorm. "I mean it, Ethan."

He ignored her, standing to the side as she tried to unlock the front door. Her coordination was shot, and she could not find the keyhole. The Vicodin was probably kicking in, swimming around in the sea of alcohol sloshing inside her stomach. What had she been thinking, mixing drugs and alcohol like that? Lena knew better.

Ethan jerked her keys out of her hand and opened the door. She tried to take them back, but he was already inside.

He said, "Which room's yours?"

"Give me my keys." Again she tried to grab them, but Ethan was too fast.

"You're shitfaced," he said. "You know that?"

"Give me my keys," she repeated, not wanting to cause a scene. The dorms were so shitty that not many professors lived here, but Lena didn't want her few neighbors poking their heads out.

Ethan was reading her name off the mailbox in the lobby. Without another word, he walked down the hall toward her room.

"Stop it," she ordered. "Just give me —"

"What'd you take?" he demanded, sorting through her keys, looking for the right one. "What were those pills you swallowed?"

"Get off my case!" she said, grabbing her keys. She leaned her head against the door, concentrating on opening the lock. When she heard the click, she allowed herself a smile, which quickly left her face when Ethan pushed her into the room.

He demanded, "What pills did you take?"

"Are you watching me?" she asked, but that was obvious.

"What did you take?"

Lena stood in the middle of the room, trying to orient herself. There was not much to see. Her living space was a two-room hovel with a private bath and a galley kitchen that smelled of bacon grease no matter how many times she cleaned it. She remembered her answering machine, but the readout showed a big fat zero. That bitch Jill Rosen still had not called her back.

Ethan repeated, "What did you take?"

Lena walked to the to the kitchen cabinet, saying, "Motrin. I've got cramps, okay?" thinking that would shut him up.

"That's all you took?" he asked, walking toward her.

"Not that it's any of your business," Lena told him, taking a bottle of whiskey out of the cabinet.

Ethan threw his hands into the air. "And now you're going to drink some more."

"Thanks for the narration, junior," she quipped, pouring herself a healthy drink and polishing it off in one gulp.

"Great," he said as she poured another.

Lena turned around, saying, "Why don't you —" She stopped. Ethan was close enough to touch, disapproval blistering off him like heat from a forest fire.

He stood stock-still, hands at his sides. "Don't do this."

"Why don't you join me?" she asked.

"I don't drink," he said. "And neither should you."

"Are you in AA?"

"No."

"You sure?" she asked, taking a sip of the whiskey and giving a big "ahhh," like it was the best thing she had ever tasted. "You sure act like a drunk on the wagon."

His eyes had followed the glass to her mouth. "I don't like to be out of control."

She held the whiskey under her nose, inhaling. "Smell that," she said, then held it close to his face.

"Get that away from me," he said, but he didn't move.

She licked her lips, making a smacking noise. He was a drunk; Lena was sure of it. There was no other explanation for his reaction. She said, "Can't you just taste it, Ethan? Come on, AA's for pussies. You don't have to go to some stupid meeting to know when to stop."

"Lena —"

"You're a man, right? Men know how to control themselves. Come on, Mr. Control."

She pressed the glass to his lips, and he clamped his mouth shut. Even when she tilted the glass, spilling the amber liquid down his chin and onto his shirt, his lips did not part.

"Well," she said, watching alcohol drip from his chin. "That was a waste of good whiskey."

He yanked the kitchen towel off its hook and slammed it into her hand. Through clenched teeth he ordered, "Clean it off. Now."

Lena was taken aback by his vehemence. It cost her nothing to clean up the mess, so she did as she was told, rubbing his shirt, then dabbing at the front of his jeans. His pants were tight at the front, and despite herself, Lena laughed.

She said, "Is that what you get off on, making people do things?"

"Shut up," he ordered, trying to snatch the towel from her.

She let him have the towel and used her hand instead, increasing the pressure on the front of his pants. He grew harder under her touch.

She asked, "Was it the whiskey? You like the way it smells? Does it turn you on?"

"Stop that," he said, but she could feel him getting more excited.

She said, "You sick little shit," and was surprised to hear the teasing note in her voice.

"Don't," he said, but he did not try to stop her when she unzipped his jeans.

"Don't what?" she asked, wrapping her hand around him. He was bigger than Lena had imagined, and there was something exciting about knowing she could either give him pleasure or cause him a great amount of pain.

She stroked him, asking, "Don't do this?"

"Oh, fuck," Ethan whispered, licking his lips. "Fuck."

She worked her hand up and down, watching his reaction. Lena hadn't exactly been a virgin before the attack, and she knew instinctively how to make him gasp.

"Oh —" Ethan opened his mouth, sucking air. He reached for her.

"Don't touch me," Lena ordered, squeezing him hard enough to let him know she meant it.

He braced his hand on the top of the refrigerator instead. She felt his knees weaken, but he managed to keep standing.

Lena smiled to herself. Men were so stupid. As strong as they were, you could have them begging on the floor if they thought you could make them come.

She asked, "Is this why you followed me home like a puppy?"

Ethan leaned in to kiss her, but Lena turned her head away. He gasped again when she rubbed the tip of his cock with her thumb.

"Is this what you wanted?" she asked, keeping her hand still, wanting him to beg for it. "Tell me," she said.

"No," he whispered. He tried to put his hand around her waist, but she touched him in the place she knew would put him on the ceiling.

"God . . ." He hissed out air between his teeth, knocking the glass off the kitchen counter as he reached for something to hold on to.

"You want to bang the rape victim?" she asked, keeping her tone conversational. "Go off and tell your little friends all about it?"

He shook his head, his eyes closed as he concentrated on her hand.

"You have a bet with somebody?" she asked. "Is that what this is about?"

He pressed his head against her shoulder, trying to remain standing.

She put her lips to his ear. "You want me to stop?" she asked, slowing down.

"No," he whispered, his hips moving as he tried to speed her up.

"What did you say?" she asked. "Did you say you wanted me to stop?"

He shook his head again, panting.

"Did you say 'please'?" she asked, bringing him to the edge. When his body started to shake, she stopped. "Was that a 'please'?"

"Yes," he exhaled, putting his hand over hers, trying to make her continue.

"Are you supposed to be touching me?"

He moved his hand away, but his hips swayed, and he was breathing hard enough to hyperventilate.

"I didn't hear you say it," Lena goaded. "Say 'please.'"

He started to say the word but stopped himself, groaning.

"Say it," she said, exerting the right amount of pressure to remind him what her hand could do.

Ethan's mouth moved as he tried to say the word, but he was either breathing too hard or too proud to make it come out.

"What's that?" she whispered, her lips just shy of kissing his ear. "What did you say?"

He made a guttural sound, like something inside of him had broken. Lena smiled when he finally relented.

"Please . . . ," he begged, and as if that were not enough, he repeated. "Please . . ."

Lena was in that dark room again, lying on her stomach. Slow, sensual kisses were making their way along her back down toward the space where her tailbone started. She stretched, feeling her pants slide down, loving the sensation of having her favorite spot kissed without realizing that she should not be able to feel these things. Her hands and feet should be nailed down to the floor. She should be on her back.

She came fully awake with a sharp intake of breath, jumping off the bed so quickly that she fell on the floor, her head banging against the wall so hard she was stunned for a few seconds.

"What's wrong?" Ethan said.

Lena slid up the wall, her heart pounding in her head. She reached down to her jeans. Only the top button was undone. What had happened last night? Why was Ethan here?

She said, "Get out," her voice dead calm, despite the fear pumping through every part of her body.

Ethan smiled at her, stretching up his arms. The bed was a twin, almost too small for Lena alone, and he was pressed up against the wall on his side. He was fully dressed, but his jeans were unbuttoned, the zipper halfway down.

"What the fuck did you do to me?" she asked, horrified at the thought that he'd touched her, might even have been inside of her.

"Hey," he said, his voice light, as if they were discussing the weather. "Chill out, okay?" He sat up in bed and reached toward her.

"Get the fuck away from me," she warned, slapping his hands away.

He stood. "Lena —"

"Get away from me!" she yelled, her voice raw in her throat.

He looked down, buttoning and zipping his pants as he said, "Come on, it's not like we're gonna have to get married or any—"

She pushed him hard in the chest. He stumbled back a step but did not fall. Instead of getting the message, he took a step toward her, his face expressionless, no words coming from his mouth as he slammed his hands into her shoulders.

She hit the wall but stayed upright, shocked by his brute strength. Lena had assumed all along that she could take him, but Ethan's body was like steel.

Ethan opened his mouth, probably to apologize. Her palm landed flat against his face. The sound echoed in the room, and before she knew what was happening, he had slapped her back, and hard.

"Bastard!" She went for him again, this time with her fists, but he caught her hands, easily overpowering her, pushing her against the wall.

"Lena —" he said, pinning her wrists. She expected pain from the earlier injury, but she was too terrified about what might have happened between them to feel anything except rage.

She tried to free herself, but he held on easily. Her knife was still in her pocket, though she knew she could not get to it with him holding her hands. She kicked him in the knee, and he bent down reflexively, giving her the opportunity to sucker-punch him full in the face. Ethan finally backed up, his hands over his nose, blood seeping out between his fingers. Lena ran into the bathroom, slamming the door behind her.

"Oh, God," she whispered. "Oh-God-oh-God-oh-God." Her hands trembled as she unbuttoned her jeans. Her nails scraped the skin on her legs as she pulled down the pants to see what damage had been done. She checked herself for bruises and cuts, then her underwear for telltale stains, even smelled them to see if there was a trace of Ethan anywhere on or near her.

"Lena?" Ethan said, knocking on the door. His voice was muffled, and she hoped she had broken his nose.

"Go away!" she ordered, kicking her foot against the door, wishing she were kicking him with the same intensity, wishing she could see him bleeding and in pain.

He banged back once so hard that the door shook. "Lena, goddammit!"

"Get out of here!" she screamed, her throat ragged and raw. Had he been inside her mouth? Was she still tasting him?

"Lena, come on," he said, moderating his tone. "Please, baby."

Lena felt her stomach clench, and she ran to the toilet as she retched, bile sputtering out of her mouth and onto the floor. She sat on her knees, heaving so hard into the bowl that she felt her guts cramp inside her like somebody had put a fist in there.

She closed her eyes, not wanting to see what was in the toilet, breathing through her mouth, trying not to be sick again.

The sound of a door bursting open made her look up, but the bathroom door was intact.

"Up against the wall," a man's voice said. She recognized Frank instantly.

"Fuck you," Ethan barked back, but she heard a familiar sound as Ethan must have been slammed into the wall. She hoped Frank was hurting him. She hoped he beat the shit out of Ethan.

Lena wiped her mouth and spit into the toilet. She sat back on her heels, putting her hand to her stomach, listening to what was going on outside the door. Her head was killing her, her heart pounding.

"Where's Lena?" Jeffrey said, an edge to his voice.

"She's not here, you bastard," Ethan told them in such a convincing tone that even she believed him. "Where's your fucking warrant for breaking down that door?"

Lena put her hand on the sink and slowly pulled herself up.

Jeffrey asked, "Where did she go?" still using the same worried tone.

"Out for coffee."

Lena looked at herself in the mirror over the vanity. A trickle of blood dribbled from her nose, but it did not feel broken. There was a bruise right under her eye, and she reached up to touch it. Her fingers were a few inches from her face when she stopped. A vivid memory from last night shot through her brain like a current of electricity. She had touched Ethan with this hand. She had reached down into his pants and stroked him while staring into his eyes, watching the effect she had on him, relishing what had seemed like power last night but felt only like something cheap and vile this morning.

Lena turned on the hot-water faucet, grabbing the soap from the dish. She lathered her hands, then put the foam in her mouth, trying to remember if she had kissed him. She scraped her tongue with her fingernails, gagging as soap went down her throat. She had done this because she was drunk. Fucking drunk. What the hell else would make her do something so fucking stupid?

Jeffrey knocked softly the door. "Lena?"

She did not answer, scrubbing her hands until they were dark red from the heat and friction. Her injured wrist was twice the size of the other one, but the pain felt good because it was something she could control. An irregular ridge on one of her scars caught under her fingernail, and the blood was welcome. She picked at the opening, trying to rip the skin, wishing she could peel it off.

"Lena?" Jeffrey knocked louder, sounding concerned. "Lena? Are you okay?"

Ethan said, "Just leave her alone."

"Lena," Jeffrey repeated, knocking hard on the door. She could not tell if he was worried or angry or both. "Answer me."

She looked up. The mirror told the story of what he would see: her vomit in the toilet, her bloody hands dripping in the sink, Lena standing there, shaking with disgust and self-loathing.

Frank said, "Break down the door."

Jeffrey warned her, "Lena, either you come out or I'm coming in."

"Just a moment, please," she called, like he was her date, waiting patiently to go to dinner.

She slid the pocketknife out of her jeans before buttoning them up again. There was a loose board in the floor of the medicine cabinet, and she slipped the knife underneath it before turning off the water in the sink.

Lena flushed the toilet as she gargled a mouthful of Scope, spitting out some and swallowing the rest, hoping her stomach could take it. She wiped under her nose with the back of her hand, then wiped the blood off on her jeans. There was no way she could button the cuffs of her shirt, but she knew that the long sleeves would cover any damage.

When she finally left the bathroom, Jeffrey was standing there, ready to break down the door. Frank stood behind Ethan, pressing Ethan's face so hard into the wall that blood from his nose was dripping down the Sheetrock. Lena stood in the doorway. She could see past Jeffrey's shoulder to the sitting area and the small kitchen. She wished there was some way to make them all go into the other room. Lena had a difficult enough time falling asleep at night without having to deal with the memory of their all being in her bedroom.

Jeffrey and Frank both looked completely shocked to see her, as if she were an apparition instead of the woman they had worked with almost every day for the last decade.

Without thinking, Frank loosened his grip on Ethan, muttering, "What happened?"

She covered the bleeding scar on her hand, telling Jeffrey, "You'd better have a warrant."

Jeffrey asked, "Are you okay?"

"Where's your warrant?"

His voice was soft. "Did he hurt you?"

Lena did not answer. She was looking at the clean comforter, the fact that it was barely wrinkled. The material was dark burgundy, and any stains would have been obvious. She let herself breathe, knowing that nothing else had happened with Ethan last night. As if what she knew *had* happened were not bad enough.

She crossed her arms, saying, "Get the hell out of my place. You're trespassing."

"We got a call," Jeffrey said, and it seemed like his resolve was kicking in. He walked over and looked at the pictures she kept tucked into the mirror over the dresser. "Domestic disturbance."

She knew that was bullshit. Lena's room was at the corner of the building, her nearest neighbor a professor who was away at a conference for the week. Even if someone had called, there was no way Jeffrey could have gotten here that fast. He and Frank had probably been outside the dorm and used the scuffle as a reason to break down her door.

"So," Jeffrey said, "what's the trouble?"

"I don't know what you're talking about," Lena said, keeping a steady gaze on him.

Jeffrey said, "Your eye, for starters. Did he hit you?"

"I fell against the sink when you broke down the door." She gave him a quick smile. "The noise frightened me."

"Right," Jeffrey said. He indicated Ethan with his thumb. "What about him?"

Lena looked at Ethan, and he managed to return her gaze out of the corner of his eye. Whatever had happened between them last night was just that — between them.

Jeffrey prompted, "Lena?"

"I guess Frank did that when he came in," she told him, not meeting the sharp look Frank gave her. They had been partners before Lena was fired, and she knew Frank well enough to know she had effectively ruined that connection. Lena had broken the code. The way she felt now, so much the better.

Jeffrey opened one of the top drawers of her dresser, glanced in it, and gave Lena a steady look. She knew he was looking at her ankle sheath, but there was no law against having a sheathed knife in your sock drawer.

"What are you doing?" Lena demanded as he slammed the drawer closed.

He opened the next drawer, where she kept her underwear, and put his hand in, pushing stuff around. He pulled out a black cotton thong she had not worn in years and gave her the same steady look before dropping it back into the drawer. She knew he was looking for similar items to the pair found in Andy Rosen's room, just as surely as she knew she would never wear a single item in that drawer again.

Lena tried to keep her tone even when she asked, "Why are you here?"

He slammed the drawer closed. "I told you yesterday. We found some evidence linking you to a crime."

She held out her hands, shocked at how calm she felt. "Arrest me."

Jeffrey backed down, as she guessed he would. "We just want to ask you a couple of questions, Lena."

She shook her head. He didn't have enough evidence to arrest her, or she would be sitting in his squad car right now.

"We can run him in instead," Jeffrey said, indicating Ethan.

"Do it," Ethan challenged.

Lena hissed, "Ethan, shut up."

"Take me in," Ethan told them. Frank pressed him closer into the wall. Ethan sucked in air but said nothing.

Jeffrey seemed to be enjoying this. He walked over to Ethan and put his lips close to Ethan's ear. He said, "Hey, Mr. Eyewitness."

Ethan struggled, but Jeffrey easily lifted

out his wallet. He thumbed through some photographs in the front and smiled. "Ethan Nathaniel White," he read.

Lena tried not to register her surprise, but she couldn't keep her lips from parting.

"So, Ethan," Jeffrey said, putting his hand to the back of Ethan's head and pressing. "How would you like to spend the night in jail?" He whispered something else in Ethan's ear that Lena could not hear. Ethan tensed, like an animal wanting to attack.

"Don't," Lena said. "Leave him alone."

Jeffrey grabbed Ethan by his shirt collar and threw him onto the bed. "Get your shoes on, boy," he ordered, kicking the black work boots out from under the bed.

Lena said, "You don't have anything to charge him with. I told you I fell against the sink."

"We'll run him down to the station, see what turns up." He turned to Frank. "The boy just *looks* guilty, don't you think?"

Frank chuckled.

Lena stupidly said, "You can't arrest people for looking guilty."

"We'll find something to hold him on." Jeffrey gave her a quick wink. For as long as she had known him, Jeffrey had never bent the law to this degree. She could see now that he was on a mission to bring her in, no matter who suffered in the process.

"Just let him go," she said. "I have to be at work in half an hour. We can talk here."

"No, Lena," Ethan said, standing. Frank pushed him down on the bed so hard the mattress bowed, but Ethan sprang back up, one of his boots in his hands. He was about to slam Frank in the face with it when Jeffrey caught him hard with a kidney punch. Ethan groaned, doubling over, and Lena put herself between the two men, trying to stop a bloodletting.

The cuff of her shirt had slid up, and Jeffrey was staring at her wrist.

She dropped her hand, telling them both, "Stop."

Jeffrey leaned down and picked up Ethan's boot, turning it over in his hand. He seemed interested in the tread. "Resisting arrest. That a good enough one for you?"

"Okay," Lena said. "I'll give you an hour."

Jeffrey threw the boot hard at Ethan's chest. He told Lena, "You'll give me as long as I damn well say."

9

Jeffrey stood in the hallway outside the interrogation room, waiting for Frank. He had been in the observation area, watching Lena through the one-way glass, but the way she stared at the mirror made him uncomfortable, even though he knew she could not see through.

He had taken Frank to Lena's apartment this morning, hoping to talk some sense into her. The night before, Jeffrey had rehearsed in his mind how it would go. They would all sit down and talk, maybe drink some coffee, and figure out what was going on. The plan was perfect — except for Ethan White's getting in the way.

"Chief," Frank said, his tone low. He had two cups of coffee in his hands, and Jeffrey took one, even though he already had enough caffeine in his system to make the hair on his arms vibrate.

"Did the file come in?" Jeffrey asked.

The fingerprints from the cup Ethan had used were not much help, but his name and driver's-license number had hit the jackpot. Not only did Ethan White have a record, he had a parole officer in town. Diane Sanders, his PO, was bringing in White's sheet herself.

"I told Marla to send her back here," Frank said, taking a sip of his coffee. "Sara find anything on the Rosen kid?"

"No," Jeffrey said. Sara had performed Andy Rosen's autopsy right after she finished with Ellen Schaffer. The body held no startling revelations, and, but for Jeffrey and Sara's suspicions, there was nothing that pointed to murder.

He told Frank, "Schaffer's definitely a homicide. There's no way the two of them aren't connected. We're just not seeing it."

"And Tessa?"

Jeffrey shrugged, his mind reeling as he tried to find a connection that would make sense. He had kept Sara awake most of the night trying to figure out how all three victims were connected. Ten minutes had passed before he realized she had finally fallen asleep at the kitchen table.

Frank looked through the small window in the interrogation-room door, watching Lena. "She say anything?"

"I didn't even try," Jeffrey said. Mostly, he did not know what to ask her. Jeffrey had been shocked to find Ethan in the room when they busted down the door, and then scared as shit when Lena did not immediately come out of the bathroom. For a split second, he had been certain she was lying dead on the floor. He would not soon forget the panic he felt before she finally came out or the horror when he realized that not only had she let that kid hit her, she was covering for him.

Frank said, "This don't seem like Lena."

"Something's going on," Jeffrey agreed.

"You think she let that punk hit her?" Frank asked.

Jeffrey took a sip of coffee, thinking about the one thing he did not want to consider. "Did you see her wrist?"

"Looks pretty bad," Frank agreed.

"I don't like any of this."

Frank said, "Here's Diane."

Diane Sanders was of average height and build with the most beautiful gray hair Jeffrey had ever seen. On the surface she was fairly unremarkable, but there was a raw sexuality underneath that always took Jeffrey by surprise. She was very good at her job, and despite her caseload she kept on top of all of her parolees.

She got right to the point. "Do you have White here?"

"No," Jeffrey said, wishing he did. Lena had made sure Ethan was given a head start before she would leave her apartment with Jeffrey and Frank.

Diane looked relieved. "Three of my guys got locked up this weekend, and I've been buried in paper. I don't need trouble from this one. Especially this one." She held out a thick file. "What are you looking at him for?"

"Not sure," Jeffrey said, handing Frank his coffee so he could open the file. The first page was a color photo of Ethan White at the time of his last arrest. His head and face were shaved clean, but he still looked pretty much like the same thug Jeffrey remembered from their earlier meetings. His eyes were dead, staring into the camera as if he wanted to make sure that whoever looked at the picture knew he was a threat.

Jeffrey flipped past the photo, looking for Ethan's arrest record. He scanned the details, feeling like someone had hit him in the gut with a brick.

"Yeah," Diane said, reading his expression, "he's been squeaky clean ever since. He keeps up the good behavior and he'll be off parole in less than a year."

"You sure about that?" Jeffrey asked, picking up something in her tone.

"As far as I can see," she told him. "I've been doing drop-ins on him almost every week."

"Sounds like you're looking for something," Jeffrey commented. For Diane to be making a special effort to do surprise visits on Ethan said a lot. She was trying to catch him at something.

"I'm just making sure he stays clean," she said ruefully.

Frank asked, "He into drugs?"

"I make him pee in a cup every week, but those guys never touch drugs. They don't drink, they don't smoke." She paused. "Everything's either a weakness or a strength with them. Power, control, intimidation — the adrenaline from that gives them their high."

Jeffrey took back his coffee and handed Frank the file, thinking that Diane could easily have been talking about Lena instead of Ethan White. He had been worried about Lena before, but now Jeffrey was scared she had gotten herself involved in something she would never be able to get out of.

Diane said, "He's doing everything he's

supposed to. Completed anger-management classes —"

"At the college?"

"No," she told him. "County health services. I don't think they have much of a need for that at Grant Tech."

Jeffrey sighed. It had been worth a shot.

"Who've you got in there?" Diane asked, glancing through the window. Jeffrey knew she could only see Lena's back.

"Thanks for the file," he said.

She got the hint and looked away from the window. "No problem. Let me know if you catch him on anything. He says he's reformed, but those guys never are."

Jeffrey asked, "What kind of threat do you think he is?"

"To society?" She shrugged. "To women?" Her mouth set in a straight line. She told him, "Read the file. It's the tip of the iceberg, but I don't have to tell you that." She indicated the door. "If that's his girlfriend in there, then she needs to get away from him."

Jeffrey could only nod, and Frank, who was reading the file, mumbled a curse.

Diane looked at her watch. "I've got a hearing I need to go to."

Jeffrey shook her hand, saying, "Thanks for bringing this by."

"Let me know if you run him in. That's one less perp to keep me up at night." She turned to go but then stopped, telling Jeffrey, "You'd better have your ducks in a row if you try to jam him up. He's sued two police chiefs before."

"Did he win?"

"They settled," she said. "And then they resigned." She gave him a meaningful look. "You make my job a hell of a lot easier, Chief. I'd hate to lose you."

"All right," Jeffrey said, taking both the compliment and the warning in stride.

She left, calling over her shoulder, "Let me know."

Jeffrey watched Frank's lips move as he read the file.

"This is bad," Frank said. "You want me to round him up?"

"For what?" Jeffrey asked, taking the file. He opened it, again skimming the pages. If Diane was right, they would have only one chance to bring in Ethan White. When they did — and Jeffrey had no doubt they eventually would — he would have to have something solid to take White apart with.

Frank said, "See if Lena will flip on him."

"You really think that's going to happen?" Jeffrey asked, feeling revulsion as he read through Ethan White's criminal history. Diane Sanders was right about another thing: The kid was good at beating a charge. He had been arrested at least ten times in as many years, but only one charge had stuck.

Frank asked, "You want me to go in with you?"

"No," Jeffrey said, checking the clock on the wall. "Call Brian Keller. I was supposed to be at his house ten minutes ago. Tell him I'll check in with him later."

"You still want me to ask around about him?"

"Yeah," Jeffrey said, though this morning he'd been planning on asking Lena to do that. Despite what had happened since, he still wanted to follow up on Brian Keller. Something was not sitting right about the man. He told Frank, "Let me know if you find out anything."

"Will do." Frank saluted.

Jeffrey put his hand on the doorknob but did not turn it. He took a breath, trying to get his thoughts together, then walked into the room.

Lena stared straight ahead at the wall as he closed the door. She was sitting in the suspect's chair, the one that was bolted to the floor and had a round eye hook in the back to attach cuffs. The metal seat was straight and uncomfortable. Lena was probably more pissed about the idea of the chair than the actual chair itself, which was exactly why he had put her there.

Jeffrey walked around the table and sat across from her, putting Ethan White's file on the table. In the bright light of the interrogation room, her injuries were on display like a shiny new car on the showroom floor. She had a bruise working its way around her eye, dried blood caked around the corner. Her hand was pulled back into her sleeve, but she held it stiffly on the table, like it was giving her pain. Jeffrey wondered how Lena could let someone hurt her after what had happened to her. She was a strong woman, and good with her fists. The thought of her not protecting herself was almost laughable.

There was something else that was getting to him, and it was not until he sat down across from her that Jeffrey realized what it was. Lena was hungover, her body radiating the smell of alcohol and vomit. She had always been self-destructive to a certain degree, but Jeffrey would have never guessed that Lena would cross the line this way. It was like she didn't care about herself anymore.

"What took you so long?" she asked. "I've got to go to work."

"You want me to call Chuck?"

She narrowed her eyes. "What the fuck do you think?"

He allowed some time to pass, letting her know she should check her tone. Jeffrey knew he should go at her hard, but every time he looked at Lena, his mind flashed onto a picture of her a year ago, when he had found her nailed to the floor, her body ravaged, her spirit broken. Pulling out those nails had been the hardest thing Jeffrey had ever done in his life. Even now the memory brought out a cold sweat, but underneath that, Jeffrey was feeling something else. He was angry — not just angry, but pissed as hell. After all she had been through, after all she had survived, why was Lena mixing herself up with trash like Ethan White?

She said, "I don't have all day."

"Then I suggest you don't waste my time." When she did not respond, he said, "Guess you had a late night last night."

"So?"

"You look like shit, Lena. Are you drinking now? Is that what's going on?"

"I don't know what the hell you're talking about."

"Don't be stupid. You smell like a bum. You've got puke on your shirt."

She had the grace to look ashamed before she caught herself and screwed her face back into an angry fist.

He told her, "I saw your stock in the kitchen." On one of the cabinet shelves, Jeffrey had found two bottles of Jim Beam lined up like soldiers, waiting for Lena to imbibe. The trash can held an empty bottle of Maker's Mark. There was an empty glass in the bathroom that smelled of alcohol and one by the bed that had been knocked over on its side. Jeffrey had lived with a drunk growing up. He knew their rituals, and he knew the signs.

He said, "That's how you're dealing with it, huh? Hiding behind a bottle?"

"Dealing with what?" she challenged.

"What happened to you," Jeffrey said, but he backed off, unable to push her in that direction. Instead he went for her ego. "You never struck me as that kind of coward, Lena, but this isn't the first time you've surprised me."

"I'm handling it."

"Yeah you are," he said, his anger sparking at the turn of phrase. His father had said the same thing when Jeffrey was growing up, and Jeffrey knew that the excuse was bullshit then, just as he did now. "How's it feel puking your guts out before you go to work every morning?"

"I don't do that."

"No? Not yet anyway." Jeffrey could still remember Jimmy Tolliver heaving into the bowl as soon as he woke up, then falling into the kitchen, where he searched for his first drink of the day.

"My life is none of your business."

"I guess the headache goes away when you spike your coffee in the morning," he said, clenching and unclenching his fists, aware that he needed to get hold of his anger before he lost control of the interview. He took out the bottle of pills he had found in her medicine cabinet and tossed it onto the table. "Or does this help get you through?"

Lena stared at the bottle, and he could see her mind working. "That's for pain."

"Pretty strong prescription for a headache," he said. "Vicodin's a controlled substance. Maybe I should talk to the doctor who's giving you these."

"It's not for *that* pain, you prick." She held up her hands, showing him the scars. "You think this just went away when I got out of the hospital? You think everything just magically healed back to how it was before?"

Jeffrey stared at the scars, one of which had a trickle of fresh blood sliding down her palm. He tried to keep his expression neutral as he took out his handkerchief.

"Here," he said. "You're bleeding."

Lena looked at her hand, then balled it into a fist.

Jeffrey left the handkerchief on the table between them, unnerved that she did not care that she was bleeding. "What does Chuck think about you showing up drunk for work?"

"I don't drink on the job," she told him, and he saw a flash of regret in her eyes even before she finished speaking. He had caught her.

To his horror, Lena started picking at the scar again, drawing fresh blood.

"Stop," he said, putting his hand over hers. He pressed the handkerchief into her palm, trying to stanch the bleeding.

He saw her throat move as she swallowed, and he thought for a minute that she might start crying.

He let her hear the concern in his voice. "Lena," he said, "why are you hurting yourself like this?"

She waited a moment before slipping her hands out from under his, tucking them beneath the table and out of sight. She stared at the file, asking, "What do you have?"

"Lena."

She shook her head, and he could tell from the way her shoulders moved that she was picking at her hand under the table. She said, "Let's get this over with."

Jeffrey left the file closed, instead taking a folded sheet of paper out of his coat pocket. He saw recognition flash in Lena's eyes as he opened the page. She had seen enough lab reports over the years to know what he had in his hand. He slid the page across the table so that it was right in front of her.

He said, "This is a comparison of a pubic hair we found on the underwear in Andy Rosen's room and a sample from you."

She shook her head, not looking at the document. "You don't have a sample from me."

"I got it from your bathroom."

"Not today," she said. "You didn't have time."

"No," Jeffrey agreed, watching realization dawn on her face. Frank had jimmied the lock to Lena's apartment while she was still at the coffee shop with Ethan. Jeffrey had been ashamed enough about their methods to keep this information from Sara last night, but he had assumed that no one would ever have to know what they had done. He had assumed they were just helping Lena when she would not help herself.

Lena's voice was small in her throat, and he could taste her sense of betrayal like a piece of sour candy. "That's illegally obtained evidence."

"You wouldn't talk to me," he said, knowing how wrong it was to turn this back around like it was her fault. He tried to explain. "I thought it would clear you, Lena. I was trying to clear you."

She slid the lab report toward her so she could read it. He saw her start to pick at the scar on her hand again. Guilt twinged in his chest as a drop of blood pooled on the white page.

She glanced at the mirror on the side of the room, probably wondering who was behind it. Jeffrey had told Frank not to let anyone in there, including Frank.

He asked, "Well?"

She sat back in her chair, her hands beside her, gripping the seat. Jeffrey was glad to see her angry, because it made her seem more like Lena. She said, "I don't know what you think you have in there" — she indicated the file — "but there's no way anything from me matched anything in that kid's room." She sat up straighter. "And besides, hair isn't admissible. All you can say is that it's microscopically similar, and you know what? Big fucking deal. Probably half the girls on campus test out similar. You don't have dick on me."

"What about your fingerprint?"

"Where did you find it?"

"Where do you think?"

"Fuck this." Lena stood but did not leave, probably because she knew that Jeffrey would stop her.

He let her stand there feeling foolish for a while before he said, "You want to talk about your boyfriend?"

She cut her eyes at him. "He's not my boyfriend."

"I didn't think you were into racists."

Her lips parted, but he could not tell if she was surprised or just trying to think of a way to answer him without giving Ethan away. "Yeah, well, you don't know much about me, do you?"

"Is he the one who's been spray-painting shit all over campus?"

She snorted a laugh. "Why don't you talk to Chuck about that?"

"I talked to him this morning. He said

he asked you to track down who's been doing it, but you seem to be dragging your ass."

"That's bullshit," she said, and Jeffrey did not know whether to believe Lena or Chuck. Two days ago the choice would have been easy. Now he did not know.

"Sit down, Lena." He waited as she took her time sitting back down. "You know Ethan's on parole?"

She crossed her arms. "So?"

Jeffrey could only stare at her, hoping that his silence might will her into being sensible.

Lena asked, "Is that all?"

"Your boyfriend nearly beat a girl to death in Connecticut," Jeffrey said. "How's the shiner, by the way?"

She touched her finger to her bruised eye.

"Lena?"

If she'd been startled by his information, she recovered quickly. "I won't be pressing charges against the department, if that's what you mean. Accidents happen."

"Maybe Tessa's stabbing was an accident," Jeffrey suggested.

She shrugged. "Maybe."

"Or maybe somebody didn't like the fact that a white girl was carrying a black man's child." She did not react. "Maybe some-body didn't like two Jewish kids on cam-pus."

"Two?"

"Don't lie to me, Lena. I know you know about Ellen Schaffer." He tapped the file with his finger. "Tell me about your boy-friend."

Lena sat up. "Ethan wasn't involved in this, and you know it."

"I do?" he asked. "Let me tell you what I know, Lena." He counted the points off on his fingers. "I know that you were in Andy Rosen's room at one time or another, and I know you lied about it. I know that Andy Rosen and Ellen Schaffer are dead, and I know that both of those deaths were staged to look like suicides."

Jeffrey paused, hoping she would say something. When she did not, he con-tinued, "I know that Tessa Linton was stabbed by a man with a lean build, close-cropped hair, and no alibi on Sunday after-noon —"

"I saw the attacker," she interrupted. "It wasn't Ethan. This guy was taller and had a thicker build."

"Yeah? Matt's description's a little dif-ferent from yours, funny enough."

"This is bullshit. Ethan wasn't involved."

"Put it together, Lena."

She found the same hole in the scenario Sara had kept coming back to last night. "You think somebody staged Rosen's suicide and then just hung around, hoping Tessa Linton would come along to pee so he could stab her? That's fucking stupid." She paused, gathering her thoughts. "And who the fuck knows who Tessa Linton is, let alone that she's banging a black guy? I sure as hell didn't know. You think people on campus give a flying fuck what some plumber is up to?" She scowled at him. "This is a waste of time. You don't have anything."

"I know you're drinking too much." He watched her body tense. "Are you having blackouts now? Maybe there's something you don't remember."

"I told you I didn't know Andy Rosen," she insisted.

"Why did you sound surprised on the hill when I said his name?"

"I don't remember that."

"I do," he said, tucking the lab report into his pocket.

"What about Chuck?" she tossed out.

Jeffrey sat back, staring at her openly, wondering if she was drinking so much that her brain was going soft. "Chuck was with you the morning we found Andy Rosen, right?"

She gave a tight nod, her face tilted down so he could not read her expression.

He walked her through it like he was talking to a third-grader. "And then he was with Andy when Tessa was stabbed." Jeffrey paused. "Unless you think he sprouted wings and took off after her and then flew right back when it was all over?"

Lena shot him a look, and Jeffrey thought she must be pretty desperate to be grasping at straws. Of course, desperation came from fear. She was hiding something, and Jeffrey had a pretty good idea what that was.

He turned the file around and opened it on the table in front of her, asking, "Ethan tell you about this?"

Lena hesitated, but curiosity eventually got the better of her. Jeffrey watched her read through Ethan's arrest jacket. She seemed to be skimming, quickly turning the pages over as she read about Ethan's sordid past.

He waited until she got to the last page before saying, "His father's some kind of white supremacist."

She nodded toward the pages. "It says here he's a preacher."

"So was Charles Manson," Jeffrey pointed out. "So was David Koresh. So was Jim Jones."

"I don't know —"

"Ethan grew up in the middle of that, Lena. He was raised on hate."

Lena sat back, her arms crossed over her chest again. Jeffrey studied her closely, wondering if any of this was news to her or if White had already explained, putting his own spin on the story.

Jeffrey said, "He was charged with assault when he was seventeen."

"They dismissed the case."

"Because the girl was too scared to testify."

She waved her hand at the file. "He's on parole for kiting some checks in Connecticut. Big deal."

Jeffrey stared at her, because that was all he could do. He tried to walk her through the evidence. "Four years ago tire marks from his truck placed him at the scene where a girl was raped and killed."

"Placed at the scene like I was?" Lena asked, sarcasm dripping from her voice.

"The girl was raped before she was killed," Jeffrey repeated. "Sperm taken from her rectum and vagina proved that at least six guys raped her before she was beaten to death." He paused. "Six guys, Lena. That's plenty to hold her down while each guy takes his turn."

She gave him a blank stare.

"Ethan's truck was there."

Lena shrugged, but he thought he saw her composure begin to slip.

"That's how they got him to flip, Lena. The tire marks matched his truck. They already knew where to find him, because he was on their sheet for this kind of thing." He tapped the file. "You know what he did? You know what your boyfriend did? He ratted out his friends so he could save his own ass, and, like every good rat, he admitted he was there, but he swore on a stack of Bibles he didn't touch her."

She said nothing.

"You think he just sat in that truck, Lena? You think he just sat there while everybody else was taking their turn? Or do you think he was out there getting his piece? You think he helped hold her hands down so she couldn't scratch them? Maybe he helped keep her feet apart so they could get a better angle, or maybe he had his hand over her mouth so she couldn't scream."

Still she was silent.

"Let's give him the benefit of the doubt,

though. You wanna do that?" Jeffrey asked. "Let's say he sat in his truck. Let's say he just sat there watching them rape her. Maybe that was enough to get him off, watching them hurt her, knowing she was helpless and he could save her but he didn't."

She started to pick at the scar again, and Jeffrey kept his eyes on hers, trying not to watch her hands.

He said, "Six guys, Lena. How long did that take, for six guys to rape her while your boyfriend sat in the truck watching — if that's what he was really doing, just watching?" Lena was silent. "And then they beat her to death. Hell, I don't know why they bothered. By the time they were finished with her, she was bleeding from every place they could fuck her."

She chewed her lip, looking down at her hands. Blood was flowing pretty steadily from her palm, but she did not seem to notice.

He let his guard down for just a moment, unable to stop himself. "How can you protect him?" he asked. "How can you be a cop for ten years and protect scum like that?"

His words seemed to be striking home, so he continued, "Lena, this kid is bad. I don't know what it is you've got going with him, but . . . Jesus Christ! You're a cop. You know how this kind of asshole can slip around the law. For every piece-of-shit little thing he's been picked up on, there are twelve big things he gets away with."

Jeffrey tried again. "His father's spent hard time — federal time — for selling guns. We're not talking handguns. He was trafficking sniper rifles and machine guns." He paused, waiting for her to say something. When she did not, he asked, "Ethan tell you about his brother?"

"Yes," she said, so quickly that he was sure she was lying.

"So you know he's in prison?"

"Yes."

"You know he's on death row for killing a black man?" He paused again. "Not just a black man, Lena. A black cop."

Lena stared at the table, and he could tell she was shaking her foot, though who knew if it was from nerves or anger.

"He's a bad kid, Lena."

She shook her head, though she had enough proof in front of her. "I told you, he's not my boyfriend."

"Whatever he is, he's a skinhead. It doesn't matter if he let his hair grow out and changed his name. He's still a racist bastard, just like his father, just like his cop-killing brother."

"And I'm half spick," she shot back. "You ever wonder about that? What's he doing with somebody like me if he's a racist?"

"That's a good question," he told her. "You might want to ask yourself that the next time you look in the mirror."

She finally stopped picking at her palm and pressed her hands together on the table in front of her.

"Listen," he began, "I'm only going to say this once. Whatever you're messed up in, whatever it is with this kid, you need to tell me. I can't help you if you get yourself dug into this any deeper."

She stared at her hands, not speaking, and he wanted to grab her and shake her, to make her say something that made sense. He wanted her to explain to him how she could be mixed up with a nasty piece of shit like Ethan White, and then he *really* wanted her to tell him that it was all some kind of big misunderstanding and that she was sorry. And that she was not going to drink anymore.

What she said was, "I have no idea what you're talking about."

He had to try again. "If there's something you're not telling me about all this . . . ," he said, hoping she would fill in the rest. Of course she did not.

He tried a different tactic. "There's no chance you'll get back on the job with this guy around your neck."

She looked up, and for the first time in a while he could read her expression loud and clear: surprise.

She cleared her throat, like she was having trouble finding her voice. "I didn't know that was an option."

Jeffrey thought about her working for Chuck now, and the situation rankled as much as it had the first day he had heard about it. "You shouldn't be working for that jerk."

"Yeah, well," she said, her voice still low. "The jerk I was working for before kind of made it obvious I wasn't wanted." She looked at her watch. "Speaking of which, I'm late for work."

"Don't leave it like this," he said, aware that he was begging. "Please, Lena. I just . . . Please."

She huffed a laugh, making him feel like an idiot. "I told you I'd talk to you," she said. "Unless you've got something to charge me on, I'm out of here."

He sat back in the chair, willing her to

explain this all away.

"Chief?" she said, putting as little respect into the word as was humanly possible.

He skimmed the file, reading aloud from the list of charges that never saw the light of a courtroom. "Arson," he said. "Felony assault. Grand theft auto. Rape. Murder."

"Sounds like the latest best-seller," she said, standing. "Thanks for the chat."

"The girl," he said. "The one who was raped and beaten to death while he sat in his truck and watched?" She did not leave, so he continued. "Do you know who she was?"

She came back fast. "Snow White?"

"No," he told her, closing the file. "She was his girlfriend."

Jeffrey sat in his car in front of the student-union building, staring at a group of women taping posters to the light poles around the courtyard. They were all young and healthy-looking, dressed in jogging outfits or sweats. Any one of them could have been Ellen Schaffer. Any one of them could be the next victim.

He was here to tell Brian Keller that his son was probably murdered. Jeffrey wanted to see what the man's reaction to the news would be. He also wanted to find out what Keller had not wanted to say in front of his wife. Jeffrey hoped that what Keller said would give him a solid lead to go on. As it was, all he had was Lena, and Jeffrey could not accept that she was involved in this.

Last night Sara had kept hitting on the differences between the Rosen and Schaffer crime scenes. If someone had staged Andy Rosen's suicide, they'd done a damn good job. Ellen Schaffer was a different matter. Even if the killer had not known about the aspirated tooth, the arrow in the yard was a pretty obvious taunt. Sara had suggested at one point that the differences between the two crimes could indicate there could be two killers instead of one. Jeffrey had dismissed her idea last night, but after seeing Lena and Ethan together this morning, he was not sure of anything.

Lena had been a different person in the interrogation room, someone he had never met before. The way she had not just defended Ethan White's past but denied that he had harmed her made Jeffrey want to question everything she had said so far in the case. He'd been a cop for a long time and seen how abusers sucker in even strong women. It was amazing how similar their methods were and how easily some women were swayed. There were thousands of women sitting in jail right now because they'd been caught holding dope for their boyfriends. Thousands more had probably committed some kind of crime because they knew that jail was the only way they could protect themselves from the abuse.

In Birmingham, back when Jeffrey was working patrol, he had been called to one woman's house at least ten times. She was the communications manager of an international company and had two degrees from Auburn. At least a thousand people all over the world answered to her, and every time Jeffrey came to her house because her neighbors had called, she stood there in the doorway, her face bleeding, her clothes torn, saying she had fallen down the stairs. Her husband was a scrawny little fuck who called himself a stay-at-home dad. In reality he was a drunk who could not keep a job and lived off his wife's money. Like most abusers, he was charming and gracious and blind to what his wife looked like when he was finished with her. These days a cop didn't need the wife's testimony to arrest her husband for abuse, but back then the laws had protected the husband.

Jeffrey remembered one time in particular. He was standing on her doorstep in the freezing cold, watching blood drip down her leg and pool at her feet from God knows what, while she insisted that her husband was a gentle man who never laid a hand on her. In fact, the only time Jeffrey ever saw the husband touch her was at her funeral. He reached into her coffin and patted her hand, then gave Jeffrey the biggest shit-eating grin he had ever seen and said, "That last step was a killer."

Jeffrey had worked two years with the medical examiner trying to get something on the asshole, but while you could show with a fair amount of certainty that someone had fallen down the stairs and broken her neck, proving she was shoved was a little more difficult.

All this brought him back to Lena and how she behaved this morning. She was right that the hair match only circumstantially linked her to Andy Rosen. The fingerprint on the book could be explained away by a good lawyer. Jeffrey had trained Lena himself, and he knew that she was more than familiar with the ins and outs of forensic investigation. She would have known to be careful. She would have known exactly how to cover her tracks.

The question was, did she have it in her? Was she so wrapped up in Ethan White that she would do anything to cover for him?

Jeffrey had to look at the facts, and the facts made Lena look suspicious as hell, especially considering her hostile attitude in the interrogation room this morning. She had all but challenged him to put the pieces together.

As much as he did not want to, Jeffrey made himself consider the two-killer scenario Sara had brought up last night, one who'd killed Andy and stabbed Tessa and one who'd killed Ellen Schaffer. The weak point they kept coming back to was Tessa's attacker in the woods. After looking at Ethan White's sheet, then talking to Lena, Jeffrey had to consider a variation on the theory.

Ethan could have killed Andy Rosen. Lena had come late to the scene. She could have called Ethan on her cell phone and told him Tessa was in the woods. There was no telling where either of them was when Ellen Schaffer killed herself, but Jeffrey knew that Lena would have noticed the discrepancy in the ammo. She knew more about guns than any man he had ever met. He took little consolation in the fact that Lena's involvement in this could be as a mere accomplice. Under Georgia law she was just as guilty as Ethan.

He rubbed his eyes with his hands, thinking he was being ludicrous. Lena was a cop, despite the fact that she wasn't carrying a badge. Crossing the line into murder, even as an accomplice, was not something she would do, no matter what kind of charm Ethan White poured on. This was crazy, and there was no reason to suspect her other than that she was being difficult. As Sara had pointed out, Lena thrived on being difficult.

He took his cell phone out of his pocket and called Kevin Blake's office. The dean of Grant Tech liked to give people the impression that he was a very busy man, but Jeffrey knew for a fact that Blake spent most of his free time on the golf course. Jeffrey wanted to make an appointment with the man to update him on the case before Blake sneaked out early. Blake's secretary put Jeffrey right through.

"Jeffrey," Blake said. He was using the speakerphone, and if the tension in Blake's voice was not enough to tell Jeffrey that someone else was in his office, the speakerphone was.

Blake asked, "Where are you?"

"On campus," he answered. Keller had told Frank he would be in his lab all day if Jeffrey wanted to talk to him alone. Before Lena this morning, Keller had been the best avenue Jeffrey had to explore. Jeffrey knew that it would be easy to get side-tracked, but there was nothing he could do with Lena right now, and he knew better than to go at Ethan White with nothing to use as leverage.

Blake said, "I've got Albert Gaines here with Chuck. We were about to call you at the station and see if you could come by."

Jeffrey suppressed the curse that wanted to come.

"Hey, Chief," Chuck said, and Jeffrey could imagine the smug look on the other man's face. "We got some doughnuts and coffee here for you."

There was a grumbling sound that was probably Albert Gaines.

Blake said, "Jeffrey, could you drop by the office? We'd like to talk to you."

"I can be there in an hour," Jeffrey told him, thinking he would be damned if he came running when they snapped their fin-gers. "I've got a lead to track down."

"Oh," Blake said, probably thinking he would have to postpone his tee time. "Sure you can't just run by here a second?"

Albert Gaines grumbled something again. He was a gruff man, and he demanded answers from his subordinates, but he had always been supportive of Jeffrey.

Blake had obviously been reprimanded. His tone was brisk when he said, "We'll see you in about an hour, then, Chief."

Jeffrey closed his phone, holding it to his chin as he watched the group of girls move on to the next section of the courtyard. He got out of the car and walked toward the student union, stopping to look at one of the posters. At the top was a blurry black-and-white photo of Ellen Schaffer and a separate, even blurrier one of Andy Rosen. Beneath these were the words "Candlelight Vigil." A time and a location were given, along with a new suicide hot-line number that had been set up through the mental-health center.

"Do you think it will do any good?"

Jeffrey jumped, startled by Jill Rosen.

"Dr. Rosen —"

"Jill," she corrected. "I'm sorry I frightened you."

"It's okay," he said, thinking that the mother looked worse than she had the day before. Her eyes were so puffy from crying that they were barely slits, and her cheeks looked gaunt. She was wearing a white long-sleeved sweater with a collar that zipped into a turtleneck. As she talked to Jeffrey, she clutched the collar together in her hand, as though she were fighting the cold.

"I look a sight," she apologized.

"I was just going to talk to your husband," Jeffrey said, thinking he had blown the opportunity to speak to Keller alone.

"He should be here soon," she told him, holding up a set of keys. "His spare set," she explained. "I told him I'd meet him here. I just needed to get out of the house."

"I was surprised to hear he was at work."

"Work restores him." She gave a wan smile. "It's a good place to hide when the world is falling down around you."

Jeffrey knew exactly what she meant. He had thrown himself into work after Sara divorced him, and if he hadn't had a job to go to every day, he would have gone crazy.

"Here," he told her, indicating a bench. "How are you holding up?"

She exhaled slowly as she sat down. "I don't know how to answer that."

"I guess it was a pretty stupid question."

"No," she assured him. "It's something I've been asking myself a lot lately. 'How am I holding up?' I'll let you know when I get an answer."

Jeffrey sat beside her, looking out at the campus quad. Some kids had wandered out onto the lawn for lunch, spreading blankets and taking sandwiches from brown paper bags.

Rosen was staring at the students, too. She had the edge of her shirt collar in her mouth. He could tell from the frayed material that this was a nervous habit.

She said, "I think I'm going to leave my husband."

Jeffrey turned to her but said nothing. He could tell that her words took effort.

She said, "He wants to move. Move away from Grant. Start over. I can't start over again. I can't." She looked down.

"It's understandable to want to get away," Jeffrey said, trying to keep her talking.

Rosen indicated the campus with a tilt of her head. "I've been here nearly twenty years. We made our lives here, such as they are. I've built something at the clinic."

Jeffrey let some time pass. When she did not add anything more, he asked, "Did he say why he wanted to move?"

She shook her head, but not because she did not know why. There was an almost unbearable sadness in her voice, as though she'd decided to admit defeat. "That's his response to everything. He's all macho bluster, but at the first sign of trouble, he runs away from it as fast as he can."

"Sounds like he's done this before."

"Yes," she agreed.

Jeffrey tried to press her. "What's he running away from?"

"Everything," she said, but she did not explain. "My working life has been built around helping people confront their past, yet I can't help my own husband stay and face his demons." She said more quietly, "I can't even help myself."

"What demons does he have here?"

"The same as mine, I suppose. Every corner I turn, I expect to see Andy. I'm at home and I hear something outside and look out the window, expecting to see him climbing the stairs to his room. It has to be harder for Brian, working in the lab. I know it's harder for him. He has to meet this deadline. A tremendous amount of money is at stake. I know that. I know all of that."

Her voice had gone up, and he sensed anger that had been brewing for a while.

He asked, "Is this about the affair?"

"What affair?" she said, and her surprise seemed genuine.

"I'd heard a rumor," Jeffrey explained, wanting to kick Richard Carter's teeth in. "Someone told me that Brian was involved with a student."

"Oh, God," she breathed, covering her lips with the collar. "I almost wish that were true. Isn't that horrible?" she asked. "It would mean he was capable of caring about something other than his precious research."

"He cared for his son," Jeffrey said, remembering the argument he had overheard the day before. Rosen had accused Keller of not caring about Andy until after he was dead.

"He cares in spurts," she said. "That car. The clothes. The television. He *bought* things. That was how he cared."

There was something else she was trying to tell him, but Jeffrey did not know what. He asked, "Where does he want to move?"

"Who knows?" she said. "He's like a turtle. Whenever anything bad happens, his response is to tuck his head in and wait for it to pass." She smiled, realizing that she had been tucking her head into her collar. "Visual aid."

He returned her smile.

"I just can't do it. I can't live this way anymore." She slid her gaze toward Jeffrey.

"Will you bill me for this session, or should I pay you now?"

He smiled again, willing her to continue.

"I suppose your job is very similar to mine in a lot of ways. You listen to people talk and you try to figure out what they're really trying to say."

"What are you really trying to say?"

She considered the question. "That I'm tired," she said. "That I want a life — any life. I stayed with Brian because I thought it would be better for Andy, but now that Andy is gone . . ."

She started to cry, and Jeffrey reached for his handkerchief. He did not notice the blood from Lena's hand until after he had handed her the cloth.

He apologized, "I'm sorry."

"Did you cut yourself?"

"Lena did," he told her, watching her reaction closely. "I talked to her this morning. She was cut under her eye. Someone hit her."

Concern flashed in the woman's eyes, but she said nothing.

"She's seeing someone," he said, and Rosen seemed to be forcing herself to keep her mouth closed. "This morning I went to her apartment, and he was there with her."

Rosen did not tell him to go on, but her

eyes were pleading with him. Her fear for Lena's safety was obvious.

"Her eye was cut and her wrist was bruised, like someone had grabbed her." He waited a beat. "This guy has a past, Dr. Rosen. He's a very dangerous and violent man."

She was on the edge of the bench, practically begging for him to continue.

"Ethan White," he said. "Does that name sound familiar to you?"

"No," she told him. "Should it?"

"I hoped it might," he said, because it would mean a clear connection between Andy Rosen and Ethan White.

"Was she hurt badly?" Rosen asked.

"From what I could see, no," Jeffrey said. "But she kept picking at her hand. She was bleeding, and she kept picking at the scar."

Rosen pressed her lips together again.

"I don't know how to get her away from him," Jeffrey said. "I don't know how to help her."

She looked off into the distance, staring at the students again. "She can only help herself," Rosen said, her tone giving a deeper meaning to her words.

"Was she a patient of yours?" Jeffrey asked, hoping to God this was the case.

"You know I can't give you that kind of information."

"I know," Jeffrey said, "but hypothetically, if you could, it would answer a question for me."

She looked at him. "What question is that?"

"When we were by the river, Chuck said your son's name, and Lena seemed surprised, like she knew him," Jeffrey said, working it out as he talked. "Now, could it be that when Lena said 'Rosen,' like she knew the name, she was saying it because she knew *you*, not because she knew Andy?"

The woman seemed to consider how she could answer Jeffrey without compromising what she believed in.

"Dr. Rosen . . ."

She sat back on the bench, drawing her collar closer. "My husband is coming."

Jeffrey tried to hide his exasperation. Keller was about fifty feet away, and Rosen could have answered Jeffrey's question if she had really wanted to.

Jeffrey greeted the man. "Dr. Keller."

He seemed confused to see his wife and Jeffrey together. He asked, "Is something wrong?"

Jeffrey stood, indicating that Keller

should sit, but the man ignored him, asking his wife, "Do you have my keys?"

She handed him the ring, barely looking at him.

"I need to get back to work," Keller said. "Jill, you should go home."

Rosen started to stand.

"I have to tell you both something," Jeffrey said, gesturing for her to stay seated. "It's about Andy."

Keller gave a look that said his son was the last thing on his mind.

"I wanted to tell you both this before it was released on campus," Jeffrey said. "I'm not certain your son's death was a suicide."

Rosen asked, "What?"

"I can't rule out the possibility that he might have been killed," Jeffrey told them.

Keller dropped his keys but did not pick them up.

Jeffrey continued, "We didn't find anything conclusive in Andy's autopsy, but Ellen Schaffer —"

"The girl from yesterday?" Rosen interrupted.

"Yes, ma'am," Jeffrey said. "There's no question she was murdered. Considering the fact that it was staged to look like a suicide, we have to question the circumstances surrounding your son's death. I can't say with all honesty that we have anything to prove he *didn't* take his life, but we have strong suspicions, and I'm going to investigate this until I find out the truth."

She sat back on the bench, her lips parted.

Jeffrey continued, "I have to tell the dean about this, but I wanted y'all to hear it first."

Rosen asked, "What about the note?"

"That's one of the things I don't have an explanation for," Jeffrey said. "And I'm sorry to say that all I can give you right now is what I suspect. We're exploring every possible avenue we can to try to find out exactly what happened, but I have to be honest: Nothing obvious is coming to mind. The two cases could be completely unrelated. It could be that at the end of all this we find out that Andy really did kill himself."

Keller exploded, and his rage was so unexpected that Jeffrey stepped back.

"How the hell can this happen?" Keller demanded. "How the hell can you let me and my wife think our son killed himself when —"

"Brian," Rosen tried.

"Shut up, Jill," he snapped, his hand flicking like he might strike her. "This is preposterous. This is . . ." He was too angry to speak, but his mouth moved as he considered words to describe how he felt. "I cannot believe . . ." He leaned down and snatched up his keys. "This college, this whole town . . ." He put his finger in his wife's face, and she backed away as if to defend herself.

Keller rose to his full height, screaming, "I *told* you, Jill. I *told* you what a hellhole this place is!"

Jeffrey stepped in, saying, "Dr. Keller, I think you need to calm down."

"I think you need to mind your own business and figure out who murdered my son!" he roared, his face contorted with rage. "You Keystone Kops think you run this town, but this is like living in a Third World country. You're all corrupt. You're all answering to Albert Gaines."

Jeffrey had had enough. "We'll talk about this some other time, Dr. Keller, when you've had a chance to absorb all this."

This time, Keller put his finger in Jeffrey's face. "You're damn right we'll talk about this," he said, then turned his back on them both and stomped away.

Jill Rosen immediately apologized for her husband. "I'm sorry."

"You don't need to apologize for him," Jeffrey said, trying to keep his own anger at bay. He wanted to follow Keller back to his lab, but both of them probably needed a few minutes to calm down.

Jeffrey told Rosen, feeling her desperation, "I'm sorry I can't give you more information that that."

She clutched her collar to her neck, asking, "Your hypothetical question from before?"

"Yes?"

"It's related to Andy?"

"Yes, ma'am," he told her, trying to shift gears.

Rosen stared out at the quad, at the students sitting on the lawn and enjoying the day. "Hypothetically," she said, "she might have a reason to recognize my name."

"Thank you," Jeffrey said, feeling an inordinate amount of relief to have at least one thing explained.

"About the other," she said, still watching the students. "The man she's seeing?"

"Do you know him?" Jeffrey asked, then amended, "Hypothetically?"

"Oh, I know him," she said. "Or at least I know his type. I know his type better than I know myself."

"I'm not sure I follow."

She pulled back her collar, taking down the zipper to show a large bruise on her clavicle. Black finger marks were pressed into the side of her neck. Someone had tried to choke her.

Jeffrey could only stare. "Who . . . ," he said, but the answer was obvious.

Rosen zipped her shirt back up. "I should go."

"I can take you somewhere," Jeffrey offered. "To a shelter —"

"I'll go to my mother's," she told him, smiling sadly. "I always go to my mother's."

"Dr. Rosen," he said. "Jill —"

"I appreciate your concern," she interrupted. "But I really have to go."

He stood there, watching her make her way past a group of students. She stopped briefly to talk to one of them, acting as if nothing had happened. He was torn between following her and tracking down Brian Keller to let him know exactly how it felt to be pushed around.

On impulse, Jeffrey chose the latter, walking toward the science building at a fast pace. As a kid, he had interrupted enough fights between his parents to know that anger only fueled more anger, so he took a deep, calming breath before opening the door to Keller's lab.

The room was empty but for Richard Carter, who stood behind the desk, tapping a pen against his chin. His expectant look quickly turned to one of disappointment when he recognized Jeffrey. "Oh," he said. "It's you."

"Where's Keller?"

"That's what I want to know," Richard snapped, clearly annoyed. He bent back over the desk, scribbling a note. "He was supposed to meet me thirty minutes ago."

"I just talked to his wife about that so-called affair he was having."

He perked up at this, a smile tugging at his lips. "Yeah? What'd she say?"

"That it wasn't true." Jeffrey warned, "You need to be more careful about what you say."

Richard looked hurt. "I told you it was a rumor. I made it very clear that —"

"You're messing around with people's lives. Not to mention wasting my time."

Richard sighed as he returned to his note. He mumbled, "Sorry," the way a child might.

Jeffrey did not let him off that easy. "Because of you, I've been chasing my tail tracking down this rumor when I could've been working on something that might actually help." When there was no response, Jeffrey felt the need to add, "People are dead, Richard."

"I'm well aware of that, Chief Tolliver, but what on earth does that have to do with me?" Richard did not give him a chance to respond. "Can I be honest with you? I know what happened was horrible, but we've got work to do. Important work. There's a group in California working on this same thing. They're not just going to say, 'Oh, Brian Keller's had a hard time lately, let's stop until he feels better.' No, sir. They're going at it night and day — night and day — to beat us to the punch. Science is not a gentleman's game. Millions, maybe billions, are on the line."

He sounded like an infomercial trying to pressure some poor sucker into buying a set of steak knives in the next two minutes. Jeffrey said, "I didn't know you and Brian worked together."

"When he bothers to show up." He threw down his pen on the desk, picked up his briefcase, and walked toward the door.

"Where are you going?"

"Class," Richard said, as if Jeffrey were stupid. "Some of us actually show up when we're supposed to."

He left in a dramatic huff. Rather than

follow him, Jeffrey went to Keller's desk and read the note: "Dear Brian, I suppose you're still busy with Andy, but we really should get the documentation together. If you need me to do it on my own, just say the word." Richard had put a smiley face next to his name.

Jeffrey read the note through twice, trying to reconcile the helpful tone with Richard's obvious irritation. It didn't jibe, though Richard was hardly the rational type.

He glanced toward the door before deciding to make himself at home and go through Keller's desk. He was kneeling down, rifling the bottom file drawer, when his cell phone rang.

"Tolliver."

"Chief," Frank said. By his tone, Jeffrey could have guessed what was coming next. "We found another body."

Jeffrey parked his car in front of the men's dorm, thinking if he never saw the Grant Tech campus again, he would be a happy man. He could not forget the blank expression on Jill Rosen's face and wondered how surprised he must have looked when she showed him her bruises. He would not have guessed in a million years that Keller was the type of man to beat his wife, but Jeffrey had been caught off guard by too many revelations today to feel stupid for missing what might have been obvious signs.

Jeffrey took out his phone, debating whether to call Sara. He did not want her at the crime scene, but he knew she needed to see the body in situ. Jeffrey tried to think of a good excuse to keep her away but finally relented, dialing her number.

The phone rang five times before Sara picked up, mumbling a groggy hello.

"Hey," Jeffrey said.

"What time is it?"

He told her, thinking she sounded better than she had last night. He said, "I'm sorry I'm waking you up."

"Hm . . . what?" she asked, and he could hear her moving around in bed. He had a flash of being there beside her and felt a stirring he had not felt in a while. There was nothing he wanted more than to slip into bed beside Sara and start this day over again.

Sara said, "Mama called about twenty minutes ago. Tessa's doing a little better." She yawned loudly. "I've got some paperwork at the morgue, and then I'm going to drive back this afternoon."

"That's why I'm calling."

There was dread in her voice. "What?"

"A hanging," he said. "At the college."

"Christ," Sara breathed. Jeffrey felt the same way. In a town where the murder rate was ten times lower than the national average, bodies were suddenly stacking up to the walls.

She asked, "What time?"

"I'm not sure yet. I just got the call." He knew what her response to his words would be, but he had to say, "You could send Carlos."

"I have to see the body."

"I don't like the thought of you on campus," he told her. "If something happened —"

"I'm not going to *not* do my job," she said, her tone making it clear there was no point arguing.

Jeffrey knew she was right. Sara did not just have a job to do; she had to live her life. He thought about what Lena had looked like this morning and the bruises on Jill Rosen's neck. Should he let them just live their lives, too?

"Jeff?"

He relented. "It's the men's dorm, Building B."

"All right," she said. "I'll be there in a few minutes."

Jeffrey ended the call and got out of the car. He steered his way past the group of boys outside the door and walked into the dorm, the strong smell of liquor enveloping him like a cloud. Back at Auburn, where Jeffrey had studied history in between warming the bench for the rest of the football team, they had partied pretty hard, but he could not remember his dorm ever smelling like a liquor store.

"Hey, Chief," Chuck said. He was standing at the top of the stairs, hands tucked into the front pockets of his tight pants. The effect was obscene, and Jeffrey wished the other man would back up from the stairs Jeffrey was about to climb.

"Chuck," Jeffrey said, watching the steps as he walked up them.

"Glad you finally showed up. Kev and I were waiting around for you."

Jeffrey frowned at the way he threw around the dean's name like they were best friends. Except for the fact that Albert Gaines was Chuck's father, Kevin Blake wouldn't have given Chuck the time of day, let alone play golf with the man. Not that Kevin would be seeing the greens anytime soon. He'd probably be spending the rest of the month fielding phone calls from anxious parents who were nervous about their kids being at a school where three of their classmates had died.

"I'll talk to him when I can make the time," Jeffrey told him, wondering how long he could postpone the meeting.

"This'n's pretty straightforward," Chuck said, meaning the suicide. "Got caught with his pants down."

Jeffrey ignored the remark and asked, "Who found him?"

"One of the other kids in the building."

"I want to talk to him."

"He's downstairs right now," Chuck said. "Adams tried to get the story out of him, but I had to take over." He gave a knowing wink. "She can be a little heavy-handed. You gotta employ some finesse in these types of situations."

"Is that right?" Jeffrey asked, looking down the hallway. Frank and Lena were standing outside a room. Guessing from their posture, the two were not sharing a happy moment.

Chuck said, "She's the one that found the needle."

"Found it?" Jeffrey asked. He had called the scene-of-crime unit less than ten minutes ago. There was no way the techs had had time to process the room.

"Lena spotted it when she walked in to

check on the perp," Chuck said, using the wrong word for the victim. "Guess it rolled under the bed."

Jeffrey suppressed a curse, knowing that whatever evidence they found in the room would be tainted, especially if it was evidence that suggested Lena had been in the room before.

Chuck laughed. "Didn't mean to show you up, Chief," he said, patting Jeffrey on the back like Jeffrey's team had lost a game of pickup basketball.

Jeffrey ignored him, walking toward Frank and Lena. When Chuck started to follow, Jeffrey said, "You do me a favor?"

"Sure, hoss."

"Stand at the top of the stairs. Make sure nobody comes up but Sara."

Chuck gave him a salute and turned on his heel.

"Idiot," Jeffrey mumbled, walking down the hall.

Frank was saying something to Lena, but he stopped talking when Jeffrey got there.

Jeffrey asked Lena, "Can you excuse us for a minute?"

"Sure," she said, taking a few steps down the hall. Jeffrey knew she could still hear them, but he did not care.

He told Frank, "Crime techs are on the way."

"I went ahead and took pictures," Frank said, holding up the Polaroid camera.

"Get Brad over here," he ordered, knowing that Sara did not want a baby-sitter. "Tell him to bring the camera. I want some clean shots."

Frank made the phone call as Jeffrey peered into the room. A chubby kid with long black hair was slumped against the bed. On the floor beside him was a yellow band of rubber like the kind addicts use to help find a vein. The body was bloated and gray. The kid had been there for a while.

"Jesus Christ," Jeffrey muttered, thinking that this room smelled even worse than Ellen Schaffer's had. "What the hell is that?"

Frank volunteered, "Not much of a housekeeper."

Jeffrey studied the scene. None of the lights were on, but the late-morning sunlight was bright enough to see by. There was a combination TV/VCR across from the body, propped up on the mattress of the bed. A bright blue screen glowed, indicating that the tape had stopped. The light gave the body an odd cast, making the skin look moldy, or maybe that particular de-

419

scription came to mind because the room smelled so bad. The place was a mess, and Jeffrey guessed most of the odor came from the food containers left to rot on the floor. Papers and books were everywhere, and he wondered how anyone managed to walk around without tripping.

The kid's head tilted down into his chest, his greasy hair covering his face and neck. He was not wearing anything other than a pair of dirty-looking white boxer shorts. His hand was shoved into the opening and Jeffrey could make an educated guess as to what it had been doing in there.

There was a pattern bruise on the victim's left arm, but Sara could better assess the mark. Jeffrey assumed from the stiff way the body sat that rigor mortis had taken over, which put the time of death within the last two to twelve hours, depending on how consistent the temperature in the room had been. Time of death was never easy to establish, and Jeffrey guessed that Sara would not be able to ballpark it any better than he could.

"Is the air on in there?" Jeffrey asked, loosening his tie. The window unit had plastic streamers on the vents, but they were still.

"No," Frank said. "The door was open when I got here, and I figured I might as well leave it that way to air the funk out."

Jeffrey nodded, thinking the room must have been pretty hot most of the night if the air had stayed off and the door had been closed. His neighbors must have been so accustomed to the bad smell by now that they had not noticed anything out of the ordinary.

Jeffrey asked, "We got a name on him?"

"William Dickson," Frank said. "Far as I can tell nobody called him that."

"What'd he go by?"

Frank smirked. "Scooter."

Jeffrey raised his eyebrows, but he was in no position to talk. He was not about to share with anyone what they had called him back in Sylacauga. Sara had used it yesterday just to rankle him.

Frank said, "His roommate's back home this week for Easter."

"I want to talk to him," Jeffrey said.

"I'll get a number from the dean when this is clear."

Jeffrey walked into the room, noticing a broken plastic syringe on the floor. Whatever was in it had dried, but he could make out a clear waffle shoe tread imprinted in what had once been fluid.

He stared at the tread, telling Frank, "Make sure Brad gets a good shot of this." Frank nodded, and Jeffrey knelt beside the body. He was about to ask Frank for some gloves when the older man tossed him a pair.

"Thanks," Jeffrey said, tugging them on. The fact that his hands were sweating made the latex stick. The light in the room was negligible, and Jeffrey looked around for a lamp Dickson might have used. There was one on the refrigerator by the bed, but the cord had been cut off, the ends of the wires sheared back to the copper. "Don't let anybody turn on the light switch until we get a look at this," Jeffrey warned Frank.

He tilted Scooter's head to the side, lifting his chin off his chest. There was a leather belt wrapped around the boy's neck that Jeffrey had not seen from the hall. Scooter's hair was so long and greasy, Jeffrey was surprised he could see it now.

Jeffrey pushed back the boy's hair, which moved in a thick clump. The belt looped around the neck, the buckle so tight it dug into the skin. Jeffrey did not want to loosen the leather, but he could see a thin piece of foam squeezing out at the top. He followed the end of the belt, finding it looped through another belt, this one made of canvas. The buckle on the second belt was looped through a large eye hook screwed into the wall. The entire length of the belts was taut, the weight of the body pulling on the bolt in the wall. From the looks of it, the eye hook had been there a while.

Jeffrey turned slightly, looking at the television opposite the body. The unit was cheap, the kind you could get at a discount store for less than a hundred bucks. Beside it was a jar of Tiger Balm edged with crusty white chunks of God only knew what. Jeffrey took out his pen and used it to press the eject button on the VCR. The label had a sexually suggestive scene drawn on it under the title *The Bare Wench Project*.

Jeffrey stood up, taking off his gloves. Frank followed him down the hall to Lena.

"You call anybody?" Jeffrey asked.

"What?" she said, wrinkling her brow. She had obviously been ready for another interrogation, but he knew his question had surprised her.

"When you got here," he said, "did you call anybody on your cell phone?"

"I don't have a cell phone."

"Are you sure about that?" Jeffrey asked. He thought Sara was the only person in

Grant who did not carry one.

"Do you know what they pay me?" Lena laughed, incredulous. "I can barely afford food."

Jeffrey changed the subject. "I heard you found the needle."

"We got the call about half an hour ago," she said, and he knew that this was the answer she had been rehearsing. "I went into the room to see if the subject was alive. He had no pulse and was not breathing. His body was stiff and cool to the touch. That was when I found the needle."

"She was real helpful," Frank said, his tone indicating the opposite. "Saw it under the bed and just thought she'd save us the trouble and fetch it for us herself."

Jeffrey stared at Lena, stating rather than asking, "Guess your prints are all over it."

"Guess so."

"Guess you don't remember what else you touched while you were in there?"

"Guess not."

Jeffrey looked into the room, then back at Lena. "You wanna tell me how your boyfriend's tread print got on the floor?"

She did not seemed fazed at all. As a matter of fact, she smiled. "Didn't you hear?" she asked. "He's the one who found the body."

Jeffrey glanced at Frank, who nodded. "I heard you already tried to interview him."

She shrugged.

"Frank," he said, "go fetch him up here."

Frank left, and Lena walked over to the window, looking out at the front lawn of the dorm. There was trash everywhere, and beer cans were piled into a monument by the bike rack.

Jeffrey said, "Looks like they had some party here."

"I guess," she said.

"Maybe this guy" — he indicated Scooter — "got carried away."

"Maybe."

"Seems to me like you've got a drug problem on this campus."

Lena turned to look at him. "Maybe you oughta talk to Chuck about that."

"Yeah, he's real on top of things," Jeffrey said sarcastically.

"Might want to see where he was this weekend."

"At the golf tournament?" Jeffrey asked, remembering the front page of the *Grant Observer*. He guessed Lena was alluding to Chuck's father, trying to remind Jeffrey that Albert Gaines could catch him by his short hairs.

Jeffrey said, "Why are you working

against me, Lena? What are you hiding?"

"Your witness is here," she said. "I'd better go check in with my boss."

"Why so fast?" Jeffrey asked. "Are you scared he's going to hit you again?"

She pressed her lips together, not giving him a response.

"Stay here," he told her, making it clear she did not have a choice.

Ethan White sauntered down the hall with Frank beside him. He was still dressed in his usual long-sleeved black T-shirt and jeans. His hair was wet, and a towel was wrapped around his neck.

"Take a shower?" Jeffrey asked.

"Yeah," Ethan said, using the edge of the towel to wipe his ear. "I was washing off all the evidence from choking Scooter to death."

"That sounds like a confession," Jeffrey said.

Ethan gave him a scathing look. "I already talked to your junior pig here," he said, staring at Lena. Lena stared back, ratcheting up the tension.

"Tell it to me," Jeffrey said. "You live on the first floor?" Ethan nodded. "Why did you come up here?"

"I needed to borrow some class notes from Scooter."

"Which class?"

"Molecular biology."

"What time was this?"

"I don't know," he answered. "Count backward about two minutes from whatever time I called her."

Lena saw the opening. She said, "I was at the security office. He didn't call me, I just happened to answer the phone."

Ethan grabbed the ends of the towel in his hands as if he were strangling it. "I left when they got here. That's all I know."

"What did you touch in the room?"

"I don't recall," he said. "I was pretty unnerved, what with walking in on my fellow classmate dead on the floor."

"You've seen a dead body before," Jeffrey reminded him.

Ethan raised his eyebrows, as if to say *So what?*

Jeffrey said, "I want you to make a formal statement at the police station."

Ethan shook his head. "No way."

"Are you impeding an investigation?" Jeffrey threatened.

"No, sir," Ethan answered smartly. He took a piece of notebook paper from his back pocket and held it out to Jeffrey. "This is my statement. I've signed it. I'll sign it again now if you want to witness it. I believe legally I'm under no obligation to do this at the police station."

"You think you're good at this," Jeffrey said, not taking the statement. "You think you know how to weasel your way out of anything." He indicated Lena. "Or beat your way out of it."

Ethan winked at Lena, like they shared a special secret. Lena tensed but said nothing.

"I'm going to get you," Jeffrey said. "Maybe not now, but you're up to something, and I'm going to nail you on it. Do you hear me?"

Ethan released the paper and it floated to the floor. "If that's it," he said, "I really need to get to class."

10

Sara drove her car from the campus back to the morgue on autopilot, mulling over every detail of last night's autopsies. There was something about Andy Rosen's death that still troubled her, and, unlike Jeffrey, she needed more than a coincidence to be able to sign off on murder. At best Sara could say only that his death was suspicious, and even that was pushing it. There was no scientific evidence suggesting foul play. The tox screen had come back clean, and the autopsy had been completely normal. It was very possible that Andy Rosen's suicide was still just that.

William "Scooter" Dickson was another deal altogether. The pornography in his VCR, the foam between the belt and Scooter's skin to prevent marking, the bolt in the wall that had obviously been there a long time — all of these pointed toward autoerotic asphyxiation. Sara had seen only one case of this in her career, but there had been several papers about it in the *Journal of Forensic Science* a few years ago, when manual strangulation had reached the height of its popularity.

"Crap," Sara said, realizing she'd passed the hospital. She continued down Main Street toward the college, then made an illegal U-turn in front of the police station. She waved at Brad Stephens, who was getting out of his squad car. He covered his eyes, pretending he didn't see her as she nearly clipped a white Cadillac parked in front of Burgess's Cleaners.

Sara passed the children's clinic, the sign outside faded and rotting because Jeffrey had chosen the only sign maker in town to cheat with when they were married. She sighed, looking at the dilapidated sign, wondering if she should attach some greater meaning to its irreparable condition. Perhaps it was foreshadowing what would eventually happen with Sara and Jeffrey. Cathy Linton liked to say that you can never go back.

Sara slammed on the brakes, almost missing the turn into the hospital again. Working around children all the time, Sara was not given to cursing, but she let loose a couple obscenities as she put the car in reverse. A couple more came out when the front wheel bumped up over the curb. She parked the car on the side of the building and took the stairs down to the morgue two at a time.

Carlos had not yet returned from the college with the body, and Jeffrey was tracking down William Dickson's parents, so Sara had the morgue to herself. She walked toward her office but stopped just outside the doorway. A large flower arrangement was on the corner of her desk. Jeffrey had not sent her flowers in years. She walked around the display, feeling a big, silly grin on her face. He had forgotten that she was not crazy about carnations, but there were other flowers, beautiful flowers, whose names Sara could not remember, and the whole office was filled with their fragrance.

"Jeffrey," she said, feeling her cheeks strain from the smile on her face. He must have ordered them this morning before all hell broke loose. She slid out the card, her smile fading when she read the note from Mason James.

Sara looked around, wondering where she could put the flowers so that Jeffrey would not see them, then giving up, because she was not a sneaky person and was not about to start hiding things.

431

She sat down in her chair, putting the card by the vase. There were plenty of other items on her desk to hold her attention. Molly, Sara's nurse at the children's clinic, had dropped off a stack of papers this morning, and Sara could probably spend the next twelve hours going through them without even making a dent. She slipped on her glasses and signed off on a stack of about sixty forms before noticing that Carlos had arrived.

She watched Carlos through the window as he set out the instruments for autopsy. He was slow and methodical, checking each piece for damage or signs of wear. Sara watched him for a few more minutes before deciding to take care of her phone messages. She noticed Carlos's handwriting on the first one. Brock had called to see when he could come to get Andy Rosen's body. She picked up the phone and dialed the funeral home.

Brock's mother answered, and Sara spent several minutes catching her up on Tessa's condition, knowing that the news would spread around town before lunchtime. Penny Brock didn't have much to do at the funeral home, and between taking naps and greeting the occasional customer, she spent most of her time gossiping on the phone.

Brock sounded his usual jovial self when he finally came on the line. "Hello there, Sara," he said. "You calling to talk about storage fees?"

She laughed, knowing he was trying to make a joke.

She said, "I was calling to see how much time I have. Is the service today?"

"Set for nine tomorrow morning," Brock said. "I was gonna do him last thing today. How bad's he messed up?"

"Not bad," Sara said. "Just the usual."

"You get him finished around three, and I'll have plenty of time."

Sara checked her watch. It was already eleven-thirty. She did not even know why she was keeping Andy Rosen in-house. His tissue and organs had been biopsied, and Brock had taken several vials of urine and blood that she could study at her leisure. There was absolutely nothing more she could think to do.

She said, "You know, just come pick him up now."

"You're sure?"

"Yes," Sara told him. With another body coming in, they probably needed the space in the freezer.

"You can have him after the service if you think of anything," Brock volunteered.

"I was gonna drop him off at the crematory around lunchtime." He lowered his voice. "I like to wait around now to make sure it's done right, if you know what I mean. People are antsy about cremation these days, on account of that rascal up in north Georgia."

"Right," Sara said, recalling the case of a family-owned crematory that had stacked bodies in car trunks and against trees on their property instead of cremating them. The state had spent nearly $10 million removing and identifying the remains.

Brock said, "It's a shame, really. Such a clean way to handle things. Not that I don't like the extra money with a ground interment, but some folks are so messed up it's just best to handle it quickly."

"His parents?" Sara asked, wondering if Keller had threatened his wife in front of Brock.

"They came by for the arrangements last night and I tell you . . ." Brock's voice trailed off. He was very discreet, but Sara could usually get him to talk. Sometimes his candor made her wonder if she had somehow stumbled into the crosshairs of one of his famous unrequited crushes.

Sara gave him some prodding. "Yes?"

"Well . . ." he began, his voice even

lower. Brock knew better than anybody else that his mother was the main artery to Grant County gossip.

He said, "His mama was a bit concerned about cremating him after the autopsy. Thought it couldn't be done. Lord, where do these people get their notions?"

Sara waited.

"My feeling was, she wasn't too happy about the whole thing to begin with, but then the daddy stepped in and said that's what the boy wanted and that's what they were gonna do."

"If those were his wishes, they should be honored," Sara said. Even though she dealt with death all the time, Sara had never considered letting anyone know how she wanted to be buried. Thinking about it now made her shudder.

"Some people come in with their pre-needs," Brock said, chuckling. "Boy, the stories I could tell you about what some folks wanna be buried with."

Sara closed her eyes, willing him not to share.

Brock took the cue from her silence and moved on. "Tell you the truth, what with them being Jewish, God bless 'em, I thought they'd wanna do it fast, but they've done it all normal-like. I guess

435

they're not real into it like some."

"No," Sara answered. As a medical examiner, she'd seen only one case where her performing an autopsy was contested by a family of Orthodox Jews. While she admired their devotion to religion, she imagined that the family was relieved to know that their father had died of a heart attack rather than purposefully driven his car into the lake.

"Well . . ." Brock cleared his throat uncomfortably, probably interpreting her silence as disapproval. "I'll be over in two shakes."

Sara hung up the phone, slipping on her glasses as she thumbed through the rest of the messages. The white noise of the morgue was punctuated by the pop and flash as Carlos took pictures of the body. Sara stopped on the last phone message, seeing that she had missed a drop-in visit from a pharmaceutical company's rep. Sara frowned, knowing he would have left more free samples for her patients had she been there to talk him into it.

Under the messages was a slick brochure from the rep advertising the fact that an asthma drug had just been approved for children. In fact, pediatricians like Sara had been prescribing the inhaler to patients for years; the drug companies used the new FDA approval for pediatric use to extend their patents on the drug so they could keep gouging the consumer and not have to worry about competition from generics. Sara often thought if they stopped paying for fancy brochures and expensive television spots, the companies might be able to drop the price on their drugs so that people could afford them.

The trash was across the room, and she threw the brochure toward it and missed just as Jeffrey came into the office.

"Hey," Jeffrey said, tossing a manila folder down on her desk. He dropped a large paper bag on top of it.

She stood up to get the brochure, and he put his hand on her arm.

"What —"

He kissed her on the mouth, something he did not tend to do in public. The kiss was chaste, more like a friendly hello or, considering how Jeffrey had behaved with Mason James the previous afternoon, a dog marking a fire hydrant.

"Hey," she said, giving him a curious look as she put the brochure in its proper place.

When she turned back around, Jeffrey was cupping one of the carnations in his hand. "You don't like these."

She was more pleased that he had remembered this detail than if he had actually sent the flowers. "No," she said, watching him take the card out of the envelope.

"Please, go ahead and read it," she offered, though he was doing just that.

He took his time tucking the card back into the envelope. "That's nice," he said, then quoted from the card, " 'I'm here if you need me.' "

She crossed her arms, waiting for him to say whatever he needed to say.

"Long morning," he said, closing the door. His expression was neutral, and she could tell he was trying to move on when he asked, "Tess the same?"

"Better, actually," she told him, slipping on her glasses as she sat down. "What did you want to talk about?"

He poked his finger at one of the flowers. "Lena was hit this morning."

Sara sat up. "She was in a car accident?"

"No," he said. "It was Ethan White, that punk I told you about. The one she's been seeing. The one who tried to push me down."

"That's his name?" Sara asked, because for some reason the name sounded harmless to her.

"One of them," Jeffrey said. "Frank and I went to talk to her this morning . . ." He let his voice trail off as he stared at the flower. Sara sat back in her chair as he recounted his morning to her, ending with Jill Rosen's showing him the bruises on her neck.

Sara stated the obvious. "She's being abused."

"Yes," Jeffrey said.

"I didn't see any signs of abuse when I autopsied Andy Rosen."

"It's possible to hurt somebody without leaving any evidence."

"Either way, an argument could be made that Rosen killed himself to stop the abuse," Sara said. "His note was to his mother, not his father. Maybe he couldn't take it anymore."

"It's possible," Jeffrey agreed. "Except for Tessa, we wouldn't suspect anything with Andy."

"How likely is it that they're not connected?"

"Shit, Sara, I don't know."

Sara reminded him. "We don't have any evidence that Andy Rosen was murdered. Maybe we should take him out of the equation and go with what we know."

"Which is?"

"Ellen Schaffer was murdered. Maybe

someone thought they would take advantage of Andy's suicide and make it seem like she copied him. That sort of chain reaction is not uncommon on college campuses. MIT had twelve suicides one year."

"What about Tess?" he reminded her. Tessa was always the wild card, the victim who did not make sense.

"That could be a different crime altogether," Sara said. "Unless we find some sort of connection, maybe we should treat them as two separate incidents."

"And this one?" Jeffrey indicated the body out in the morgue.

"I have no idea," she said. "How did his parents take it?"

"About as well as you would expect," he said, but he didn't elaborate.

"We might as well get started," she told him, moving the brown paper bag off the folder so she could read the report. Jeffrey had made copies of his notes, and there was an inventory from the scene. Sara skimmed these, but out of the corner of her eye she could see Jeffrey touching one of the bell-shaped purple flowers.

When Sara had finished, she pointed to the stack of journals in the only other chair in the office. "You can put those on the floor."

"I'm sick of sitting," he said, kneeling beside her desk. He rubbed his hand on her leg. "You get enough sleep?"

She put her hand over his, thinking she should have Mason send her flowers every day if it made Jeffrey this attentive.

"I'm okay," she told him, returning her attention to the file. "You got these back fast," she said, meaning the scene-of-crime photos.

"Brad did them in the darkroom," he told her. "And you might want to watch it the next time you take a U-turn in front of the police station."

She gave an innocent smile, then indicated the brown paper bag. "What's this?"

"Prescription bottles," he said, dumping the contents on her desk. She could tell from the black powder on the containers that they had already been dusted. There had to be at least twenty bottles.

She asked, "All of these belonged to the victim?"

"His name's on them."

"Antidepressants," Sara said, lining up the bottles one by one across her desk.

"He was shooting Ice."

"Handsome *and* smart," Sara noted wryly, still lining up the bottles, trying to classify them into sections. "Valium, which

441

is contraindicated with antidepressants." She studied the labels, all of which had the same prescribing doctor. The name didn't ring any bells, but the scripts were setting off all kinds of alarms in Sara's head.

She started to read off the prescriptions. "Prozac, about two years old. Paxil, Elavil." She paused, noting the dates. "Looks like he tried them all and settled on the Zoloft, which is —" She paused, then let out a "Wow."

"What?"

"Three hundred fifty milligrams of Zoloft a day. That's high."

"What's the average?"

Sara shrugged. "I don't give this to my kids," she told him. "Educated guess for an adult would be fifty to one hundred milligrams tops." She continued with the bottles. "Ritalin, of course. His generation grew up on that crap. More Valium, lithium, amantadine, Paxil, Xanax, cyproheptadine, busiprone, Wellbutrin, Buspar, Elavil. Another of Zoloft. Another." She grouped the three bottles of Zoloft together, noting that they had each been filled at different pharmacies on different dates.

"What are these for?"

"Specifically? Depression, sleeplessness,

anxiety. They're all for the same thing, but they work in different ways." She rolled her chair back to the shelf by the filing cabinet and found her pharmacological guide. "I'll have to look these up," she said, rolling back to the desk. "Some of them I know, but I have no idea about the others. One of my Parkinson's kids is on busiprone for anxiety. Sometimes you can take these together, but not all of them. That would end up being toxic."

"Could he be selling them?" Jeffrey asked. "He had the needles. We found a stash of pot and ten tabs of acid in his closet."

"There's not really a market for antidepressants," Sara told him. "Anybody can get a prescription for them nowadays. It's just a matter of finding the right — or in this case the wrong — doctor." She indicated a couple of the bottles she had set aside. "Ritalin and Xanax have street value."

"I can go to the elementary school and score ten pills of each for around a hundred dollars," Jeffrey pointed out. He held up a large plastic bottle. "At least he's taking his vitamins."

"Yocon," she said, reading the ingredients. "Might as well start with this one."

Sara thumbed through the book, finding the appropriate entry. She scanned the description, summarizing, "It's a trade name for yohimbine, which is an herb. It's supposed to help the libido."

Jeffrey took back the bottle. "It's an aphrodisiac?"

"Not technically," Sara answered, reading further. "Supposedly it helps with everything from premature ejaculation to maintaining a harder erection."

"How come I've never heard of it?"

Sara gave him a knowing look. "You never needed to."

Jeffrey smiled, setting the Yocon back on her desk. "He's a twenty-year-old kid. Why would he need something like this?"

"The Zoloft could cause him to be anorgasmic."

Jeffrey narrowed his eyes. "He couldn't come?"

"Well, that's another way of putting it," Sara allowed. "He could achieve and maintain an erection but have a problem ejaculating."

"Jesus Christ, no wonder he was choking himself."

Sara ignored his comment, double-checking the drug in her guide just to be sure. " 'Side effects: anorgasmia, anxiety, increased appetite, decreased appetite, insomnia . . .' "

"That might explain the Xanax."

Sara looked up from the book. "No doctor in his right mind would prescribe all of these pills together."

Jeffrey compared some of the labels. "He used about four different pharmacies."

"I don't imagine one pharmacist would fill all of these. It's too reckless."

"We'll need something solid to get a warrant for pharmacy records," he said. "Do you recognize the doctor?"

"No," she said, sliding open the bottom drawer of her desk. She pulled out the phone book for Grant County and surrounding areas. A quick search revealed that the man was not listed. "He's not affiliated with the health clinic or the school?"

"No," Jeffrey told her. "He could be in Savannah. One of the pharmacies is listed there."

"I don't have a Savannah phone book."

"They've got this new thing," Jeffrey said, teasing her. "It's called the Internet."

"All right," Sara said, forgoing the lecture on how wonderful technology was. She could see its application for someone like Jeffrey, but as far as Sara was concerned, she saw too many pasty, overweight kids in her practice to appreciate the benefits of staring at a computer all day.

Jeffrey suggested, "Maybe it's not a doctor?"

"Unless the pharmacist knows you, you have to have a DEA number when you call in a script. It's on a database."

"So maybe someone stole a number from a retired doctor?"

"He's not prescribing narcotics or Oxy-Contin. I imagine these wouldn't throw up any red flags with government regulators." Sara frowned. "Still, I'm not sure what the purpose is. These aren't stimulants. You can't really get high off any of them. The Xanax can be addictive, but he's got the methamphetamine and pot, which do a hell of a lot better jobs."

Carlos would count and classify the pills later, but on impulse Sara opened one of the Zoloft bottles. Without taking them out, she compared the yellow tablets to the drawing in the book. "They match."

Jeffrey opened the next bottle while Sara took the third. He said, "Mine don't."

Sara peered into the bottle. "No," she agreed, opening the top drawer of her desk. She found a pair of tweezers and used them to remove one of the clear capsules. A fine white powder was packed inside. "We can send it off and find out what's in it."

Jeffrey was checking each bottle in turn. "Is there money in the budget for a rush?"

"I don't think we have a choice," Sara told him, slipping the capsule into a small evidence bag. She helped him check the contents of the other bottles, but all of them had some sort of imprint identifying the maker or drug name.

Jeffrey said, "He could be using the capsule shells for other drugs."

"Let's test the unknown ones first," Sara suggested, knowing how expensive a wild-goose chase would be. If they were in Atlanta, she would certainly have the resources, but the budget in Grant County was so tight that some months Sara had to borrow latex gloves from the clinic.

She asked, "Where is Dickson from?"

"Right here," Jeffrey said.

Sara tried her earlier question, thinking Jeffrey was in a better place to talk about it now.

"How did his parents take the news?"

"Better than I thought," Jeffrey said. "I gathered he was a handful."

"Like Andy Rosen," Sara pointed out. She had filled him in on Hare's impression of the Rosen family during the drive back from Atlanta.

"If our only connection here is that we've got two spoiled twenty-something boys, that means half the kids at the school are in danger."

"Rosen was manic-depressive," Sara reminded him.

"Dickson's parents said he wasn't. He never mentioned anything about therapy. As far as they knew, their son was as healthy as a horse."

"Would they have known?"

"They don't seem very involved, but the father made it clear he was paying all the bills. Something like that would have come up."

"He could see someone at the health center on campus for free."

"It might be tricky getting access to clinic documents."

Sara suggested, "You could ask Rosen again."

"I think she's tapped out," Jeffrey told her, a dark expression on his face. "We interviewed the entire dorm, and nobody knew a damn thing about the kid."

"From the smell in his room, I'd guess he spent most of his time there."

"If Dickson was dealing, nobody's going

to admit to knowing him anyway. Every toilet in the dorm started to flush when it got around that we were asking questions."

Sara mulled over what they had. "So both he and Rosen were isolated loner types. Both were into drugs."

"Rosen's tox screen was clear."

"That's hit or miss," Sara reminded him. "The lab only tests for the substances I specify. There are thousands of other drugs he could have used that I just didn't know to screen for."

"I think somebody wiped down Dickson's room."

She waited for him to continue.

"There was a bottle of vodka in the fridge, half full, but no prints. Some beer cans and other stuff had prints from the victim and a couple of latents probably from the store clerk or whoever sold them to him." He paused. "We're gonna try to run the syringe to see what was in it. The one on the floor is pretty trashed. They scraped the wood, but I don't know if they'll be able to get a good sample." He paused again, as if there was something else he did not want to say. "Lena found the syringe."

"How'd that happen?"

"She saw it under the bed."

"Did she touch it?"

"All over."

"Does she have an alibi?"

"I was with Lena all morning," Jeffrey said. "She was with White all night. They alibi each other."

"You don't sound convinced."

"I don't trust either of them right now, especially considering Ethan White's criminal background. You don't wake up one day and stop being a racist. The only thing that ties all of them together, including Tess, is something to do with race."

Sara knew where he was going with this. "We've talked this through already. How would anyone know I was going to bring Tessa to the scene? It's too improbable."

"Lena just keeps popping up too much in this for her to not be a part of it."

Sara knew what he meant. They were having the same problem with Andy Rosen's alleged suicide. Coincidences were seldom really that.

"This White," Jeffrey began, "he's a nasty piece of shit, Sara. I hope you never meet him." His tone turned harsh. "What the hell is she doing with somebody like that?"

Sara sat back in her chair, and she waited for his attention. "Considering what Lena's been through, it's no wonder she's mixed up with someone like Ethan White. He's a dangerous man. I know you keep calling him a kid, but from what you've told me, he doesn't act like a kid. Lena could be attracted to that danger. She's going with the known quantity."

He shook his head, like that was something he could not accept. Sometimes Sara wondered if he knew Lena at all. Jeffrey tended to see people the way he *wanted* to see them rather than the way they really were. This had actually been a running problem in Sara's marriage, and she did not like being reminded of it now.

Sara said, "Except for Ellen Schaffer, this could be a series of coincidences, compounded by you and Lena being in the pissing contest to end all pissing contests." She put her finger to his mouth to shush him. "I know what you're going to say, but you can't deny that there's hostility between you and Lena. As a matter of fact, she could be protecting White just to piss you off."

"It's possible," he agreed, much to her surprise.

Sara sat back in her chair. "Do you really think she's been drinking?" she asked. "Drinking enough to have a problem?"

He shrugged, and Sara was reminded again of how much Jeffrey hated alcoholics. His father had been a violent drunk, and though Jeffrey claimed to have transcended his abusive childhood, Sara knew that an alcoholic could set Jeffrey off more quickly than a murderer could.

Sara said, "Being hungover doesn't mean she has a problem — it just means she had too much to drink one night." Sara let that sink in before continuing. "And what about this?" she asked, paging through the pictures. She showed him the photo of the stomped syringe on the floor.

"I'm pretty sure she didn't do that," he admitted. "Eyeballing the tread with White's shoe, it's almost identical."

"No," Sara said. "You're missing the bigger question. Dickson had two syringes of the purest meth you can buy. If he wanted to kill himself — or if someone wanted to make it look like he killed himself — why not use the second syringe? The meth was so strong that the second dose would have killed him almost instantly."

"Scarfing is a pretty embarrassing way to go," Jeffrey pointed out, using the slang for autoerotic asphyxiation. "Could be somebody who hated him."

"That hook was in the wall a long time," Sara told him, finding the photograph. "The belts show wear patterns to indicate they've been used like this before. The foam would keep the leather from marking his neck. He had it all set up, including the porn on the television." She fanned through the pictures as she talked. "He probably thought he was safe sitting down. Most of these cases are closet rods and chairs that slip out from under their feet." She indicated the prescription bottles. "If he was anorgasmic, he would certainly be looking for a better way to build a mousetrap."

Jeffrey could not let Lena go. "Why would Lena contaminate the scene if she didn't have anything to hide? She never did anything like that before."

Sara could not answer his question. "If White is the perpetrator, what's his motivation for killing Scooter?"

Jeffrey shook his head. "No reason that I can see."

"Drugs?" Sara asked.

"White checks out clean every week as part of his parole, but Lena had some Vicodin in her apartment."

"Did you ask her about it?"

"She said it's for the pain from what happened to her last year."

Unbidden, an image of Lena during the rape exam came to Sara's mind.

Jeffrey said, "She had a valid prescription."

Sara realized she had lost track of the conversation for a moment. She asked, "Schaffer didn't use drugs?"

"No."

"Dickson doesn't sound like an ethnic name."

"Southern Baptist, born and bred."

"He wasn't seeing anyone?"

"Smelling like that?" Jeffrey reminded her.

"Good point." Sara stood, wondering where Brock was. "Can we start? I told Mama I would drive back as soon as I can."

Jeffrey asked, "How's Tessa?"

"Physically? She'll recover." Sara felt herself tearing up. "Don't ask me about the rest, okay?"

"Yeah," he agreed. "Okay."

She opened the door and stepped out into the morgue. "Carlos," she said, "Brock's going to be here soon. You can take your break when he gets here."

Jeffrey seemed curious but did not ask the obvious question. He told Carlos, "Good call on that tattoo. You were right."

Carlos smiled, something he never did when Sara complimented him.

She tied the gown around her waist as she walked over to the lightbox to look at the X rays Carlos had taken of William Dickson. After she was certain she had given each film a thorough review, she walked back to the body.

The scale hanging over the end of the table swayed in the breeze, and even though Carlos never forgot, Sara checked to see that the weight was set back to zero. Brock had said he would be right over, but he had yet to show. Sara did not want to start the formal autopsy until he was gone.

She said, "I'll do a cursory exam before Brock gets here."

She put on a pair of gloves and pulled back the sheet, exposing William Dickson to the harsh overhead lights. A perfect impression of the belt looked painted in black on his neck. His left hand was still wrapped around his penis.

Sara asked Jeffrey, "He was left-handed?"

"Does it matter?"

"Really?" Sara asked, surprised. Granted, she had not given it any thought, but she had always assumed that a man would use his dominant hand.

Jeffrey looked away as she unwrapped

William Dickson's hand from his penis. The fingers remained curled, but the rigor was slowly dissipating in the upper body, where it had first started. The tips of his fingers were dark purple, and his penis showed vividly where his hand had been.

"Ouch," Carlos whispered, and it was the first time he had ever commented on anything Sara had found. He was looking at the pronounced cork-colored bilateral ridges around the testicles.

"Are those knife wounds?" Jeffrey asked.

"It looks more like electrical burns," Sara said, recognizing the color. "Fresh, probably within the last few days. This could explain the electrical cord by the bed." She picked up a swab and pressed it to the burn, rolling off a slick glob that looked like ointment. She sniffed it, saying, "This smells like Vaseline."

Carlos held out a bag for the swab.

Jeffrey asked, "Are you supposed to use that on burns?"

"No, but considering his medicine cabinet, he doesn't strike me as the type to read the directions." She studied the burns. "He could have been using the Vaseline as a lubricant."

Carlos and Jeffrey exchanged a look of disagreement.

Jeffrey said, "He was probably using Tiger Balm. There was a jar of it by the TV."

Sara remembered the jar from the picture, but she had thought nothing of it. "Isn't that for sore muscles?"

Neither one of them answered, so Sara returned to the burns. "He might have been using electrical stimulation to help him reach orgasm."

Jeffrey said, "That's not the first thing that would pop into my mind to take care of that."

"He was shooting pure meth. I doubt he was thinking clearly most of the time." She asked Carlos, "Can you help me turn him over?"

The young man put on a pair of gloves, and they both maneuvered Dickson onto his stomach. There was pronounced lividity on the dead boy's buttocks and a long horizontal mark on his back where he had been leaning up against the bed.

She examined William Dickson from head to toe, not really certain what she was looking for. Finally she found something to remark upon.

"There's scarring around his anus," she told Jeffrey, who was looking at the sinks.

"He was gay?" Jeffrey asked.

"Not necessarily," Sara said, snapping off her gloves. She walked over for a new pair, saying, "There's no telling when or how it was done. Some heterosexual men are into that sort of thing."

Jeffrey squared his shoulders as if to say, *Not this heterosexual man.*

He pointed out, "If he was gay, this could be some kind of hate crime."

"Do you have any other evidence that he was gay?"

"No one is saying anything about him."

"What about the tape he was watching?"

"Straight," Jeffrey conceded.

"You might want to go back and look for something he could use on himself. Considering what else he was into, I wouldn't be surprised if he had an anal plug or —"

Jeffrey stopped her. "Something like a giant red pacifier?"

She nodded and he scowled, probably remembering that he had touched it.

Sara went back to work. She took photographs of what she had found, then asked Carlos to help her turn the body again. Dickson was loosening up, but the rigor still made it awkward.

She repeated the examination on the front of Dickson's body, checking every nook and crevice. His jaw was loose enough for her to force open his mouth and she could not see anything obstructing the airway. The furrow marks around his neck and the petechiae dotting the skin around his bloodshot eyes were all consistent with strangulation.

She told Jeffrey, "Pressure against the carotid arteries, which take oxygenated blood to the brain, would bring about transient cerebral hypoxia. It takes about ten to fifteen seconds before loss of consciousness from the occlusion."

Jeffrey asked, "In English."

"The object is to cut off the blood flow to the head in order to increase the pleasure from masturbation. Either he mistimed it or got carried away or passed out from the loss of blood, or he came down too hard from the meth . . ." Sara let her voice trail off, knowing that Jeffrey was considering all of these things. She said, "I'll check the hyoid and thyroid cartilages when I open the neck, but I doubt they've been crushed. Most of the pressure was on the carotids. I'm telling you, between the hook and the padding on the belt, it looks like he knew what he was doing."

"Looks like," Jeffrey repeated, but Sara could not share his skepticism.

"I guess we can go ahead and start," she

said, thinking the internal examination would give them something more conclusive.

"You don't want to wait for Brock?"

"He's probably been held up," she said. "We'll just start and take a break when he comes."

Sara tapped on the Dictaphone and proceeded with William Dickson's autopsy, calling out the usual findings, examining every organ and every patch of skin under the magnifying glass until she was certain there was nothing else she could do. With the exception of a fatty liver and a softening in the brain consistent with long-term drug use, there was nothing remarkable about the boy other than the way he had died.

She ended the dictation with the same conclusion she had given Jeffrey earlier. "Death is due to the occlusion of the carotid arteries with cerebral hypoxia." She tapped off the mike, removing her gloves.

"Nothing," Jeffrey summarized.

"Nothing," Sara agreed, putting on a fresh pair of gloves. She was sewing the chest together with a standard baseball stitch when the service elevator by the stairs dinged.

Carlos was gone before the doors opened.

"Hey, lady," Brock said, rolling a stainless-steel gurney into the morgue. "Sorry I'm late. Some recently bereaveds showed up I had to deal with. I woulda had Mama call, but you know." He smiled at Jeffrey, then back at Sara, unable to say that he couldn't trust his own mother. "Anyway, I figgered you folks could use the extra time."

"That's fine," Sara assured him, walking toward the freezer.

"I'm not getting this one," Brock said, indicating Dickson. "Parker's over in Madison got 'em." The gurney caught on a broken tile, and Brock stumbled.

Jeffrey asked him, "Can I give you a hand?"

Brock chuckled, righting himself. He said, "I got my license and registration, Chief," as if Jeffrey had pulled him over for a traffic stop.

Sara wheeled out Andy Rosen and started to help Brock transfer the body.

Brock asked, "You need your bag?"

"Just bring it by sometime tomorrow," she told him. Then, thinking of Carlos, she amended, "Actually, do you mind using yours?"

"I'm like the Boy Scouts," he told her, reaching under the gurney and removing a dark green body bag with the Brock and Sons emblem printed in gold across the side.

Sara tugged the zipper while he laid out the bag on his gurney.

"Nice incision," Brock noted. "I can just glue that together and stick some cotton on it, no problem."

"Good," Sara told him, not knowing what else to say.

"Took a look at him yesterday when I was here just to see what the embalming would be like." He gave a resigned sigh. "Guess I can use some putty to patch the head. That sucker'll leak sure as I'm standing here."

Sara stopped what she was doing. "What will leak?"

He pointed to the forehead. "The hole. Thought you saw that, Sara. I'm sorry."

"No," Sara said, grabbing the magnifying glass off the clip. She pushed back Andy Rosen's hair, finding a small puncture wound in the scalp. The body had been sitting for a while, giving the skin time to contract away from the hole. Sara could easily see it without the magnifier.

She said, "I can't believe I missed this."

"You examined his head," Jeffrey told her. "I saw you do it."

"I was so tired last night," she said, thinking that was a poor excuse. "Goddammit."

Brock was visibly shocked by the utterance. Sara knew she should apologize, but she was too angry. The puncture wound on Andy Rosen's forehead was obviously from a needle. Someone had given him an injection in his scalp, hoping the small wound would be hidden by the hair follicles. Had Brock not pointed it out, she would have never seen it.

She told Jeffrey, "I need Carlos. We're going to take blood and tissue samples again."

Jeffrey asked, "Is there any blood left?"

Brock said, "We don't —"

"Of course there is," Sara interrupted. Then, more to herself, she said, "I want to excise this area around his forehead. Who knows what else I missed?"

She took off her glasses, so angry her vision was blurred. "Goddammit," she repeated. "How could I have missed this?"

"I missed it, too," Jeffrey said.

Sara bit her lower lip so that she would not explode. She told Brock, "I need him for at least another hour."

"Uh, yeah," Brock told her, anxious to leave. "Just call me when you're finished."

★ ★ ★

Sara sat at her kitchen counter, staring at the microwave, wondering if she was going to give herself cancer sitting this close to the machine. She was so tired she did not care, and so angry with herself for missing the needle puncture in Andy Rosen's scalp that she almost welcomed the punishment. Three hours of the most intricate physical examination Sara had ever performed in her life had revealed nothing else on Rosen. From there she had performed the same detailed examination on William Dickson's body, making Carlos and Jeffrey follow her every move to triple-check what she was doing.

She had spent another hour with her eyes pressed to the microscope, studying the pieces of Ellen Schaffer's scalp that had been recovered at the scene. By then Jeffrey was able to convince Sara that even if the evidence was not damaged beyond detection, she was too tired to find it. She needed to go home and get some sleep. He had promised that after she got some rest, he would drive her back to the morgue so she could review everything again. The idea had seemed right at the time, but guilt and the need for answers had kept Sara from even thinking about closing her eyes.

She had missed something crucial to the case, and but for Brock, Andy Rosen would have been cremated, destroying all hope of Sara's finding the one thing that would prove he was murdered.

The oven timer beeped, and Sara pulled out the chicken-and-pasta dinner, knowing before she peeled off the film that she would not be able to eat it. Even the dogs turned up their noses at the smell, and she contemplated taking the meal to the outside garbage before laziness won over and she dumped it down the garbage disposal in the sink.

The refrigerator did not have much on offer, except for a tangerine that had shriveled up and glued itself to the glass shelf and two fresh-looking tomatoes of questionable origin. Sara stared blankly into the fridge, debating her options, until her stomach started to grumble. She finally decided and ate a tomato sandwich sitting at the kitchen island so she could look out at the lake. There was a rumble of thunder outside. The storm had followed them back from Atlanta.

Sara noticed the row of plates and glasses sitting in the strainer by the sink where Jeffrey had washed them, and for some silly reason tears came into her eyes.

No amount of flowers or pretty compliments could ever measure up to a man who did housework.

"Oh, me," Sara laughed at herself, wiping her eyes, thinking that sleep deprivation and stress were turning her into a basket case.

She was considering taking a long shower and washing off the day's filth when a sharp knock came at the front door. Sara groaned as she stood, assuming that a well-meaning neighbor was dropping by to get the latest news on Tessa. For a split second she thought about pretending she was not home, but the slim chance of the neighbor's having brought a nice casserole or at least some cake compelled her to answer the door.

"Devon," she said, surprised to see Tessa's boyfriend standing on her front porch.

"Hey," he returned, tucking his hands into his pockets. There was a duffel bag at his feet. "What's the cop for?"

Sara waved at Brad, who'd been parked across the street since she got home. "Long story," she told him, not wanting to bring up Jeffrey's fears.

Devon rested his foot on the duffel bag. "Sara, I —"

"What?" she asked, her heart jumping in her chest as she realized that something must have happened to Tessa. "Is she . . . ?"

"No," Devon assured her, holding out his hands like he might need to catch her if she fainted. "No, I'm sorry. I should have said. She's fine. I just came back to —"

Sara put her hand to her heart. "My God, you scared me to death." She waved him in. "Do you want something to eat? I've only got —" She stopped because he did not follow.

"Sara," Devon began, and then he looked down at the bag. "I got Tessa's things for you. Some things she said she wanted."

Sara leaned up against the open door, a tingling sensation tickling the hairs on the back of her neck. She knew why he was here, what the bag was for. He was leaving Tessa.

She said, "You can't do this to her, Devon. Not now."

"She told me to go," he said.

Sara did not doubt that Tessa had done this, just as she did not doubt that Tessa meant the exact opposite.

"It's the only thing she's said to me in two days." Tears slid down his cheeks. " 'Leave,' just like that. 'Leave.' "

"Devon —"

"I can't stay up there, Sara. I can't see her like this."

"Wait a couple of weeks at least," she said, aware she was begging. No matter what Tessa had told him, Devon's leaving at this point would be devastating.

"I've gotta go," he said, picking up the bag and tossing it into the foyer.

"Wait," Sara said, trying to reason with him. "She only told you to go to make sure you wanted to stay."

"I'm just so tired." He looked over her shoulder, staring blankly down the hall. "I should have my baby right now. I should be taking pictures and passing out cigars."

"Everyone's tired," she told him, thinking she did not have the strength to do this. "Give it some time, Devon."

"You know, you guys are so together. You're up there rallying around and being there for her, and that's great, but —" He stopped, shaking his head. "I don't belong up there. It's like y'all're a wall around her. This thick, impenetrable wall that's protecting her, making her stronger." He stopped again, looking straight at Sara. "I'm not a part of that. I'm never gonna be a part of that."

"You are," she insisted.

"You really think that?"

"Of course I do," Sara told him. "Devon, you've been at every Sunday dinner for the last two years. Tessa adores you. Mama and Daddy treat you like you're their son."

Devon asked, "Did she tell you about the abortion?"

Sara did not know what to say. Tessa had considered having an abortion when she found out she was pregnant, but it had been her choice to keep the child and start a family with Devon.

"Yeah," he said, reading her expression. "I thought so."

"She was confused."

"And you were just moving back from Atlanta," he said. "And she had already broken up with the guy."

Sara had no idea what he was talking about.

"God punishes people," Devon said. "He punishes people when they don't do right by Him."

She said, "Devon, don't say that," but her mind was reeling. Tessa had never told Sara anything about an abortion. Sara reached for his hand, saying, "Come inside. You're not making sense."

"She could've dropped out of college," he said, staying on the porch. "Hell, Sara, you don't need a bachelor's degree to be a plumber. She could have moved back here and raised the kid on her own. It's not like your folks would have disowned her."

"Devon . . . please."

"Don't make excuses for her," he said. "We all live with the consequences of our actions." He gave her a rueful look. "And sometimes other people have to live with them, too."

Devon turned around as Jeffrey's car pulled into the driveway. Sara could see that Devon had parked his van in the street, as though he wanted to make a fast getaway.

"I'll see you around," Devon said, tossing her a wave, like this meant nothing to him.

"Devon," Sara called, walking after him. She followed him into the yard but stopped when he started to jog toward his van. She would not chase him. Sara owed that much to Tessa.

Jeffrey walked up to her, watching Devon leave. "What's wrong?"

"I don't know," she said, but she did. Why had Tessa never told her about the abortion? Had she been feeling guilty all these years, or had Sara just been too involved in her own life at the time to notice what her sister was going through?

Jeffrey led her back to the house, asking, "Did you eat dinner yet?"

She nodded, leaning into him, wishing he could make the last three days go away. She was exhausted, and her heart ached for Tessa, knowing that the abortion was one more time when Sara had not been there for her sister.

"I'm so . . ." She searched for a word, but nothing came to mind that could describe how she felt. Every last bit of life had been drained out of her.

He guided her up the front steps, saying, "You need some sleep."

"No." She stopped him. "I need to go to the morgue."

"Not tonight," he told her, kicking the duffel bag out of the way.

"I have to —"

"You have to sleep," he told her. "You can't even see straight."

She knew he was right, and Sara relented. "I need to take a bath first," she said, thinking of everything she had done at the morgue. "I feel so . . ."

"It's all right," he said, kissing the top of her head.

Jeffrey led her to the bathroom, and Sara stood motionless as he undressed her, then himself. She watched silently as he turned on the water, checking the temperature before helping her into the shower. When he touched her, she felt a familiar reaction, but sex seemed to be the last thing on his mind as he held a washcloth under the stream of warm water.

She stood motionless in the shower, letting him do all the work, relishing the fact that someone else was in charge. Part of Sara felt like she was waking up from a horrible dream, and there was something so restorative about his touch that she started to cry.

Jeffrey noticed the change. "You okay?"

Sara felt overwhelmed with such need that she could not respond to his question. Instead she leaned back, pressing into him, willing Jeffrey to understand how much she needed him. He hesitated, so she moved his hand slowly up her body, cupping her breast, feeling the muscles in his hand flex as his fingers teased out all the right sensations. His other hand cupped her below, and Sara gasped at how good it felt to have part of him inside her. She felt greedy, wanting all of him, but Jeffrey kept the pace slow and sensual, taking his time, touching every part of her with deliberate intention. When Jeffrey finally pressed her back into the cold tiles of the shower, Sara felt alive again, as if she had been in the desert for days and just now found her oasis.

11

"You got it?" Chuck asked for the hundredth time.

"I've got it," Lena snapped, twisting her pocketknife in her right hand while she held the grate for the air vent with her left. A flash of lightning came through the windows, and Lena's shoulders hunched at the sound of thunder that followed. The whole lab lit up like someone had flashed a picture.

"I can get a screwdriver," Chuck said just as the grate came loose.

Lena pulled her Mag-Lite out of her pocket and directed the beam into the air vent.

Some asshole had picked today to leave one of the cages open in the lab. Four mice had escaped, each of them worth more to the school than Lena made in a year, and every available body had been called in to help find them. That had been around noon, and it was after six now, and only two of the beady-eyed fuckers had been found.

Lena had changed her clothes after leaving the station, but the day's search had made her sweaty again. She could feel her shirt clinging to her back, and she was still shaky from the night before. Her head was about to split open, and she had the worst cotton mouth she had ever experienced in her life. A drink would have fixed most of this or at least taken the edge off, but Lena had made a promise to herself sitting in the interrogation room this morning. She was not ever going to touch a drop of alcohol again.

She could see now the mistakes she had made, and most of them were connected to the whiskey. The rest could be directly traced back to Ethan, and for that, she had made another promise: He was out of her life. This had held up for all of two hours. Then Chuck had made Lena answer the phone at the security office. Ethan had been panicked on the other end of the line, his voice squeaking like a girl's, when he told her about finding Scooter. The idiot had even wiped down the room, as if there were not a good explanation for his fingerprints to be in there. As if Lena did not know how to cover her own ass, too.

Outside Scooter's dorm Lena had told Ethan to fuck off, and still he would not leave her alone. He had even volunteered to help look for the missing mice, and for the last six hours he had done everything he could to get her attention. As far as Lena was concerned, she had said everything this morning that she planned on ever saying to Ethan Green or White or whatever the fuck his name was. She was finished with him. If Jeffrey ever let her back on the force, her first priority would be making sure the little asshole was locked up in the nearest jail. Lena would personally throw away the key.

"Stick your head in so you can get a better look," Chuck said, hovering over her like an overbearing mother. As with every other shit job he had Lena do for him, Chuck had plenty of advice on how it should be done and no intention of helping her.

Lena tucked her knife into her pocket and did as she was told, sticking her head into the dusty metal box. She realized too late that her ass was in the air, and she got the unpleasant sensation that Chuck was enjoying the show.

She was about to call him on it when a

very angry voice yelled, "What the hell are we doing about all this? I have important work to do."

Lena banged her head on the vent as she backed out. Brian Keller was standing about two inches from Chuck, his face red with rage.

Chuck said, "We're doing everything we can, Dr. Keller."

Keller did a double take when Lena stood. A lot of the professors who had worked with Sibyl did this, and Lena was used to it.

Lena tossed a wave, making an attempt to be pleasant. Keller had the unfortunate distinction of being in the adjacent lab. The constant noise and interruptions had gotten to him around one o'clock, and he had called off the rest of his classes with a few well-chosen expletives aimed at Chuck. He was the kind of guy Lena could learn to like. Unlike Richard Carter, who chose this moment to pop his head into the classroom.

He said, "How's it going?"

Chuck sniped, "No girls allowed," and Richard batted his eyes, giving him a coquettish look. Chuck was about to say more, but Richard's attention was squarely on Brian Keller.

"Hey, Brian," he said, smiling like a new-born with gas. "I could take over your classes if you want to leave. I'm finished for the day. It's really no trouble."

"Classes were over two hours ago, you idiot," Keller growled.

Richard deflated like a balloon. "I just . . ." he began, an edge of petulance to his tone.

Keller turned on his heel, showing Richard his back as he jabbed his finger at Chuck. "I need to talk to you *right now*. I cannot have these disruptions to my work."

Chuck gave a curt nod, and passed on the ass-chewing to Lena before leaving with Keller. "Don't leave until you've searched that vent thoroughly, Adams."

Lena mumbled, "Jerk," as they both left the room. She expected Richard to voice his agreement, but the man looked stricken.

She asked, "What?" but Richard was already talking over her.

"I am a colleague in this department," he hissed, his jaw clenched so tight she was surprised he could speak. He pointed his finger at the empty doorway. "He has no right to talk to me that way in front of other people. I deserve — I have *earned* — at least a modicum of respect from that man."

"Okay," she said, wondering why he was so ticked. From what she had gathered, Brian Keller talked to everybody the same way.

"He has a class tonight," Richard said. "I was offering to take his night class."

"Uh," Lena began. "I think he canceled it."

Richard stared at the doorway like a pit bull waiting for an intruder. Lena had never seen him mad before. His eyes bulged and his whole face was red except for his thin, white lips, which were pressed together in a straight line. She did not know whether to back away or laugh.

She said, "Lookit, fuck him," and wondered if that was what the real problem was. While it did not say much about Richard's taste in potential sexual partners, it would explain a lot about his current behavior.

He jabbed his hands into his hips. "I don't have to take that kind of treatment. Not from him. We are equals in this department and I will not tolerate that sort of —"

She tried again. "Come on, the guy just lost his son."

Richard dismissed this with a brusque wave of his hand. "All I ask is to be treated like an adult. Like a human being."

Lena didn't have time for this, but she knew Richard would never leave if she did not find some sympathy for him. "You're right. He's a prick."

Richard finally looked at her, then did a double take. His question surprised her, though it shouldn't have. "Who hit you?"

"What?" she asked, but she knew he meant the cut under her eye. "No. I fell. I hit it on the door. I was just being stupid." The urge to offer more excuses overwhelmed her, but Lena made herself stop. She knew from being a cop that liars had a hard time shutting up. Still, she could not help but add, "It's nothing."

He gave her a sly wink, letting her know he wasn't buying it. His whole attitude from before with Keller was changed when he said, "You know, I've always felt close to you, Lena. Sibyl talked about you all the time. She saw all the good in you."

Lena cleared her throat but said nothing.

"All she ever wanted to do was help you. To make you happy. That's all that mattered in the world to her."

Lena felt an uncomfortable tingling in the soles of her feet. "Yeah," she said, hoping he would move on.

"What happened to your eye?" he pressed,

but his tone was gentle. "It looks like someone hit you."

"No one hit me," she countered, aware she was talking more loudly than was necessary: another common mistake with liars. Inwardly, she cursed herself. She used to be good at this.

"If you ever wanted help . . ." He let his words trail off, probably realizing how stupid his offer sounded to someone like Lena. He changed tactics. "If you ever want to talk about anything. Believe it or not, I know how you feel."

"Yeah," she said, but the pope would be scrambling eggs in hell before Lena ever confided in Richard Carter.

He slid up onto one of the lab tables, his feet dangling over the side. From the concerned look he gave her, she expected him to renew his offer, but he asked instead, "Did y'all find out who opened the cages?"

"No," Lena said. "Why?"

"I heard that a couple of sophomores were late on some class projects, so they created a . . . diversion."

Lena gave a disgusted laugh. "I wouldn't be surprised."

"Hey, I'm supposed to have dinner with Nan tonight," he said. "Why don't you come along? It'll be fun."

"I've got work to do," Lena told him. Then, to emphasize this, she opened her knife.

"Lord A'mighty." Richard slid off the table to get a better look. "What do you need that for?"

She was about to say it was a good way of getting rid of annoying people who wouldn't mind their own business when his cell phone started to ring. Richard fumbled in the pockets of his lab coat before finding it. He looked at the screen, a huge smile breaking out on his face.

He told Lena, "I'll catch up with you later. We can talk more about this." He touched the skin under his eye, letting her know what he meant.

She wanted to tell him not to bother, but settled on, "See you around." It was a waste of her breath anyway. Richard scooted out of the classroom before she had time to finish the sentence.

Lena went back to the vent, using the knife to twist the screws back in. Chuck was right, this would have gone a lot faster with a screwdriver, but she did not want to have to ask for one. She was the only person in the room, and this was the first time all day she'd had any time alone. What she really needed to think about was how she was going to get back into Jeffrey's good graces.

She had tried to hand him Chuck on a silver platter, but Jeffrey had completely missed her meaning. So Chuck was at a golf tournament last weekend. He could still be involved in some kind of drug-trafficking scheme at school. Scooter had made it clear the security office was involved. Chuck was not a complete idiot. Even he couldn't miss that kind of action going on right under his nose. Knowing Chuck, though, Lena was sure he was not directly involved. It was more his style to sit on his fat ass and demand a cut of the profits.

Thunder rolled again, and Lena was so startled that the knife slipped, slicing the side of her left index finger. She hissed a curse, untucking her shirt so she could wrap the excess material around the cut. Chuck promised every month to order her an extra-small uniform, but he never did. The baggy clothes were just another trick he had to make her feel like she did not belong.

"Lena."

She did not look up. Even though Lena had only known him for less than a week, she recognized Ethan's voice.

She squeezed the shirt around her finger, trying to stop the bleeding. The wound ran deep, and blood quickly soaked the material. At least she had cut the same hand that was already injured. Maybe she could get a two-for-one if she went to the hospital.

As if she had not heard him, Ethan repeated, "Lena."

"I told you I don't want to talk to you."

"I'm worried about you."

"You don't know me well enough to worry about me." Lena refused the hand he offered as she stood. "Remember? It's not like we're gonna have to get married."

Ethan looked contrite. "I shouldn't have said that."

Lena dropped her hand to the side, feeling blood rush to the cut. "I really don't give a flying fuck what you said."

"You don't have to be embarrassed about last night."

"You're the one who grunts like a pig when he comes." She grabbed his arm and pushed his sleeve up before he could stop her.

He jerked away, sliding his sleeve back down, but she had seen a tattoo of barbed wire circling his wrist and something that looked like a soldier with a rifle on his arm.

"What's that?" she asked.

"It's just a tattoo."

"A tattoo of a soldier," she clarified. "I know about you, Ethan. I know what you're into."

He stood completely still, a deer caught in the headlights. "I'm not that person anymore."

"Yeah?" She pointed to her eye. "Which person did this?"

"It was just a reaction, a gut reaction," he said. "I don't like being hit."

"Well, who the hell does?"

"It's not like that, Lena. I'm trying to straighten myself out here."

"How's your parole working for you?"

That threw him off. "Did you talk to Diane?"

Lena did not answer, but a smile played at her lips. She knew Diane Sanders well. Finding out the rest of Ethan's history would be a cinch.

She asked, "What were you doing in Scooter's room this morning?"

"I wanted to see if he was okay."

"Yeah, you're such a good pal."

"He had a lot of meth," Ethan said. "He doesn't know when to stop."

"He's not in control like you are."

He did not take the bait. "You've got to

believe me, Lena. I didn't have anything to do with this."

"Well, you'd better find a convincing alibi, Ethan, because Andy Rosen and Ellen Schaffer were Jews, and Tessa Linton was screwing a black man —"

"I didn't know —"

"Doesn't matter, sport," she told him. "You've got a bull's-eye painted on your chest because of that shit you pulled with Jeffrey. I told you to stay out of it."

"I am out of it," he said. "That's why I moved here, to get away from it."

"You moved here because the friends you sent to jail were probably looking to settle some scores."

"I'm even with them," he said, his tone bitter. "I told you I got out, Lena. You think that didn't have a price?"

"I guess your girlfriend was the price?" she said. "And now you're sniffing around me, a spick. Is that what you and your buddies call it? Wetback?" She paused for effect. "Or is it my dyke sister you want to talk about? Or her lover, the bush-whacking school librarian?" She laughed at his reaction. "I wonder what the folks back home would think about all that, Ethan *White*."

"It's Green," he told her. "Zeek White is

my stepdad. My real dad walked out on us." His voice was firm, insistent. "I'm Ethan Green, Lena. Ethan Green."

"What you are is in my way," she told him. "Move."

"Lena," he said, and there was a desperation in his tone that made her look in his eyes. Since the attack she had made a habit of avoiding people. Lena realized she had never really looked into Ethan's eyes, even when she was touching him last night. They were a startling clear blue, and she imagined that if she got close enough, she would be able to see the ocean in them.

He said, "I'm not that person anymore. You have to believe me."

She stared at him, wanting to know why he cared.

"Lena, we've got something going here."

"No we don't," she said, but not with as much conviction as she wanted.

He tucked her hair behind her ear, then gently traced his finger over the cut under her eye. He said, "I never wanted to hurt you."

She cleared her throat. "Well, you did."

"I promise you — promise — it'll never happen again."

She wanted to tell him that he would never have the opportunity, but she could not look away from him, could not break the spell.

He smiled, probably seeing the impact his words were having. "You know, I haven't even kissed you," he said, tracing her lips with his fingers. Parts of Lena she thought were dead reacted to his touch, and she felt tears come to her eyes. She had to stop this now before it got out of hand. She had to do something to get him out of her life.

"Please," he said, a smile tugging at his lips. "Let's just start over."

She said the one thing she knew would stop him. "I want to be a cop again."

He jerked his hand away as if she had spit at him.

She told him, "It's who I am."

"It's not," he insisted. "I know who you are, Lena, and you're not a cop."

Chuck came back, hitching his belt so that his keys rattled. She was so relieved to see him that she smiled.

"What?" Chuck said, suspicious.

Ethan told Lena, "I'll talk to you later."

"Okay," she said, dismissing him.

He did not move to leave. "I'll talk to you later."

"All right," she agreed, thinking she would say anything to get him out of this room. "We'll talk later. I promise. Go."

He finally left, and Lena looked down at the floor, trying to regain control of herself. She saw blood on the floor. The cut on her finger was dripping like a leaky spigot.

Chuck crossed his fat arms over his chest. "What was that all about?"

"None of your business," she answered, smearing the blood on the floor with her shoe.

"You're on the clock, Adams. Don't steal my time."

"I'm getting overtime now?" she asked, which was bullshit. The college made everyone take comp time, and Chuck conveniently forgot when Lena was owed.

She showed him her finger. "I need to go back to the office and take care of this."

"Let me see it," he said, like she might be faking.

"It's practically to the bone," she told him, peeling off the shirt. Pinpricks of pain made her hand feel hot and cold at the same time. "It might need stitches."

"It doesn't need stitches," he said, like she was being a big baby. "Go back to the office. I'll be there in a few minutes."

Lena left the lab before he could change his mind or realize that the huge white box bolted to the wall that said FIRST AID might at least have a Band-Aid in it.

The rain that had been threatening to fall all week broke as soon as Lena was halfway across the quad. Wind kicked up so hard that the rain blew sideways, slicing into her face like tiny slivers of glass. She kept her eyes closed to slits, her hand a few inches in front of her, trying to see her way to the security office.

After she had spent five minutes looking for her key and trying to work it into the lock, the door finally opened, blowing back on its hinges. Lena grabbed the knob and braced her feet as she pulled the door closed.

She flipped the light switch several times, but the power was out.

Muttering a curse, Lena pulled out her flashlight and used it to find the first-aid box. When she did, the damn thing would not open, and she had to use the long side of her ankle knife to pry up the plastic lid. Her hand was so slippery that the knife popped out of her hand, and the contents of the kit clattered to the floor.

She used her flashlight to find the things she needed, leaving the rest on the floor. Chuck could clean it up if it bothered him that much. Hell, he probably had enough cash coming through here every week to pay someone to clean the office himself.

Lena hissed out a "Shit" between her teeth as she poured alcohol on the open cut. Blood pooled with the alcohol onto the desk. She tried to use her sleeve to wipe it off, but that only made things worse.

"Fuck it," she muttered.

A poncho was in her locker, but Lena had never used it. The collar only had snaps on one side, a manufacturing defect that Chuck had not considered a problem when Lena had pointed it out to him. Of course, Chuck's poncho was fine, and Lena decided she would borrow it to walk home in.

Chuck's locker jimmied open with a couple of tugs on the latch. The raincoat was still in its plastic pack on the top shelf, but Lena decided to take advantage of the situation and search his locker.

Aside from a scuba-diving magazine, which seemed to be more about the half-naked models sporting the latest in thigh-baring rubber diving suits, and an unopened box of Powerbars, there was nothing of interest. She grabbed the poncho and was about to close the locker when the door blew open and Chuck walked in.

"What the fuck are you doing?" he demanded, crossing the room more quickly than she thought him capable of. He slammed his locker closed so hard it popped back open.

"I wanted to borrow your poncho."

"You've got your own," he said, snatching it out of her hand and tossing it onto his desk.

She said, "I told you there's something wrong with mine."

"I think there's something wrong with you, Adams."

Lena was aware that he was standing way too close to her. She took a step back just as the power came back on. The fluorescent light flickered, casting a shadowy gray light over them. Even in the partial light, she could see that Chuck was ready for a fight.

Lena went to her locker. "I'll use my own."

Chuck leaned his ass on the desk. "Fletcher called in sick. I need you to work the night shift."

"No way," Lena protested. "I should've been off two hours ago."

"That's the way it is, Adams," he said. "Tough."

Lena opened her locker and stared at the

contents, not recognizing anything.

"What are you doing?" Chuck asked, slamming the locker closed.

Lena jerked back her hand so it would not get smashed in the door. She had opened Fletcher's locker by mistake. Two Baggies were on the top shelf, and Lena could guess what was in them. They were so sure they would not get caught that they were just leaving the shit lying around.

"Adams?" Chuck repeated. "I asked you a question."

"Nothing," she said, thinking there was a reason Fletcher never reported any incidents on his night log. He was too busy selling dope to kids.

"All right," Chuck said, probably thinking she had acquiesced. "I'll see you in the morning. Call me if you need me."

"No," Lena said, picking up his poncho. "I told you I'm not doing it, Chuck. You're just going to have to work for a change."

"What the hell does that mean?"

Lena snapped out the coat and wrapped it around her. The extra-large was enormous, but she did not care. The storm was still raging, but, knowing her luck, it would pass as soon as she got home. She would have to find some way to secure the door to her apartment. Jeffrey had busted the lock this morning when he barged in. God only knew if the hardware store would still be open.

Chuck said, "Where are you going, Adams?"

"I'm not working tonight," she told him. "I need to go home."

"Bottle calling you, huh?" Chuck asked, a nasty smile twisting his lips.

She realized he was blocking the door. "Get out of my way."

"I could stick around for a while if you want," Chuck told her, and there was a glint in his eyes that put Lena on alert.

"I've got a bottle in my desk drawer," he said. "Maybe we could sit down and get to know each other a little better."

"You have *got* to be kidding."

"You know," Chuck began, "you'd be kind of pretty if you put some makeup on and did something with your hair."

He reached out to touch her, and she moved her head away. "Get the fuck away from me," she ordered.

"I guess you don't need this job as bad as you say," he said, that same nasty look on his face.

Lena bit her bottom lip, feeling the sting of his threat.

"I read about what that guy did to you,"

he said. "In the paper."

Her heart thumped over in her chest. "So did everyone else."

"Yeah, but I read it more than once."

"Your lips must've gotten really tired."

"Let's see if yours can," he said, and before she knew what was happening, he had wrapped his big hand around the back of her head and jerked her down toward his crotch.

Lena balled her hand into a fist and punched him between the legs with all her strength. He groaned and fell to the floor.

Lena's door opened before she reached her room.

"Where have you been?" Ethan demanded.

Her teeth were chattering. She was so wet that her clothes were chafing her as she walked. She did not care how Ethan had gotten into her apartment or what he was doing here. She walked straight to the kitchen to get herself a drink.

"What happened?" Ethan asked. "Lena, what happened?"

Her hands were shaking too much to pour the drink, and he took over for her, filling up the shot glass to the rim. He held the glass to her mouth the same way she had done for him the night before. She drank it all down in one gulp.

Ethan's tone was soft. "Are you okay?"

She shook her head, trying to pour another drink even as her stomach clenched. Chuck had touched her. He had put his hand on her.

"Lena?" Ethan asked, taking the glass from her. He poured another drink, this one a little less generous, and handed it to her.

Lena swallowed it down, her throat clenching. She put her hands on the edge of the kitchen sink, trying to control the emotions that were welling up.

"Baby," Ethan said. "Talk to me."

He stroked her hair back from her face, and Lena felt the same revulsion Chuck had inspired earlier.

"No," she said, swatting him away. The effort from speaking made her start coughing, her airway seizing up as if she were being strangled.

"Come on," Ethan said, rubbing her back with the palm of his hand.

"How many times," Lena began, her voice straining in her chest, "do I have to tell you not to touch me?" On this last part she jerked away from him.

"What is *wrong* with you?" Ethan demanded.

"Why are you here?" she shot back, feeling violated all over again. "What the fuck makes you think you have a right to be here?"

"I wanted to talk to you."

"About what?" she asked. "About that girl you beat to death?"

He stood completely still, but she could see every muscle in his body tense. Lena wanted to make him feel the way Chuck had made her feel, like he was trapped. Like he had nowhere to go.

He said, "I explained what —"

"You just stayed in the truck, huh?" she asked, walking around him. He was like a statue in the middle of the room. "Did that give you a good view?" she asked. "Could you see them fucking her, beating the shit out of her?"

"Don't do this," he warned, his voice as cold as steel.

"Or what?" she asked, managing to laugh. "Or you're gonna do the same thing to me?"

"I didn't do anything." His muscles were still tensed, his jaw clenched tight like it was taking every ounce of his self-control to remain calm.

"You didn't rape that girl?" Lena asked. "You stayed in the truck, all innocent, while your buddies got a nut off?"

She pushed his shoulder, but it was like pushing a mountain; he did not move.

"You get hard watching them?" she asked. "Huh, Ethan? Did it turn you on watching her suffer, watching her realize there was nothing she could do but get screwed?"

"No."

She asked, "What was it like sitting there, knowing she was gonna die? Did you like that, Ethan?" She pushed his shoulder again. "Did you get out of your truck and join in? Did you hold her arms still while they fucked her? Did you fuck her? Were you the one who ripped her open? Did the blood turn you on?"

He warned her again. "You don't want to do this, Lena."

"Let's see what you've got under here," she said, snatching at his shirt. He did it himself, ripping off the black T-shirt. Lena's mouth dropped open when she saw the large tattoos covering his torso.

He roared, "Is this what you wanted? Is this what you wanted to see, you bitch?"

She slapped him, and when he did not respond, she slapped him again, then again. She slapped him until he threw her into the wall and they both fell onto the floor.

They struggled, but he was stronger,

pushing himself on top of her, yanking down her pants, his fingernails digging into her stomach. Lena screamed, but he put his mouth over hers, jamming his tongue so far down her throat that she gagged. She tried to knee him in the groin, but he was too fast, pushing her thighs apart with his knees. With one hand he kept both of her arms pinned over her head, nailing her wrists to the floor, trapping her.

"Is this what you want?" he screamed, spit flying out of his mouth.

Ethan reached down and unzipped his pants. She felt dizzy and sick, and everything she saw was washed in red. She gasped, tensing when he entered her, tightening herself against him.

Ethan stopped midthrust, holding himself inside her, his lips parted in surprise.

She could feel his breath on her face and the pain in her wrists where he rested his weight on her hands. None of this meant anything to her. She felt it all, and she felt nothing.

Lena looked into his eyes — deep into his eyes — seeing the ocean. She moved her hips slowly, letting him feel how wet she was, how much her body wanted him.

He shook from the effort of remaining still. "Lena . . ."

"Shh . . . ," she hushed.

"Lena . . ."

His Adam's apple moved, and she put her lips to it, kissing it, sucking it. She moved up to his mouth, giving him a hard, probing kiss.

He tried to let go of her wrists, but she grabbed his hand, keeping herself pinned.

He begged her, like that would work again. "Please . . . ," he said. "Not like this . . ."

She closed her eyes, arching her body up to his, pulling him in deeper.

Wednesday

12

Kevin Blake paced around his office, glancing at his watch every two minutes. "This is horrible," he said. "Just horrible."

Jeffrey shifted in his chair, trying to act like he was paying attention. Thirty minutes ago Jeffrey had told Blake that Andy Rosen and Ellen Schaffer were murdered, and the dean had not shut up since. The man had not asked one question about the students or the investigation. His sole focus was on what this would mean for the school and, by extension, him.

Blake threw his hands into the air with a great sense of drama. "I don't have to tell you, Jeffrey, but this is the sort of scandal that can break the school."

Jeffrey thought that it would not be the end of Grant Tech so much as the end of Kevin Blake's tenure there. As good as the dean was at shaking hands and asking for money, Kevin Blake was a little too good-ol'-boy to be running a school like Grant Tech. His golf weekends and annual fund-raisers worked for the most part, but Blake was not aggressive enough to seek new sources of funding for research. Jeffrey would have placed a sizable bet on Blake's getting ousted in at least a year, replaced by some energetic but mature woman who would drag the school into the twenty-first century.

"Where is that idiot?" Blake asked, meaning Chuck Gaines. Chuck was at least ten minutes late for their seven o'clock meeting. "I've got important things to do."

Jeffrey did not express his own feelings on the matter, which were that he could have spent the extra half hour in bed with Sara instead of waiting around in Blake's office for a meeting that would be as tedious as it was unproductive. He had a lot to do today, primarily following up with Brian Keller.

Jeffrey offered, "I can go look for him."

"No," Blake said, plucking a glass golf ball off his desk. He tossed it into the air and caught it. Jeffrey made a noise like he was impressed, but he had never understood golf and did not have the patience to learn.

"Played in the tournament this weekend," Blake said.

"Yeah," Jeffrey answered. "I saw it in the paper." That must have been the right answer, because Blake's face lit up. "Shot two under par. Beat the pants off Albert."

"That's great," Jeffrey said, thinking it was probably not wise to beat the president of the bank at anything, let alone golf. Of course, Blake had the upper hand with Albert Gaines. He could always fire Chuck and make his daddy have to find him another job.

"I'm sure Jill Rosen will be glad to hear this get out."

"Why is that?" Jeffrey asked, thinking there was something spiteful about the way Kevin said the woman's name.

"Did you see the write-up in the paper? 'College Psych Can't Throw Her Son a Rope.' For God's sake, how tacky, but still . . ."

"Still what?"

"Oh, nothing." He grabbed a club out of the bag in the corner. "Brian Keller made overtures about resigning the other day."

"That so?" Jeffrey asked.

Blake gave an exasperated sigh, twisting the club in his hand. "He's sucked on the university tit for twenty years, and now that he's finally come up with something that might make the school some money, he's talking about resigning."

"Doesn't the research belong to the school?"

Blake snorted at Jeffrey's ignorance. "He can lie his way out of that, and even if he can't, all he needs is a good lawyer, which I'm sure any pharmaceutical company in the world would be able to provide."

"What's he come up with?"

"An antidepressant."

Jeffrey thought of William Dickson's medicine cabinet. "There are tons of those already on the market."

"This is hush-hush," Blake said, lowering his voice even though they were alone in his office. "Brian's been playing this real close to his chest." He gave another laugh. "Probably so he can bargain his way into a bigger share, the greedy bastard."

Jeffrey waited for him to answer the question.

"It's a pharmacological cocktail with an herbal base. That's the marketing key — make people think it's good for them. Brian claims it has zero side effects, but that's bullshit. Even aspirin has side effects."

"His son didn't take it?"

Blake looked alarmed. "You didn't find a

patch on Andy, did you? Like one of those Nicotine-control patches? That's how it's delivered, through the skin."

"No," Jeffrey admitted.

"Phew." Blake wiped his forehead with the back of his hand to exaggerate his relief. "They're not ready for human testing, but Brian was in D.C. a couple of days ago showing his data to the big boys. They were ready to cut the check right then and there." Blake lowered his voice. "Truth be told, I took Prozac myself a couple of years back. Couldn't tell it made a damn bit of difference."

"How about that," Jeffrey said, his standard answer-without-giving-an-answer.

Blake leaned over the club, as if he were on the golf course instead of standing in the middle of his office. "He didn't say anything about Jill leaving with him, though. I wonder if there are problems."

"What kind of problems would there be?"

Blake swung the club in a wide arc, then stared out the window like he was following the ball.

"Kevin?"

"Oh, she just takes a lot of time off." He turned back to Jeffrey, leaning on the club. "I don't think a year has gone by since Jill got here that she hasn't used every last one of her sick days. And vacation days. We've had to dock her pay more than once for taking too much time."

Jeffrey could take a good guess as to why Jill Rosen needed to stay home some days, but he did not share that with Kevin Blake.

Blake looked out the window, lining up another imaginary shot. "She's either some kind of hypochondriac or allergic to work."

Jeffrey shrugged, waiting for him to continue.

"She got her degree about ten, fifteen years ago," Blake said. "One of those late bloomers. You see that a lot these days. The kids get a little older, and Mommy gets bored, so she takes some classes at the local school, and next thing you know she's working there." He winked at Jeffrey. "Not that we don't appreciate the extra money. Continuing ed has been the backbone of our night school for years."

"I didn't know you offered that kind of training here."

"She got her master's in family therapy from Mercer," Blake said. "Her doctorate is in English lit."

"Why didn't she teach?"

"We've got more than enough English teachers. You can't shake a tree without six of them dropping down and wanting tenure. It's science and math teachers we need. English professors are a dime a dozen."

"How'd she get hired at the clinic?"

"Frankly, we needed more women on staff, and when the position opened up for a counselor, she went through the licensing to become a therapist. It's worked out well." He frowned, adding, "When she shows up to work."

"What about Keller?"

"Welcomed with open arms," Blake said, opening his arms to illustrate. "He came from the private sector, you know."

"No," Jeffrey answered. "I didn't know." Generally, professors left colleges to go to the private sector, where more money and status awaited them. He had never heard of a professor going backward, and he said this to Kevin Blake.

"We lost half our faculty in the early eighties. They all fled to the big companies." Blake took a swing, then groaned, as if the shot had gone wide. He leaned on his club again and looked at Jeffrey. "Of course, most of them came crawling back a few years later when their jobs were cut."

"What company was he with?"

"You know, I don't recall," Blake answered, taking the club in hand. "I remember shortly after he left, they were bought out by Agri-Brite."

"Agri-Brite, the agricultural firm?"

"That's right," Blake answered, taking another swing with the club. "Brian could have made a fortune. Oh" — he went to his desk and picked up his gold Waterman pen — "that reminds me. I should give them a call and see if they're interested in touring the university." He pressed a button on his phone. "Candy?" he said, calling his secretary. "Can you get me the number for Agri-Brite?"

He smiled at Jeffrey. "I'm sorry. What were you saying?"

Jeffrey stood, thinking he had wasted enough time. "I'll go look for Chuck."

"Good idea," Blake said, and Jeffrey left the office quickly, before he could change his mind.

Candy Wayne was typing on her computer outside Blake's office, but she stopped when Jeffrey walked by. "You leaving already, Chief? That's the shortest meeting I think he's had since he got here."

"Is that a new perfume?" he asked, giving her a smile. "You smell as pretty as a rose garden."

She laughed, tossing back her hair. This might have been attractive on a woman who was not on the tail-end side of seventy, but as it was, he worried she might throw out her shoulder.

"You old dog," she said, every line in her face gathering into a smile of sheer delight. Blake probably resented the hell out of the fact that he could not hire a twenty-year-old slut to take his dictation, but Candy had been at the school longer than anyone could remember. The alumni board would get rid of Blake before they let him get rid of Candy. Jeffrey had a similar situation with Marla Simms at the station, though he was more than happy to keep the older woman around.

Candy asked, "What can I do you for, hon?"

Jeffrey leaned on her desk, careful not to knock over the thirty or so framed pictures of her great-grandchildren. "Now, why would you think I want something?"

"Because you always want something when you're being nice," she said, then pouted her lips. "But it's never the right thing."

He tried the smile again, knowing it worked no matter what she said. "Can I get the number for Agri-Brite?"

She turned back to the computer, all business. "Which department?"

"Who would I need to talk to about someone who worked at one of their other companies about twenty years ago?"

"Which company?"

"That I don't know," Jeffrey admitted. "Brian Keller worked there."

"Why didn't you say so?" she asked, giving a sly smile. "Hold on a sec." She rose from her desk, surprisingly spry in her tight velour miniskirt and Lycra top. She walked across the room in high heels that would have broken a lesser woman's ankles, flicking back her platinum white hair as she pulled open one of the file drawers. She was not overweight by any means, but a flap of skin under her arm jiggled as she ran her finger along a series of folders.

She said, "Here you go," pulling out a file.

"That's not on computer?" he asked, walking over to see what she had.

"Not what you want," she told him, handing him a sheet of paper.

He read Keller's employment application, which had Candy's notes neatly written in the margin. Jericho Pharmaceuticals was the name of the company that had been sucked into Agri-Brite, and

Candy had spoken with Monica Patrick, the then head of personnel, to verify Keller's employment and make sure he was not leaving in disgrace.

Jeffrey said, "He was at a pharmaceutical company?"

"Assistant to the assistant director of research," she told him. "He made a lateral move salary-wise to come here."

"He could have made more money if he'd stayed."

"Who knows?" she said. "Those big-time mergers back in the eighties cut off everybody at the knees." She shrugged. "Some might say he was smart getting out when he did. Nothing rewards mediocrity like the world of education."

"You'd call him mediocre?"

"He hasn't exactly set the world on fire."

Jeffrey read aloud from Keller's typed comments, " 'It is my desire to get back to the fundamentals of scientific research. I am tired of the backbiting corporate world.' "

"So he came to a university." She laughed long and hard. "Ah, the ignorance of youth."

"How can I get in touch with this Monica Patrick?"

Candy put her finger to her lip, thinking.

"I don't guess she's still there. When I talked to her, she sounded old as the hills." The look she gave Jeffrey told him to keep his mouth closed. "I bet I could make a couple or three phone calls and find a current number for you."

"Oh, I can't let you do that," Jeffrey offered, hoping she would.

"Nonsense," she said. "You don't know how to talk to these corporate muckety-mucks. You'd be as helpless as a one-legged man in a butt-kicking contest."

"You're probably right," Jeffrey allowed. Then, "Not that I don't appreciate it, but —"

Candy looked over her shoulder to check that Blake's office door was still closed. "Between you and me, I never liked the man."

"Why is that?"

"Something about him," she said. "I can't put my finger on it, but I learned a long time ago that first impressions are generally right, and my first impression of Brian Keller was that he was a creep who couldn't be trusted."

"What about his wife?" Jeffrey asked, thinking he should have talked to Candy yesterday.

"Well," she began, tapping a finely manicured finger to her lip, "I don't know. She's stayed with him this long. Maybe there's something about him that I'm just not seeing."

"Maybe," Jeffrey said. "But I think I'll trust your instincts. We both know you're the smartest person here."

"And you are the devil," she said, though he could tell she was pleased with the characterization. "If I was forty years younger . . ."

"You wouldn't give me the time of day," he told her, kissing her cheek. "Let me know when you track down that number."

She either gave a low purr or cleared something in her throat. "Will do, Chief. Will do."

He left before she said something that embarrassed them both, taking the stairs instead of waiting for the elevator. The distance between the administration building to the security office was a short one, but Jeffrey made it a stroll. He had not been for a run in almost a week, and his body felt sluggish, his muscles tight and strained. The storm last night had done some damage, debris scattered all over the quad. Campus maintenance people were mulling around, picking up trash, pressure-washing the sidewalk with enough bleach in the mixture to make Jeffrey's nose burn. They were smart to clear up the areas around the main buildings first, where people who would complain about the mess were most likely to work.

Jeffrey pulled out his notebook, reading through his notes, trying to figure out how his day would best be spent. The only thing he could do at this point was talk to more parents and recanvass the dorms. He wanted to talk to Monica Patrick, if she was still alive, before he went back at Brian Keller. People did not leave high-paying jobs in the private sector to take a pay cut and teach. Maybe Keller had falsified data or taken one too many shortcuts. Jeffrey would ask Jill Rosen why her husband had left his job. She had talked about re-building her life. Perhaps she had done it once before and knew how hard it would be to do again. Even if she could not offer any new information, Jeffrey wanted to talk to the woman and see if there was anything he could do to help her get away.

Jeffrey tucked his notebook into his pocket as he opened the door to the security office. The hinges squeaked loudly, but he barely heard them.

"Damn," Jeffrey whispered, looking over his shoulder to see if anyone was watching.

Chuck Gaines was lying on the floor, the soles of his shoes facing the door. His neck was wide open like a second mouth, what was left of the esophagus lolling out like another tongue. Blood was everywhere — on the walls, the floor, the desk. Jeffrey looked up, but there was no blood on the ceiling. Chuck had been leaning down when he was cut, or maybe sitting at the desk. The chair had been knocked on its side.

Jeffrey knelt down so he could see under the desk without contaminating the scene. He saw the glint of a long hunting knife under the chair.

"Damn," he repeated, this time with more passion. He knew that knife. It belonged to Lena.

Frank looked mad as hell, and Jeffrey could not blame him.

"This isn't her," Frank said.

Jeffrey drummed his fingers on the steering wheel. They were sitting outside Lena's dorm, trying to decide the best way to do this.

"You saw the knife, Frank."

Frank shrugged. "Big deal."

"Chuck's throat was sliced open."

Frank blew out air between his teeth.

"Lena's not a murderer."

"This could tie back to Tessa Linton."

"How? The kid was with us when it happened. She chased the fucker into the woods."

"And lost him."

"Matt didn't think she was slowing down."

"She did when she twisted her ankle."

Frank shook his head. "The White kid — him I could see."

"She might have recognized him in the forest and tripped on purpose so he'd get away."

Frank kept shaking his head. "This is not the kind of thing I signed up for."

Jeffrey wanted to tell him that he was not crazy about it himself, but instead he said, "You saw the knife she's been carrying on her ankle. Are you telling me it's not like the one we found under the desk?"

"It could be a different one."

Jeffrey reminded him of the forensic evidence that had brought them here. "Her fingerprints are on the knife, Frank. In blood. She was either there when he was cut and touched the knife, or she was holding it when it happened. There's no other explanation."

Frank stared out at the building, not

blinking. Jeffrey could tell he was trying to figure out how this could not be Lena. Jeffrey had had the same reaction less than half an hour ago when the computer had made a positive match on three of the prints. Even then Jeffrey had pulled the card and made the tech do the comparison point by point.

Jeffrey looked up as a professor came out of the dorm. "She hasn't left all morning?"

Frank shook his head.

"Give me a good explanation for her fingerprints being stamped on that knife in blood and we'll drive away right now."

Frank's mouth set in an angry line. He had been sitting in front of the dorm for a good hour, probably trying to think of anything that would exonerate Lena.

"This ain't right," he said, but, without anything further, he opened the car door and got out.

The faculty dorm was fairly deserted, most of the professors already at classes. Like most colleges, things slowed down toward the end of the week, and with the Easter holiday coming up, a lot of kids had already left for home. Jeffrey and Frank did not see anyone as they walked down the hallway toward Lena's room. They stood outside the door, and Jeffrey could see that the knob was cockeyed from when they had kicked it in yesterday morning. If Jeffrey had managed to find something on Lena then, if his gut had let him believe she was culpable, Chuck Gaines might still be alive.

Frank stood to the side of the door, his hand on his weapon, not drawing. Jeffrey knocked twice, calling, "Lena?"

A few moments passed, and he strained to hear if anyone was in the room.

He tried again, saying, "Lena?" before opening the door.

"Shit," Frank said, pulling his gun. Jeffrey did the same, his instincts kicking in before he saw that Lena was just pulling on her pants, not going for some kind of weapon.

Jeffrey asked the question he knew Frank was thinking. "What the hell happened to you?"

Lena cleared her throat, which had dark bruises around it. When she spoke, her voice was raspy. "I fell."

She was wearing only pants and a bra, the material white against her olive skin. She covered herself with her hands in a flash of modesty. There were round fingertip bruises on her upper arms, as if someone had grabbed her too hard. A

520

mark on her shoulder looked like it was from a bite.

"Chief," Frank said. He had cuffed Ethan White and was holding him by the arm. The boy was dressed but for his socks and shoes. His face was black and blue, the lip split down the center.

Jeffrey picked up a shirt off the floor, meaning to offer it to Lena so that she could cover herself. He stopped when he realized what he was holding was evidence. Dark blood stained the bottom.

"Jesus," he whispered, trying to get Lena to look at him. "What have you done?"

13

Sara pulled up outside the Heartsdale Medical Center, parking beside Jeffrey's car in the parking lot. He hadn't given her any information other than that he needed her at the hospital to take some physical evidence from two suspects. He wouldn't say their names over the phone, but Sara had been privy to his thought processes long enough to know he meant Ethan White and Lena.

As usual, the emergency room was empty. Sara glanced around, looking for the nurse on duty, but the woman must have been on a break. Down the hall she could see Jeffrey talking to an older man of average height and thick build. Beyond them Brad Stephens stood in front of a closed exam-room door, his hand resting on the butt of his gun.

Sara could hear the man talking to Jeffrey as she got closer, his tone of voice shrill and demanding. "My wife has been through too much already."

"I know what she's been through," Jeffrey said. "I'm glad to see you're concerned for her well-being."

"Of course I am," the man snapped. "What are you trying to imply?"

Jeffrey noticed Sara and motioned for her to come over. "This is Sara Linton," he told the man. "She'll do the physical exam."

"Dr. Brian Keller," the man said, barely glancing at Sara. He held a woman's purse at his side, which she guessed belonged to his wife.

"Dr. Keller is Jill Rosen's husband," Jeffrey explained. "Lena asked me to call her."

Sara tried not to register her surprise.

Jeffrey told Keller, "If you'll excuse us," and then led Sara back up the hall to a small exam room.

"What's going on?" she asked. "I told Mama I'd be in Atlanta this afternoon."

He closed the door before saying, "Chuck's throat was slit."

"Chuck Gaines?" she said, as if there were another Chuck it could be.

"We've got Lena's prints on the murder weapon."

Sara reeled for a moment, trying to understand what he was saying.

He asked, "Did you remember the rape kit?"

For a moment Sara didn't know what he meant.

"When we were talking about the DNA on the underwear. Did you remember the rape kit we did on Lena?"

She tried to think of the best way to answer him but knew that this was too black-and-white to say anything but "Yes."

Jeffrey's face was a study in anger. "Why didn't you tell me, Sara?"

"Because it's not right," she said. "It's not right to use that against her."

"You tell that to Albert Gaines," Jeffrey said. "You tell that to Chuck's mama."

Sara kept her mouth closed, because she still could not accept that Lena was in any way connected to the crimes.

"I want you to do White first," Jeffrey said, his tone still sharp. "Blood, saliva, hair. Full-body comb. Just like an autopsy."

"What are we looking for?"

"Anything that ties him to the crime scene," Jeffrey said. "We've already got Lena's shoe prints in blood." He shook his head. "Blood was everywhere."

Jeffrey opened the door and looked down the corridor. He did not leave, so

Sara knew he had more to tell her.

She asked, "What?"

The anger in his tone went down a notch. "She's messed up pretty bad."

"How bad?"

Jeffrey looked down the hall again, then back to Sara. "I don't know if there was a struggle or what. Maybe Chuck attacked her and she defended herself. Maybe White went nuts."

"Is that what she's saying?"

"She's not saying anything. Neither of them is." He paused. "Well, White's saying they were together in her apartment all night, but people at the school say White left the lab after Lena did." He indicated the hall. "Brian Keller was actually one of the last people to see her."

"Lena asked for his wife?"

"Yeah," Jeffrey said. "I've got Frank listening in the other room in case she says anything."

"Jeffrey —"

"Don't give me a lecture about doctors and patients, Sara. I've got too many dead people stacking up."

Sara knew that arguing the point would only waste time. "Is Lena all right?"

"She can wait," he told her, obviously meaning to cut off further questions.

"Do you have a warrant for this?"

"What are you, a lawyer now?" He didn't let her answer. "Judge Bennett signed off on it this morning." When she didn't respond, he said, "What? You want to see it? You don't trust me to tell you the truth anymore?"

"I didn't ask —"

"No, here." He took the warrant out of his pocket and slammed it down on the counter. "See how that goes, Sara? I tell you the truth about things. I try to help you do your job the right way so that more people don't get hurt."

She stared at the document, seeing Billie Bennett's tight signature across the line. "Let's get this over with."

Jeffrey stepped back so she could leave, and Sara felt a sense of dread welling up into her like nothing she'd felt in a long while.

Brian Keller was still standing in the hall, holding his wife's purse. He stared blankly as Sara walked by, and he looked so harmless that she had to remind herself that he beat his wife.

Brad tipped his hat to Sara before opening the door, saying, "Ma'am."

Ethan White stood in the middle of the room. He was dressed in a light green hospital gown, his muscular arms crossed over his chest. He'd been hit in the nose recently, and dried blood traced a thin line down to his mouth. A large red spot under his eye was slowly turning into a bruise. There were intricate tattoos of battle scenes on what she could see of both arms. His bare calves had geometric designs and flames climbing up the sides.

He looked like an average kid with close-cropped hair and a body that revealed he spent too much free time in the gym. Muscles pulsed across his shoulders, straining the material of the hospital gown. He was a small person, a good six inches shorter than Sara, but there was something about him that filled the space around him. White seemed angry, like at any moment he would spring up and attack her. Sara was glad that Jeffrey had not left them alone in the room.

"Ethan White," Jeffrey said. "This is Dr. Linton. She's going to take samples ordered by the court."

White's jaw was clenched so tight his words came out with a slur. "I want to see the order."

Sara put on a pair of gloves as White read the warrant. Glass slides and a DNA-testing kit were on the counter, along with a black plastic comb and tubes for drawing blood. Jeffrey had probably arranged for the nurse to have all these things ready, but Sara was curious as to why he had not asked the woman to stay and help. She wondered what he did not want anyone else to see.

Sara slipped on her glasses, thinking she would ask Jeffrey to send in a nurse.

Before she could say anything, Jeffrey told White, "Take off the gown."

"That's not —" Sara stopped mid-sentence. White dropped the gown to the floor. There was a large swastika tattooed on his belly. On his right upper chest, there was a faded likeness of Hitler. A row of SS soldiers on his left chest saluted the image on the other side.

Sara could not bring herself to do anything but stare.

White snarled, "You like what you see?"

Jeffrey's hand slammed into the boy's face, pushing him into the wall. Sara jumped back until she was pressed against the counter. She saw Ethan's nose move, fresh blood dripping down into his mouth.

Jeffrey spoke in a low, angry tone that Sara hoped she would never hear again. "That's my wife, you motherless fuck. You understand me?"

White's head was clamped between Jeffrey's hand and the wall. He nodded once, but there was no fear in his eyes. He was like a caged animal who knew one day soon he would find a way out.

"That's better," Jeffrey said, backing off.

White looked at Sara. "You're a witness, aren't you, Doctor? Police brutality."

Jeffrey said, "She didn't see anything," and Sara cursed him for including her in this.

"Didn't she?" White asked.

Jeffrey took a step toward him, saying, "Don't give me a reason to hurt you."

White gave a surly, "Yes, sir." He wiped the blood from his nose with the back of his hand, keeping his eyes locked on Sara. He was trying to intimidate her, and she hoped he could not see that it was working.

Sara opened the oral-DNA kit. She walked over to White with the scraper in her hand, saying, "Open your mouth, please."

He did as he was told, opening wide so she could scrape for loose skin. She took several swabs, but her hands were shaking when she started to prepare the slides. Sara took a deep breath, trying to reconcile herself to the task ahead of her. Ethan White was just another patient. She was a doctor doing her job, nothing more, nothing less.

She could feel his eyes boring into her back as she labeled the specimens. Hate filled the room like a noxious gas.

She said, "I need your date of birth."

He paused a second, as if he was telling her of his own free will. "November twenty-first, 1980."

Sara recorded the information on the label along with his name, her name, the location, the date, and the time. Each piece of evidence would have to be cataloged this way, then either stored in a paper evidence bag or collected onto a slide.

She picked up a sterile paper wafer with a pair of tweezers and held it in front of his mouth. "I need you to moisten this with your saliva."

"I'm not a secretor."

Sara kept the tweezers steady until he finally stuck out his tongue so she could place the paper in his mouth. After an appropriate amount of time, she removed the wafer and logged it into evidence.

She followed procedure, asking, "Would you like some water?"

"No."

She continued through the preliminaries, feeling his eyes watch every move she made. Even when she was standing at the counter with her back to him, Sara could feel Ethan's eyes fixed on her like a tiger preparing to attack.

Her throat closed when she realized she could no longer postpone actually touching him. His skin was warm under her gloves, the muscles tense and unrelenting. Sara had not drawn blood from a living patient in years, and she kept missing the vein.

"I'm sorry," she apologized after the second try.

"No big deal," he said, his polite tone contrary to the hateful look in his eyes.

Using a thirty-five-millimeter camera, Sara documented what looked like defensive wounds on his left forearm. Four superficial scratches were on his neck and head and there was a crescent-shaped indentation, probably from a fingernail, behind his left ear. The area around his genitals was bruised, the glans red and irritated. A short fingernail scratch went down his left buttock, a longer one up the small of his back. Sara had Jeffrey hold a scale close to the injuries while she photographed each of them with the macro lens.

She said, "I need you to lie down on the table."

Ethan did as he was told, watching her closely.

Sara went to the counter, turning away from him. She unfolded a small white sheet of paper and turned back around again, saying, "Lift up so I can put this underneath you."

Again he did as he was told, his eyes never leaving her face.

Several foreign hairs raked out when she combed his pubic hair. The root strands were still attached to the shafts, indicating that the hairs had been torn from the body. With a sharp pair of scissors, she cut out a matted area of hair on his inner thigh, dropping it into an envelope and labeling it with the appropriate information.

She used a wet swab to obtain samples of dried fluids on his penis and scrotum, her jaw clenching so tight that her teeth ached. She scraped his fingernails and toenails, photographing a broken nail on his right index finger. By the time she was finished with the exam, the counter was filled with evidence. Everything was either cool-air-drying in the swab dryer or collected into paper evidence bags, which Sara had sealed and labeled with a now steady hand.

"That's it," she said, taking off her gloves and dropping them on the counter. She left the room as quickly as she could without running. Brad and Keller were still in the hallway, but she passed by them both without saying a word.

Sara went back to the empty exam room, fear and anger surging through every inch of her body. She leaned down to the sink, turning on the faucet full blast so she could splash cold water in her face. Bile stuck in her throat, and she gulped water, willing herself not to be sick. She could still feel Ethan's eyes following her, searing into her flesh like a branding iron. She could smell the soap he used, and, when she closed her eyes, Sara could see the slight erection he had gotten when she swabbed his penis and combed his pubic hair.

The faucet was still running, and Sara turned off the water. She was drying her hands with a paper towel when she suddenly realized that she was standing in the same room she had used to perform Lena's rape kit last year. This was the table Lena had lain on. This was the same counter she had filled with Lena's evidence, much as she had just done with Ethan White's.

Sara wrapped her arms around her waist, staring at the room, trying not to let the memories swallow her.

After several minutes Jeffrey knocked on the door and let himself in. He had taken off his coat, and she could see his gun in its holster.

"You could have warned me," she said, her voice catching. "You could have told me."

"I know."

"Is this how you pay me back?" she said, aware that she was going to start either crying or yelling.

"It wasn't payback," he said, and she did not know if she believed him or not.

Sara put her hand to her mouth, trying to suppress a sob. "Jesus Christ, Jeff."

"I know."

"You don't know," she said, her voice loud in the room. "My God, did you see those tattoos?" Sara did not let him answer. "He's got a swastika —" She could not continue. "Why didn't you warn me?"

Jeffrey was silent. Then, "I wanted you to see," he said. "I wanted you to know what we're dealing with."

"You couldn't *tell* me?" she demanded, turning on the faucet again. She scooped water into her hand so she could wash the bad taste out of her mouth. "What took you so long?" she asked, remembering the way he had pounded Ethan's head back into the wall. "Did you hit him again?"

"I didn't hit him in the first place."

"You didn't hit him in the eye?" she demanded. "His nose was bleeding, Jeffrey. The blood was fresh."

"I told you, I didn't hit him."

She grabbed his hands, checking his knuckles for cuts or bruises. They were clean, but she still asked, "Where's your class ring?"

"I took it off."

"You never take that ring off."

"Sunday," he said. "I took it off Sunday before I talked to your folks."

"Why?"

He relented angrily, "There was blood, Sara. Okay? There was blood from Tess."

Sara dropped his hand. She asked the question she would not let herself think when she was in the same room with White. "Do you think he could have stabbed Tessa?"

"He doesn't have an alibi for Sunday. Not a good one."

"Where was he?"

"He says in the library," Jeffrey answered. "No one remembers him. He could have been in the woods. He could have killed Andy, then waited around in the woods to see what was going on."

Sara nodded that he should continue.

"He wasn't waiting for Tessa, Sara. She just came along, and he took advantage of the situation."

Sara gripped the counter again, closing her eyes, trying to reconcile the man in the next room with Tessa's stabbing. Sara had been in the presence of a murderer before, and what had struck her about that man was that he was so normal, so ordinary. With his clothes on, Ethan White had seemed the same way. He could be just another kid on campus. He could have been one of her patients. Somewhere, back in his hometown, there could be a pediatrician just like Sara who watched Ethan White grow into a man.

When she could speak, she asked, "Where does Lena fit into all of this?"

"She's seeing him," Jeffrey said. "She's his girlfriend."

"I can't believe . . ."

"When you see her," Jeffrey began, "when you see her, Sara, I want you to remember that she's involved with White. She's protecting him." He pointed at the wall, indicating the next exam room. "That thing you saw in there, that animal — she's protecting him."

"Protecting him from what?" Sara asked.

"It's her fingerprints on the knife. She's the one who worked with Chuck."

"You'll understand when you see her."

"Is this another surprise?" she asked, thinking she could not handle another one, especially if it had anything to do with Lena. "Does she have a swastika, too?"

"Honestly," Jeffrey began, "I don't know what to make of her. She looks bad. Bad like she's been hurt."

"Has she been?"

"I don't know," he repeated. "Somebody worked her over."

"Who?"

"Frank thinks Chuck did something."

"Did what?" Sara asked, dreading what he might say.

"Attacked her," Jeffrey said. "Or maybe he just pissed her off. She told White, and White went ballistic."

"What do *you* think happened?" Sara asked.

"Honestly, who the hell knows?" he said. "And she's not telling me anything."

"Did you ask her the same way you asked White?" she said. "With your hand pressed into her face?"

The hurt in his eyes made her wish she could take back her words, but Sara knew that would accomplish nothing. She still wanted an answer to her question.

He asked her, "What kind of person do you think I am?"

"I think . . . ," Sara began, not knowing what to say, "I think we both have jobs to do. I think we can't talk about this right now."

"I want to talk about it," he said. "I need you with me on this, Sara. I can't fight you and everybody else at the same time."

"Now isn't the time," she told him. "Where's Lena?"

Jeffrey stepped back into the hall, indicating that she should see for herself.

Sara dried her hands on her pants as she walked past Brad toward the next room. She reached down to open the door just as Frank was coming out.

"Hey," Frank said, looking somewhere past her shoulder. "She wanted some water."

Sara walked into the room. The first thing she saw was not Lena but the rape kit that had been left on the counter. Sara froze, unable to move until Jeffrey put his hand to her back and gently pushed. She wanted to rail against him, to pound her fists into his chest and damn him for making her do this again, but all the spirit had been drained out of her. She felt completely empty of everything but sorrow.

Jeffrey said, "Sara Linton, this is Jill Rosen."

A small woman dressed in black stood with her back against the wall. She said something, but all Sara heard was a clicking of metal against metal. Lena was sitting on the bed, her feet hanging over the side. She was dressed in a green hospital gown with a ribbon at the neck. She was moving her hand back and forth in what looked like a nervous twitch, and the handcuff around her wrist was clicking on the bar at the foot of the bed.

Sara bit her lip so hard she tasted blood. She said, "Get those handcuffs off her right now."

Jeffrey hesitated but did as she instructed.

When he had removed the cuffs, she told him, "Get out," in a voice that invited no discussion.

Again he hesitated. She looked him right in the eye and crisply enunciated the two words. "Get. Out."

Jeffrey left, the door snicking closed behind him. Sara stood with her hands on her hips, a few feet away from Lena. Though the handcuffs were off, Lena's hand continued to move back and forth as if in a palsy. Sara had thought Jeffrey's leaving would make the room feel less small, but the walls were still closing in on her. There was a palpable fear in the room, and Sara felt a sudden coldness overwhelm her.

Sara asked, "Who did this to you?"

Lena cleared her throat, staring at the floor. When she tried to speak, her voice was barely more than a whisper. "I fell."

Sara put her hand to her chest. "Lena," she said, "you've been raped."

"I fell," Lena repeated, her hand still shaking.

Jill Rosen crossed the room and wet a paper towel at the sink. She walked back to Lena, patting the towel to her face and neck.

Sara asked, "Did Ethan do this to you?"

Lena shook her head as Rosen tried to wipe away some of the blood.

She said, "Ethan didn't do anything."

Rosen placed the towel on the back of Lena's neck. She might have been wiping away evidence, but Sara did not care.

"Lena," Sara said, "it's okay. He's not going to hurt you anymore."

Lena closed her eyes, but she let Rosen wipe under her chin. "He didn't hurt me."

"This is not your fault," Sara said. "You

don't have to protect him."

Lena kept her eyes closed.

"Did Chuck do this?" Sara asked. Rosen looked up, startled.

Sara repeated, "Was it Chuck?"

Lena whispered, "I haven't seen Chuck."

Sara sat on the edge of the bed, wanting to understand. "Lena, please."

Lena turned her head away. The gown slipped, and Sara could see a deep bite mark just above her right breast.

Rosen finally spoke. "Did Chuck hurt you?"

"I shouldn't have called you," Lena told the other woman.

Rosen's eyes watered as she tucked Lena's hair behind her ear. She was probably seeing herself twenty years ago.

Lena told her, "Please go."

Rosen looked at Sara as if she didn't quite trust her. "You have the right to have someone here," Rosen said. Working on campus, the woman must have gotten calls like this before. She knew the system, even if she never used it for herself.

"Please go," Lena repeated, her eyes still closed, as if she could will the woman away.

Rosen opened her mouth to say something more but seemed to decide against it.

She left the room quickly, like a prisoner escaping.

Lena's eyes remained closed. Her throat worked, and she coughed.

"It sounds like your trachea is bruised," Sara told her. "If your larynx is damaged —" Sara stopped, wondering if Lena was even listening. Her eyes were closed so tightly it looked as if she wanted to shut out the world.

"Lena," Sara said, her mind going back to the forest with Tessa, "are you having any trouble breathing?"

Almost imperceptibly, Lena shook her head once in a tight no.

"Do you mind if I feel?" Sara asked, but she did not wait for an answer. As gently as she could, Sara tested the skin around Lena's larynx for pockets of air. "It's just bruised," she said. "It's not fractured, but it'll hurt for a while."

Lena coughed again, and Sara got her a glass of water.

"Slowly," Sara told her, tilting down the bottom of the glass.

She coughed again, looking around the room like she could not remember how she had gotten here.

"You're at the hospital," Sara said. "Did Chuck hurt you and Ethan found out? Is that what happened, Lena?"

She swallowed, wincing from the pain. "I fell."

"Lena," Sara breathed, feeling such deep sadness that she could barely talk. "My God, please, just tell me what happened."

Lena kept her head down, mumbling something.

Sara asked, "What?"

She cleared her throat, finally opening her eyes. The blood vessels were broken, tiny red dots scattered in the whites.

She said, "I want to take a shower."

Sara looked at the rape kit on the counter. She did not think she could do this again. It was too much for one person to handle. The way Lena just sat there, helpless, waiting for Sara to do whatever she had to do, broke her heart.

Lena must have sensed her trepidation. "Please just get this over with," she whispered. "I feel so dirty. I have to take a shower."

Sara made herself slide off the bed and walk over to the counter. She felt numb when she checked to make sure there was film in the camera.

Following procedure, Sara asked, "Have you had consensual sex with anyone in the last twenty-four hours?"

Lena nodded. "Yes."

Sara closed her eyes. "Consensual sex?" she repeated.

"Yes."

Sara tried to keep her tone steady. "Have you douched or showered since the attack?"

"I wasn't attacked."

Sara walked over, standing in front of Lena. "There's a pill I can give you," she said. "Like the one I gave you before."

Lena's hand still shook, rubbing against the sheet on the bed.

"It's for emergency contraception."

Lena moved her lips without speaking.

"It's also called a morning-after pill. Do you remember how it works?"

Lena nodded, but Sara told her anyway.

"You'll need to take one now and another one in twelve hours. I'll give you something for the nausea. Was the nausea bad last time?"

Lena might have nodded, but Sara was not certain.

"You might have cramping, dizziness, spotting."

Lena stopped her. "Okay."

"Okay?" Sara asked.

"Okay," she repeated. "Yes. Give me the pills."

★ ★ ★

Sara sat at her desk in the morgue, her head in her hands, the telephone cradled between her ear and shoulder as she listened to her father's cell phone ring.

"Sara?" Cathy answered, concern straining her voice. "Where are you?"

"Didn't you get my message?"

"We don't know how to check that," her mother said, as if it were obvious. "We were starting to get worried."

"I'm sorry, Mama," Sara said, looking at the clock out in the morgue. Her parents had been expecting her to call an hour ago. "Chuck Gaines has been killed."

Cathy was too shocked to be worried anymore. "The boy who ate your macaroni in the third grade?"

"Yes," Sara answered. Her mother always remembered people from Sara's childhood by something stupid they had done as kids.

Cathy said, "Well, how horrible," not making the connection that Chuck's death could somehow be related to Tessa's stabbing.

"I've got to do the autopsy, and there are some other things." Sara did not want to tell her mother about Lena Adams or anything else that had happened at the hospital. Even if she tried, Sara did not think she could articulate her feelings. She felt raw and exposed and wanted nothing more than to be with her family right now.

"Can you come in the morning?" Cathy asked, a strange tone to her voice.

"I'm going to come tonight as soon as I can," Sara said, thinking she had never wanted to leave town more than she did right now. "Is Tess okay?"

"She's right here," Cathy said. "Talking to Devon."

"Well," Sara said. "Is that a good thing or a bad thing?"

"Probably first one," Cathy answered cryptically.

"How about Daddy?"

Cathy paused before answering. "He's okay," she said, in a way that was far from convincing.

Sara tried to hold back her tears. She felt like she was barely treading water as it was. The added strain of worrying about her relationship with her father was going to pull her under.

"Baby?" Cathy asked.

Sara saw Jeffrey by the shadow that fell over her desk. She looked up, but not at him. Through the window she saw Frank and Carlos talking by the body.

Sara said, "Jeff's here, Mama. I need to get started."

Cathy still sounded concerned, but she said, "All right."

"I'll come as soon as I can," Sara told her, then hung up.

Jeffrey asked, "Is something wrong with Tess?"

"I just need to see her," Sara said. "I need to be with my family."

Jeffrey got the implication that this did not include him. "Are we going to talk about this now?"

"You handcuffed her," Sara said, torn between hurt and outrage. "I can't believe you handcuffed her."

"She's a suspect, Sara." He looked back over his shoulder. Frank was staring at his notebook, but Sara knew he could hear every word they said. Still, she raised her voice just to make sure.

"She was raped, Jeffrey. I don't know by whom, but she was raped, and you shouldn't have handcuffed her."

"She's part of a murder investigation."

"She wasn't going anywhere in that room."

"That wasn't the point."

"What *was* the point?" she demanded, still trying to keep her voice low. "To torture her? To make her break?"

"That's what I do, Sara. I get people to confess."

"I'm sure you get them to say a lot of things just to stop you from hitting them."

"Let me tell you something, Sara, a guy like Ethan White responds to one thing."

"Oh, did I miss the part where he told you what you wanted to know?"

Jeffrey stared at her, clearly trying not to yell. He finally asked, "Can't we just go back to how things were this morning?"

"This morning you hadn't handcuffed a rape victim to a hospital bed."

"I'm not the one that withheld evidence from you."

"That's not withholding evidence, you ass. That's protecting a patient. How would you like it if someone used my rape kit to frame me?"

"Frame you?" he echoed. "Her fingerprints are on the murder weapon. She looks like somebody beat the shit out of her. Her boyfriend has a criminal record as long as my dick. What the hell else am I supposed to think?" He made a visible effort to check his temper. "I can't dictate my job by what pleases you."

"No," she said, standing. "Or by common decency either."

"I didn't know —"

"Don't be stupid," she hissed, slamming the door closed. She had stopped wanting Frank to hear. "You saw what she looked like, what he did to her. You must have the pictures now. Did you see the lacerations on her legs? Did you see the bite marks on her breast?"

"Yes," he told her. "I saw the pictures. I saw them." He shook his head as though he wished he had not.

"Do you really think Lena killed Chuck?"

"Nothing ties White to the scene," he told her. "Give me something that ties him to the scene. Give me something other than her bloody fingerprints on the murder weapon."

Sara could not get past one point. "You shouldn't have handcuffed her."

"Am I supposed to ignore the fact that she might have killed somebody just because I feel sorry for her?"

"Do you?"

"Of course I do," he told her. "Do you think I like seeing her like that? Jesus Christ."

"It could have been self-defense."

"That's for her lawyer to decide," Jeffrey said, and though his tone was harsh, Sara knew that he was right. "I can't let how I feel about her interfere with my job, and neither should you."

"I guess I'm just not as professional as you are."

"That's not what I'm saying."

"Eighty percent of all women who are raped experience a second attack at some point in their lives," she told him. "Did you know that?"

His silence answered her question.

"Instead of charging her with murder, you should be looking for someone to charge with rape."

Jeffrey held his hands up in a shrug. "Didn't you hear?" he asked, so glib that she wanted to smack him. "She wasn't raped. She fell."

Sara threw open the door, knowing she could not talk to him anymore. As she walked into the morgue, she could feel Jeffrey staring at her, but she did not care. No matter what the autopsy revealed, she would never be able to forgive Jeffrey for handcuffing Lena to the bed. The way she was feeling now, Sara could not care less if she never talked to him again.

She walked over to the X rays, not really seeing the films. Sara concentrated on her breathing, trying to make her mind focus on the task at hand. She closed her eyes, pushing Tessa and Lena from her mind, banishing Ethan White from her memory. When she thought that she had recovered, she opened her eyes and walked back to the table.

Chuck Gaines was a large man with broad shoulders and a smattering of hair on his chest. There were no defensive wounds on his arms that Sara could see, so he must have been taken by surprise. His neck was splayed open, bright red, with arteries and tendons hanging out like twigs on a vine. She could see clear through to his cervical spine, a piece of which had become dislodged from its normal place.

"I black-lighted him earlier," Sara said. A black light could pick up body fluids and show if there had been recent sexual activity. "He's clean."

Jeffrey countered, "He could've worn a condom."

"Did you find one at the scene?"

"Lena would know to take that away."

Sara jerked down the overhead light, making her irritation apparent. She concentrated the light so she could better see the area around the wound. "There's one hesitation mark," she said, indicating the cut that had not gone all the way through. Whoever had stabbed Chuck had needed at least one try before he or she broke skin.

"So," Jeffrey surmised, "it wasn't a strong person."

"It took a lot of strength to cut through the cartilage and bone," Sara countered, wishing he would not editorialize but not wanting to call him on it in front of Frank. Jeffrey had probably brought Frank along for just this reason.

She asked, "Do you have the weapon?"

Jeffrey held up a plastic evidence bag that contained a bloody six-inch-long hunting knife. He said, "The empty sheath was in her bedroom. The knife fits perfectly."

"You didn't look for anything else?"

Jeffrey took the dig in stride. "We tossed her room and White's. This was the only weapon." He added, "Of any kind."

Sara studied the knife. The blade was serrated on one side and sharp on the other. There was black fingerprint powder on the handle, and she could see the faint outline of the bloody print they had removed with tape. Other than that, there was not much blood on the weapon. Either the murderer had cleaned it off or Jeffrey had the wrong knife. Sara could make an educated guess at to which was the case, but she wanted to be sure before she said anything definitive.

Sara put on two pairs of gloves. The only other mark on the body was a penetrating stab wound high on the left chest. The opening was big enough for the blade Jeffrey had shown her, but the edges did not account for the serration. Chuck's attacker had probably slashed him across the neck, then stabbed him in the chest. The chest wound was at an angle, indicating that the person doing the stabbing was standing over the body when it had been delivered.

Jeffrey asked, "Wasn't that where Tess was stabbed?"

Sara ignored the question. "Can you help me roll him to his side?"

Jeffrey went to get a pair of gloves off the wall dispenser.

Frank offered, "You need me to help, too?"

"No," Sara told him. "Thanks."

Frank patted his chest, looking visibly relieved. Sara could see that the skin on the back of his knuckles was cut and bruised. He saw her notice and tucked his hand into his pocket with an apologetic smile.

Jeffrey said, "Ready?"

Sara nodded, waiting for him to get into place.

As Chuck's head had been nearly separated from his neck, moving him was an awkward job. Compounding the problem, the body was still stiff. The legs slid toward the edge of the table, and Sara had to move quickly to keep the body from rolling onto the floor.

Jeffrey said, "Sorry."

"It's okay," she told him, feeling some of her earlier anger slipping away. She pointed to the tray. "Can you hand me that scalpel?"

Jeffrey knew that this was not routine. He asked, "What are you looking for?"

Sara estimated the trajectory of the blade before making a small incision in Chuck's back just below the left shoulder.

"The knife was the only weapon you found?" Sara asked him to clarify, pointing to another instrument on the tray.

"Yes," Jeffrey said, handing her a pair of stainless-steel tweezers.

Sara reached into the wound with the tweezers, digging around with the point until she found what she was looking for.

Jeffrey said, "What's going on?"

She pulled out a piece of metal as her answer.

Frank said, "What's that?"

Jeffrey looked sick. "The tip of the knife."

Sara added, "It broke off against his shoulder blade."

Frank's confusion was obvious. "Lena's blade wasn't broken." He picked up the plastic bag. "The tip's not even bent."

Jeffrey's face had turned completely white, and the distress in his expression made Sara regret everything she had said to him before.

Frank said, "What the hell is going on here?"

"It wasn't her knife," Jeffrey said, his voice thick with emotion. "It wasn't Lena."

14

Lena woke with a start, pushing herself up on her hands. Her ribs ached with every breath, and her wrist was pounding even though it was finally in a fiberglass cast. She sat up, looking around the small cell, trying to remember how she had gotten here.

"It's okay," Jeffrey said.

He was sitting on the cot across from her, his elbows on his knees, hands clasped in front of him. She was in holding, not general lockup behind the station. The cell was dark, the only light coming from the monitoring booth up the hallway. The cell door was open, but Lena did not know how to interpret that.

"It's time for your other pill," he told her. There was a metal food tray on the bed beside him, with a plastic cup and two pills. He picked it up, offering it to her like a waiter. "The smaller one is so you won't feel sick."

Lena put the pills in her mouth, then washed them down with a swig of cold water. She tried to put the cup back in the hole on the tray, but her coordination was off, and Jeffrey had to do it for her. Water spilled on his pants, but he took no notice.

She cleared her throat several times before she could ask, "What time is it?"

"About a quarter to midnight," Jeffrey told her.

Fifteen hours, Lena thought. She had been in custody for nearly fifteen hours.

"Can I get you anything?" Jeffrey asked. The light caught his face when he leaned down to put the tray on the floor, and she could see that his jaw was set. "Are you feeling okay?"

She tried to shrug, but her shoulder was too tender. The parts of her body that weren't numb were stiff and sore. Even her eyelids hurt when she blinked.

"How's the cut on your hand?"

Lena looked down at her index finger jutting from the cast. She wondered how much time had passed since she'd cut herself trying to screw the air-conditioning grate back in. An eternity had passed. She wasn't even that person anymore.

"Is that how the blood got on your knife?" Jeffrey asked, leaning forward into the light again. "When you cut your hand?"

She cleared her throat again, but the pain only increased. Her voice was raspy, just above a whisper. "Can I have more water?"

"Do you want something stronger?" he asked. She studied him, trying to understand what he was doing. Jeffrey was playing good cop now, and she needed someone to be nice to her so badly that she would probably fall for it. She ached to tell someone what had happened, but her mind could not bring itself to think the words that her mouth would need to form.

Holding out the cup, Jeffrey said, "Let's start with water, okay?"

Lena drank, glad the water was cold. He must have gotten it from the cooler in the main lobby instead of the faucet.

Lena handed him the cup, then sat against the wall. Her back was sore, but the cement block was solid and reassuring. She looked down at the cast, which started just below her fingers and stopped halfway down her arm. Moving her fingers, she felt a quiver through her arm.

"The pain medication is probably wearing off," Jeffrey told her. "Do you want more? I can get Sara to prescribe something."

Lena shook her head, though she wanted nothing more than to be oblivious.

"Chuck's B-negative," he said. "You're type A."

She nodded. The DNA tests would take about a week, but they could type blood themselves at the hospital.

Jeffrey said, "Type A was on the knife and the desk and the tail of your shirt."

Lena waited for the rest.

"We didn't find any B-negative any-where." He added, "Anywhere except the office."

She had been holding her breath in her chest, and she kept it there, wondering how long she could hold it.

"Lena . . . ," he began. To her surprise, his voice cracked, and before he looked down at his hands, she could see how upset he was.

He said, "I should never have cuffed you."

Lena wondered what he meant. She could not remember much of anything past what had happened with Ethan the night before.

"I would've handled it completely differ-ently, if only . . ." He looked up at her, his eyes glistening in the light from the hall. "I didn't know."

Lena suppressed a cough, wishing she could have more water.

He said, "Lena, tell me what happened. Tell me who did this to you so I can punish him."

Lena could only stare. She had done it to herself. What more could he do to punish her?

"I should have never cuffed you," he repeated. "I'm so sorry."

Lena exhaled slowly, feeling a pain in her rib.

She asked, "Where's Ethan?"

Jeffrey's body tensed. "He's still locked up."

"What charge?"

"Parole violation," he told her, but did not explain further.

"Is he really dead?" she asked, thinking about the last time she had seen Chuck.

"Yeah," Jeffrey said. "He's dead." He looked at his hands again. "Did he do this to you, Lena? Did Chuck hurt you?"

She cleared her throat again, her neck hurting from the strain. "Can I go home?"

He seemed to think about it, but she knew from what he had told her that there was not much to hold her on.

She told him, "I just want to go home," but the home she was thinking about was not the shithole she lived in at the college. She was thinking of the house she used to own and the life she had when she lived in it. She was thinking about the Lena who did not attack people or force them into doing things they did not want to do. The good Lena. The Lena she was before Sibyl died.

Jeffrey said, "Nan Thomas is here. I called her to pick you up."

"I don't want to see her."

"I'm sorry, Lena. She's outside waiting for you, and I can't — I won't — let you go home alone."

Nan was silent on the drive back to her house. There was no telling how much or how little she knew. None of that really mattered to Lena right now. She had stopped caring about anything after the storm hit last night.

Lena stared out the window, thinking that she hadn't taken an evening car ride in a long while. Usually she was in bed by now, sometimes sleeping, sometimes looking out the window and waiting for day to come, but never outside. Never somewhere she didn't feel safe.

Nan pulled into the driveway and cut the engine. She tucked the ignition key over the visor, giving Lena a goofy grin. Nan trusted people too much. Sibyl had been the same way, right up until some maniac killed her.

The house Sibyl and Nan bought a few years ago was a small bungalow of the kind that was all over Heartsdale. Two bedrooms were on one side, with a bath off the hallway and a kitchen, dining room, and living room on the other side. The second bedroom had been converted into an office for Sibyl, but Lena did not know what Nan used the room for now.

Lena stood on the front stoop, bracing her hand against the side of the house so she would not fall over as Nan took her time unlocking the door. Exhaustion was becoming a way of life for her; another thing that had changed.

Three short beeps from an alarm panel greeted them when Nan opened the door. Considering Nan's lack of concern about safety, Lena was surprised to see that she had bothered to get an alarm.

Nan must have read her mind. "I know," she said, punching Sibyl's birth date into the pad. "I thought it would make me feel safe after Sibyl . . . and then you . . ."

"A dog would be better," Lena suggested, then felt guilty when she saw the concerned look on Nan's face. "The noise from the alarm can scare off people, too."

"I kept setting it off when I first got it. Mrs. Moushey across the street nearly had a heart attack."

"I'm sure it's fine," Lena told her.

"Why don't I believe you?"

Lena leaned her hand on the back of the couch, thinking she did not have the strength for such an inane conversation.

Nan seemed to pick up on this. "Are you hungry?" she asked, turning the lights on as she walked through the dining room to the kitchen.

Lena shook her head, but Nan didn't see her.

"Lena?"

"No," Lena said. She traced her fingers along the couch as she walked toward the bathroom. She was cramping from the medication, and she felt a burning like maybe she had a bladder infection.

The bathroom was narrow, with black and white tiles on the floor. Beaded wood ran around the top part of the walls, with white tile below it. A medicine cabinet with a warped mirror had a picture of Sibyl tucked into its frame. Lena looked into the mirror, then back at Sibyl, comparing the two images. Lena looked ten years older, even though the photograph had been taken a month or so before Sibyl was killed. Lena's left eye was swollen, the cut underneath bright red and sensitive to the touch. Her lip was split in the center, and there were scratches and what looked like one giant bruise wrapped around her neck. No wonder she was having trouble talking. Her throat was probably as raw as a piece of meat.

"Lena?" Nan said, knocking on the door.

Lena opened the door, not wanting Nan to get worried.

"Do you want some tea?" Nan asked.

Lena was going to say no but then decided the tea might help her throat. She nodded.

"Tummy Mint or Sleepy Bear?"

Lena wanted to laugh, because it seemed ludicrous that, after what had happened, Nan was standing at the bathroom door asking Lena if she wanted Tummy Mint or Sleepy Bear.

Nan smiled. "I'll decide for you," she said. "Do you want to change?"

Lena was still wearing the prison uniform they had given her at the jail, because her clothes had been bagged as evidence.

Nan said, "I've still got some of Sibyl's things if you want . . ." They both seemed to realize at the same time that neither of them would feel comfortable with Lena in Sibyl's clothes.

"I've got some pajamas that will fit you," Nan said. She went into her room, and Lena followed her. There were more pictures of Sibyl by the bed, and Sibyl's Pooh bear from when she was little.

Nan stood in the room, watching her.

"What?" Lena asked, holding her mouth tight, trying to keep her lip from splitting back open.

Nan went to the closet, standing on the tips of her toes to root around the top shelf. She pulled out a small wooden box.

"This was from my father," she said, opening the box. A mini Glock rested in the molded velvet interior. A full magazine was beside it.

"What are you doing with that?" Lena asked, wanting to take the gun out of the box just to feel its weight. She had not held a gun since she resigned from the force.

"My father gave it to me after Sibyl died," Nan said, and Lena realized that she hadn't even known that Nan's father was still alive.

Nan said, "He's a cop. Like your dad was."

Lena touched the cold metal, liking the

way it felt under her fingers.

"I don't know how to use it," Nan said. "I can't stand guns."

"Sibyl hated them, too," Lena said, though surely Nan knew that Calvin Adams, their father, had been shot on a traffic stop.

Nan closed the box and handed it to Lena. "You keep this if it makes you feel safer."

Lena took the box, holding it to her chest.

Nan walked to her dresser and pulled out a pair of pastel blue pajamas. "I know they're not your style, but they're clean."

"Thank you," Lena said, appreciating the effort.

Nan left, pulling the door closed. Lena wanted to lock it but thought Nan might hear the sound and take it personally. She sat on the bed, opening the wooden box on her lap. She traced her finger along the barrel of the gun the same way she had traced her fingers along Ethan's cock. Lena scooped the gun into her hand, fumbling to load the magazine. The cast on her left arm made it difficult, and when she tried to pull the slide to load a bullet into the chamber, the gun nearly slipped from her hand.

"Dammit," she said, squeezing the

trigger several times just to feel the click.

Out of habit Lena ejected the magazine before putting the gun back into the box. With some difficulty she changed into the blue pajamas. Her legs were so sore she did not want to move them, but she knew that movement was the only way to fight the stiffness and pain.

When she got to the kitchen, Nan was pouring tea. She smiled at Lena, trying not to laugh, and Lena looked down at the dark blue cartoon dog on the pocket of the pajama top.

"I'm sorry," Nan apologized around sniggers. "I just never pictured you wearing something like that."

Lena gave a weak smile, feeling her lip split back open. She put the wooden box on the table. The gun was useless if she couldn't chamber a round, but having it close made her feel safe.

Nan noticed the gun but said, "Well, they look better on you than they do on me."

Lena felt a slight trepidation and decided to clear the air. "I'm not gay, Nan."

Nan fought a smile. "Oh, Lena, even if you were, I don't think I'm ever gonna be at a point in my life where I even *think* somebody could replace your sister."

Lena gripped the chair, not wanting to talk about Sibyl. Bringing her into the room would bring her into what had happened. Lena felt a searing shame at the thought of Sibyl's ever knowing what had happened to her. For the first time ever, Lena was glad her sister was dead.

"It's late," Lena said, reading the clock on the wall. "I'm sorry you got dragged into all this."

"Oh, don't worry about it," Nan said. "It's kind of neat being up after midnight for a change. I've been going to bed at nine-thirty like an old lady since Sibyl —"

"Please," Lena asked. "I can't talk about her. Not like this."

"Let's sit you down," Nan said. She put her arm around Lena's shoulders and tried to guide her to the chair, but Lena did not move.

"Lena?"

Lena bit her lip, opening the cut even more. She licked it with the tip of her tongue, remembering how she had licked Ethan's neck.

Without warning she started to cry, and Nan put her other arm around her. They stood in the kitchen, Nan holding her, comforting her, until Lena could not cry anymore.

Thursday

15

Ron Fletcher looked like a deacon at a church. His brown hair was parted neatly to the side, held in place with some kind of shiny gel. He was wearing a suit, like he was here for a job interview, though Jeffrey had told him on the phone he was needed only to help fill in some background information about Chuck Gaines. By the smell of Fletcher, he was a smoker. By what they found in his locker at the security office, nicotine was the least of his addictions.

"Good morning, Mr. Fletcher," Jeffrey said, sitting across from him at the table.

Fletcher flashed a quick, nervous smile at Jeffrey, then made a point of turning around and looking at Frank, who stood by the door like a military guard.

"I'm Chief Tolliver," Jeffrey told him. "This is Detective Wallace."

Fletcher nodded, patting his hair. He was a perpetual stoner, a forty-year-old man who had not aged past his teens. "Hey. How y'all doing?"

"Pretty good," Jeffrey said. "Thanks for coming down here this early."

"I work nights," Fletcher told him, his speech slow and labored from a lifetime of pot. "I'm usually just going to bed about now."

"Well" — Jeffrey smiled — "we appreciate you coming in." He sat back in his chair, leaving his hand on the table.

Fletcher turned around and looked at Frank again. Frank could be imposing when he wanted to be, and the old cop had squared his shoulders to make that known.

Fletcher looked back at Jeffrey, flashing the same nervous smile.

Again Jeffrey returned the smile.

"I, uh . . . ," Fletcher began, slumping forward, his elbow on the table. "I guess y'all found the pot."

"Yep," Jeffrey told him.

"That's not mine," Fletcher tried, but Jeffrey could tell from the way he said it that the man knew that the excuse was weak. Ron Fletcher was in his midforties, and, going by his employment file, had never had a steady job for longer than two years.

"It's yours," Jeffrey said. "We found your

fingerprints on it."

"Damn," Fletcher groaned, smacking his palm on the table.

Jeffrey could see Frank smile. They had found fingerprints on the bags, but Fletcher's were not on file at the station to make a comparison.

"What else are you selling?"

Fletcher shrugged.

"We're gonna toss your place, Ron."

"Oh, man!" Fletcher put his head down on the table. "This is so whacked." He looked up, imploring, "I ain't never been in trouble with the law. You gotta believe me."

"I already ran your record," Jeffrey told him.

Fletcher's mouth twitched. His record had been clean except for a parking ticket, but there could have been something else that had not shown up because no charges were filed. Fletcher was of the generation who thought that cops were a lot more powerful than they actually were.

Jeffrey asked, "Who were you selling to at school?"

"Just some kids, man," Fletcher said. "Just a little at a time to keep myself going, you know? Nothing big."

"Did Chuck know about it?"

"Chuck? No, no. Course not. He wasn't real on top of things, you know, but if he found out I was doing this . . ."

"You know he's dead?"

Fletcher paled, his mouth dropping open.

Jeffrey let some time pass until Fletcher twitched nervously.

Jeffrey asked, "Were you encroaching on anyone at the school?"

"Encroaching?" Fletcher repeated, and Jeffrey was about to explain to him what the word meant, but Fletcher said, "No, man. I don't know who else was dealing, but nobody ever said anything to me about it. I wasn't doing enough to cut into anybody's market. Honest."

"No one ever approached you, intimated they didn't like what you were doing?"

"Never," Fletcher insisted. "I was careful, you know. I only had a handful of kids I sold to. I wasn't looking to make a lot of money, just enough to keep me in weed."

"Just weed?"

"Sometimes some other stuff," Fletcher said. The man was not completely stupid; he knew that pot was a relatively minor offense compared to some of the other hard narcotics.

"Who were the kids you sold to?"

"Not many, just three or four."

"William Dickson?" Jeffrey asked. "Scooter?"

"Aw, no, not Scooter. He's dead. I didn't sell him that shit. Is that what this is about?" He became agitated, and Jeffrey indicated he should calm down.

"We know Scooter was dealing. Don't worry about Scooter."

"Oh, wow." Fletcher put his hand to his chest. "You scared me there for a minute."

Jeffrey thought he would go out on a limb. "We know you sold to Andy Rosen."

Fletcher's mouth worked but he did not speak. He looked from Frank to Jeffrey, then back to Frank again. "No way," he finally said. "I want a lawyer."

"A lawyer's going to change the whole tone of this interview, Ron. You bring in your lawyer, I've gotta bring in mine."

"No way. No way."

"If I file charges, that's it. You're in the system. No deal. You'll do hard time."

"This is so bogus. This is entrapment."

"It's not entrapment," Jeffrey corrected. Technically, since Fletcher had asked for a lawyer, this was merely a violation of his Miranda rights. "We're not looking to nail you, Ron. We just want to know what you sold to Andy Rosen."

"No way, man," Fletcher challenged. "I know how this works. If he smoked some dope before he jumped off that bridge, y'all are gonna pin this on me — I mean, on whoever sold him the shit."

Jeffrey leaned across the table. "Andy didn't jump, Ron. He was pushed."

"No shit?" Fletcher asked, staring from Jeffrey to Frank again. "Man, that is wrong. That is just so wrong. Andy was a good kid. He had some trouble, but . . . shit. He was a good kid."

"What kind of trouble did he have?"

"Couldn't get off the dope," Fletcher said, throwing his hands into the air. "Some people, they wanna and they just can't."

"He really wanted to?"

"I thought," Fletcher said. "I mean, you know. I thought he did."

"Until?"

Fletcher grimaced. "Oh, I don't know."

"Until when, Ron? Did he try to buy something from you?"

"He didn't have any money," Fletcher said. "He was all like" — he hunched his shoulders and started rubbing his hands together — " 'I will gladly pay you Tuesday for some rock today.' "

Jeffrey asked, "So did you?"

"Hell no, man. Andy tried to burn me before. He tried to burn everybody."

"Did he have enemies because of this?"

Fletcher shook his head. "You could push him and get it back. I felt sorry for the little dude about that. He was all tough and shit, but all you had to do was push him around some and he was like, 'All right. Here's the money. Don't hurt me.'" Fletcher stopped, realizing what he had said. "Not that I would hurt him. That's not my game, man. I'm all about being mellow, exploring your, you know, your . . ." Fletcher looked for the word. "No, that's not right. Expanding. You gotta expand your mind. Open yourself up."

"Right," Jeffrey said, thinking that if Fletcher's mind expanded any more he'd be drooling.

"I felt bad for him. He had some good news. He was ready to do some celebrating."

Jeffrey shot Frank a look. "What was he celebrating?"

"Didn't say," Fletcher answered. "Didn't say, and I didn't ask. That was how Andy was. He liked to keep his secrets, you know. Even if he was just going to the bathroom to take a crap, it was all a big se-

cret, like he was fucking James Bond."
Fletcher feigned a laugh. "Ha, ha. Not like
he was fucking the dude."

"What about Chuck?" Jeffrey asked.
"How was he involved in this?"

Fletcher shrugged. "I don't want to
speak ill of the —"

"Ron?"

He groaned, rubbing his stomach. "He
mighta been getting some money off the
top. You know, for, like, rent and all."

Jeffrey sat back in his chair, trying to
figure out how Chuck could be connected
to the recent murders. Drug dealers only
killed people who crossed them, and then
they did it in a spectacular way to serve as
a warning to would-be rivals. Staging the
deaths to look like suicides would be contrary to good business.

Fletcher had grown nervous over Jeffrey's silence. "Do I need a lawyer?" he
asked.

"Not if you cooperate." Jeffrey pulled
out a notebook and a pen. He slid them
over to Fletcher, saying, "I know this is
your first offense, Ron. We'll try to keep
you from doing jail time, but you've got to
tell us what's in your apartment. If I go
there and find something that you haven't
mentioned, then I'm going to tell the judge

to give you the maximum sentence."

"Okay, man," Fletcher said. "Okay. Meth. I've got a little meth, and it's under my mattress."

Jeffrey indicated the pen and paper.

Fletcher started to write, offering a running narrative of his house. "There's some pot in the fridge, in the butter-dish area. What's that you call where the butter goes?"

Jeffrey offered, "Butter compartment?"

"Yeah, yeah." Fletcher nodded, going back to his pad.

Jeffrey stood, thinking he had better things to do than this. He left the door open so he could watch Fletcher from the hallway.

Frank asked, "What's up?"

Jeffrey lowered his voice, telling Frank, "I'm going to go talk to Jill Rosen again, see what she can give me."

"How's the kid doing?"

Jeffrey felt his mood darken at the thought of Lena. "I talked to Nan Thomas this morning. I dunno. Maybe I'll go by and see if she's willing to press charges."

"She won't do it," Frank said, and Jeffrey knew he was right.

Jeffrey said, "You could talk to her," and Frank reacted as if Jeffrey had suggested he slap his own mother with a wet rag. Since Lena's attack Frank had not known how to deal with his ex-partner. Jeffrey sometimes understood the other man's reaction, but he could not imagine anything that would make him abandon his own partner. There were cops back in Birmingham that Jeffrey had not seen in years who could call him anytime and he would be in his car in seconds on the way to Alabama.

Jeffrey said, "I'm not going to order you to go see her, but I think if you reached out —"

Frank coughed into his hand.

Jeffrey tried again. "She trusts you, Frank. Maybe you could lead her down the right path."

"Looks to me like she's already chosen which path she wants to take." He got a steely look to his eyes, and Jeffrey remembered how hard it had been to pull Frank off Ethan White yesterday. If Jeffrey had left him to it, White would probably be dead right now.

"She'll listen to you," Jeffrey said. "You might be our last chance to get through to her."

Frank ignored this so smoothly that Jeffrey wondered if he had even said it.

With a wave of his hand, Frank indicated Fletcher, who was already working on the second page of his confession. "You want me to toss his place?"

"Yeah," Jeffrey said, aware of the distinct possibility that Fletcher was a very convincing liar. "Go ahead and process him for the pot in his locker. We'll see what sticks on him at the end of the day."

"What about White?" Frank said. "You gonna cut him loose?"

Jeffrey had called on the Macon sheriff to keep White in lockup, not trusting his own people to leave the kid alone. "I'm going to hold him as long as I can, but if Lena doesn't file charges, there's not a hell of a lot I can do."

"What about DNA?"

"You know that takes a week at least," Jeffrey reminded him. "And even if it comes back, it doesn't matter if she keeps insisting it was consensual."

Frank gave a tight nod. "You going to Atlanta tonight?"

Jeffrey said, "Yeah, probably," even though the last thing Sara had said to him last night was to leave her alone for a while. There was going to come a day when she'd say that to him and really mean it. He hoped like hell that was not now.

Jeffrey walked to the Rosen-Keller house, needing the time to clear his mind. Guilt was piling up this week, from Tessa's stabbing to Lena's attack. Last night in the jail, all he had wanted to do was put his arm around her and make it better. He had known in his gut that this was the last thing Lena needed, and the next best thing Jeffrey could do was find out who had started all of this in the first place. No physical evidence had shown an intruder in the security office. There was no one who had a specific grudge against Chuck and, other than the general consensus that he was an asshole, no one could think of a reason for someone to kill him. Even if he was skimming something off the top of Fletcher's drug trade, it was Fletcher who would be punished, not Chuck.

The red Mustang was still parked in the driveway where Jeffrey had seen it last. He walked to the front porch and knocked on the door, tucking his hands into his pockets as he waited. A few minutes passed, and he peered into the window, wondering if Jill Rosen had really left her husband.

He knocked on the door a couple more times before leaving. Jeffrey was halfway down the driveway when he changed his mind. He walked toward the back of the house, to Andy Rosen's apartment. Fletcher had said that Andy wanted to celebrate Saturday night. Maybe Jeffrey could figure out what the boy was so happy about.

Jeffrey knocked on the door to the apartment, not wanting to interrupt Jill Rosen if she was packing up her son's things. He tried the doorknob.

"Hello?" he called, walking into the small apartment. Much like the main house, whoever decorated the interior of Andy's apartment had not been back since. An orange shag rug covered the floor, and the walls were a dark pine paneling that bowed out in places. There was a bathroom right beside the door with a sitting room behind it. Tattered posters for rap groups were taped haphazardly over the walls. Two pyramids of beer cans stacked about three feet high flanked either side of a big-screen television.

An easel by the window held a rough sketch of another nude woman, this one thankfully not in color. Jeffrey picked through the plastic crate of art supplies on the floor, finding several cans of paint thinner and a couple cans of aerosol paint.

At the bottom of the crate, he found two tubes of airplane glue and a used-looking rag. He sniffed the rag and nearly passed out from the chemicals.

"Christ," Jeffrey said. Under the sink he found four more aerosol cans. In the small bathroom were four cans of spray toilet-bowl cleaner. Either Andy Rosen was a neat freak or he was huffing — inhaling glue and aerosols to get high. Sara would not have found that on the tox screen unless she had specified that the lab look for it.

Jeffrey scanned the room for other signs of drug use. Scattered on the floor was paraphernalia for a video-game player and several CDs that were out of their cases. The entertainment center had a DVD player, a VCR, a CD player, an elaborate stereo receiver, and a surround-sound speaker. Either Andy was dealing or his parents had taken out a second mortgage to keep him in electronics.

The bedroom of the apartment was sectioned off by a series of wooden screens. Behind them the bed was unmade and wrinkled. The scent of sweat and cocoa-butter hand lotion hung in the air. A lamp by the bed had a red scarf draped over its shade, as if to set the mood.

The drawers and closet in the bedroom had already been searched, but Jeffrey felt compelled to check again. Three or four shirts hung in the closet, T-shirts overflowing from shelves built into the sides. Three pairs of worn-looking blue jeans were on the top shelf, and he unfolded them, checking the pockets of each one before throwing them back onto the shelf.

Several shoe boxes were on the floor of the closet, most of them containing shiny new sneakers. One of them held a stack of photographs and a bunch of Andy's old report cards. Jeffrey read the report cards, which showed a hell of a lot more promise than his own had, then looked through the photographs. Jill Rosen and Brian Keller remained pretty much the same in each picture, but the scenery behind them changed, from roller coasters to water slides, from the Smithsonian to the Grand Canyon. Andy was in very few of the photographs, and Jeffrey imagined that he had elected himself family photographer.

There was a separate stack of black-and-white prints at the bottom of the box. Jeffrey picked these up. The rubber band holding them together was so old it broke off in his hand. The first photo was of a young woman sitting in a rocking chair holding a baby. Her hair was cut into the shape of a football helmet and sprayed to within an inch of its life, the same way Jeffrey's mother had worn hers when he was in high school.

In other pictures the woman was playing with the child, her hair growing longer in each shot as the boy aged. There were ten pictures in all, stopping around the time the kid was three. Jeffrey stared at the last shot, which showed the woman sitting alone in the rocking chair. She was staring right at the camera, and there was something familiar about the shape of her face and her long eyelashes. Jeffrey turned the last photo over, reading the date, trying to put the pieces together. He stared back at the woman, wondering again why she looked so damn familiar.

He flipped open his phone and dialed Kevin Blake's office. Candy answered after three rings.

"Hey there, hon," she said, sounding pleased to hear his voice. "I was just about to call you."

"Did you track down Monica Patrick?"

"Yep," she said, not sounding happy about it. "She's been dead three years now."

Jeffrey had feared as much. "Thanks for trying."

"Sure," she said. "Don't know what good she would've been. I guess you were looking for some kind of scandal?"

"Something like that," Jeffrey allowed, staring at the photograph as if he could force it to make sense.

"I went through all of that when I screened him," she said. "Brian's not exactly Albert Einstein, but he's one of those workhorse types. Does the jobs nobody else wants to do. Stays until midnight making sure everything's done. We call it anal retentive now, but back then it just meant you had a work ethic."

Jeffrey tucked the photographs into his pocket and put the shoe box back where it belonged. "I got the impression from his wife that he's still like that."

"Well, she should know," Candy said. "Though it's a bit late in the game to start complaining about it."

Jeffrey closed the closet door, looking around the room. "What do you mean?"

"That's how they got together," she told him. "Jill was his secretary back at Jericho."

"You're joking?"

"Why would I joke about that?" she asked. "There's nothing wrong with being a secretary."

"No, not that," Jeffrey said. "It's just that neither of them ever mentioned it."

"Why would they?" Candy asked, and she had a point. "Didn't you ever wonder why they have different names?"

"Not really," he told her, hearing a car door slam in the driveway. He walked into the living room to look out the front window. Brian Keller was leaning into the backseat of a tan Impala. He pulled out a couple of large white boxes, leaning them on his thigh while he shut the car door.

"Chief?"

"I'm here," Jeffrey told her, trying to pick back up on the conversation. "What were you saying?"

"I'm saying he probably divorced her by now."

"Divorced who?" Jeffrey asked, watching Keller try to manage the boxes as he walked toward the garage.

"The girl he was married to when he started seeing Jill Rosen," she told him, then added, "Not that she's a girl now. Hell, she's probably in her fifties. I wonder what happened to the son?"

"The son?" Jeffrey repeated, hearing Keller's footsteps on the stairs. "What son?"

"His son from his first marriage," she

588

said. "Are you paying attention to me at all?"

"He has a son by his first marriage?" Jeffrey said, taking out the photograph.

"That's what I've been telling you. He just up and left them. Never even mentioned them to Bert. You remember Bert Winger — he was dean before Kevin came along. Not that Bert woulda given two shakes about Brian's family situation. He had two kids of his own from a previous marriage, and let me tell you, those children were the sweetest little things I ever —"

"I need to go," Jeffrey said, closing the phone. He finally knew why the kid in the photo looked so familiar.

The old saying was true. A picture really was worth a thousand words — or in this case, a free ride to the police station in the back of a squad car.

Keller walked in the door and startled at the sight of Jeffrey, nearly dropping the boxes. "What are you doing here?"

"Just looking around."

"I can see that."

"Where's your wife?" Jeffrey asked.

Keller's face paled. He leaned over, dropping the boxes onto the floor with a heavy thud. "She's at her mother's."

"Not that one," Jeffrey said, holding up the photograph. "Your other one."

"My other —"

"Your first wife," Jeffrey clarified, showing him another picture. "The mother of your oldest son."

16

Lena shuffled into the kitchen, every joint in her body grating like rusted metal. Nan was sitting at the table reading the newspaper while she ate a bowl of cereal.

"Sleep okay?" Nan asked.

Lena nodded, looking around for the coffeemaker. The kettle on the stove was steaming. A cup was on the counter with a tea bag beside it.

"Do you have coffee?" Lena asked, her voice barely a whisper.

"I've got instant," Nan said, "but it's decaffeinated. I could run up to the store before I go to work."

"That's okay," Lena said, wondering how long it would be before she started to get a caffeine-withdrawal headache.

"You sound better this morning," Nan said, trying to smile. "Your voice. It's more like a whisper instead of a croak."

Lena slumped into a chair, exhaustion

pulling at her bones. Nan had taken the couch, leaving the bed to Lena, but Lena had not been able to get comfortable. Nan's bed was underneath a bank of windows that looked out into the backyard. All of them were at ground level, and none of them had blinds or even curtains. Lena had not been able to close her eyes, afraid that someone would crawl in through the windows and grab her. She had gotten up several times, checking the locks, trying to see if anyone was outside. The backyard was too dark for her to see more than a few feet, and Lena had finally ended up with her back to the door and the gun in her lap.

Lena cleared her throat. "I need to borrow some money."

"Of course," Nan told her. "I've been trying to give you —"

"Borrow it," Lena insisted. "I'll pay you back."

"Okay," Nan agreed, standing up to wash her bowl at the sink. "Are you going to take a little time off? You're welcome to stay here."

"I need to hire a lawyer for Ethan."

Nan dropped her bowl in the sink. "Do you think that's wise?"

"I can't leave him in jail," Lena said,

knowing that the black gangs would kill Ethan as soon as they saw his tattoos.

Nan sat back down at the table. "I don't know if I can give you the money for that."

"I'll get it from somewhere," Lena said, though she did not know where.

Nan stared at her, lips slightly parted. She finally nodded. "All right. We'll go to the bank when I get home from work."

"Thank you."

Nan had more to say. "I didn't call Hank."

"I don't want you to," Lena insisted. "I don't want him to see me like this."

"He's seen you like this before."

Lena gave her a warning look, letting Nan know that was not open for discussion.

"All right," Nan repeated, and Lena wondered if she was saying it more to herself. "So I've got to get to work. There's an extra key by the front door if you go out."

"I'm not going anywhere."

"That's probably best," Nan said, glancing at Lena's neck. Lena had not looked in the mirror this morning, but she could imagine how bad she looked. The cut on her cheek felt warm, like it might be infected.

Nan said, "I'll be back at lunchtime,

around one. We're going to start inventory next week, and I need to get some things done."

"That's okay."

"Are you sure you don't want to come to school with me? You could stay in the office. No one would see you."

Lena shook her head. She did not ever want to return to campus again.

Nan scooped up her book bag and a set of keys. "Oh, I almost forgot."

Lena waited.

"Richard Carter might drop by."

Lena muttered a curse that Nan had obviously never heard from a woman.

Nan said, "Oh, my."

"Does he know I'm here?"

"No, I didn't know you were going to be here. I gave him the key last night at dinner."

"You gave him the key to your house?" Lena asked, incredulous.

"He worked with Sibyl for years," Nan defended. "She trusted him with everything."

"What does he want?"

"To go through some of her notes."

"He can read Braille?"

Nan fidgeted with her keys. "There's a translator at the library he can run it through. It's going to take him forever."

"What's he looking for?"

"God knows." Nan rolled her eyes. "You know how secretive he can be."

Lena agreed, but she thought this was odd behavior even for Richard. She would find out what the hell he was up to before he even got near Sibyl's notes.

"I'd better scoot," Nan said. She pointed to the cast on Lena's wrist. "You're supposed to keep that elevated."

Lena raised her arm.

"You've got my number at school." Nan indicated the keypad. "Just press the 'stay' button if you like."

"Right," Lena said, though she had no intention of setting the alarm. A spoon clanging against a frying pan would be more effective.

"It gives you twenty seconds to close the door," Nan said. Then, when Lena didn't respond, she pressed the "stay" key herself. "The code's your birthday."

The pad started beeping, counting down the seconds Nan had to leave through the front door.

Lena said, "Great."

"Call me if you need me," Nan told her. "Bye!"

Lena closed the front door and locked

the bottom latch. With one hand she dragged a chair over and propped it under the knob so Richard couldn't surprise her. She pulled aside the curtain and looked out the little round window in the door, watching Nan back out of the driveway. Lena felt stupid for breaking down in front of Nan last night, but part of her was glad that the woman had been there. She was finally understanding after all these years what Sibyl had seen in the mousy librarian. Nan Thomas wasn't that bad after all.

Lena grabbed the cordless phone off the coffee table on her way to the kitchen. She found the Yellow Pages in the drawer by the sink and sat at the table. The ads for lawyers took up five pages, each one of them colorful and tacky. Their headlines beseeched those suffering from car accidents or sucking off disability to call right now for help.

Buddy Conford's ad was the biggest one. A picture of the slick bastard had a cartoon balloon coming out of his mouth with the words "Call me before you talk to the police!" written in fat red letters.

He answered on the first ring. "Buddy Conford."

Lena chewed at her lip, reopening the cut. Buddy was a one-legged bastard who thought all cops were crooked, and on more than one occasion he'd accused Lena of using illegal methods. He had busted a few of her cases wide open on stupid technicalities.

"Hello?" Buddy said. "All righty, counting to three. One . . . two . . ."

Lena forced herself to say, "Buddy."

"Yep, you got 'im." When she did not say anything, he prompted, "Speak."

"It's Lena."

"Come again?" he said. "Darlin', I can barely hear you."

She cleared her throat, trying to raise her voice. "It's Lena Adams."

The lawyer let out a low whistle. "Well, I'll be," he said. "I heard you were in the pokey. Thought it was a rumor."

Lena kept enough pressure on her lip to cause pain.

"How's it feel to be on the other side of the law now, partner?"

"Fuck you."

"We'll discuss my fee later," Buddy said, chuckling. He was enjoying this even more than she had imagined he would. "What are you charged with?"

"Nothing," she told him, thinking that that could change at any minute, depending on what kind of day Jeffrey had.

"This is for somebody else."

"Who's that?"

"Ethan Green." She corrected herself. "White, I mean. Ethan White."

"Where's he at?"

"I'm not sure." Lena closed the phone book, sick of looking at the cheap ads. "He's charged with some sort of parole violation. The original charge was bad checks."

"How long've they had him locked up?"

"I'm not sure," Lena said.

"Unless they have something solid to charge him with, they mighta already cut him loose."

"Jeffrey won't cut him loose," Lena told him, certain of that one thing. He only knew Ethan White from his rap sheet. He had never seen the good side of Ethan, the side that wanted to change.

"There's something you're not telling me here," Buddy said. "How'd he end up on the chief's radar?"

Lena ran her fingers along the pages of the book. She wondered how much she could tell Buddy Conford. She wondered if she should tell him anything at all.

Buddy was good enough to know what was coming. "If you lie to me, it only makes it harder to do my job."

"He didn't kill Chuck Gaines," she said. "He wasn't involved in any of that. He's innocent."

Buddy gave a heavy sigh. "Honey, let me tell you something. *All* my clients are innocent. Even the one that ended up on death row." He made a disgusted sound. "*Especially* the one that ended up on death row."

"This one's really innocent, Buddy."

"Yeah," he said. "Maybe we should do this in person. You wanna swing by my office?"

Lena closed her eyes, trying to visualize herself out of the house. She couldn't do it.

Buddy asked, "Something I said?"

"No," Lena told him. "Can you come here instead?"

"Where's here?"

"I'm at Nan Thomas's house." She gave him the address, and he repeated the numbers back to her.

"It'll be a couple of hours," he said. "You gonna be around?"

"Yeah."

Buddy said, "I'll see you in a couple."

She hung up the phone, then dialed the number at the police station. She knew that Jeffrey would do everything he could to hold Ethan in lockup, but she also knew that Ethan was well aware of how the law worked.

"Grant Police," Frank said.

Lena had to force herself not to hang up the phone. She cleared her throat, trying to make her voice sound normal.

She said, "Frank? It's Lena."

He was silent.

"I'm looking for Ethan."

"Yeah?" he grumbled. "Well, he ain't here."

"Do you know where —"

He slammed the phone down so hard the sound echoed in Lena's ear.

"Shit," she said, then started coughing so violently she thought her lungs were going to pop out of her mouth. Lena went to the sink and drank a glass of water. Several minutes passed before the coughing fit passed. She started opening drawers, looking for some cough drops to soothe her throat, but found nothing. She found a bottle of Advil in the cabinet over the stove and shook three capsules into her mouth. Several more came out, and she tried to catch them before they fell on the floor, smacking her hurt wrist against the refrigerator in the process. The pain made her see stars, but she breathed through it.

Back at the table, Lena tried to think

where Ethan would go if he was let out of jail. She did not know his number at the dorm and knew better than to call the campus office to try to get it. Considering that Lena had been in jail last night, she doubted that anyone would want to help her.

Two nights ago she had plugged in her answering machine in case Jill Rosen called back. Lena picked up the phone and dialed her home phone number, hoping she had hooked up the machine right. The phone rang three times before her own voice greeted her, sounding foreign and loud. She punched in the code to play back her messages. The first one was from her uncle Hank, saying he was just checking in and was glad she had finally decided to get an answering machine. The next was from Nan, sounding very worried and asking Lena to call her as soon as she could. The last message was from Ethan.

"Lena," he said. "Don't go anywhere. I'm looking for you."

She pressed the three button, rewinding the message to play it again. There was no time or day stamp on the machine because she had been too cheap to spend the extra ten bucks, and the three rewound all the messages, not just the last one, so she had to listen to Hank and Nan again.

"Don't go anywhere. I'm looking for you."

She hit the three again, suffering through the first two messages before she heard Ethan's voice. Lena pressed the phone closer to her ear, trying to decipher his tone. He sounded angry, but that was nothing new.

She was listening to the message a fourth time when a knock came at the door.

"Richard," she mumbled under her breath. She looked down at her clothes, realizing she was still wearing the blue pajamas. "Fuck."

The portable phone beeped twice in quick succession, the LED screen flashing that the battery was low. Lena pressed the five key, hoping that would save Ethan's message.

She walked into the living room, dropping the phone in the charger. A dark figure was standing at the front door, the outline of his body showing through the curtains. She called, "Just a minute," her throat straining from the effort.

In Nan's bedroom she looked for something to cover herself. The only thing on offer was a pink terry-cloth robe, which was just as ludicrous as the blue pajamas.

Lena walked to the hall closet and took out a jacket. She put it on as she walked to the front door.

"Hold on," she said, removing the chair. She unlocked the dead bolts and opened the door, but no one was there.

"Hello?" Lena said, walking onto the front porch. No one was there either. The driveway was empty.

She could hear the alarm keypad beeping inside and remembered that Nan had set it before she left. The alarm was on a twenty-second delay, and Lena ran back into the house, entering the code into the keypad just in time.

She was walking toward the kitchen when the sound of breaking glass stopped her. The curtain on the kitchen door moved, but not from a breeze. A hand reached in, feeling for the latch. Lena stood, paralyzed for a few seconds, until panic took hold and she darted into the hallway.

Footsteps crunched across the kitchen floor. She ducked into the spare bedroom and hid between the open door and the wall, watching the hallway through the crack. The intruder made his way across the house in purposeful strides, his heavy shoes thunking across the hardwood floor.

In the hallway he stopped, looking left, then right. Lena could not see his face, but could tell he was wearing a black shirt and jeans.

She squeezed her eyes shut, holding her breath as he walked toward the spare room. She pressed her back into the wall as hard as she could, trying to make herself invisible behind the door.

When she dared to open her eyes, he was turned away from her. Lena could only stare. She had been sure the man was Ethan, but the shoulders were too broad, the hair too long.

The closet was packed floor to ceiling with boxes. The intruder started pulling them out one by one, reading their labels before stacking them neatly onto the floor. After what seemed like hours, he found what he wanted. Sitting on his knees in front of the box, he offered his profile to Lena. She recognized Richard Carter instantly.

Lena thought of the Glock in Nan's room. Richard had his back to her, and if she walked carefully, she might be able to clear the door and lock herself in Nan's room.

She held her breath, stepping out from behind the door. She was retreating slowly from the room when Richard sensed her presence. His head snapped around, and he stood quickly. White-hot anger flashed in his eyes, quickly replaced by relief. He said, "Lena."

"What are you doing here?" she demanded, trying to sound strong. Her throat scratched with every word, and she was certain he could hear the fear in her voice.

He furrowed his brow, clearly confused by her anger. "What happened to you?"

Lena put her hand to her face, remembering. "I fell."

"Again?" Richard gave a sad smile. "I used to fall that way myself. I told you I know what it's like. I went through the same thing."

"I don't know what you're talking about."

"Sibyl never told you the stories?" he asked, then smiled. "No, of course she wouldn't tell secrets. She wasn't that way."

"What secrets?" Lena asked, reaching behind her, trying to find the doorway.

"Family secrets."

He took a step toward her and Lena stepped back.

"It's a funny thing about some women," he said. "They get rid of one wife beater and run right to the next one with open arms. It's like deep down that's what they really want. It's not love unless they're getting the shit beaten out of them."

"What are you talking about?"

"Not you, of course." He waited long enough to let her know that was exactly what he meant. "My mother," he provided. "Or, more specifically, my stepfathers. I had several of them."

Lena took a small step away from him, her shoulder brushing the doorjamb. She bent her left arm, keeping her cast clear of the leaded glass knob. "They hit you?"

"All of them did," Richard said. "They would start off with her, but then they always came to me. They knew something was wrong with me."

"Nothing's wrong with you."

"Of course there is," Richard told her. "People sense it. They know when you need them, and what they do is they punish you for it."

"Richard —"

"You know what's funny? My mom always protected them. She always made it clear that they were more important to her than I was." He gave a sad laugh. "And then she turned around and did it to them. None of them were ever as good as the one who got away."

"Who?" Lena asked. "Who got away?"

He inched closer to her. "Brian Keller." He laughed at her surprise. "We're not supposed to tell anybody."

"Why?"

"His faggot son from his first marriage?" Richard said. "He said if I told anybody, he would stop talking to me. He would cut me completely out of his life."

"I'm sorry," Lena said, taking another step back. She was a few feet into the hallway now and she had to fight her instinct to run. The look in Richard's eyes made it clear that he would chase her. "I'm expecting the lawyer here soon. I need to get dressed."

"Don't move, Lena."

"Richard —"

"I mean it," he said, standing less than a foot away from her. His shoulders were squared, and she sensed that Richard could really hurt her if he put his mind to it. "Don't move an inch."

She stood still, holding her left arm to her chest, trying to think of anything she could do. He was at least twice her size. She had never noticed what a large man he was, perhaps because she had never seen him as a threat.

She repeated, "The lawyer will be here soon."

Richard reached past her shoulder and turned on the hall light. He looked her up and down, taking in her cuts and bruises. "Look at you," he said. "You know what it's like to have someone preying on you." He gave her a sly smile. "Like Chuck."

"What do you know about Chuck?"

"Only that he's dead," Richard said. "And that the world's a better place without him."

Lena tried to swallow, but her throat was too dry. "I don't know what you want from me."

"Cooperation," he said. "We can help each other. We can help each other a lot."

"I don't see how."

"You know what it's like to be second best," he told her. "Sibyl never talked about it, but I know that your uncle favored her."

Lena did not respond, but in her heart his words rang true.

"Andy was always Brian's favorite. He was the reason they left town in the first place. He was the reason they abandoned me with my mom and Kyle and Buddy and Jack and Troy and every other asshole who thought it was fun to get drunk and beat the shit out of Esther Carter's little faggot son."

"Did you kill him?" Lena asked. "Did you kill Andy?"

"Andy was blackmailing him. He knew that Brian didn't come up with the idea on his own, let alone implement the research."

"What idea?"

"Sibyl's idea. She was about to submit her research to the committee before she was killed."

Lena glanced at the boxes. "Are those her notes?"

"Her research," he clarified. "The only proof left that it was hers." A look of sadness crossed his face. "She was so brilliant, Lena. I wish you could understand how truly gifted she was."

Lena could not hide her anger. "You stole her idea."

"I worked with her on it every step of the way," he defended. "And when she was gone, I was the only one who knew about it. I was the only one who could make sure her work was continued."

"How could you do that to her?" Lena asked, because she knew that Richard had cared for Sibyl. "How could you take credit for her work?"

"I was tired, Lena. You of all people should understand that I was tired of being the second choice. I was tired of watching

Brian waste everything on Andy when I was right there, ready to do anything for him at any cost." He pounded his hand into his fist. "I was the good son. I was the one who translated Sibyl's notes for him. I was the one who brought it to him so we could work together and create something that —" He stopped, his lips a thin line as he tried to hold back his emotions. "Andy didn't give a fuck about him. All he cared about was what car he could get or CD player or video game. That's all Brian was to him, a cash machine." He tried to reason with her. "He was blackmailing us. Both of us. Yes, I killed him. I killed him for my father."

Lena could only ask, "How?"

"He knew Brian couldn't do this," Richard said, indicating the boxes. "Brian's not exactly a visionary."

"Anyone would know that," Lena said, getting to the heart of the matter. "What was his proof?"

Richard seemed impressed that she had worked it out. "The first rule of scientific research," he said. "Write it down."

"He kept notes?"

"Journals," Richard said. "He wrote down every meeting, every phone call, every stupid idea that never panned out."

"Andy found the journals?"

"Not just the journals — all the notes, all the preliminary data. Transcripts from Sibyl's earlier research." Richard paused, visibly angry. "Brian wrote down every goddamn thing in those journals, and he just left them lying around for Andy to find, and of course Andy's first reaction isn't, 'Oh, Dad, let me return these.' It's, 'Hm, how can I get more money for this?' "

"Is that how you got him to meet you on the bridge?"

"Smart," he said. "Yes. I told him I was going to give him the money. I knew he would never stop. He would just keep demanding more and more money, and who knows who he'd talk to?" Richard gave an exasperated snort. "All Andy ever cared about was himself and how he was going to get his next high. He couldn't be trusted. It was always going to be take, take, take for him, and everything I worked for, all the sacrifices I made to *help* my father, to give him something to work on that he could be proud of — that *we* could be proud of — would be smoked away by that little ungrateful piece of shit."

The hatred in his voice took Lena's breath away. She could only imagine what it must have felt like for Andy to be trapped on the bridge with Richard.

"I could have made him suffer." Richard moderated his tone, obviously trying to sound reasonable. "I could have punished him for what he was doing to me — to the relationship I worked to build with my father — but I chose to be humane."

"He must have been terrified."

"He was so huffed up on Tidy Bowl he could barely see," Richard said, disgusted. "I just steadied him with my hand here" — he put his hand a few inches in front of Lena's chest — "gently leaned him against the railing, and injected him with succynil-choline. Do you know what that is?"

She shook her head, praying he would move his hand away from her.

"We use it at the lab to put down animals. It paralyzes you — paralyzes everything. He just fell into my arms like a rag doll and stopped breathing." Richard inhaled sharply, his eyes wide in surprise, illustrating Andy's reaction. "I could have made him suffer. I could have made it horrible, but I didn't."

"They'll figure it out, Richard."

He finally dropped his hand. "It's not traceable."

"They'll still figure it out."

"Who?"

"The police," she told him. "They know it's murder."

"I heard," he said, but he did not seem threatened by the information.

"They'll trace it back to you."

"How?" he asked. "There's no reason for them even to suspect me. Brian won't even admit I'm his son, and even if Jill didn't have her head in the sand, she's too afraid to say anything."

"Afraid of what?"

"Afraid of Brian," Richard said, as if that were obvious. "Afraid of his fists."

"He beats his wife?" Lena asked. She couldn't accept that Richard was telling the truth. Jill Rosen was strong. She wasn't the type to take shit from anyone.

Richard said, "Of course he beats her."

"Jill Rosen?" she said, still incredulous. "He beats Jill?"

"He's beaten her for years," he said. "And she's stayed with him because no one's helped her like I can help you."

"I don't need help."

"Yes you do," he said. "Do you think he's just going to let you go?"

"Who?"

"You know who."

Lena stopped him. "I don't know what you're talking about."

"I know how hard it is to get away," he told her, putting his hand to his chest. "I know you can't do that kind of thing on your own."

She shook her head.

"Let me take care of him for you."

"No," she said, taking a step back.

"I can make it look like an accident," he told her, closing the space between them.

"Yeah, you've done such a great job so far."

"You could give me some advice," he said, holding up his hand so she wouldn't interrupt. "Just a little advice is all. We can help each other get out of this."

"How can you help me?"

"By getting rid of him," Richard said, and he must have seen something in her eyes, because he gave a sad smile. "You know it, don't you? You know that's the only way you're ever going to get him out of your life."

Lena stared at him. "Why did you kill Ellen Schaffer?"

"Lena."

"Tell me why," she insisted. "I need to know why."

Richard waited a beat before saying, "She looked right at me when I was in the woods. She stared at me while she was calling the cops. I knew it was just a matter of time before she told them."

"What about Scooter?"

"Why are you doing this?" Richard asked. "You think I'm going to offer this long confession and then you're going to arrest me?"

"We both know I can't arrest you."

"Can't you?"

"Look at me," she said, holding her arms out to the side, drawing attention to her battered body. "You know better than anybody else what I'm mixed up in. Do you think they're going to listen to me?" She put her hand to her bruised neck. "They can barely even hear me."

He gave a half smile, shaking his head as if to say he could not be suckered in.

"I need to know, Richard. I need to know I can trust you."

He gave her a careful look, trying to decide whether to continue. Finally he said, "Scooter wasn't me."

"Are you sure?"

"Of course I'm sure." Richard rolled his eyes, for just a moment the girly Richard she knew from before. "I heard he was scarfing. Who's stupid enough to do that anymore?"

Lena resisted his cattiness as an invitation to let down her guard. "And Tessa Linton?"

"She had this bag," he said, suddenly agitated. "She was picking up stuff on the hill. I couldn't find the necklace. I wanted that necklace. It was a symbol."

"The Star of David?" she said, remembering how Jill had clung to it in the library. That day seemed like a lifetime ago.

"They both had one. Jill bought them last year, one for Brian and one for Andy. Father and son." He exhaled sharply. "Brian wore it every day. Do you think he would do something like that for me?"

"You stabbed Tess Linton because you thought she had the necklace?"

"She recognized me somehow. I saw her putting it together. She knew why I was there. She knew I had killed Andy." Richard paused, as if to gather his thoughts. "She started yelling at me. Screaming. I had to shut her up." He wiped his face with his hands, his composure slipping. "Oh, Jesus, that was hard. That was so hard to do." He looked down at the floor, and she could feel his remorse. "I can't believe I had to do that. It was so horrible. I stayed around to see what happened and . . ." His voice trailed off, and he was silent, as if he wanted Lena to say it was okay, that he had not been given a choice.

He said, "How do you want to do this?"

Lena did not answer.

"How do you want me to get rid of him?" Richard asked. "I can make him suffer, Lena. I can hurt him just like he hurt you."

Lena still could not answer. She looked at her hands, thinking about Ethan in the coffee shop and how angry she had been when he hurt her. She had wanted to pay him back, to make him suffer for the pain he caused.

Richard lightly tapped his finger on the cast. "I had more than my share of these growing up."

She rubbed the cast. The scar on her hand was still red, dried blood around the edges. She picked at it as Richard laid out his plan.

"You won't have to do anything," he said. "I'll make sure everything is taken care of. I've helped women like you before, Lena. Just say the word and I can make him go away."

She could feel the scar give under her fingernails, peeling back like the sticker on an orange. "How?" she whispered, playing with the edge of skin. "How would you do it?"

Richard was watching her hands, too. "Will it do any good?" he asked. "Will it make you stop hurting yourself?"

She clutched her right hand around the cast and held it low on her waist, shaking her head, saying, "I just need to get him out of my life. I just need to get away."

"Oh, Lena." He put his fingers under her chin, trying to get her to look up. When she did not move, he leaned down, putting his hands on her shoulders, his face close to hers. "We'll get through this," he said. "I promise you. We can do it together."

With both hands Lena rammed the cast up into his throat as hard as she could. The cast cracked underneath his jaw, clamping his teeth down on his tongue, throwing his head back whiplash fast. Richard stumbled backward, his arms flailing as he fell hard against the doorjamb. She bolted down the hallway toward Nan's room, slamming the door behind her, working the ancient thumb latch just before Richard turned the knob from the other side.

Nan's gun was under the bed. Lena dropped to her knees, pulling out the box. The cast had split open at the top, and she managed to use both hands to jam the magazine into the gun and release the

618

safety before Richard broke down the door. He came in so fast that he tripped over her, knocking the gun from Lena's hand. She scrambled to reach the weapon, but he was faster than she was. She stood slowly, hands in the air, as he pointed the gun at her chest.

"Get on the bed," he told her, blood and saliva spraying from his mouth. His words were thick from where he had bitten his tongue, and his breathing was labored, like he was not getting enough air. He kept the gun on her and put his free hand to his throat, coughing once. "I could have helped you, you stupid bitch."

Lena stayed where she was.

Despite his injury, his voice filled the room. "Get on the fucking bed!"

When she still did not move, Richard raised his hand to hit her.

She did as she was told, lying on her back with her head on the pillow. "You don't have to do this."

Richard moved deliberately onto the bed, straddling her legs, keeping her in place. Blood dripped from his mouth and he wiped it on his sleeve. "Give me your hand."

"Don't do this."

"I can't knock you out," he said, and she

knew that Richard's only remorse came from the fact that her being awake made things more difficult for him. "Put your hand on the gun."

"You don't want to do this."

"Put your fucking hand on the gun!"

When she did not obey, Richard grabbed her hand and forced it around the gun. She tried to push the glock away, but he had the advantage of height. He pressed the muzzle to her head.

She said, "Don't."

Richard hesitated for half a second, then pulled the trigger.

Shards of glass rained down, and Lena put her hands over her head, trying to protect herself as the window exploded above her.

Richard was blown back onto the floor. That was how it happened: The window shattered, and he was on the floor. Empty space was above her, nothing but the ceiling fan in Lena's line of vision. She sat up so she could see Richard. There was a large hole in his chest, blood pooling around him.

Lena turned, looking behind her. Outside the broken window, Frank stood with his gun still drawn on Richard. The threat was unnecessary. Richard was dead.

17

Sara sat at Mason's desk, the phone propped between her shoulder and ear as she listened to Jeffrey describe what had happened at Nan Thomas's house.

"Frank hung up on Lena when she called the station. He felt guilty and went by to talk to her," Jeffrey explained. "Then he heard Richard screaming and ran around the back."

"Is Lena okay?"

"Yeah," he said, but she could tell from his tone of voice that she wasn't. "If Richard knew how to load a gun, she would be dead right now."

Sara sat back in the chair, trying to process everything he had said. "Has Brian Keller said anything?"

"Nothing," Jeffrey told her, sounding disgusted. "I brought him in for questioning, but his wife was here an hour later with a lawyer."

"His wife?" Sara asked, wondering how anyone could be so self-destructive.

"Yeah," Jeffrey said, and she could tell he agreed with her. "I can't hold him without a charge."

"He stole Sibyl's research."

"I'm meeting with the DA and the school's attorney in the morning to see exactly what we can charge him with. I guess we'll go with theft of intellectual property, maybe fraud. It's going to be complicated, but we'll get him in jail somehow. He's going to pay for this." He sighed. "I'm used to cops and robbers. These white-collar crimes are way over my head."

"You can't prove he was an accomplice to the murders?"

"That's the thing. I'm not sure if he is," Jeffrey told her. "The way Lena tells it, Richard copped to all of them: Andy, Ellen Schaffer, Chuck."

"Why Chuck?"

"Richard didn't exactly spell it out. He was just trying to get her on his side. I think he liked her. I think he thought he could help her."

Sara knew that Richard Carter would not be the first man who tried to save Lena Adams and failed spectacularly. She asked, "What about William Dickson?"

"Accidental death, unless you can figure out a way to pin it on Richard."

"No," Sara told him. "He never implicated Keller?"

"Never."

"Why did he make up that lie about the affair, then?"

Jeffrey sighed again, clearly exasperated. "Just to stir up more shit, I guess. Or maybe he thought it would make Brian come to him for help. Who knows?"

"Succynilcholine would be kept under lock and key at the lab," Sara offered. "There should be a log to account for its usage. You could check to see who had access."

"I'll follow up on it," he said. "But if both of them had access, it'll be hard to prove the case." Jeffrey paused. "I have to say, Sara, if Keller was going to kill one of his sons, it would have been Richard, and not with a needle."

"It's a nasty way to die," she told him, imagining the last few minutes of Andy Rosen's life. "His limbs would have been paralyzed first, then his heart and lungs. It doesn't affect the brain, so he would have been completely cognizant of what was happening right up until the last minute."

"How long would it take?"

"Depending on the dosage, twenty, thirty seconds."

"Jesus."

"I know," she agreed. "And it's nearly impossible to find postmortem. The body breaks it down too quickly. They didn't even have a way to test for it until about five years ago."

"Sounds like it'd be expensive to find."

"If you can put the succynilcholine in Keller's hands, I'll find money in the budget to run the test. I'll pay for it myself if I have to."

"I'll do everything I can," Jeffrey said, but he did not sound hopeful. "I know you'll give your folks the news, but do you want to wait until I get there to tell Tessa?"

"Sure," Sara said, but she had hesitated a second too long.

He paused before saying, "You know what? I've got a lot of work to do here anyway. I'll see you around."

"Jeffrey —"

"No," he said. "You stay up there with your family. That's what you need right now, to be with your family."

"That's not —"

"Come on, Sara," he said, and she could hear the hurt in his voice. "What are we doing here?"

"I don't know. I just . . ." Sara searched for something to tell him but came up blank. "I told you I need time."

"Time's not going to change anything," he said. "If we can't get past this, past what I did five years ago —"

"You make it sound like I'm being unreasonable."

"You're not," he said. "And I'm not trying to push you, I just . . ." He groaned. "I love you, Sara. I'm tired of you sneaking out every morning. I'm tired of this damn hokeypokey where you're half in and half out of my life. I want to be with you. I want to marry you."

"Marry me?" She laughed, as if he had asked her to go for a walk on the moon.

"You don't have to sound so shocked."

"I'm not shocked. I'm just . . ." Again she was at a loss for words. "Jeff, we were married before. It wasn't exactly successful."

"Yeah," he said. "I was there, remember?"

"Why can't we just go on how we are now?"

"I want something more than that," he told her. "I want to have a really shitty day at work and come home to you asking me what's for dinner. I want to knock over

Bubba's water bowl in the middle of the night. I want to wake up in the morning to the sound of you cussing because I left my jockstrap on the doorknob."

She smiled despite herself. "You make it all sound so romantic."

"I love you."

"I know you do," she said, and even though she loved him, too, Sara could not bring herself to say the words. "When can you get up here?"

"That's okay."

"I want you to tell her," she said. When he did not respond, she told him, "They're going to have questions I can't answer."

"You know everything I do."

"I don't think I can tell them," she said. "I don't think I have the strength right now."

He waited a beat before saying, "This time of day it'll be about four and a half hours."

"Okay." Sara gave him Tessa's room number. She was about to hang up but said, "Hey, Jeff?"

"Yeah?"

Now that she had stopped him, Sara did not know what to say. "Nothing," she told him. "I'll see you when you get here."

He gave her a few seconds to add more,

but when she did not, he said, "All right. I'll see you then."

Sara hung up the phone feeling as if she had just walked a tightrope over a lake of alligators. So much had happened this week that she could not even process what Jeffrey had said to her. Part of her wanted to pick the phone back up and tell him she was sorry, that she loved him, but another part of her wanted to call him and tell him to stay home.

Outside the door she could hear doctors being paged and codes being called. Shadowy figures walked by the glass, their images flashing like strobe lights as they ran to help patients. It felt as though a hundred years had passed since Sara had been an intern. Everything seemed more complicated now, and though she was certain that life had been just as overwhelming when she was younger, Sara could only think of those days with nostalgia. Learning to be a surgeon, treating critical cases that took every ounce of her discipline, had been as addictive as heroin. She still got a rush when she thought about working at Grady. At one time in her life, the hospital had been more important than air. Even her family had paled in comparison.

Making the decision to return to Grant had seemed so easy at the time. Sara had wanted — needed — to be with her family, to get back to her roots and feel safe, to be a daughter and a sister again. The role of town pediatrician had been a comfortable one to slip into, and she knew that it had given her some amount of peace to be able to give back to the town that had given her so much growing up. Still, not a week had gone by since Sara had left Atlanta that she did not find herself wondering what her life would have been like if she had stayed on. She had not realized until this moment how much she missed it.

Sara glanced around Mason's office, wondering what it would be like to work with him again. As an intern, Mason had been incredibly meticulous, which made him a very good surgeon. Unlike Sara, he let this trait spill over into his personal life. He was the sort of man who could not leave a plate unwashed in the sink or a load of clothes wrinkling in the dryer. The first time Mason had visited her apartment, he had nearly gone into apoplexy over the basket of unfolded clothes that had been sitting on her kitchen table for two weeks. When Sara had awakened the next morning, Mason had folded all the clothes before starting his 5:00 a.m. shift.

A knock on the door took Sara out of her reverie.

"Come in," she called, standing.

Mason James opened the door, carrying a pizza box in one hand and two Cokes in the other. "Thought you might be hungry," he said.

"Always," she returned, taking the Cokes.

Mason laid several napkins on the coffee table, holding the pizza aloft as he told her, "I left one with your folks."

"That was sweet of you," she said, setting down the cans to help him with the napkins.

Mason gave her the pizza box so he could put napkins under the cans. "You used to love this place in med school."

" 'Shroomies," she read off the top of the box. "Did I?"

"You ate there all the time." He rubbed his hands together. "Voilà."

Sara looked down. He had lined up the napkins into a perfect square. She handed him the box. "I'll let you put it down the right way."

He laughed. "Some things never change."

"No," she agreed.

"Your sister's looking good," he told her, placing the box squarely on the table.

"She's moving around a lot better than she was yesterday."

Sara sat down on the couch. "I think my mother's been pushing her."

"I can see Cathy doing that." He opened a napkin and put it in her lap. "Did you get the flowers?"

"Yes," she said. "Thank you. They're gorgeous."

He popped open the Cokes. "Just wanted to let you know I was thinking about you."

Sara played with the napkin, not sure what to say.

"Sara," Mason began, draping his arm on the couch behind her shoulders. "I never stopped loving you."

She felt a flush of embarrassment, but before she could respond, he leaned over and kissed her. To her surprise, Sara kissed him back. Before she knew what was happening, Mason moved closer, gently pushing her back on the couch until he was lying on top of her. His hands ran up the inside of her shirt as he pressed his body into hers. She put her arms around him, but instead of the mindless euphoria she usually felt at this point, all Sara could think was that the person she was holding was not Jeffrey.

"Wait," she said, stopping his hand on the button of her pants.

He sat up so quickly that his head hit the wall behind the couch. "I'm sorry."

"No," she said, buttoning her shirt, feeling like a teenager who had just gotten caught in the back of a movie theater. "I'm sorry."

"Don't apologize," he said, crossing his ankle over his knee.

"No, I —"

He shook his foot. "I shouldn't have done that."

"It's all right," she told him. "I did it back."

"You sure did," he said, exhaling in a short huff. "God, I want you."

Sara swallowed, feeling like she had too much saliva in her mouth.

He turned to her. "You're so wonderful, Sara. I think you might have forgotten that."

"Mason —"

"You're just extraordinary."

She felt herself blushing, and he reached over, tucking her hair behind her ear.

"Mason," she repeated, putting her hand over his.

He leaned in to kiss her again, and she tilted her head away from him.

Mason backed off just as quickly the second time.

Sara said, "I'm sorry. I just —"

"You don't have to explain."

"I do, Mason. I have to tell you —"

"Really, you don't."

"Stop telling me not to," she ordered, then barreled into an explanation. "I've only been with Jeffrey. I mean, since I left Atlanta." She moved away from him, scared that if she stayed too close, he would kiss her again. And worse, that she would return the kiss. "It's just been him since then."

"That sounds like a habit."

"Maybe it is," she said, taking his hand. "Maybe . . . I don't know. But this isn't the way to break it."

He looked down at their hands.

She told him, "He cheated on me."

"Then he's an idiot."

"Yes," she agreed. "He is sometimes, but I'm trying to tell you that I know how that feels, and I'm not going to be responsible for making someone else feel that way."

"Turnabout is fair play."

"It's not a game," she said, then reminded him, "And you're still married, Holiday Inn or not."

He nodded. "You're right."

She had not expected him to capitulate so easily, but Sara was used to Jeffrey's dogged tenacity, not Mason's casual repose. Now she remembered why it was so easy to leave Mason behind, like everything else she left in Atlanta. There was no spark between them. Mason had never had to fight for anything in his life. She wasn't even sure he wanted her now so much as that she was just convenient.

Sara said, "I'm going to go check on Tess."

"Why don't I call you?"

If he had phrased it differently, she might have said yes. As it was, she told him, "I don't think so."

"All right," Mason said, giving her one of his easy smiles.

She stood to leave, and he did not speak again until she was walking out the door.

"Sara?" He waited for her to turn around. He was leaning back on the couch, his arm still draped along the edge, legs casually crossed. "Tell your folks I said to take care."

"I will," she said, then shut the door.

Sara stood at the window of her sister's hospital room, watching traffic inch by on the downtown connector. Tessa's steady breathing behind her was like the sweetest music Sara had ever heard. Every time she looked at her sister, it took everything Sara had not to get into bed with her just to hold her and know that she was safe.

Cathy came into the room holding a cup of tea in each hand. Sara flashed back to the Dairy Queen almost a week ago, when Tessa had been unbearably irritable. Sara wanted that moment back so badly she could almost taste it.

Sara asked, "Is Daddy okay?" Her father had been overcome when Sara had told them about Richard Carter. He had walked away before Sara had finished telling them what had happened.

"He's standing at the end of the hall," Cathy said, not really answering the question.

Sara took a sip of the tea and scowled at the taste.

"It's strong," Cathy agreed. "Will Jeffrey be here soon?"

"Should be."

Cathy stroked Tessa's hair. "I remember watching y'all sleep when you were babies."

Sara used to love hearing her mother talk about their childhood, but she had such a clear sense of before and after now that it hurt to listen.

Cathy asked, "How's Jeffrey?"

Sara drank the bitter tea. "Fine."

"This was hard on him," she said, taking a tube of hand lotion out of her purse. "He's always been like a big brother to Tessa."

Sara had not let herself consider this before, but it was true. As horrified as she had been in the woods, Jeffrey was just as frightened.

"I'm beginning to see why you can't stay mad at him," Cathy said as she rubbed lotion into Tessa's hand. "Do you remember that time he drove to Florida to pick her up?"

Sara laughed, but more from her own surprise that she had forgotten the story. Years ago, when Tessa was on spring break from college, her car had been totaled by a stolen beer truck, and Jeffrey had driven down to Panama City in the middle of the night to talk to the local cops and bring her home.

"She didn't want Daddy to come get her," Cathy said. "Wouldn't hear of it."

"Daddy would have said 'I told you so' all the way back," Sara reminded her. Eddie had said only an idiot would take a convertible MG down to Florida with twenty thousand drunken college kids.

"Well," Cathy said, rubbing lotion into Tessa's arm, "he was right."

Sara smiled but withheld comment.

"I'll be glad when he gets here," Cathy said, more to herself than Sara. "Tessa needs to hear it from him that this is over."

Sara knew that her mother had no way of knowing what had happened between her and Mason James, but she felt exposed anyway.

"What?" Cathy asked, always able to sense when something was wrong.

Sara confessed easily, needing to unburden herself. "I kissed Mason."

Cathy seemed nonplussed. "Just kissed him?"

"Mama," Sara said, trying to hide her embarrassment with outrage.

"So?" Cathy squirted more lotion into her palm and rubbed her hands together to warm it. "How'd it feel?"

"Good at first, then . . ." Sara put her hands to her cheeks, feeling the heat.

"Then?"

"Not so good," Sara admitted. "I just kept thinking about Jeffrey."

"That should tell you something."

"What?" Sara asked, wanting more than anything for her mother to tell her what to do.

"Sara," Cathy sighed. "Your greatest downfall has always been your intelligence."

"Great," Sara said. "I'll be sure to tell my patients that."

"Don't get haughty with me," Cathy snipped, her tone low, the way it always got when she was annoyed. "You've been so damn restless lately, and I'm sick and tired of watching you pine after the life you could have had if you'd stayed here in Atlanta."

"That's not what I'm doing," Sara said, but she had never lied well, especially to her mother.

"You have so much in your life now, so many people who love you and care for you. Is there anything you want for that you don't have?"

Sara could have made a list a few hours ago, but now she could only shake her head.

"It might do you some good to remember that at the end of the day, no matter how smart that brain of yours is up there, it's your heart that needs looking after." She gave Sara a pointed look. "And you know what your heart needs, don't you?"

Sara nodded, though honestly she wasn't sure.

"Don't you?" Cathy insisted.

"Yes, Mama," Sara answered, and somehow she did.

"Good," she said, squeezing more lotion into her hand. "Now go talk to your father."

Sara kissed Tessa, then her mother, before leaving the room. She saw her father at the end of the hallway, standing at the window watching traffic the same way Sara had been doing in Tessa's room. His shoulders were still stooped, but the faded white T-shirt and worn-out jeans he had on were unmistakably Eddie. Sara was so like her father sometimes that it frightened her.

She said, "Hey, Daddy."

He didn't look at her, but Sara could feel his grief as clearly as she could feel the cold coming off the window. Eddie Linton was a man who was defined by family. His wife and children were his world, and Sara had been so focused on her own suffering that she hadn't noticed the struggle her father had endured. He had worked so hard to build a safe and happy home for his children. Eddie's reticence toward Sara this week had not been because he blamed her; it was because he blamed himself.

Eddie pointed out the window. "See that guy changing a tire?"

Sara saw a bright greenish yellow box van, one of the HERO squads the city of Atlanta hired to keep traffic moving. They were equipped to change tires, give a jump start or a free gallon of gas if you broke down on the side of the road. In a city where the average commute could be two hours and it was perfectly legal to carry a concealed handgun in your glove box, this was tax money well spent.

"In the box van?" she asked.

"They don't charge for that. Not a dime."

"How about that?" she said.

"Yeah." Eddie let out a long breath. "Tessie still sleeping?"

"Yes."

"Jeffrey on his way?"

"If you don't want him —"

"No," Eddie interrupted, his tone definitive. "He should be here."

Sara felt a lightness in her chest, as if a heavy weight had been lifted.

She said, "Mama and I were just talking about the time he drove to Florida to pick up Tess."

"I told her not to drive that damn car down there."

Sara looked at the traffic, hiding her smile.

Eddie cleared his throat more times than needed, as if he did not already have Sara's undivided attention. "Guy walks into a bar with a big lizard on his shoulder."

"O-kaaay . . . ," she said, drawing out the word.

"Bartender says, 'What's your lizard's name?'" Eddie paused. "The guy says, 'Tiny.' The bartender scratches his head." Eddie scratched his head. "Says, 'Why do you call him tiny?'" He paused for effect. "Guy says, 'Because he's my newt!'"

Sara repeated the punch line out loud a few times before she finally got it. She started laughing so hard that she got tears in her eyes.

Eddie merely smiled, his face lighting up as if the sound of his daughter laughing was pure joy to him.

"God, Dad," Sara said, wiping her eyes, still laughing. "That's the worst joke ever."

"Yeah," he admitted, putting his arm around her shoulders, pulling her close. "That was pretty bad."

Friday

18

Lena sat on the floor in the middle of her dorm room, surrounded by boxes containing everything she owned in the world. Most of her belongings would be stored at Hank's until she could find a job. Her bed was going to Nan's, and she would sleep in the spare room until she had enough money to move out on her own. The college had offered her Chuck's job, but under the circumstances she never wanted to see the security office again. That bastard Kevin Blake had not even given her severance pay. Lena took consolation in the fact that the board had announced this morning that they were going to start looking for a replacement for Blake.

The door creaked as Ethan pushed it open. The lock had not been fixed since Jeffrey broke it days ago.

He smiled when he saw her. "You put your hair up."

Lena resisted the temptation to take it

down. "I thought you were leaving town."

Ethan shrugged. "It's always been hard for me to leave where I'm not wanted."

She gave a thin smile.

"Besides," he said, "it's kind of hard to transfer out right now, considering the university's under investigation for ethics violations."

"I'm sure it'll get worked out," Lena said. She had worked at the college for only a few months, but she knew how scandals operated. There would be fines and a lot of stories in the papers for a few months, but a year later the stories would be gone, the fines would still be unpaid, and some other asshole professor would be stabbing someone in the back — literally or figuratively — to ensure his own fame and fortune.

"So," Ethan began. "I guess you squared things with the cop."

Lena shrugged, because she had no idea where things stood with Jeffrey. After interviewing her about Richard Carter, he had told her to show up at the station bright and early Monday morning. There was no telling what he had to say.

Ethan asked, "They ever figure out about the panties?"

"He jumped to the wrong conclusion. It

happens." Again, she shrugged. "Rosen was a freak. He probably stole them from some girl." She could imagine Andy sniffing more than glue on a lonely Friday night. As for the book, Lena could have read it on one of her own lonely nights, buying some peace in the library before it was time to go back to her hovel and try to sleep.

Ethan leaned against the open door. "I wanted you to know that I'm not leaving," he said. "In case you see me around."

"Will I see you around?"

He shrugged, noncommittal. "I don't know, Lena. I'm trying real hard to change here."

She looked at her hands, feeling like a monster. "Yeah."

"I want to have something with you," he said. "But not like that."

"Sure."

"You could move somewhere and start over." He waited before saying, "Maybe when I find a transfer, we could go together?"

"I can't leave here," she told him, knowing he would never understand. Ethan had left his family and his way of life without looking back. Lena could never do that to Sibyl.

He said, "If you change your mind . . ."

"Nan will be back soon," she told him. "You'd better go."

"All right," Ethan nodded, understanding. "I'll see you around, right?"

Lena did not answer.

He gave her back her own question. "Will I see you around?"

His words hung in the air like fog. She let herself look at him, taking in his baggy jeans and black T-shirt, his chipped tooth and his blue, blue eyes.

"Yeah," she said. "See you around."

He pulled the door to, the latch not catching. Lena stood up, dragging a chair over to the door and propping it under the knob to keep it closed. She would never be able to do that again without thinking of Richard Carter.

She walked to the bathroom. Her reflection in the mirror over the sink was a little better now. The bruises around her neck were turning greenish yellow, and the cut under her eye was already scabbing over.

"Lena?" Nan said. She heard the door hit against the chair as Nan tried to open it.

"Just a minute," Lena said, opening the medicine cabinet. She jiggled the bottom board loose and pulled out her pocketknife. Traces of blood were still on the handle, but the rain had washed most of it away. When she opened the blade, she saw that the tip had broken off. With some regret Lena realized that she would never be able to keep it.

The chair under the door popped against the knob again. Nan's voice was filled with concern. "Lena?"

"On my way," Lena called. She closed the blade with a snap, tucking it into her back pocket as she went to let Nan in.

Acknowledgments

The first thing I always read in a book is the acknowledgments, and I hate when there is a long list of people I don't know being thanked for stuff that has nothing to do with me. Having written three books now, I understand why these lists are necessary. I know you can't put pearls on a pig, but the following folks have gone above and beyond the call of duty promoting the Grant County series here and abroad, and I am eternally grateful for all of their hard work.

At Morrow/Harper: George Bick, Jane Friedman, Lisa Gallagher, Kim Gombar, Kristen Green, Brian Grogan, Cathy Hemming, Libby Jordan, Rebecca Keiper, Michael Morris, Michael Morrison, Juliette Shapland, Virginia Stanley, Debbie Stier, Eric Svenson, Charlie Trachtenbarg, Rome Quezada, and Colleen Winters.

At Random House UK: Ron Beard, Faye Brewster, Richard Cable, Alex Hippisley-

Cox, Vanessa Kerr, Mark McCallum, Susan Sandon, and Tiffany Stansfield.

There are countless others, and my apologies for leaving anyone out.

My agent, Victoria Sanders, inspires me to reach great heights. Editors Meaghan Dowling and Kate Elton are the Dynamic Duo. I consider it a gift that we all work so well together. Dr. David Harper, Patrice Iacovoni, and Damien van Carrapiett helped me keep the medical passages as true to life as you can be when you're writing fiction. Cantor Isaac Goodfriend wrote "Shalom" for me in twenty different languages. Beth and Jeff at CincinnatiMedia. com are two of the best, most authoritative author Website designers/administrators around. Jamey Locastro answered some very frank questions about never you mind. Rob Hueter talked to me about Glocks and took me shooting. Remington.com has a killer online tutorial about shotgun safety that kept me entertained for hours. Speaking of which, special thanks to online friends whose Siren song pulls me away from work. Please stop. I am begging you.

Fellow authors VM, FM, LL, JH, EC, and EM deserve many thanks for listening to me whine. (You *were* listening, right?) My daddy has always supported me, and not just with no-interest loans. Judy Jordan is the best mother and friend I could ask for. Billie Bennett, my ninth-grade English teacher, deserves all the praise she'll allow — which is never enough.

On a more personal note, thanks to the Boss, Diane, Cubby, Pat, Cathy, and Deb for making New York not such a horrible place to visit these last few times. Y'all just don't know.

Lastly, to D.A. — I could as soon forget you as my existence.

About the Author

KARIN SLAUGHTER grew up in a small south Georgia town and lives in Atlanta. She is currently writing the fourth Grant County novel, *Indelible*.

We hope you have enjoyed this Large Print book. Other Thorndike, Wheeler or Chivers Press Large Print books are available at your library or directly from the publishers.

For more information about current and up-coming titles, please call or write, without obligation, to:

Publisher
Thorndike Press
295 Kennedy Memorial Drive
Waterville, ME 04901
Tel. (800) 223-1244

Or visit our Web site at:
www.gale.com/thorndike
www.gale.com/wheeler

OR

Chivers Large Print
published by BBC Audiobooks Ltd
St James House, The Square
Lower Bristol Road
Bath BA2 3SB
England
Tel. +44(0) 800 136919
email: bbcaudiobooks@bbc.co.uk
www.bbcaudiobooks.co.uk

All our Large Print titles are designed for easy reading, and all our books are made to last.

/